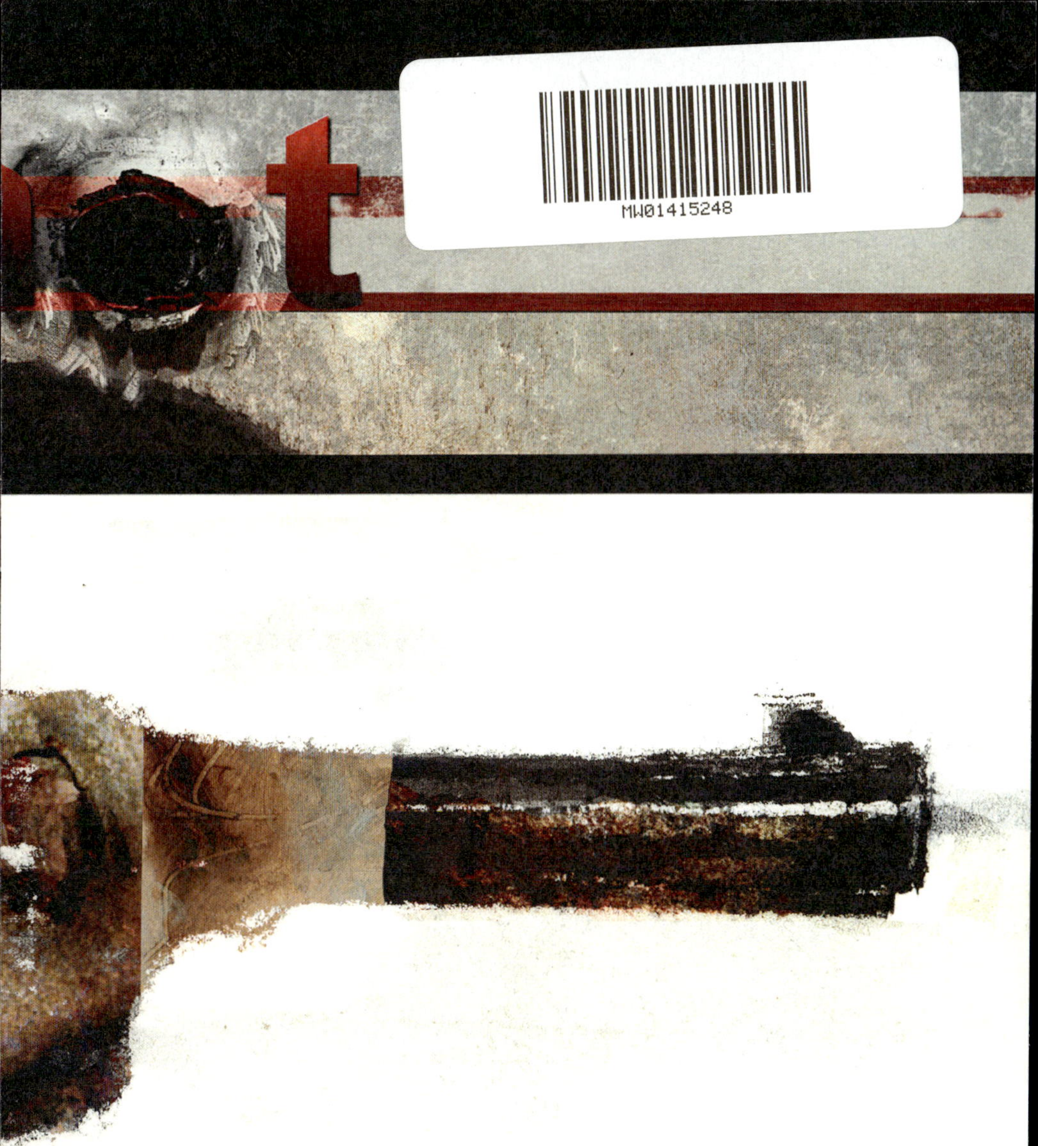

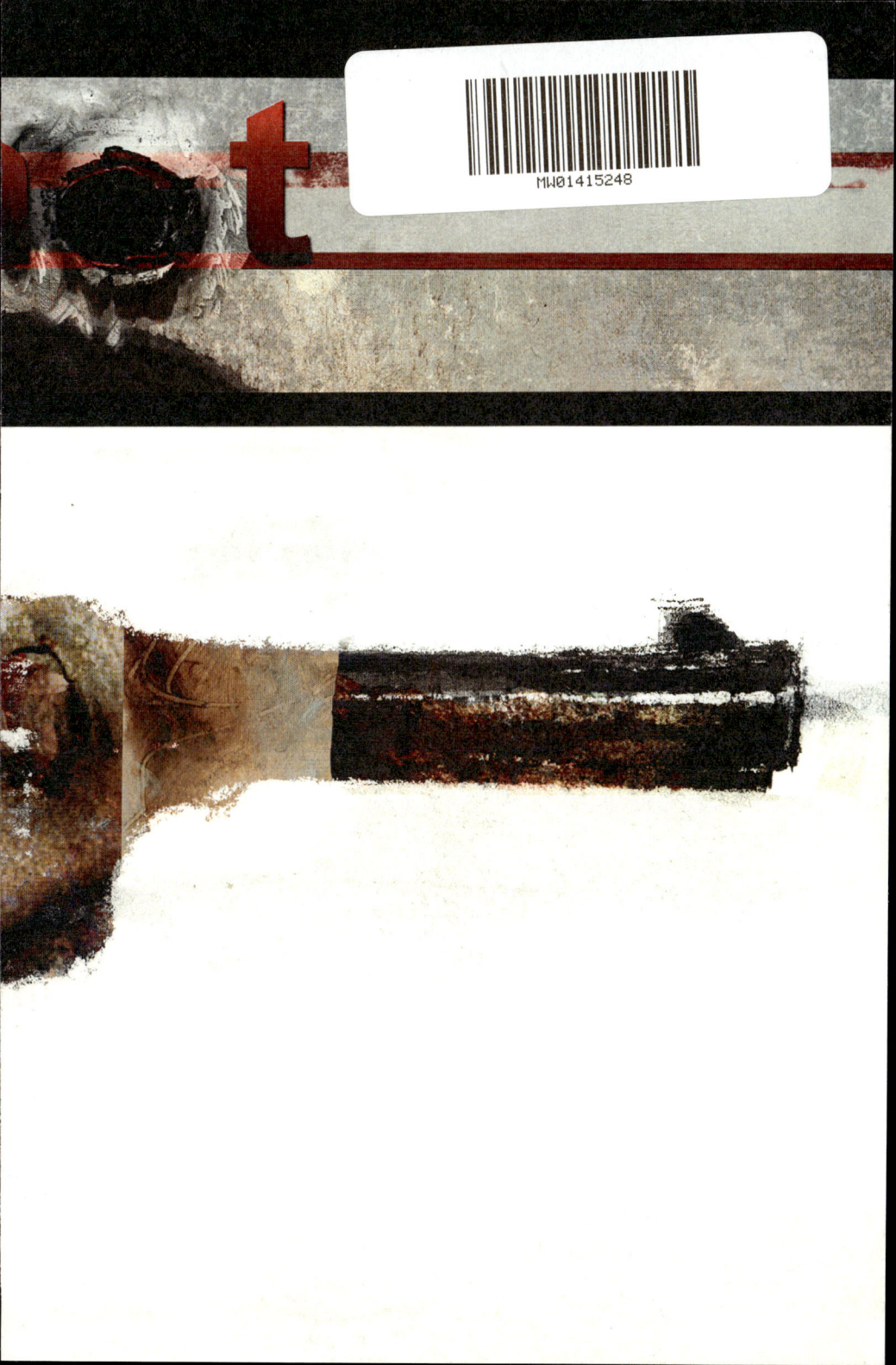

Gutshot
Weird West Stories

Gutshot
Weird West Stories

Edited by
Conrad Williams

GUTSHOT

'The Ghost Warriors' by Michael Moorcock first appeared in
Tales from the Texas Woods, published by Mojo Press,
and is © 1997 Michael and Linda Moorcock.
All other stories are © 2011 by their respective authors.

INTRODUCTION
Copyright © Conrad Williams 2011

COVER ART
Copyright © Caniglia 2011

Published in October 2011 by PS Publishing Ltd. by arrangement with the authors. All rights reserved by the authors. The rights of the contributors to be identified as the Authors of this Work have been asserted by them in accordance with the Copyright, Designs and Patents Act 1988.

First PS Edition

ISBN
978-1-848632-13-4
978-1-848632-14-1 (signed)

This book is a work of Fiction. Names, characters, places and incidents either are products of the authors' imaginations or are used fictitiously.
Any resemblance to actual events or locales
or persons, living or dead, is entirely coincidental.

Design by Jupper Peep
www.jupperpeep.com

Printed in England by MPG Books Group

PS Publishing Ltd / Grosvenor House / 1 New Road /
Hornsea / HU18 1PG / England

editor@pspublishing.co.uk / www.pspublishing.co.uk

CONTENTS

Introduction IX
Passage by Alan Peter Ryan 5
The Black Rider by James Lovegrove 21
The Alabaster Child by Cat Sparks 33
The Ghost Warriors by Michael Moorcock 51
Blue Norther by Zander Shaw 79
In the Sand Hills by Thomas Tessier 95
White Butterflies by Stephen Volk 107
El Camino de Rojo by Gary McMahon 123
The Bones that Walk by Joe R Lansdale 137
Ghosts by Amanda Hemingway 155
The Boy Thug by Christopher Fowler 165
Kiss the Wolf by Simon Bestwick 179
Waiting for the Bullet by Mark Morris 191
Carrion Cowboy by Paul Meloy 213
Some Kind of Light Shines from Your Face by Gemma Files 217
Splinters by Peter Crowther and Rio Youers 233
All Our Hearts are Ghosts by Peter Atkins 259
Beasts of Burden by Sarah Langan 271
What God Hath Wrought? by Adam Nevill 283
Those Who Remember by Joel Lane 311

INTRODUCTION

I used to play Cowboys and Indians in the school playground. Maybe I was among the last generation to do so. One of my favourite T-shirts bore the imposing face and headdress of a Native American chief. I could lay claim to being at the tail-end of an era in which you could switch on the TV on Saturday mornings to find black-and-white episodes of *Champion the Wonder Horse*. *The High Chaparral* and *Bonanza* were around too, as was *Branded*. The Milky Bar Kid and Texan bars (sure is a mighty chew) relieved me of my pennies at Boughey's corner shop. At the cinema up until the late 1960s, some of the biggest-grossing movies still featured gun battles, horses and Stetsons. Cowboys were cool.

But now, although still being explored on the silver screen thanks to the rejuvenating successes of *Dances with Wolves* (1990) and *Unforgiven* (1992)—both won the Oscar for Best Film, the first Westerns to do so since *Cimarron* in 1930—the Old West in fiction seems to be as dead as any of the gunslinging varmints you'll find within these covers.

Zane Grey and Louis L'Amour, phenomenally popular in their day, have been ousted from the bookshops. Maybe they've retained a couple of inches of shelf space in your local library. Maybe you'll find some behind the box of unwanted toys in the charity shop. Sharston Books, my go-to place for secondhand treasures in Manchester, has a selection of

Western fiction, but the books are old and dusty and liable to crumble to powder if you so much as turn towards them. Pulp indeed. But once, this was a very busy genre. Every continent had its pages of inscrutable strangers, showdowns, sunsets. Tales of the American frontier, the gaucho literature of Argentina and stories of the settlement of the Australian Outback. New lands being discovered. Isn't that what genre writing is all about? And that's why these pale riders won't go away for good.

Elmore Leonard's angle of attack might be different these days, his novels filled with modern-day gangsters and deadbeats, but his Westerns have recently been reprinted by Orion in this country, fifty years after their first publication. Cormac McCarthy's latest couple of novels (and I include *The Road*) remain resolutely Western in their themes and approaches, despite a contemporary, or future setting. Who else is sticking to their guns? Precious few, but there are those flirting with the genre while ploughing their own unique furrow—you'll find a number of them in this anthology.

The cowboy, the pioneer, the outcast. The consumers and practitioners of literature's dark edges perhaps recognise a little of themselves in those mysterious, troubled figures. And perhaps that is how the Western will survive, by relocating in time, slipping into bed with another genre. We've seen, in *Westworld* for example, how successful this option can be. Other films such as *Straw Dogs*, *Outland*, *Dead Men's Shoes*, *Eden Lake*, *The Burrowers* and, in the year that this book goes to print, *Rango* and *Cowboys and Aliens* either borrow the tropes of the Old West and dress them accordingly, or go for a straight 'mash-up'. It is in this spirit that the book you hold was conceived.

The Western might well be dead, but we readers and writers of the weird, more than anybody else, know that isn't necessarily the end of things.

Conrad Williams
Manchester, UK
June 2011

Gutshot
Weird West Stories

For my parents.
And to the memory of Alan Peter Ryan (1943–2011).

PASSAGE
Alan Peter Ryan

Chapter One

"**W**ell, he's lost," said Beauchamp.

He kicked his right boot free of the stirrup and crossed that leg over the horn and the other leg, then dipped two fingers into his shirt pocket and brought out the makings.

Trask sat in silence beside him on Ulysses, looking down into the valley below.

"I don't know," he said.

Beauchamp lit his cigarette. The red mare smelled the new grass higher up on the rocky shelf where they stood and she would have liked to go back there and crop at it, but Beauchamp stroked her neck a couple of times and she settled down to wait.

Together they looked out from the high shelf. Below them a valley stretched north and south, green but darkening now towards end of day, its shadows long and spiky, bigger than the things that made them. At the far side of the valley, the land rose into a vast array of scattered hills, like shapeless mounds dripped or dropped upon the earth by an inattentive god, mostly rocky, with only scrub and a little struggling grass to relieve the bare roughness, and that not much at all. Men around there called them the Hills of Hell. Even the Comanche called that treacherous and shadowy maze the Tortured Path, which meant roughly the same as Hell in their own tongue. Yet the Comanche had always loved those hills and the torturous narrow trails winding among them and had roamed there and camped there and even dwelt there from time unremembered. A Comanche could pass a full lifetime in those hills, sire a tribe of his own, and never come out unless it was to kill, or unless the thing to be killed went into those hills of its own volition and presented itself for death.

"Maybe he went into the hills," Beauchamp said.

"I don't know," Trask said again. He threw away the butt end of the cigarette he was smoking and began to construct another.

"Or maybe he just plain got lost," Beauchamp said. "I don't know either. I know he's new in this country but I was there when you described the trail to him. Alameda's not hard to find. It's not a straight ride but it's not hard to find."

"Maybe," Trask said.

"He got lost twice before. You remember? You sent him out twice and he got lost both times. I thought that second time, now there's a man can't find a buffalo in a rain barrel."

Trask stirred at that. "Sure he could," he said. "I think he could find it alright. Problem is he just doesn't care, not about the buffalo and not about the barrel."

"Well, I reckon that's worse still," said Beauchamp. "Worse still than not being able to find it in the first place."

"You don't like him," Trask said.

Beauchamp considered that.

"No," he said after a moment. "I don't. I didn't like him from the day he rode in and you gave him a job. I can't rightly tell you why, so don't ask. He's just not right. It's almost like something you can smell about a man sometimes, something you can feel, like when the hair stands up on the back of your neck. You going to tell me you didn't feel that with Sarney?"

Trask sighed. "Maybe I did," he said.

"You gave him the job."

"He deserved a chance like any other man and I needed a rider," Trask said.

"Well," Beauchamp said. "I'll say no more."

They were tired. Trask had sent Sarney to Alameda on a simple errand, a two-day ride there and another two days back, and now it was five days and Trask was worried. He shouldn't have sent Sarney, a new man, on a little-used trail in country he didn't know, but that was why he'd hired him, so his known and reliable riders could keep at their regular work. And now here was the result, Sarney not back and Beauchamp and himself spending the whole livelong day out looking for him and now it was coming on to dark and Sarney still not found.

"Maybe he went into the hills," Beauchamp said. "Which I believe I said before."

"I told him not to," Trask said.

"I know that," Beauchamp said. "I heard you myself. But maybe he did. Man who doesn't care about either the buffalo or the barrel might just go into those hills even so."

"Well, I reckon you might be right," Trask said.

They both looked out across the valley below towards the hills that were starting to grey and become patched with shadows as twilight set in. There were a lot of those hills and in the dimming light they rippled and misted and faded away as far as forever.

"Let's go," said Trask. "We can get across the valley and make camp on the other side while there's still light. That way we can start into the hills first thing in the morning."

"Sure," said Beauchamp. He got his leg down and his boot in the stirrup.

"Beauchamp," Trask said.

Beauchamp looked at him.

"I did feel what you said. That funny warning thing. But I can't not give a decent-seeming man a job because of a thing like that."

"Sure," Beauchamp said again and, by way of emphasis, he nodded his head.

They lifted the reins and backed the horses away from the edge of the shelf and turned them to where a steep trail led downward.

"I didn't think we'd be out all day," Trask said as they started off. "Reckon I should have. You bring any food?"

"Got a tin of beans in each saddlebag," Beauchamp said. "Got a chunk of bacon. Brought them just in case."

Trask shook his head a little. "You think of everything," he said.

"No," said Beauchamp. "You do. That's your problem."

Chapter Two

Those hills would be muffled in darkness and shadow so they waited until dawn before they set out. The red sun had just slid into view and turned the land a fresh but unnatural orange colour, broken by lengthy shadows, as they saddled up the horses. Everything in view, the grass before them and the rocks and the scattered trees and the scrubby hills above had in that light an edge sharp enough to cut.

They rode through the narrow V-shaped passages that snaked this way and that around and between the hills. Rarely was there room to ride side-by-side and mostly Trask took the lead. The passages all looked alike. The hills all looked alike. Through eons of time some of the rock above had broken and crumbled and tumbled down the slopes and lay like rubble from a smashed and shattered pueblo. The horses disliked the uncertain footing. They had to pick their steps with care and the going was slow.

The sun was well up now and beginning to heat the rocky slopes around them.

"Come noon," said Beauchamp, "a man could bake like a biscuit in here."

Some of the taller and steeper of the hills still offered a diminishing slice of shadow. They reined in the horses in the shade beside a nearly straight wall of rock to get out of the sun for a few minutes and let the laboring horses breathe.

"What do you call that thing where you get in and you can't get out?" said Beauchamp. "You told me about it one time, something out of an old book."

"A labyrinth," said Trask.

"That's it," said Beauchamp. "I reckon we're in one now."

"We'll get out," said Trask. "Worse comes to worst, we can scramble up one of these hills and see where we are and how to get out."

"Not if we get in too far," Beauchamp said.

"We get in too far, there's still the sun to give us direction," Trask said.

Beauchamp was silent for a few seconds. "Sun in the sky can see things a man on the ground can't," he said.

"Best push on," Trask said.

They rode on for another hour or more, following the twisting pathways between the hills and, except for the still shrinking shadows, would not have known which way they were facing. They scanned the ground without cease, looking for any sort of sign, a hoofprint where there was a bit of sand or soil, a struggling small green thing broken, a scratch from a horseshoe on a rock where there was none. They watched for horse droppings in the narrow passages and, where there was a large rock or a stunted tree just above the passages they scouted for human droppings or the tiny white butt of a cigarette but there was nothing, nothing at all to indicate that either horse or man had ever passed this way in all the ages of time.

The hills were alike in their steep individual rising but irregular in their layout and here and there the riders came to a flat open space among them. Wind-blown grass seed had taken root here and rain ran down the rocky slopes and gathered in little pools, so these places were green and fresh. The riders stopped a couple of times and the horses cropped at the grass and men and horses took a little of the cool water.

"A man could live a long time in these hills," Trask said. "If he was willing to live slow."

"A man could die here slow too," said Beauchamp.

"You're taking a very dark view of things these days," Trask said.

"Way I'm seeing it," said Beauchamp. "I don't like it here. I've got that feeling again, only stronger."

"Well, I do too," Trask said. "It's just I'm trying not to."

"I know that," Beauchamp said.

They rode some more and then stopped in another open space where there was grass and water and made coffee and drank that for their midday meal.

Maybe fifteen minutes after they set out again, they found Sarney and it was clear at once that he had died slow.

Chapter Three

He had been a big man and he was still big but now he was turned nearly inside out. The body lay curving backward over a rounded and slanting rock, perfect for the purpose. It was naked, not even boots or socks, and the neck and wrists and ankles were roped and tied down to picket stakes jammed in beneath the edges of the rock to pin the body firmly in place. The dirty toes were splayed upward as if in continuing pain. The genitals were gone, a gaping bloody gash left in their place. But there they were on the ground. A length of filthy frayed rope, good for no other use, lay on the grass. At one end, lying between the wide-spread feet, was a little noose and caught in the noose were what was left of the bloody private parts, private no longer. The other end of the worn rope was crimped, as if it might have been tied to a bridle or rope hackamore and then pulled free and tossed there after it was used. The body was split open, breast and belly to just below the waist, with side cuts to facilitate opening, leaving the ribs exposed and the guts swelling and bulging outward. The eyes were pinned open with cactus thorns through the lids. The head was scalped, leaving visible a pate of white bone smeared with blood.

Trask and Beauchamp looked at all of this with their mouths open and their guns in their hands and didn't even know they had drawn. Ulysses and the red mare, who had both smelled more blood than any horse should ever have to, snorted and tossed their heads and each took a step backward. After that first moment, the men snapped their heads upward and twisted around and scanned the rocky heights above them.

In silence, Trask gestured towards a passage at their left that had a little grass at its opening to muffle the sound of their horses. They rode into the passage. The grass gave way to sand and, a little farther on, to gravel. They stopped the horses on the sand and moved them close together. As they did that, they both caught sight of Sarney's horse, just where the gravelly surface of the passageway curved out of view. It was picketed but still saddled.

Trask leaned sideways to Beauchamp and whispered.

"Comanche," he said. "Just one, I think."

"I saw pony tracks in the grass back there. One. He must be close."

Trask glanced at the ancient hills as if it were somehow possible to extract their stony secrets.

"We can't search," he breathed. "He could be anywhere and he'd hear us coming. Leave the horses. We'll go back and wait there. He'll come back to admire his work."

"Hope he doesn't come this way where the horses are," said Beauchamp.

"So do I," Trask said.

They went back on foot, guns ready, and crossed the grassy opening and carefully ascended the rocky slope on its far side and found niches in which to hide and wait. There was nothing else to do. They crouched and sweated in the growing heat and checked their guns and looked down towards the splayed body of Sarney maybe thirty feet below and tried not to.

"If he shows," Trask whispered, although it was barely even a whisper, "I'll call out and you shoot him in the right hand and I'll shoot him in the right foot."

"Best shoot him in the head," said Beauchamp, but Trask shook his head no, just once, and they resumed the vigil.

In less than an hour, the Comanche appeared. It was obvious he had come from a different direction and had not seen the horses or gone to look at Sarney's horse. He was a young man and he rode a wiry mountain pony, white and dappled brown, without a saddle, only a small piece of blanket that hung down a little at the sides, and he used a rope hackamore. He was wearing leather britches and moccasins, his chest was bare, and his black hair was in long braids. His face was painted red and black. A knife hung at his waist but he had no gun. When he slid to the ground from the horse, he stood a moment and contemplated Sarney's body from a little distance. Then he walked close to it, leaned over, and spat into the gaping dead mouth.

"Hey!" Trask shouted.

The Indian spun around and Trask and Beauchamp both shot him.

Both bullets went apparently true because the Indian spun around nearly three times, leaped into the air, came down twisting, and crashed sideways against a large rock and then tumbled to the ground beside it. He was twitching violently and his mouth was working. Trask stood up and aimed his gun and whanged a bullet off the rock beside the Indian's face, spraying grit into his eyes that made his head jerk, and Beauchamp slugged another into the soft ground beside his trembling left hand. The hand spasmed and clutched at the ground and the Indian lay still.

After a moment, Beauchamp said, "Simple as that." He was breathing very hard.

Guns pointed, they made their way with all due care down the treacherous irregular slope to the flat grassy circle below, crossed it, and went to look at the Comanche.

He was maybe eighteen or nineteen, above medium height, well built with a fine chest, strong arms, and not at all bad-looking or murderous-looking, except for the paint. He had washed himself somewhere and he was clean and there was none of Sarney's blood on him. His eyes were closed but you knew they would be bright and fierce and smart.

Trask stood over him. "You'd best hope you understand English," he said. "We're going to take your knife."

He leaned over and shoved the hot barrel of his gun, hard, against the Indian's left temple and Beauchamp bent over and pulled away the knife from his waist and put it in his own belt.

"Stand up," Trask said. "Do it now."

The Indian opened his eyes and looked at him.

"I can't," he said. "My foot's shot." The muscles in his face were bunched in hard knots and there was terrible pain in his voice but he was controlling it.

"Do it anyway," Trask said. "If you don't, I'm going to let you lie where you are and I'll stake you down and while you're lying there I'm going to tie a noose around your business and tie the other end to your own pony and then whack him hard and let him pull your business off same as you did to that man yonder."

The Indian might almost have been weighing the benefits and deficits of various options for a moment but then he blinked his eyes and stirred. He got awkwardly to one knee, biting his lip and visibly trying not to cry out. He put out his right hand to steady himself against the rock, realised the hand was broken and bloody and flaming with pain, fell over on top of it, and choked back a scream.

"Stand up," said Trask.

The Indian tried again, slowly and with great deliberation, but he managed it, half bending and supporting himself on his left foot with his left hand against the rock behind him. He was breathing with difficulty and sweating hard but he was breathing and he looked more or less alert, all things considered.

"You listen to me," Trask said. "I'm going to tell you what I think. You listen carefully and I want you to tell me if I'm right, but if I have to repeat it you won't be around to hear me. It's your choice. You can die like a dog or you can die like a Comanche."

That seemed to have a striking effect on the Indian. His eyes glowed with scorn and hatred but he looked directly at Trask and his gaze displayed as much attention as it did pain.

"Best step back, Trask," Beauchamp said. "We're too close. I don't trust him. I don't trust him."

Their guns were aimed at the Indian's heart and he was standing on one foot and his leg was trembling, they could plainly see, but they cautiously stepped back and away.

"This is a ritual, isn't it," Trask said, but it wasn't a question. "You're declaring yourself a warrior in the old ways of your grandfathers." He had to stop. He was short of breath and his chest was heaving. "A warrior. That's what you want to be. In the old way. Prove yourself. You want to prove yourself. And this is the ritual for it."

The Comanche's leg was shaking now. He shifted his position slightly and moved his left hand an inch on the rock where he leaned. Both guns moved a fraction of an inch with him and the fingers on the triggers flexed. The Comanche saw that and, except for his shaking leg, he froze.

Trask made a sound deep in his throat and Beauchamp glanced at him. Trask's face was covered with sweat.

"You alright, Trask?" Beauchamp said.

Trask shook his head. "No," he said. "I believe I'll need to sit down."

"What is it, Trask?" Beauchamp said.

"Make that boy sit too," Trask said. "He just gained a few minutes of life."

Trask backed farther away and swept a glance behind him. There was a flattish rock twenty feet away at the edge of the grass and Trask moved toward it, mostly backward but still watching the Indian, and a little unsteadily. When he got to the rock he sat down on it and put his elbows on his knees and kept the gun pointed where it had been. With his left hand he lifted his hat and then wiped his sleeve quickly across his wet face.

Beauchamp had moved to the side to be out of Trask's line of fire. He too backed away and stopped when he stood beside Trask.

"What is it, Trask?" he said.

The Indian had not moved and his fierce eyes followed them.

Beauchamp lifted his chin toward him and said, "Sit down."

The Indian stood still for a few seconds more, then leaned to his left and rested his hip on the rock he'd been using for support. Then he bent his good leg and lowered himself to the ground, but the leg was weak now and still trembling and it gave away beneath him and he landed hard on his ass. A spasm of pain rippled up his body and across his face but he did not cry out.

"Trask," Beauchamp said. "You going to be sick?"

"No," Trask said.

"We've seen men dead and hurt bad before this," Beauchamp said.

"Watch him," Trask said. He lowered his head and let the gun sink earthward and put his head down low between his spread knees and breathed in deeply. Beauchamp locked his gaze on the Indian and the Indian licked his dry lips repeatedly and watched both of them. Finally Trask lifted his head and sat up and raised the gun once more.

"What is it, Trask?" Beauchamp asked.

"It's not what's been done," Trask said slowly. "It's not what that Comanche did to Sarney." He used his left hand again to lift his hat and wipe the sweat from his face. When he'd done that, he sat up straight and when he spoke his voice was steady.

"It's what I'm going to have to do to him," he said.

"And you too," he added. "You're going to have to do it with me."

Chapter Four

Beauchamp squatted down and Trask remained seated on the stone like some shaman or curandero making pronouncements. Their guns did not waver from the subject.

"They come off the reservation and into these hills," he said. "A few of them, now and then, one by one, still. They won't accept the reservation. Can't say as I blame them. I wouldn't either, I reckon. But there they are. Then you get one like this. He's either the best they have and destined to be their leader and he knows it, he feels it, but he thinks too that he has to prove it, prove himself, maybe even prove that he's worthy. I can see how that might be. I can see it all too plain. So he wants to restore things to the way they used to be, the way he knows inside his head is the right way. He wants to put everything in order the way his granddaddy did and his granddaddy's granddaddy. I can see that. Yes, I can."

He looked across the open green space at the young Comanche and the Comanche, whose face was turning ashen, looked at him.

"Or else," Trask went on in the same low steady voice, "he is nothing more than the worst they have. He was a bad boy and now he's a bad young man. His daddy tried to make him behave and he wouldn't. His daddy let him go to the school to learn English and he learned English and nothing else. He doesn't want to learn. He just wants to break things."

The Comanche rolled his weight maybe two inches over to ease his hip on the hard ground and the barrels of the guns moved with him, even twenty feet away.

"Which one are you?" Trask asked him.

The Indian stared coldly at him but then as a coil of pain flared up in his mangled hand or his torn foot he blinked a couple of times rapidly in spite of himself.

His teeth were clenched together but he spoke distinctly.

"You are a pig," he said.

Trask stood up.

"I am going to teach you about rituals," he said.

"What are we doing, Trask?" Beauchamp asked.

Trask told him and Beauchamp nodded and said, "Alright."

Trask held his gun on the Indian and Beauchamp walked out of the clearing. A few minutes later he came back, leading the red mare and Ulysses and Sarney's horse. Sarney's horse was one of the Welch horses and it looked happy to be with its fellows again. When they came into the clearing, the three of them looked warily across at the Indian pony and the Indian pony looked just as warily at them. Beauchamp lined up the three horses at the side of the clearing opposite the Comanche, facing him. He took a coil of rope from the horn of his saddle and squatted down and using his own knife from his belt cut four short lengths of it. Then, with the ropes dangling from his hand, he walked across and stood beside Trask. The Comanche looked at the ropes.

"Wait a minute," Trask said and, as if by way of apology, added, "I never did this before. Never will again, either, I hope."

He walked slowly over to the Indian pony. It didn't like either his look or his smell and it eyed him nervously and edged away. Trask spoke softly to it and reached out slowly and rubbed it under the jaw. It tossed its head once but let him do it. Trask continued talking softly, then stroked its neck a couple of times and then its face. It had almost certainly never been rubbed or stroked or petted before. It looked anxious but willing. Trask continued talking to it, then took hold of the rope hackamore and led it over close to where Beauchamp stood with his gun aimed at the man on the ground.

"We're going to tie your hands behind your back," Trask told the Indian, "and then we're going to tie your feet and then you're going to stand up. You can make it easy or you can make it hard but we are going to do it. And then we are going to set you on your feet and you are going to stand up like a man."

The Indian's eyes went to the ropes in Beauchamp's hand and back to Trask's face. He didn't move.

Trask signalled with his chin and they bent over and rolled the Indian onto his belly. He gasped but made no other sound. Beauchamp dropped his gun into his holster and separated a length of rope. He lifted the Indian's arms, avoiding the bloody hand, and looped the rope around the wrists as if they were the legs of a calf. He jerked the rope tight. Then he did the same with the legs, looping the rope around the ankles and jerking it tight. The Indian, thus trussed up, seemed to sink closer to the ground. Trask dropped his own gun into its holster and thumbed the loop into place.

"Alright," he said.

Beauchamp dropped the two remaining lengths of rope on the ground. They bent over the Indian and Trask took hold of his shoulders and Beauchamp of his hips and they lifted him up and set him more or less upright. The Indian's face twisted in pain. He could not support himself on one foot and Beauchamp grasped him around the waist and kept him from falling.

Trask turned away and stepped over to the worried pony and led it close in behind the Indian. The pony rolled its eyes but stood its ground. Beauchamp gave a heave and shoved the Indian up against the pony, just forward of its left shoulder, and held him there. The pony, surprised, shifted, but not far. Trask quickly bent and got one of the remaining ropes and looped it over the Indian's throat and around the horse's neck and pulled it into a knot. He and Beauchamp stepped back and the Indian sagged. The rope was cutting into his throat and the back of his head was pressed tight against the pony's neck but he was not choking and he was more or less upright. The pony liked none of these proceedings but stood very still.

"Alright," Trask said again. He turned away and walked over to where the three horses stood and came back with his rifle and Beauchamp's and handed Beauchamp's to him. Like soldiers under inspection, which in a sense they were, they broke the rifles in perfect synchronicity and checked the loads. Trask stepped back. Beauchamp did the same and they held the rifles by the barrels at their sides, butt ends on the ground.

"Listen to me," Trask said to the Indian. The Comanche's eyes were beginning to dim in his pale face. "This is our ritual. This is the way we put things right." He thought for a second. "This is the way we put things right," he said again. "That's all you need to know."

Beauchamp looked at him.

"Use his horse blanket," Trask said.

Beauchamp picked up the one remaining length of rope and then pulled the sour-smelling piece of blanket from the pony's back. The pony tried to watch him and pawed the ground once and the Indian's body swayed.

The Comanche's eyes opened wider. He tried to turn his head but he couldn't.

Trask nodded and took hold of Beauchamp's rifle and Beauchamp stepped forward and raised the piece of blanket. Now the Indian realised what was happening and his eyes flew open wide as if to take in all the earth in the moment that remained. Then Beauchamp had folded the piece of blanket and wrapped it around his head like a bulky mask and wrapped the length of rope around the blanket to secure it in place.

"Pig!" came the Indian's voice from behind the blanket. "You shoot a horse too!"

"That animal is in no kind of danger," Trask said.

He stepped away to where the rocky slope rose up behind him at the other side of the grass. The three horses watched all of this with interest. Beauchamp came and joined him. Together they faced the doomed man.

"I'm going to say, 'Ready, Aim, Fire,'" Trask said.

Beauchamp nodded and they raised the rifles to their shoulders and took aim.

"Ready," Trask said. And then, "Aim." And then, "Fire."

They fired as one and in that instant a black hole and then a small red flower blossomed in the middle of the Indian's chest. The body was punched backward and the pony tossed his head and snorted and stepped sideways but otherwise held his ground. The body sagged heavily back at an angle. The other three horses snorted and tossed their heads but stayed where they were.

The two men laid their rifles on the ground. Then they walked across and Beauchamp got his knife and cut through the rope that secured the dead man to the pony. They let the shapeless weight down to the ground. Beauchamp pulled away the piece of blanket. The Indian's eyes were open.

"Got to do it right," Trask said.

He took out his gun and aimed it and fired a bullet into the centre of the Indian's forehead.

Chapter Five

It took mostly the rest of the day to thread their way out of the labyrinth of those hills. Sarney's horse and the Indian pony didn't like carrying dead men and were skittish and reluctant all the way. When they finally emerged and reached the open grass of the valley, they rode toward the nearest clump of cottonwoods and, tired as they were, dug two graves and laid their burden to rest. Then they rode on another mile or so and, in the final golden light of day, Beauchamp spotted a fat hen in the tall grass and Trask shot it. They made camp by the river and built a fire and roasted the bird.

They still had coffee and they made it and sat drinking it and smoking.

After a while, Beauchamp said, "What was it happened back there?"

Trask thought for a while to choose his words.

"Way I see it," he said, "if a man's a man at all, he ought to be trying all the time to get to the top of the mountain. May be he can't even see the top some days for the clouds. But I reckon he ought to try. Course, the trouble with a mountain is, the trail is upgrade all the way. Reckon just then I was looking up and saw a pretty rough patch to get through. Steep and rough. Made me a little dizzy."

"Alright," said Beauchamp.

"I'm alright now," said Trask.

"Alright," Beauchamp said again and, after a while, he said, "Well, I've seen easier days."

"So have I," said Trask.

They sat in silence for some minutes. A half-burned piece of wood in the fire crumbled away in sparks and Beauchamp stretched out a leg and pushed the unburned part back into the fire with his boot.

PASSAGE

"His eyes were open behind the blanket," he said.

"I saw that," Trask said.

"You know what?" said Beauchamp.

"What?" said Trask.

"When I saw that," Beauchamp said, "it made me think, now here's a man who cared about the buffalo and the barrel both."

"I reckon so," said Trask. "I reckoned that from the minute we saw Sarney and what he did to him. Took a lot of time and a lot of hard work to do it right, working all alone. That's why I figured we owed it to that Comanche to do right by him."

"Well, I reckon we did," Beauchamp said.

"I reckon so," said Trask.

The fire was still crackling merrily and doing a good job of holding back the dark.

"You want more of this coffee?" Beauchamp asked.

"I'm going to turn in," Trask said. He pitched the butt of his cigarette into the fire.

"Me too," said Beauchamp.

He leaned back on his side of the fire and rested his head against his saddle and pulled up his blanket.

Trask did the same on his side.

"Good night," said Beauchamp across the fire.

"Good night," said Trask.

Alan Peter Ryan authored four novels and two collections of short stories, before his untimely death in 2011. Several of his novels and stories have been optioned for films in the United States, England, and France, and his work has been published in the United Kingdom and translated into twelve languages. He also edited five volumes of speculative fiction and five of travel writing.

His book reviews appeared in the *Washington Post*, the *Chicago Tribune*, the *Atlanta Journal-Constitution*, *USA Today*, the *Raleigh News & Observer*, the *Cleveland Plain Dealer*, the *San José Mercury News*, *New York Newsday*, the *New York Times*, the *Los Angeles Times*, and many other newspapers. For six years he served as Vice President for Awards of the National Book Critics Circle.

His awards include the Lowell Thomas Travel Journalism Award and the World Fantasy Award for Best Short Story of the Year.

Gutshot

This, the first story Alan sold on a return to writing genre fiction after a considerable period away, is one of a number of tales featuring Trask. "It seems to me that the frontier is a natural setting for fantasy, especially dark fantasy," Alan said. "This is where the known meets the unknown, where light meets dark, where men are truly tested. The wilderness, both literal and figurative, is a rich source of material, I think, for any sort of speculative fiction."

THE BLACK RIDER
James Lovegrove

You're dying. You know it.

You know it not so much because of the pain, which is close but feels distant, but because of the birds circling overhead, which are distant but feel close. Black wings outspread, the birds wheel on the waning updraughts. They sense the nearness of death. The scent of it reaches them all the way up there in the sky, whose pure blue has become tainted with the purples and greys of twilight.

Blood on your hands—your own blood, tacky-black. You've been trying to keep it in, stop it leaking out from the wound. But fingers make for an inefficient dam.

Then you hear the sound.

Hoofbeats.

Coming.

"Coming?"

This was the first thing Viv said after Graham opened the window and leaned out. Graham had been roused by the soft *tick* of a piece of gravel hitting the glass, shortly followed by the *thwack* of a much larger stone that had left a diagonal crack across the pane. He hadn't moved quickly enough for Viv's liking, which is to say he had moved at the normal pace for a sluggish, just-woken twelve year old.

"What time is it?" he asked, yawning.

"Gone six."

"Too early!"

"No, it isn't. We've got a lot to do today. Today's a special day."

"Is it?"

"Course it is. Aren't they all?"

Graham sighed, got dressed, tiptoed downstairs to the kitchen, grabbed a glug of gold-top milk straight from the bottle, then headed outside. Vaguely it occurred to him that he should leave a note for his mother to let her know where he and Viv were going, but (a) he had no idea where they were going and (b) his mother would be sleeping off last night's Babycham binge till midday at least and there was every chance he would be back by then.

"Mum's going to crucify me about that windowpane," he told Viv.

"If she notices," Viv replied, "which she won't. Tell her a pigeon flew into it. They do. It happens."

Viv was astride his Raleigh Chopper. It was *the* bike, one that was universally envied and coveted. It had a purple frame, the only colour worth having, and Viv had customised it with every fitting and accoutrement imaginable. Rainbow rubber tassels dangled from the ends of the handgrips. Bright red insulation tape was wrapped round the "apehanger" handlebars, creating a barber's pole effect. Playing card spokey-dokeys rattled, machinegun-like, as the wheels turned. There was a plethora of lights. There was a bottle carrier. There were panniers. There was even a set of chrome wing mirrors, as on a mod's scooter.

Next to this dream machine, the sensible Dawes three-speed town bike which Graham hauled out from behind the garage looked very staid indeed.

"I've got snacks." Viv indicated his panniers. "I've got something else as well," he added with an enigmatic smile.

"What?"

"It's a surprise. Let's go."

Viv sat back in the Chopper's banana seat and started pedalling.

It was pointless asking for some kind of schedule or itinerary. Viv Bentall had a plan, and Graham's role, as Viv's best and only friend, was to shut up and go along with it.

Graham took off after him.
The sun was coming up.

A shadow falls across the setting sun. Man on horse, in perfect silhouette, so that it's hard to make out where man ends and horse begins, and vice versa.
Horse whinnies. Man reins in, looks down.
"Howdy, pardner."
You know who this is. The voice is halfway between a hiss and a croak, sandpapery, painful. The voice of someone whose throat was damaged by hanging, so the story goes. He dangled but survived. And man and horse, you now see, are not merely silhouetted—they are all in black. The man wears black from top to toe, from Stetson to spurs. The horse's glossy hide is the pure black of a starless night.
It can be but one person.
They say to meet him is to meet death.
He cannot be out-drawn. He cannot be out-ridden. He haunts the land like a dark spectre. You can search for him, but you will not find him unless he wants you to, and if he wants you to, you might wish he never had.
He is . . . the Black Rider.

The two boys rode out of town, past the newly minted sign which boasted to all-comers that their tucked-away little Sussex conurbation had recently been twinned with somewhere unpronounceable in France and further twinned—tripleted?—with somewhere even more unpronounceable in Germany. Traffic was light on the roads. They encountered a Citroën 2CV, a Morris Minor, a motorbike with canvas-roofed sidecar, a Bond Bug three-wheeler (like a motorised wedge of orange cheese), a Rover P6 and, at last something that wasn't crap, a Triumph Spitfire. Viv set a fast pace but Graham had no trouble keeping up. Choppers had small wheels. They were bikes meant for parading up and down the street, stately showing-off, wheelies, giving "backsies" to your mates, not for speed. Graham's Dawes wasn't glamorous but had a far superior effort-to-output ratio.

Two miles, three, four they went, into the dawning day that was gradually getting hotter and promising to scorch like a furnace later. Past woodland, farmland, along hedgerow-lined lanes, and the sweat was trickling into Graham's eyes, and on they rode.

○ ○ ○

The Black Rider dismounts. His stallion, which has never been favoured with a name, stands stock-still, head low, barely flicking its tail. The Black Rider crosses over to where you lie on the ground. Rowels jingle. Leather creaks. The Black Rider hunkers down beside you.

His face is masked, sheathed in a black silk bandanna. The only part of his body visible is his eyes, and they are black too. Oh so black.

"Bullet to the gut," he says. Almost imperceptibly he shakes his head. "Slow. Nasty. Ain't no comin' back from that one. Ya know the snake who did this to ya?"

You nod.

"Friend a yers?"

Nod again.

"Caught ya unawares?"

A third and final nod.

"Least it weren't in the back. That's the worst, when a friend shoots a friend in the back."

Graham and Viv had been friends for nearly a year, virtually since the day Graham moved into town with his mother. He had arrived fatherless and forlorn, tagging along behind a woman who'd given up on men in disgust and entered into a long-term relationship with the bottle instead. Graham's mother wasn't an aggressive or violent drunk, she was a sentimental, melancholy one, and when sober she was even-tempered but perpetually groggy, just about capable of keeping a household running but not much more. Her culinary skills stretched to assembling a Vesta meal and heating up canned soup. Mostly Graham lived on cereal, Marmite sandwiches, cold baked beans, Sodastream drinks, and a steady intake of pear drops, kola kubes and Aztec bars from the sweetshop, "Pleasant Confections", down the road.

Nobody talked to him on his first day at his new school except Viv, and Viv talked to him mainly because nobody ever talked to Viv either. Viv was the class weirdo, a rich kid with a screw loose, whose barrister dad and solicitor mum gave him everything, everything he could wish for, except their time and attention. His nickname was Mental Bentall, which he hated. He got ribbed about his first name, too, but that didn't bother him nearly so much.

"'Vivian'?" someone might sneer. "Isn't that a girl's name?"
"Who's the world's greatest living batsman?" Viv would retort.
"Uhh..."
"I'll tell you. It's Vivian Richards. Now you go and tell Viv Richards that he's got a girl's name."

He just couldn't stand being called Mental Bentall, though. It drove him... well, mental. Once, he attacked a boy in the year above who'd yelled the nickname across the playground. He went at the kid with a pair of compasses, in a berserker rage, and very nearly took his eye out. After that, few were so bold as to use the nickname to his face, although they muttered it behind his back often enough.

Graham and Viv soon established that they had two things in common. One was that they were both, to all intents and purposes, parent-free. Viv's mother and father were forever at work. Graham's mother was forever lost in a booze haze while his father was forever in another part of the country, a long way away, and forever with the woman ten years his junior whom he'd left his wife for.

The other thing they had in common was that they both loved TV westerns. *Bonanza, The High Chaparral, The Virginian, Alias Smith And Jones*, you name it, if it had horses, six-guns and dusty desert towns in it, Graham and Viv were fans. They liked other types of programmes too. *Starsky And Hutch* was good, *The Six Million Dollar Man* wasn't bad, and *Charlie's Angels* was worth watching for Farrah's hair, Farrah's teeth and Farrah's other parts. But it was westerns that truly floated their mutual boat.

And one series stood out above all the others. One series, for them, was truly unmissable.

It wasn't on often. It appeared irregularly, whenever, it seemed, the BBC had a hole in the schedules that needed filling. The boys scoured the Radio Times every week to make sure they knew whether and when an episode was going to be aired, and then they made sure to memorise the day and time and be there in front of the television at least ten minutes early, so as not to miss a single second. If they could, they would watch it together, preferably at Viv's place, where there was a colour set (Graham's mother had a measly little black-and-white). If not, separately, and then they would discuss it, endlessly, the next day.

The Black Rider.

○ ○ ○

The Black Rider gazes down at you.

"Reckon help's comin'?"

You can't speak. Too much effort. You try to nod one more time, but now even that is beyond you. You're too weak. You hope your eyes give the Black Rider his answer.

"Help ain't comin'," he informs you, almost sadly. "If'n it were, it'd be here by now. Yer slippin' away, pardner. No two ways about it, and I ain't gonna lie to ya or soften the blow. Ya got mebbe ten minutes left, a quarter-hour at most. What ya need to do now is ya need to make yer peace with the world and get ready to move on. But rest assured, I'm gonna stick with ya to the end. I'll see ya through this. It ain't so bad, dyin'. Hurts, but then any mother'll tell ya that givin' birth hurts too, an' birth's the opposite a dyin', so pain ain't the best way to judge the value a somethin'."

The Black Rider flicks the brim of his hat upwards.

"So let's just set here a spell, the two a us," he says, "an' wait. Won't be long."

"Not long now," said Viv, looking over his shoulder, in reply to a question Graham hadn't asked but wanted to. "Not far."

That gave Graham an inkling what their destination was, and a few panting minutes later his suspicion was proved correct.

The White Hole.

It was a quarry that had been hacked out of the South Downs hillside, a broad, deep gouge where Victorian workmen once mined gypsum for use in the building trade and making plaster of Paris. Sheer chalk cliffs formed an amphitheatre around a floor contoured with mounds, dips and slopes. Perfect for stunt biking and re-creating, on a more modest scale, the kind of daredevil leaps pioneered by Evel Knievel. Perfect, also, for hide and seek, kick the can, and other similar games, as there were profuse outcrops of buddleia, brambles and hawthorn all over the site.

The two boys stopped. They feasted on pickled onion flavour Monster Munch and Sherbet Dib-Dabs. Then they got to playing.

There was only one game worth playing as far as Graham and Viv were concerned. They were lawmen, and they were on the trail of the Black Rider. They had their cap guns, their holsters, their six-point-star badges. Viv, being Viv, also had a fringed suede waistcoat,

THE BLACK RIDER

a hat and a pair of crisscrossing bandoliers which he sometimes let Graham borrow, if he was in a generous mood.

The Black Rider was a no-good varmint, everyone knew that. What he had done initially to deserve this reputation, what heinous crime had led to him being permanently on the run, was never made clear in the series, but it must have been something terrible because Sheriff Tom Maclennan and his sidekick Deputy Cletus Grace had dedicated their lives to pursuing him and bringing him to justice. Each episode brought him just within their grasp, only for them to lose him at the last moment, usually because some other crisis—a cattle stampede, a goldmine cave-in, a rogue Indian on a scalping spree, a handsome young widow who needed help defending her ranch against rustlers—demanded their attention and they were too honourable to ignore a cry for help.

"Next time," Sheriff Maclennan would say, ruefully, just before the end credits rolled. "Next time we'll git that darn Black Rider."

In the boys' pretend version of *The Black Rider* Viv was always Maclennan, naturally, while Graham, no less naturally, was always Deputy Grace, and they would start the proceedings off by repeating together the voiceover spiel that introduced every episode, growled over the picking of a lone steel guitar before the rollicking jug-band theme tune kicked in.

"They say to meet him is to meet death," they intoned. "He cannot be out-drawn. He cannot be out-ridden. He haunts the land like a dark spectre. You can search for him, but you will not find him unless he wants you to, and if he wants you to, you might wish he never had. He is..."

Deep breath. Drop an octave.

"The Black Rider."

Then the game began.

Today, Viv had decided the scenario was that the Black Rider had been sighted somewhere up near Devil's Gulch, for which location the White Hole was standing in. Maclennan and Grace had travelled there to investigate, and now found themselves under fire from the man himself. There would, Viv promised, be rockslides to contend with, an earthquake, and possibly also a forest fire, which the Black Rider would ignite in order to smoke them out.

Exciting stuff.

For two hours they played—running, leaping, rolling, shooting, spotting the Black Rider, aiming, just missing him, getting shot at in return, avoiding falling boulders, fleeing flames, and much else besides. Graham, as Grace, took a bullet in the arm, but it was only a graze, a flesh wound. Maclennan bandaged it up with a handkerchief and Graham was soon back in the fray and a few minutes later had forgotten he'd even been injured.

Flesh wounds, in *The Black Rider*, seldom troubled anyone for long.

"Bullet wounds bleed bad, don't they?" says the Black Rider. "Bleed like crazy. Make a mess a yer body as well. Rip through the skin, tear up the flesh. Ya seen that fer yerself. There's things down there"—he gestures to your belly with a black-gloved hand—"things pokin' out that got no right to be pokin' out. Things that weren't never s'posed to see the light a day. Death's a helluva messy business, pardner."

You're happy simply to listen to him, that raspy cold voice of his grating on your ears but also strangely soothing. No matter what he's saying, it's nice to hear words, something other than the wails of the birds spiralling above. The Black Rider's words drown out the birds' ugly, impatient glee.

"Ya came lookin' fer me," he goes on, "an' now ya've found me. So whaddaya think? Ain't quite what ya expected, huh? Folks'll tell you I'm a bad guy, and I admit I done some deeds I ain't particularly proud of, but in situations like this one, well, you know what? I guess I'm just 'bout the best buddy a man could have."

Finally the two best friends had had their fill of the game. Worn out from their exertions, they collapsed on their backs on a patch of grass and lay staring up into cloudless blue infinity for a while.

Then Viv said, "Remember I told you I'd brought along a surprise, Graham?"

Graham didn't. Then he did.

"Want to see?"

"Sure." *Sure.* Graham was still speaking in a Wild West drawl.

"I'll go fetch it."

Viv rummaged in one of his bike panniers and returned with an object wrapped in a yellow dustcloth. Slowly, like a conjuror revealing a trick, he unpeeled the dustcloth from the corners, to expose . . .

A gun.

THE BLACK RIDER

A proper gun. Graham could tell that straight away. Not a kids' plastic six-shooter that took a roll of caps for ammunition. A solid, man-sized revolver made of dimly glinting metal.

"Belonged to my grandfather," Viv said. "Mark VI Webley service revolver. Granddad died last year and my dad inherited it. He's been keeping it in a drawer in the desk in his study. Didn't think I knew it was there, so he didn't think the drawer needed locking. Isn't it cool? Granddad had it during World War Two. To think he might actually have killed Nazis with this..."

Anyone with any sense knew that there was nothing cooler than killing Nazis.

"Is it loaded?" Graham asked.

"Oh no. You can tell. Look."

He held the revolver towards Graham, barrel first.

"See?" he said. "The holes in the cylinder—there's nothing in them. That's how you know."

Graham nodded, gazing in wonder at this chunky, rugged instrument of death-dealing.

"Let me hold it."

Viv passed the revolver to him instantly, without question. Graham closed his hand round the grip. Such weight. You never got that from films or telly, how much a gun actually weighed. Like hefting a large rock in your hand. And the smell, faint but distinct, a combination of grease and fireworks.

He held it up to his eye. Sighted along the slender barrel. Loosed off a couple of imaginary shots without pulling the trigger. *"P-kow! P-kow!"*

"My go," said Viv.

Graham handed the Webley back. Viv did the same as he had done. Then he inserted his forefinger inside the trigger guard. He turned to Graham.

"I am the Black Rider," he said, grinning from ear to ear, a wicked brightness in his eyes. "Time you got what's coming to you, Deputy Grace."

He raised the gun.

P-KOW!

You wince, recalling the noise. Like a clap of thunder, with you right at the heart of it. A full orchestra compared with the feeble solo pop-pop-pop of the caps.

Gutshot

Birds flew up from cover, startled by the detonation—the same birds whose tatter-edged T-shapes are now pivoting in the sky around a ghost moon, like water going down the plughole. Soon you will be carrion. They know.

"Cain't see all the rounds in a cylinder," says the Black Rider. "'Specially not the one in the chamber that's at the top."

You realise that. You realised it the moment you were thrown back onto the ground by an almighty punch to the abdomen.

"Someone shoulda broken the gun open. Someone shoulda checked."

"I should've checked."

Viv's voice—panicky, hiccupping, shot through with raw terror.

"Oh my God I should've checked. I thought . . . Oh my God. Oh Jesus. Are you OK, Graham?"

Graham was sprawled on the ground. His stomach was on fire. Of course he wasn't bloody OK.

"I don't think you're . . . I think I missed any vital organs," said Viv. "Yeah. Stomach, that's not so bad, is it?"

"Feels . . . pretty bad," Graham wheezed.

Viv glanced down at the still-smoking Webley in his hand. His stare was accusing, as if what had just happened had been entirely the gun's fault.

"Look, you'll be fine," he said, recovering some of his self-assurance. "I know you will. I'm just going to . . . well, go. You lie there. Someone'll come along, I'm sure. I can't stay here. If I'm caught with you, it'll be bad. People will know what I did, and that'll be bad for my mum and dad. Their son can't break the law. They have to resign if I do. It's the law. So you stay where you are. It'll be all right. Honest it will. And when someone comes, just tell them you were on your own, you had an accident. Yeah? All right?"

He backed off toward his Chopper.

"Viv!" Graham yelled, and the penalty for crying out like that was a fresh burst of agony from his midsection.

"You'll be fine," Viv replied, getting onto the bike, heeling up the kickstand, not looking back. "It's just a flesh wound."

It wasn't, though. Graham's hands came away from clutching his stomach awash with gore. This was nothing like any onscreen flesh wound he had ever seen.

"Viv . . ." he groaned.

THE BLACK RIDER

A crunch of tyres, a click of the crossbar-mounted gearshift, and Viv was gone.

"Nearly gone," says the Black Rider. *He sounds almost kindly now. And you are. You are nearly gone.* The world has grown dim around you, as though it is a ship at sea, carrying on to somewhere else, heading over the horizon and leaving you behind.

"I think ya kin stand up."

The Black Rider offers you his hand. You take it. It is cool to the touch. With his assistance, miraculously, you rise.

"This way, pardner."

He leads you to his horse. He mounts first, then hauls you up into the saddle behind him, easily, as if you weigh nothing.

"They say to meet me is to meet death," he whispers. "I cain't be out-drawn. I cain't be out-ridden. I haunt the land like a dark spectre. You kin search fer me, but you will not find me 'less I wants ya to, and if I wants ya to, ya might wish I never had. I am..."

But he doesn't need to say his name,

Not any more.

And together, you with your arms tight around his waist, the two of you ride off on that black horse, into the sunset.

James Lovegrove was born on Christmas Eve 1965 and is the author of over 35 books. His novels include *The Hope*, *Days*, *Untied Kingdom*, *Provender Gleed*, the *New York Times* bestselling *Pantheon* series (*The Age of Ra*, *The Age of Zeus*, *The Age of Odin*), and *Redlaw*, the first volume in a trilogy about a policeman charged with protecting humans from vampires and vice versa. In addition he has sold more than 40 short stories, the majority of them gathered in two collections, *Imagined Slights* and *Diversifications*. He has written a four-volume fantasy saga for teenagers, *The Clouded World*, under the pseudonym Jay Amory, and has produced a dozen short books for readers with reading difficulties, including *Wings*, *Kill Swap*, *Free Runner*, *Dead Brigade*, and the series *The 5 Lords Of Pain*.

James has been shortlisted for numerous awards, including the Arthur C. Clarke Award, the John W. Campbell Memorial Award and the Manchester Book Award, and his work has been translated into 15 languages. His journalism has appeared in periodicals as diverse as *Literary Review*, *Interzone* and *BBC MindGames*, and he is a regular reviewer of books for the *Financial Times* and contributes features and reviews about comic books to the magazine *Comic Heroes*. He lives with his wife, two sons and cat in Eastbourne, a town famously genteel and favoured by the elderly, but in spite of that he isn't planning to retire just yet.

James says, "*The Black Rider* is my nostalgic tribute to the TV western series I grew up watching in the 1970s, shows like *The Virginian*, *Alias Smith and Jones* and their eccentric cousin *The Wild Wild West*. I fused those with other shows I remember fondly, such as *The Invaders* and *The Fugitive*, to generate a fictional TV western that I'd have loved to have seen: *The Black Rider*. Of course, when you're a kid the line between reality you live in and the fantasy you imbibe often blurs, and in some instances it damn near ceases to exist..."

THE ALABASTER CHILD
Cat Sparks

The whole time we'd beat him, Chaedy had leered at me as if he knew some goddamn awful secret. Just another sly dog relic dealer, same as all the others. I still don't know how he got out of that cage.

He was old enough to be my grandfather—not that I'd ever had one. Him and his kind had picked the verge bone clean, yet somehow good stuff was still getting scrounged. Relics worth big coin in Sammarynda. Broke Highway was the pot o'gold, he'd confessed through shattered teeth. Eventually. It took us half the night.

I hated the filthy smirk upon his face and the fact that none of us could smack it off him. He seemed amused that Dartmoor was sending *me*. Laughed himself sick over it. I took the job anyway—why wouldn't I? Us stateless types can't afford to be too picky.

Three weeks on and I'd had to kill a stranger. My knife remained embedded in his chest. I knelt beside his lifeless form, groped blindly for the handle. Warm, sticky blood ran down my hand as I raised the blade at the sound of approaching footsteps.

He'd lunged at me unexpectedly, his weapon drawn and ready. Not the first to try it on when he saw I was a girl. Won't be the last one either but I'm tougher than I look. Harder too. The road sure takes it out of you.

A woman's face ghosted from a flicker of torchlight. She stepped towards the fallen man, paused a moment, kicked him hard. Then once more in the ribs for good measure.

"Serves him right," she said smugly. "Deserved everything he got, and anyway, who's going to speak for him out here?"

She didn't give my knife a second glance. "Did he get you, love? Hurt you very bad?"

"He came out of nowhere," I explained. "I didn't—"

"Ah, don't sweat it any. You did his wives back home a favour. But whatever are you doing on Broke Highway all alone?"

Looking for something, of course—aren't we all? According to Chaedy, that artefect had come from some place near here. A curious relic of brass and shiny silver. A *special* place, he'd called it—said I'd know it when I saw it. But he'd have said anything at that point of proceedings. So far I'd seen nothing of value. Just a lonely desert highway strewn with ruins of a thousand lifetimes past.

"Come sit by the fire, then. You'll catch your very death." The woman gave the corpse a final kick. "Get that warm robe out from under him. Won't be needing it where that bastard's gone."

Not in the mood for arguing, I tugged the robe free while the woman held the torchlight firm and steady.

"Name's Ennah," she said. "Got business in Brokehart. Obviously." She indicated her swollen belly with the hand not holding the torch.

"You're pregnant?"

"Aren't you?"

I shook my head.

"Thought that was why he was after you. Oh well. His mistake."

His mistake, alright. I hadn't meant to kill him. I hadn't meant to do so many things, amongst them following Chaedy's cryptic hints to the arse end of the world.

Ennah led me back through darkness to a campfire where two young women huddled close. Both looked up when we approached but neither spoke.

"That one's Lahela, the other one's called Ruth. Ruth, fix the lass here some beans. What did you say your name was?"

"Gehenna Diel." I told the truth. There didn't seem to be much point to lying.

"Fix Miz Diel here old Shithead's share. He landed on the sharp end of her blade."

Ruth scrambled to her knees and filled a bowl from the blackened cooking pot. She passed it over, admiration glowing on her filth-streaked face. Neither girl seemed troubled by news of *Shithead's* death.

"By Grace, it's good to have someone to talk to," Ennah said. "Shithead didn't like us signing. Treated us like cattle to market he did."

Lahela looked to be no older than Ruth, fourteen, maybe fifteen. Both were pregnant. I wondered if they were sisters. They seemed so terribly young and vulnerable. Like they'd already seen far more of life than was good for them.

"Neither of you can speak?"

Both shook their heads, their faces flush with something resembling shame.

"They've been fixed," said Ennah.

"Fixed? What is 'fixed?'"

"Show her."

Ruth sat forward on her haunches. She took my hand, opened her own mouth and placed the tip of my index finger inside. I reeled back in disgust at the thing I touched. The stump of a tongue, crudely cauterised. The girl lowered her eyes.

"Who did this to you?"

Ennah shrugged. "Their own people quiet them, I guess."

Quiet them? No matter how far I travelled, cruelty never seemed too far behind. Some days I was glad I remembered nothing of my own childhood. Other times that empty gap of years was all I thought about. "Why are you going to Brokehart?" My beans, uneaten, sat beside me on the ground.

"Only two reasons anyone bothers with that town. The Manor House or the Tide."

I'd never heard of either but I didn't want to tell them that. The three looked harmless but out here in the Badlands, things were rarely exactly what they seemed.

"I'll take his papers, pay the brokerage fee," said Ennah. "Wrap my face and cover up with his cloak. No one'll be the wiser. If they are, I'll pay 'em off. It's not like I got anywhere else to go."

She shot me a look that said I didn't understand. She was right. I didn't.

"And what about them?"

Ennah shrugged. "They birth at the Manor House. At least they'll be fed and warm for a time, then paid when they deliver. They got papers. Forged, but good enough. They'll be all right once we're through the gate."

The girls seemed unconcerned to hear their futures plotted out by others. Both were captivated by the fire, watching yellow and orange flames dance along the burning thornbush twigs.

"We're going to have to bury him," said Ennah thoughtfully. "Otherwise dogs'll be bothering us all night."

That got the girls' attention. They scampered off into the darkness, making strange sounds in their throats that I later recognised as tongueless laughter. When they eventually dragged it to the fire, the naked corpse was missing genitals and a face. Rocks had evidently been used to perform the mutilations.

The four of us dug a shallow grave with hands and knives. When the burying was done, Lahela retrieved the dead man's possessions: boots, his coin purse and a shirt.

I eyed the shirt distastefully.

"Have you seen yourself?" said Ennah.

Even in the low light of the fire, I could see my own shirt was filthy, ingrained with dirt, dried blood and who knew what else. The boots were mine if I wanted them. The coins we split four ways.

Once the excitement was over, Lahela and Ruth curled together by the fire. Dogs howled hungrily in the distance. At least I hoped they were dogs.

"You from 'round here?" Ennah asked.

I shook my head. My origins were uncertain. I didn't even know how old I was but she didn't need to know that. Most folks guessed me somewhere around thirty.

"Broke Highway sees a lot of travelers. They come to Brokehart for Tide harvest thinking to strike it rich. Mind you watch your back and your front. Nobody in Brokehart can be trusted."

"I'll mind," I assured her. "I'm not here for any harvest."

"Sure you are," she smiled. "One way or another, that's what everybody comes for."

No wall protected Brokehart from the savagery of the desert. No gate or bridge, just scattered stones and a lopsided canvas awning propped on ancient poles. Underneath, a fat man dozed, nestled comfortably amidst a stack of faded mats. His desk was a packing crate inscribed with heat-etched symbols. Upon it huddled a thick pile of brittle papers, weighted against occasional breezes with a rock.

"You must give him a coin and tell him a name," Ennah whispered.

"What coin? What name?"

"Doesn't matter."

The fat man raised a bushy eyebrow. He swigged from a glass bottle as the four of us approached.

Her face and body wrapped up tight against prying eyes, Ennah thrust a wad of papers at him impatiently.

"Family business?" he inquired, eyeing Ruth and Lahela with casual interest. He rifled through the topmost pages before directing a sideways glance at me.

Ennah tossed a pouch of hammered silver down. He picked it up, gauged the weight then pocketed it with a swift, well-practiced motion.

In exchange for my own coin I received a clumsy disc of clay stamped with what looked to be a number. Once that was done he waved us though.

Out of earshot, Ennah shrugged. "Some days you gotta fight for it. Some days no one cares. Luck's on your side today, Gehenna Diel. Hope she stays with you. You're gonna need her when the Tide comes in. No one leaves this cursed town 'til it does."

"Tell me more about this tide."

Too late. Ennah was already distracted by the cluster of women in loose-fitting shifts gathered before the black gates dead ahead.

"Sorry friend, but it's the end of the line. Ask anyone about the Tide. It's what they're here for."

Ennah unwrapped her face and affixed a cosmetic smile. I did my best to appear disinterested as women converged on the three of them, patting their bellies as if they were long lost family members, which, for all I knew, they might have been.

The walls of the Manor House were high and topped with fearsome shards of broken glass. Beyond its black-lacquered railings, well-muscled guards patrolled. There was even a garden, a patterned scattering of succulents. At its centre, a pillar upon which sat a statue. An alabaster child, its arms outstretched in search of comfort. Something I suspected there'd be little of in the whitewashed buildings behind.

Offering coin for babes seemed harsh, yet perhaps no more so that the lives Lahela and Ruth could have offered children on their own.

Ennah's, I sensed, was a different story, but she hadn't chosen to share it and I'd decided not to ask.

Now and then young women, sometimes pregnant, sometimes not, would cross the well-manicured courtyard bearing baskets of laundry. The guards ignored them and, eventually, I did, too. There were no children, babes or otherwise. The buildings beyond the metal gates were silent.

Brokehart's main street extended in a sullen strip edged with rows of dilapidated shopfronts. Most were made of mud bricks, the occasional extravagant porch of sun-warped wood. Discord radiated, a sense of menace lurking just below the surface.

The street was wide enough to take four waggons side-by-side. Five if they were the coastal type rather than the all-terrain vehicles of the interior. Further along, the buildings became much grander, the tallest of them topped with domes and spires. Everything in Brokehart was old as time and covered in a clingy film of dust.

Brokehart's transient inhabitants were a mix of races: dark skin, light skin, faces inked and plain. Some wore clothing faded from former opulence. Others appeared to have stitched themselves into sacking.

I went for a casual promenade—an unwise move that drew too much attention. Only hawkers and traders walked the street. Women with hair bound tight in scarves balanced baskets of bread on their hips, selling miserly strips of it to the hungry. Water sellers, too, bulging 'skins slung across bent backs. The Tide was the only topic of conversation amongst the thin-shouldered men and women whispering in whatever scraps of shade the dilapidated awnings offered.

At the far end of the street stood a whitewashed building with smooth oval windows. Scantily clad girls and pretty boys slouched on benches through the glassless frames, fanning themselves against the morning's heat. I turned my back on the brothel. Nothing in Brokehart resonated like Chaedy threatened it would. There was nothing to do but to wait for the mysterious Tide. A wait I hoped would not be a long one.

A spot at a verandah's edge offered paltry shade but conversation was lively. I sat, cross-legged, my back against the crumbling mud brick wall. Here, prospectors with more hope in their hearts than meat on their bones traded enthusiastic stories of other times and other Tides. I strained my ears, gleaning as much detail as I could.

"The '57 was the one. Whole family's fortune grew from that tiny globe. Weren't no bigger than a baby's fist."

"What the jeepers was it?"

"Never did find out. Something from the old time. The damn thing glowed when you set it down on stone."

"I don't believe it. I been 'specting this stretch for a decade. Dug out metal aplenty but never nothing worth big money."

"You gotta know where to look, Cleve. Gotta dig down deep, not just go pecking away at the surface like a chicken."

Laughter erupted amongst the red-faced folks.

"Depends where you're set to digging, don't it? All depends on luck o' the Tide. Isn't nothing clever about it. Just plain ol' luck is all."

Cleve snorted. "They don't tell us all they know. Can't tell me they don't got inklings of what's in there and what ain't."

"They don't know any more than ordinary folks, Cleve. You've done all right. Don't know what you're whining on about."

I waited until hunger made my stomach growl before breaking out my meagre rations. How long would we sit here baking in the sun waiting for something to happen? A few hours at most, I'd thought, but by mid afternoon nothing had changed. People seemed to take things in their stride.

"Will the Tide come in today?" I eventually asked one of the women.

She laughed. "Your first Tide is it, dear? You gotta have patience. Tide comes when Tide comes. Nothing anyone can do about it."

I nodded, wishing I'd held my tongue. The oppressive heat was making me drowsy, sending me to think of other places, other things.

As shadows lengthened and the last dregs of sunlight filtered from the sky, the lines began to break up a little. Some folks apparently had places to go. Others would be sleeping where they sat. Small fires sprang up, with enterprising peddlers hauling carts of dried dung up and down mainstreet. Some, like the woman before me, had supplies of their own. When her fire was going, she, Cleve and the others nudged over to make room for me. I tried not to appear as grateful as I felt.

When they asked for my story, I made one up: how a savage storm had torn me from my caravan. Each had sympathy to spare, a storm tale of their own, and dried meat and figs which they shared without hesitation. Stories, it seemed, ran thicker here than blood. Every one of them had lost a friend or a loved one to the Badlands' unpredictable turbulence.

"This will be my last Tide, for certain," the woman, whose name was Shereet, explained. "I'm getting too old to be digging up a Tidefront. Oughta be home before a hearth fire, grandchildren settling on my knees."

"You don't got any grandchildren," sniffed Cleve.

"Might do. How would you know? Nobody knows what goes on in Sammarynda. Could have ten of 'em by now!"

My ears pricked up, alerted by the name. Long had I ached to visit the coastal cities.

"My Lara went to Sammarynda. Least that's where she said she was heading. Got berth on a 'van heading thataway." She gestured vaguely into the distant darkness. "The 'van come back next season without her. Camel drivers said she made it to the sea, if you can trust what those old dogs have to say."

"I haven't seen any waggons. Nor camels."

Cleve laughed. "That's 'cos the Tide ain't come yet, stupid girl. There's never nothing to see before Tidefall."

"Shush you," said Shereet, glaring at Cleve till he bowed his head to stare at the fire's consolatory embers. "She's new here and she don't know the truth of it—weren't you listening? Didn't you hear about how she got lost from all her kin?"

Shereet leaned in closer and patted me on the hand. "My Lara's about your age, give or take. Wherever she is, I hope someone's feeding her up and sharing their fire. Tide'll come in tomorrow, or a day after. When it does, this dump will come to life. There'll be kites in the air, camels on the road and you can find someone to take you wherever you want, providing you got coin. What matters most is what you scavenge. You're young and quick and nimble with your hands. Not old and slow like me."

"You'll be lucky to find your own arse out there tomorrow," said Cleve, sniggering.

"Will you shut up, you old fool!" said Shereet. "Whose figs you think you're gnawing on right now? Should've left you back in Arrowfell where I found you, camels or no camels."

"She's so green she don't even got a sack!" said Cleve. He pointed at my humble swag. "That bedroll's no good. What's she gonna fit in that?"

Shereet angled her body, allowing a little more firelight to spill upon me. "No sack? Mercy, he's right! You'd better buy yourself one tomorrow. Got any coin?"

"A little."
Shereet paused to think. "Cleve, give her one of yours."
Cleve sat bolt upright. "What did you just say?"
"You heard me. Give her one of your spares. You always bring too many. You can give her one."
"She ain't your daughter, Sher. Not your business to be looking out for her."
Shereet gazed at me thoughtfully. "No, she ain't my Lara. But all the same, you'll give her a sack, and a sup of wine. Two if she really needs it. And you'll quit your complaining or I swear you'll be out there on your own tomorrow, scratching the sand alone with no one to watch your back."
Cleve turned his face away in disgust. But a few hours later he untied a roll of coarse hessian from his pack and tossed it my way, and the wineskin was passed into my hands. When I settled down to sleep that night, the last thing I noticed before drifting off was that Shereet had moved, and was now lying next to Cleve, his arm draped protectively across her stomach.

The first warm streaks of dawn brought Tidesign, a pale shimmer ghosting the horizon, soon to become a seething borealis.
You'll know what you're looking for when you see it. Take me at my word, Gehenna Diel.
Old Chaedy had been mighty sure of himself. I understood why when I caught sight of the raw blue wall of power, with its roiling clouds and stabbing forks of lightning. The blooming Tide held the whole town to ransom. Pots boiled over, prospectors stopped their bickering mid-feud.
The longer I stared at it, the harder it was to wrench my gaze away. Tidescent filled my nostrils, flooding my mouth with a sharp, metallic tang. Bolts of errant lightning lanced the sand, hardening to fangs of smoky glass.
A brace of camel riders came from nowhere, each with a band of bright blue cloth around their arm. They bore weapons, guns and knives. Brokehart prospectors were made to work in a single line that stretched across the sand, evenly spaced. Clay discs issued at the gate determined order. When whistles blew, we began to forage. Those camel riders kept us all in line.

Gutshot

The line advanced at a snail's pace. Tidestorm hung heavy above us, like a richly curdled curtain. I could sense the weight of it, felt the sand beneath my boots shudder each time lightning struck the ground.

We combed the churned-up sand for relics, items spewed forth from the peculiar turbulence. I copied the others—picked up things and shoved them in my sack. Bits of metal dating from the old time. Cogs and discs and coloured twists of wire. I found a brass spoon, a plastic comb and some polished wood. The tip of a spear, hammered from some sort of silver alloy, obviously of worth. A resin disc, bright, clean and flat. Was everything the Tide brought in so beautiful?

Above, the Tidestorm boiled and spat silvery bolts. Gusts of erratic wind blew my headwrap loose, sending my hair into a wind-whipped frenzy. Forcing myself to look away, I focussed my attention downwards, scanning for irregularities. Signs that hinted treasure lay below.

My sack was a fifth full before I encountered something I didn't want to touch. A dead animal, half burned. Nothing I'd ever seen before. Like a rat only much larger, with vicious claws and elongated teeth. Whatever it was, it hadn't been dead long. Perhaps the lightning had killed it?

Not far away, two boys with rough blue tattooed swirls on their faces froze suddenly, eyes cupped to peer into the haze. Something shiny jutted from the sand ahead. I could see it, too. Without a word, they broke the line and ran for it. One tugged it free, shouting loudly to his friends, waving his prize above his head. The second boy whooped for joy, leaping and punching the air with his fist. The boys fought a mock battle for possession of the metal, shoving each other violently to the sand. A third boy scolded harshly, gesturing madly at the forage line. Reminding them where they were supposed to be.

Distracted by the boys, I might have missed it altogether had my boot not struck something hard. Shimmering and smooth, a wheel with smaller wheels inset. Expertly crafted. Nothing from our time. My heart raced. Without doubt, a companion piece to Chaedy's precious artefect. I slipped the machine-thing casually into Cleve's sack, glancing furtively around to see if anyone had noticed.

A clap of thunder sounded. One of the boys leapt suddenly, running past me, hurtling towards the thick of the Tidestorm, howling like a wild beast. Had he lost his mind?

THE ALABASTER CHILD

The camel riders were soon upon him. One of them swung a lasso. The rope easily found its mark. The boy toppled. He struggled valiantly, shouting obscenities, harsh sounds muted by the breeze. The grim-faced camel rider raised his gun then shot him like a dog.

Nobody stopped what they were doing. Nobody said a thing. The boy was left where he had fallen, prospectors stepping over him as if he were a branch.

From this point on were slender pickings. No breaks were called for rest. Folks did not share idle conversation. The forage line went on, no matter what. Back towards the town, I glimpsed small children scrabbling in the sands already passed. Now and then one would spot a treasure. Shouting with glee, they'd run back to the safety of the buildings, delivering the precious item to an adult. The camel riders ignored them. Apparently once the line had swept the sand, the forage became a free for all.

Further on I found another of the dead, rat-like creatures. I passed it over but the family beside me did not. A skinny daughter snatched it up and stowed it within her sack, despite its head being horribly bloodied and crushed.

Suddenly I felt sorry for the lot of them. There was no generosity out here. Life was harsh. Every mouthful must be fought for, even a dead rat too precious to be ignored.

Hours passed with little to distinguish each one from the next. Occasionally a cry of excitement would issue from up or down the line. A rich find inspiring hope in some, envy in others. Such cries solicited nothing but scowls of contempt from the family sweating in the sun beside me.

At other times, singing would commence. Mournful, repetitive dirges that served to keep up the rhythm of stepping, bending and digging. I did not join in and wouldn't have, even if I'd known the words. The body of the slaughtered boy lay baking in the sun. Would no one come to claim it? Not while the Tide harvest ran, apparently.

Finally, the light began to fade and foragers broke formation to head back to town in small clusters. I joined them with an aching back and a growling belly. My sack was heavy, my mind focussed on the precious relic within. Chaedy and his riddles be damned—the only question left was why Dartmoor's raiders hadn't yet taken Brokehart and its precious Tide by force.

"There you are!" said a familiar voice as I trudged across the sand. "We was worried for you when that boy got done. Saw you staring with yer mouth hanging open. Doesn't pay to mind nobody else's business, girl. Didn't I tell you? Didn't nobody tell you?"

I threw up my hands in protest, but I couldn't stop Shereet's clumsy embrace.

"They murdered him."

Shereet shook her head. "Those Badlanders know how it goes. If they're stupid enough to step out of line, it's their own doing."

I was too tired to argue. Shereet hooked her arm through mine and dragged me back to where Cleve and two others stood waiting. Between them they had amassed several sackloads of goods. My own haul was pitiful by comparison.

"There's always a rush for tallying, but I say it's best to wait. Come eat with us. We can go for tallying together."

The Brokehart we returned to was completely different to the town we'd left. The place had literally come to life. Drab verandahs were hung with coloured banners advertising food and drink and other wares. The air was thickly scented with the smell of roasting meat. Laughter too as friends slapped each other on the back, congratulating themselves on fortunes made.

Children scampered underfoot. Music blared behind saloon doors and the lineup at the whorehouse stretched halfway down the street. Other lines snaked in and out of doorways. "Tally rooms," said Shereet, "But we don't want to be bothering with those just yet."

Individual campfires glowed up and down the length of mainstreet and it was to one of these that Shereet and the others headed. I followed obediently, enticed by the delicious smells. I didn't care if it was camel, rabbit or giant rat. Shereet directed me to a square of scrappy matting. I sat, nursing my sack of curiosities. Shereet shoved the others along and squeezed in beside me. Each campfire sported a couple of men standing watchfully over the others, ancient rifles cocked and at the ready.

"Got enough to see you by?" asked Shereet.

I shrugged. "I don't know what anything's worth. I don't even know what half this stuff is for."

Shereet laughed. "No matter what it's for, so long as someone's willing to pay for it." She shouted across the fire. "Hurry up with that meat, some of us are dying of hunger back here."

My belly growled in agreement. Shereet laughed again. She leant in closer, pulling her sandcloak tight across her shoulders. "You look like you're from the coast. Things is different there. Things stay the same, season to season, year to year. But here in the Badlands, things is always changing. Every day is different from the next. Few things stay certain other than pain and death. Head yourself back to the coast tomorrow. Hang around this town too long..." She scowled and shook her head. "Most likely you'll wind up somebody's dinner, be they beast or man."

I accepted a skewer of glistening meat, tearing into it quickly, lest it turn out to be a mirage and vanish into nothing before my eyes.

"My Lara was smart," Shereet continued. "She got out when she could. I laughed at her. Told her she had airs and graces, but she proved me wrong 'cos she never came back to this stinking place."

Shereet chewed hungrily, juice dribbling down her chin. I wanted to ask about her daughter, how she knew so much about her when they'd had no contact for years. But I knew better. Sometimes believing was better than knowing. Who wouldn't want their child to have found a better life than Brokehart had to offer?

Two skins were passed, one of water, a smaller one of wine. I drank from both while listening to the banter. I felt at home beside Shereet, as though I'd known her years. Someday I'd go searching for my mother. Find out why she'd had to give me up.

"Show us what you scored, then," she said, wiping her hands clean on the hem of her skirt.

I hesitated before revealing the relic with the tiny wheels, each one set so tight inside the other.

"That'll be worth a pretty penny," said a long-faced, ginger-stubbled man. The others nodded silently in agreement.

The wine was flushing my bones with warmth. I leant in closer to whisper conspiratorially. "Don't s'pose any of you ever met a man called Chaedy?"

Beards were stroked, heads were shook. "Can't say rightly that I did," said Cleve, his forehead creasing into frown.

"Who owns this town? Who stops the gangs from claiming it as their own? That Tideline seems an orderly kind of business."

"A boy was killed today, just like you said," whispered Shereet. "Nothing much that's orderly 'round here."

The fireside had fallen silent. The weight of a dozen pairs of eyes bore down on me.

I'd said the wrong thing and did my best to deflect it with a shrug. Before too long harmless chatter started up again. More wine and meat was passed from hand to hand.

Shereet stared at me for a very long time, the firelight lending her features an unusual harshness. "There's nothing to be knowing in Brokehart, child. Can't say I didn't do my best to warn you."

She tightened her grip on my hand then let it go.

"More wine?" Cleve offered brightly.

I said yes.

"Get some sleep," was the last advice Shereet had to offer. "You never know what troubles tomorrow will bring."

I drew my sandcloak close against my skin then curled around my sack of treasures feeling more comfortable and contented that I had in a good many years.

The cold woke me. I smelled old ash and wondered where I was. Ice and cramp had set in to my joints. My head ached abominably. When I eventually mustered the balance to sit upright, I found myself alone beside the fire's dregs. Where were Shereet, Cleve and the others? Why did my head hurt so much? Silence hung in a deathly pall across the street. My stomach roiled and then I panicked, realising that my waterskin and my sandcloak were gone. I staggered to my feet, clutching at my belly. No, the 'skin was still there beside me, half covered in sand as though someone had tried to disguise it. But the sandcloak was definitely missing, as was my sack of treasures.

As I stumbled along mainstreet, I tried to piece together the previous evening's events. So many small details—the wine skin passing to my hands, Shereet insisting I should go back to the coast. Had I drunk so much? Surely no more than a few mouthfuls to be polite. The drink had made me sleepy and then there was nothing after that.

I staggered to the nearest building and slumped my back against it, fighting the urge to be sick with all my strength. Doubling over, I waited until the wave of cramps eased up. Beads of cold sweat collected on my forehead. I wiped them away with my fist. *Had I been poisoned? Had anyone else drunk from that second smaller wineskin?*

The few people who were about moved slowly. Campfires smouldered, releasing thin grey wisps of smoke.

Mainstreet was drained of all the evening's vitality and colour. Broken bottles littered the ground. Bodies too, some of them in pools of blood. There had been brawls the night before, the easy camaraderie of wealth turning ugly with nothing more to fuel it than a spilled drink or a misinterpreted glance.

No. It could not be true. Shereet would not have robbed me. Shereet had been so kind. Another cramp racked me and this time I could not hold it in. Falling onto my hands and knees, I vomited, shuddering violently until the deed was done. I sat back on my haunches as relief spread through my body, breathing in great greedy gulps of air.

Searching would be pointless. Shereet and Cleve would be long gone on waggon trains bound for larger towns, departed at dawn with nothing but scuffed ground and camel dung to mark their berths. Soon, even the dung would be scavenged by those ill-fated enough to be left behind.

I walked to the end of the street, staring past the edge of the farthermost building at the Tide's ragged remains. A dull smudge of deep azure was all that was left of it. A few sandcombers, children mostly, sacks dragging limply along behind them.

I turned my back on it and walked dejectedly through town. There were people about but none would meet my eye. Was it always this way when the Tide had passed? Everyone gone but those that gambling, greed and violence had got the better of?

My own carelessness and stupidity were to blame for my predicament. Mulling over the events of the past two days, I found myself at a standstill outside the building Ennah had called the Manor House.

I had paid so little attention to it the day I arrived. Now that everything else had been stripped away, the house might be the only chance I had.

The big black gates were firmly locked, with armed guards patrolling the courtyard beyond. Large men in dark garb with rifles slung across their shoulders, they eyed me suspiciously, but neither did any more than that. I posed no threat on the far side of the gate. Each patrolled their section of yard, now and then glancing aggressively through the bars into the street beyond.

Around the back, iron gates merged into brick. In all, the barrier enclosed three multi-storey structures, one of them with massive wooden doors. There was no way in or out of the place, save through the front gates.

Peering through the bars, I could see someone moving about in the rear courtyard. A pregnant woman in a white ankle-length shift.

"Ennah?"

The woman turned. It was not Ennah. She eyed me distastefully before disappearing through a darkened arch. No guards were posted in the rear courtyard. They probably didn't need them.

I wandered back up front again, slow footed, heavy hearted. In the centre of the cactus garden, the alabaster child regarded me with empty eyes, its outstretched arms reaching past me to the Tideline's fast degrading stain. Something about it made me feel uneasy.

So engrossed was I in my own pathetic misery, I almost missed what happened next: first the opening of the farthest building's massive wooden doors. Waggons! Four of them, the horseless kind, with mighty wheels of inch-thick butyl, treads designed to transverse all but the thinnest sand.

Next, a line of stick-thin waifs, boys and girls in shirts and pants the colour of stained parchment. One by one they climbed aboard the waggons, none of them stopping to give a glance behind.

I stared at them hard. So hard I forgot to breathe. *Chaedy, you godforsaken bastard.*

It was not the Tideline he had wanted me to see, but this. The alabaster statue of the child. That child had once been me. In the courtyard, others like me. Orphans sold into the trade—whatever fancy name they had for it. Orphans by intent, not accident.

I held no memories before the age of five. Few I'd call on willingly before adulthood. Was this where the emptiness began, right here behind these shiny metal gates? I gripped them tight, pressed my face against cold black. Found myself thrown back suddenly when they groaned and shuddered open.

Little memories, cold and hard as stone. Songs and dances learned by rote. Other lessons known as *tricks of trade*. They all came flooding back in a relentless, sickening wave. Images that would stay with me forever.

I'd kill Chaedy when next I saw him. Not clean and easy either, no sharp blade through the heart.

As the waggons thundered down mainstreet, only one of the children met my gaze. A little thing with big brown eyes, her hair cropped close, uneven. She didn't smile or try to wave, just stared without expression. I raised my open arms to her in parody of the alabaster child, hoping to god she couldn't read my thoughts.

Cat Sparks is fiction editor of *Cosmos* magazine and is known for her award-winning editing, writing, graphic design and photography. She managed Agog! Press, an Australian independent press that produced ten anthologies of new speculative fiction from 2002-2008.

A graduate of the inaugural Clarion South writers' workshop and a Writers of the Future prize winner, more than fifty of her short stories have been published since 2000.

She is currently working on a dystopian/biopunk trilogy and a suite of post-apocalypse tales set on the New South Wales south coast.

In the '90s she worked as an archaeological photographer in Jordan. The stark, distinctive landscape inspired several dystopian desert tales including *The Alabaster Child*. For more information, visit www.catsparks.net

THE GHOST WARRIORS
Michael Moorcock

Chapter One
El Lobo Blanc

Shorty, Pinto Pete, The Breed Papoose, and some of the other hands were up on the West Range pretending to mend fences and find strays but were actually, as their boss was aware, searching out shade and sweet water because the heat was so hard and dry it felt like a sack of old cement on your sweat-soaked back. The real reason Tex, head wrangler and owner of the outfit, had sent them up there was to keep some kind of look out, which was just as well because Shorty squints up from where he's standing neck high in a pool of mud and shades his eyes and says to his dozing compadres "Ain't that Swedish Charlie makin' dust yonder?"

Shorty was the binoculars of the Circle Squared Ranch on account of his extreme long-sightedness, so it was a while before his identification was confirmed. It was indeed, the rest agreed, Swedish Charlie, sometimes known as "Sarajevo", who was riding in as if he'd eaten ten bowls of chilli and was about to soil his breeches. He was standing in his stirrups when he reached us and brought his pony to a spectacular "Mexican skid" so that he was on the ground before his mare knew she had stopped galloping. He was all dust. His eyes shone out of the dirt like frightened diamonds, and it only took him two words to explain his condition.

"*El Lobo*," he said, and pointed behind him. He went off to relieve himself against a yucca while Shorty and the others saddled up and checked their Winchesters.

"Damn," said Shorty, cinching himself into his gear and wishing he'd paid more attention to his weapons when he should have. "I thought that sucker was supposed to be six feet under!" He took his Peacemaker from its battered holster and tried to spin the chamber. "Oh, god-damn!" From one chamber he dug out a disgusting mixture of oil and hair, but the gun was no better for his attention. He put it away, relying as usual on his rifle.

"I've been sayin' about that pistol," said Grumpy with deep satisfaction, swinging up alongside him.

"You've been sayin' 'I told you so' all your life, Grumpy," says the Breed Papoose, squinting his handsome eyes to show he spoke in fun. "I'm lookin' forward to the day I take an arrow or a bullet an' find your ugly mug leanin' over me to tell me how I should've seen it comin'." And he patted his own holster. "An' when it happens, Grumpy, don't say I didn't warn you..."

Emphatically the Papoose turned down the brim of his wide Mexican sombrero and kicked his pony forward, whistling *The Streets of Laredo* in that ostentatious, elaborate way of his.

Over his shoulder Charlie told them that at least one war party of Kiowa Apache, employing their usual clever strategies, were maybe twenty miles off but moving in fast. He had seen two other distant warbands and heard of more—though they could be reports of the same parties. If the Apache's leader wasn't the real *El Lobo Blanco* he had certainly convinced the Indians that he was.

One thing was certain—they were coming together and their War Chief bore the Black Lance, the lost totem, their legendary symbol of redemption and revenge. Following this potent weapon, which was also their ginam, nothing less than an Apache army was on its way. News was that they'd already taken and gutted the Pecos Express and destroyed tramlines as far as De Quincey, making it impossible for the army to bring up troops quickly.

Charlie said that the general wisdom was that the White Dog Society was on the warpath because *El Lobo Blanco* had returned from the dead and was leading them. He had been the most feared Apache on the border—cunning, clever and supernaturally lucky, and he had nearly destroyed the Circle Squared once before. Leaving Grumpy, Windy O'Day and Swedish Charlie to follow as rearguard, the other cowboys took off like bullets for the relative security of the Brady Ranch.

The big sprawling fortified house and its various outbuildings were arranged around a good, deep well. The ranch was capable of withstanding for months anything but overwhelming numbers. Its situation, on a lush plain, gave it every advantage, and it could not be taken by surprise. Tex Brady's father had built the place in the years when Indian raids were common and there was no cavalry station nearby to make a savage think twice. Here, single-handedly, he had defended his cabin while his wife gave birth to his son and half the Apache nation seemed to descend on them as if some instinct told the Coaxinca, the Merengo, the Kakatanawa and the Chirichaua that a great warrior was being born to the whites—a warrior who, if he survived, would become their noblest and most admired adversary! They seemed determined that he should not survive.

But survive he did—and grew to young manhood at Dulwich College in England—until recalled hastily to Texas with the news that his father was murdered and the Circle Squared Ranch possessed by Mr Paul Minct, the notorious land-grabber. That tale of vengeance, redemption and love has been told already.

Now the boys skidded into the compound and dismounted in a storm of dust, their chaps flapping about their legs as they ran towards the big house just as Jenny Brady, Tex's beautiful and very recent bride, and Don Lorenzo, his grey-haired old mentor, came out onto the porch. Shorty wasted no time conveying to his mistress and her friend what Swedish Charlie had conveyed to him.

Jenny and Don Lorenzo immediately sprang into action. Barricades were raised, rifle-slits were tested, ammunition was brought out, and two Gatling guns were mounted on their swivels, covering the greater part of the surrounding range while a rider was sent to Los Pinos to warn the citizens and bring the boss back.

Tex was helping out at the circuit court where his friend, the "Prairie Green Incorruptible," Judge Abraham Peakiss, was dispensing that evenhanded law which had made him the most respected authority from Galveston to Port Sabatini. When Shorty found Tex he was about to enjoy an evening drink in the Gin-U-Wine Oyster Bar just down the street from the old French courthouse. The judge was with him and so was one of the plaintiffs the judge had just fined, shaking him by the hand, buying everybody a drink and thanking the old man for his verdict.

Swiftly the foreman blurted out the news. Nobody asked him to repeat himself. Judge Peakiss hurried off to send some telegrams. Captain Gideon went to order an express rider to Austin requesting urgent reinforcements. Mayor Borden called a general town meeting. Lizzy La Paine demanded someone's protection, preferably Tex's. Sheriff Omar Hunt was at the MacGregor farm delivering the usual writ. The plaintiff goggled, turned pale and seemed to be looking around for something to kill himself with. *El Lobo* had that kind of credibility.

Tex Brady ran to his hotel, grabbed up his simple kit and followed Shorty to the ostlers, where his greathearted stallion Geoffrey was already saddled and waiting. As always, he was eager to be off. His ancestors had borne the chivalry of Arabia and galloped with the British at Alhambra, Bengazi and Wadi-al-Djinn. Toledo steel was in his bones. Marekshi powder was in his blood.

Soon the two cowboys were riding hell-for-leather across the open prairie. The only difference was that now Tex Brady wore the famous blue-and-red costume with the black mask and white sombrero of his *alter ego*—the legendary Masked Buckaroo! His reason for donning the costume was his reputation amongst all Indians as an honest broker. That might be the edge which saved their lives. Everyone respected the Masked Buckaroo.

They used neither quirts nor spurs, simply calm, encouraging words, to maintain that wild pace. There was not a motor—steam or electric—to match them in their own element where man and mount became the same creature, thinking and acting as one. Tex's father had always maintained that justice and kindness made simple economic sense. "You get more out of an animal and more out of an Indian if you treat 'em with respect."

A stern disciplinarian and a great patriarch, that old Cattle Baron thought cruelty made no sense at all. He had coexisted with the Indians by acknowledging their ancient rights and customs, for which they were perfectly prepared to allow him some modern rights and customs.

THE GHOST WARRIORS

He knew that a balance of power existed and that if he was ever at a disadvantage, depending upon their prevailing mood and practical needs, they would finish him and everyone else on his ranch. They assumed the same of him without understanding that he believed alternatives to be available. He had no romantic notions about the kind of people they were. They saw their fundamental survival to be dependent upon their military ascendancy, their reputation as vicious conquerors. They had been practising tribal genocide as a way of life since time began.

Like the Indians, he was acting from what he took for profound moral imperatives. He did not know how much invisible power he derived, in Indian eyes, from those people in Washington he so despised. For the times, however, his views were enlightened. Behind his back, because they dare say nothing to his terrible, battle-scarred face, the other ranchers and towners called Meredith Brady an Indian-lover.

The mystical Secret Circle of the Kiowa Apache known as the White Dog Society had tested his sentiments. As he said, "It was one of those cults which catches on and spreads from tribe to tribe faster than slurry through a swimming-hole. A desperate substitute for real power, maybe, but it causes a lot of trouble while it's running."

The chief shaman of the White Dogs was a Kiowa Apache troublemaker called Ulrucha-na-o, which means "Pale Wolf" in his dialect. They believed that, as a presentiment of his coming death, a warrior saw a pale wolf following him. However, if the wolf ran ahead of him, that meant his life ran on also, so long as he followed the wolf.

Pale Wolf's charismatic personality as much as his religious proselytising drew in bored young braves with no future and a history of defeat who believed it might be possible to drive back the whites with magic and drugs as well as courage. When Ulrucha gave the word and lifted up the Black Lance they were ready to take the war-path confident in the understanding that they were protected by powerful magic and that their weapons were equally charmed. This made them even braver and their attacks all the fiercer. And it carried the luck of the devil. For eight months they did seem to lead charmed lives, running roughshod over Texas in one last, cruel, spiritually enhancing bloodletting. This seems common to the generality of religions, whose adherents justify the most elaborate horrors and torments in the promotion and establishment of their faith.

No one called Colonel Meredith Brady an Indian-lover after he had led the war against Ulrucha and his White Dog Ghost Soldiers. The final battle between him and the fighting shaman was a proud legend amongst both peoples. Suffice to say, Ulrucha's scalp was brought back to his enemy's lodge. How Brady's son made reconciliation with the Kakatanawa Apache and became their bloodbrother is another story. After it was over Tex had thought there could never be war between Apache and Texican again. Yet here was the worst news possible!

Hours later, after some tense moments and faster than seemed physically possible, the two men reached the compound of the Circle Squared and threw themselves off their exhausted ponies, calling for hot water and fresh ammunition. After a few moments they noted the eerie silence of the ranch. Though it was evening, no lamps had been lit. From somewhere came the noises of chickens and hogs, the whicker of a horse, the sound of a hammer rising and falling, but no human voices greeted them. Shorty silently pointed out the still, dark shape on the porch. The body of a black Labrador retriever. It had been shot through the eye with a white-fletched Kiowa Apache arrow.

"You ever seen that dog before, Shorty?" murmurs Tex, putting fingers to the creature's throat.

"Nope," says Shorty. "Looks like a man's good hound dog, though."

A sharp sound from somewhere inside.

Tex Brady grew instantly alert, his hands falling onto the pearl handles of his twin revolvers.

"There's something funny going on here, Shorty," he gritted. "And I have to admit I don't like the smell of it..."

Chapter Two
The Scent of the Wolf

As the two men listened, the slow, regular hammering continued to come from the bunk house. Their guns in their fists, the young cowboys warily approached the big building, kicking open the doors and ducking quickly into the shadows.

In the middle of the common room, tied to chairs which had in turn been placed on the old oaken table at the centre, were Grumpy, Pinto

THE GHOST WARRIORS

Pete, Windy O'Day, Swedish Charlie and The Breed Papoose. They were wearing nothing but their pink union suits, boots and hats. They were gagged. Some of the other boys were equally discommoded, lying in corners of the room. The Breed Papoose had made the noise rapping on the table with his fancy silver boot heels.

"Somehow," said The Masked Buckaroo as his Bowie knife expertly sliced through rope and cloth, "this has none of the earmarks of an Apache raid."

"What about the arrow?" Shorty said. "That looks and smells right."

But Tex said nothing, merely frowning as he thought the problem over. He would make no judgements until he had heard the boys out.

Windy O'Day, Tex's oldest sidekick and confidant, told what had happened. Not four hours after the hands had ridden in to the Circle Squared the entire ranch house and its outbuildings had been surrounded by shadowy Apache riders who arrived with the dusk.

"It was right spooky," said the fungus-faced oldster, rubbing at his wrists and ankles and glancing around at his companions for confirmation of his view, "like they was dead. Not a sound out of any of 'em, and all kinda glowin' with that faint, silvery light."

"Natural phosphorescent paint found in the Guadalupe Mountains of New Mexico can give that effect. It is a favourite warpaint of the Kakatanawa Apache and is said to scare the bejeezus out of their enemies." The Masked Buckaroo helped Windy outside to his usual rocking chair.

"Well, boss, I guess it scared the wixwax out of us, too," said Windy philosophically, "because we was impressed. Especially when they didn't attack. They seemed to be darin' us to shoot at 'em. This stand-off went on for a couple of hours and then they kinda faded back into the darkness. We didn't feel too easy about this and were waiting for their next trick when this mist came up all of a sudden, and we heard this single voice calling against a wild wind. My blood ran colder than a Wyomin' weasel..."

"He's right, boss," confirmed the usually sceptical Pinto Pete. "It did things to yore insides, that singin'."

"Couldn't have been worse than Windy's yodelling." Shorty winked at his old friend.

"Come to think of it, it *did* sound a little bit familiar!" The Breed Papoose joined in the fun.

"Well," said Windy, "I don't know about the rest of you boys, but I was barely in control of my bowels *or* my bladder."

Suddenly sober, the experienced old hands nodded their agreement. The scene, the noise, the fog had all combined to terrify them and somehow blind them to the fact that the Indians were sneaking into the compound, weaving in with the mist, getting through the doors and taking over the entire ranch without a single blow falling or a shot fired. When the boys got a hold of themselves again, they were tied up and sitting on the table. Miss Jenny and Don Lorenzo were in the hands of the Apache. And no time seemed to have passed between the events. They did not feel like they had slept or been drugged.

"It was more like a dream," said Grumpy, after some thought. "Like magic might be..."

"Yet it didn't seem bad or crazy, did it?" said Pinto Pete. "We weren't threatened..."

"They took Jenny and Don Lorenzo," said the young vigilante very quietly, his steel-blue eyes glittering behind his mask. "I would call that an act of aggression, I think."

"They didn't seem scared, either," offered Windy. "And I can always tell, boss, when Miss Jenny's scared."

This set the Masked Buckaroo to thinking for a moment. Then he was forced to put intellectual speculation behind him and turn to more pressing action. The Indians had been gone only three or four hours and had left a substantial trail, heading South West towards the US border. The Buckaroo had no trouble following. Not for nothing was he respected by the Kakatanawa as "Pa-ne-e-ha-ska-na-o-nee-pa-no-sta" or Sniffing Dog.

"They have made no attempt to hide their trail. This in itself is significant," said the Buckaroo, reining in on a bluff as the vast, bloody sunset turned them all into black silhouettes and the yellow sky darkened against the blue of the night to reveal a silver wash of stars. He pushed back his sombrero and brushed dust from his face. "They mean for us to follow them."

As soon as his loyal riders were gathered around him, the Masked Buckaroo explained his strategy. They would camp here for the night, but the two men with the freshest mounts would ride out before dawn racing for Port Sabatini via San Antonio with all the information Colonel R.G. "Thunderclap" Meadley could be given. Once they had delivered their messages to Colonel Meadley in San Antonio they would then ride to see Captain Blackgallon Jones, the Welsh Engineer, and hand over the remaining documents.

"The army has some of the best modern inventions at its disposal," the Buckaroo assured his audience. "The wild Indian of today has little chance against such resources. Now we shall see how Texas's investment in modern transport and communications pays off.

"But meanwhile," he reminded his listeners, his voice growing deeper and sterner and his fists hardening around Geoffrey's reins, "my wife and oldest friend are prisoners of these mysterious 'Ghost Warriors', and my guess is they're luring us into a trap."

"But why?" The Breed Papoose had already dismounted and was lifting the saddle off his tired bronc. "They could've taken us all at the ranch. They only had to wait for you, Buckaroo."

"That's what's puzzlin' me," admitted the young vigilante, "and that ain't the only thing. There's a whole lot to this affair which stinks higher than a Pecos fish pond in summertime. No Apache I ever came across behaved like these hombres. Sarajevo, did you ever get to see any of the atrocities you heard they'd committed?"

Sarajevo removed his battered sombrero and scratched his head. "I can't say I did, boss."

"And did you ever meet a man who had seen anything at first hand?"

Sarajevo frowned and thought back carefully. After a while he shook his head. "Nope."

"What are you drivin' at boss?" the Papoose wanted to know.

But the young rancher was not yet ready to speak. While the others made camp, he took his portable writing kit from his saddlebags and penned messages to the necessary personnel. This done, he sealed each envelope, then stretched out with his head on his saddle to sleep.

The Buckaroo was up before his companions, waking them to the smell of fresh coffee on a boisterous fire. Windy unlimbered his pans and provisions and began preparing the hearty breakfast all the boys looked forward to when on the trail. Then messengers were despatched, full of ham, eggs, beans and java, riding like the wind, and the Buckaroo issued instructions to his remaining men.

Soon the little party on the bluff was reduced by a further two. As the sun rose into a blue, misty sky and moonhawks sailed far overhead, the Masked Buckaroo and his loyal companion Windy O'Day continued on the trail the Apache had left for them. Tex knew he was taking a chance, but he was a natural born gambler. He was staking not only his own life and that of his companion—he was staking the liberty and well-being of his wife and mentor.

Soon the two partners were the only moving objects to be seen for scores of miles in that bleak landscape on which the sun fell with savage intensity, casting the long shadows of cactus and jedediah tree across the stirring dirt. Yet the Apache trail was impossible to lose.

"They've driven a highway for us," said Windy, still puzzled. He was used to having a harder time than this tracking Apache. "Is this a band sent to draw us off while something bigger happens somewhere else?"

"I've allowed for the possibility, Windy," the Buckaroo reassured the old-timer. "As I've suggested, modern communications coupled with the most up-to-date transport systems should solve that particular problem. But the mystery remains—where are they leading us and for what purpose?"

"Maybe just one of their devilish tricks," suggested Windy. "Who can figure what goes on in the head of an Apache?"

"I can usually make a pretty good guess," Tex answered modestly. He had, after all, lived the life of an Apache brave and gone through the harshest trials of manhood to the approval of his bloodbrothers. In other words, Tex could think like an Indian. This affair, however, baffled him.

An hour later they arrived at the Telegraph Station to find it a gutted, smouldering shell. The wires had been cut and used to bind the operator and his wife. The couple had been laid across the nearby tram-tracks which had been dynamited and were unuseable from this point on. Their personal property had been removed from the station and piled nearby on the line, as if the thief had ridden off in haste.

As the Buckaroo swung out of his saddle and stopped to cut the man and woman free he looked meaningly at Windy. "Ever hear of the Apache doing this?" he asked.

Windy scratched at his tangled beard and frowned hugely. "Can't say I ever did, boss."

The telegraph operator was, as so many in his profession, a mute, but his pretty and agreeable young wife spoke enough for both of them. Not that she had any clear idea what had happened to her. The Indians had turned up out of nowhere and surrounded the station. "They just sat there on their ponies staring in at us." They had the look of ghosts, she said, but she guessed they were wearing some kind of warpaint. Their leader carried a massive blackbladed war-lance and had, she would swear, the eyes of the devil—"Red and glaring like the fires of hell!" She blushed and apologised for her language.

"Ma'am," said the Buckaroo quietly, "There are some experiences which call for strong language. I suspect this is one of them. What happened next?"

She was not sure. She spoke of a silvery mist growing so thick that it entered the cabin. In some way she could not quite remember the Apache had entered the station. The chief had spoken a few words, but she had not understood them. The sound was awful and made something inside her head hurt. She had been lying on the tracks, watching the fire, before she realised what had happened to them. She was unable to remember earlier events. It was, she said, as if certain things had simply not happened.

"As if Time itself had been cut up at random and then put back together again with pieces missing?" suggested the Masked Buckaroo.

"Exactly," she gasped. "How did you know?"

But the young Texan did not reply. His mind was elsewhere. He was trying to recall a book he had read long ago while at school in England. The book had been in Old German and had been given to him to study. He had become fascinated by its arguments and its odd narrative; and something about this business reminded him of that book, but he could not think what.

Remembering his manners, the Buckaroo touched his gloved hand to his hat. "Just a hunch, really," he answered. "Well, ma'am, we're expecting a track-mendin' team along soon. I don't expect you'll be bothered by the Apache again. Are you willin' to wait here until the army arrives?"

"Since your trail clearly leads after the Indians," she said, "I think I would prefer to await the army." She went to help her balding, red-faced little husband to his feet. She dusted at him vaguely with a cloth. Beaming, he accepted this attention as a show of affection.

"Excellent!" exclaimed the young Texan, taking out his writing set. "I will leave a message with you. It can be despatched as soon as Colonel Meadley's 'Flyin' Tracklayers' arrive and fix everything up."

Clearly delighted that the famously romantic old soldier was on his way, the woman accepted the envelope the Buckaroo handed her.

A moment later Tex was mounted again. Geoffrey's forelegs stamped against the air. He was impatient to be off.

"Good luck, Buckaroo!" The woman waved with the envelope as Tex and Windy disappeared rapidly in a dust cloud of their own making.

Chapter Three
The English Detective

Hours later after following a waddy for a few miles, they found themselves in semi-desert with nothing but the jaspers, joshuas, jedediahs, jeremiahs, mesquite and tumbleweed for company. In the far distance was a scattering of bluffs while even further away they made out the faint, blue outline of a mountain range. They reined in to take stock of the trail. It looked as if the Indians were heading for the mountains. They determined to press on while there was still daylight left.

Windy O'Day was uncertain, however. "What if these redskins are leading us off so they can do something really bad?" the greybeard proposed.

"I have sent the appropriate messages, Windy." The Buckaroo brandished a grey glove he had discovered on the trail. "This means they're leading us to Jenny," he said. "And, old pard, that's all I reckon I care about just now..."

Windy could not disagree with him.

He was about to reply when a voice sounded behind them, startling them both.

Tex whirled in his saddle, his fingers falling to the handles of his revolvers. Then he relaxed, laughing.

"There's only one hombre could sneak up on The Masked Buckaroo like that," he said with admiring respect as he stuck out his hand and addressed the newcomer. "And that's Sir Seaton Begg! Good evening, my old friend. What brings you to this part of the prairie?"

It was indeed the famous English detective, who had last worked with The Masked Buckaroo on the exhilarating *Case of the Glass Armadillo* when the two lawmen had joined forces to solve a particularly sticky mystery and rounded up some pretty ornery hombres in the process.

Sir Seaton was dressed for the bush with a wide-brimmed hat, hunting whites and a voluminous dust-coat. His horse was a sturdy black Arab. In her long holsters were two rifles—a Winchester and a Purdy's. The rest of the detective's simple kit was rolled behind the saddle. He himself was a man in middle years, lean and fit and with an alertness of bearing which might have belonged to a much younger individual. His aquiline features emphasised the eagle sharpness of his grey-blue eyes, displaying a superb intelligence, one that for many years had been used to singular effect against the criminal fraternity.

"I picked you up a couple of hours ago," the detective told his friend. "And because I couldn't initially be sure it was you, I took my time revealing myself. Besides, I rather enjoyed the fun of wondering when you'd spot me."

"I couldn't want a better companion in this escapade," declared the young Buckaroo. "But what are you doing here, Sir Seaton, if I might ask?"

"I would guess it is what you are doing," the detective replied. "I am on the trail of a first-class troublemaker."

"Would he be known by any chance in these parts as Pale Wolf?" asked the Buckaroo.

"That is not the name by which he is most familiar to me," declared the detective, "but I am aware of it. What is your business with him?"

Laconically the Masked Buckaroo recounted the events of the last couple of days.

As they continued to ride, Sir Seaton took out his big onyx pipe and packed it full of his favourite ope. Soon the surrounding air was filled with the wonderful smell of aromatic M&E.

"It certainly doesn't sound like Apaches," opined Windy, after the Buckaroo had finished his tale.

"Well, I think you'll find Apaches are involved," Sir Seaton gestured with the pipe, "and perhaps more than you have bargained for. You are right, however, in suggesting that these are not Apache tactics. They are, in fact, the tactics of the man I seek."

"And who is that?" Tex squinted his eyes against the darkling sky. He could no longer see the range, but the buttes stood black and tall with the sun behind them.

"I am not sure he has a name you would recognise, Tex," said Sir Seaton, "save one, of course. His Kakatanawa Apache name."

"Lib-nu-pa-na-da?"

"He is called that in many languages. I mean the name he has adopted."

"Ulrucha?"

"Just so. For it is not his true name. He adopted it from the first Ulrucha—the man your father fought so long ago. That man was killed in a famous duel."

"I know the story," said the Buckaroo, "and I've seen the evidence for it. Ulrucha's long, white scalp hung in my father's smoking shed for a number of years. Until I gave it back to the Apache."

"You gave it back? Aha!"

As it grew too dark to ride the three riders headed for a sheltered gulch, making camp some distance from the water and preparing the surrounding ground against the mob of varmints which would be attracted to them in the night. Windy O'Day had soon cooked up a tasty meal, and they ate in silence for a while, looking up at the bright stars and listening to the distant song of the coyotes.

"There's nothing like a night spent under the stars in the American wilderness," said Sir Seaton offering his pouch of M&E to his friends.

They agreed enthusiastically as they packed their pipes.

Soon all three men were smoking thoughtfully, their eyes on imagined scenes, as they considered their situation.

After some time Windy spoke. "I reckon they ain't hostiles at all," he said. "Not in the regular sense, anyway."

"Your instincts are perfect as always, Windy," said Sir Seaton. "How do you explain their apparent ability to make themselves invisible?"

"Indians believe they're invisible. Sometimes that's enough, they're so tricky at not being seen, anyway." But even Windy realised his explanation did not fit the stories they had heard, let alone his own experience. "I just can't see how they slipped past us. Hardly a man in the bunkhouse ain't an experienced Injun fighter, and Don Lorenzo knows more about Apache than Geronimo. Yet we wasn't drugged. Unless there was somethin' in that smoke. How could so many get past us?"

"It might not have been many. One, with the appropriate skills, would be sufficient. It's an old trick," Sir Seaton spoke abstractedly, his mind elsewhere.

"Almost a favourite, I'd say."

"You mean you know how it was done, Sir Seaton?" Tex wanted to know.

"I believe I do, Tex. Indeed it is his timeless method. That isn't the mystery. What interests me is how he was able to employ it here."

"Were we drugged, Sir Seaton?" asked Windy, his whiskers bristling.

"Not exactly, Windy. We are dealing with forces which don't need to slip anyone a mickey finn in order to do their work. You may think me mad or worse, gentlemen, but I believe we are dealing with nothing less than the supernatural!"

"You mean we really are fightin' ghosts!" Windy's eyebrows leapt to join his unruly mop of grey hair.

"After a fashion." Sir Seaton fell again into a thoughtful silence, unable or unwilling to answer Windy's many questions.

Tex, too, said nothing but stared into the heart of the fire. It was clear to Windy that his mind was not on supernatural speculation but on the fate of his beautiful young wife, Jenny. It was the Buckaroo's way to make little of his personal fears, but there was no doubt he was in an agony of anxiety.

A little later when the moon came out and turned the whole prairie into a silver fantasy, Sir Seaton got up. They saw him sit down on a rock to inflate an Association soccer ball. When they finally put their heads to their saddles, Sir Seaton was still out there amongst the cactus and the jerrymanda punting the ball expertly through the assymetric goalposts formed by a bent yucca, muttering to himself, making complicated, almost mystical passes with the ball and puffing periodically on his vast pipe.

They were up again before dawn and on the trail with Tex leading the way. He was even more anxious than before to catch up with the men who had captured his wife. For the first time since he had set out in pursuit he began to wonder if he would ever see her again.

Sir Seaton apologised if he had disturbed them with his activities. "I have a rule about exercise," he said. "Especially when I need to think something over. And, of course, usually I have a rod with me. But here—" With a helpless gesture he indicated the dusty, waterless plain.

The mountains were now clearly distinguishable. Glowing like copper in the sunlight, the ancient, eroded peaks were the most south-easterly tip of the Nova Guadalupes, close to where they joined the Guadalupes proper. As they rode Sir Seaton explained what had brought him to this bleak plain.

Gutshot

Called upon to investigate the third theft of the Fellini Chalice, otherwise known as the Garth Cup, this time from the rooms of his own brother-in-law, the detective had uncovered an extraordinary story which had already brought him face-to-face with the League of the Cobbler's Last, the Gateshead Leopard Men and the lost tin miners of Cornwall, and had him crawling through an endless succession of tunnels, storm drains, deep galleries, shafts and corridors in pursuit of his quarry. "For most of my recent experiences, I must say, have taken place underground! A week ago you would have found me sailing the five great subterranean canals which meet at the Quai des Hivers in Paris. I found it rather a relief to take the express zeppelin to Austin and then ride alone under these wide skies."

"What led you to Texas?" asked the Masked Buckaroo, leaning to rebuckle a strap.

"That's a very long story indeed," Sir Seaton told him. "As I said, I am on the trail of the one who has been called Pale Wolf by the Apache. I believe he has gained possession of the Garth Cup and means to use it in a ceremony intended to increase the power of Chaos in our world!"

"Are we talkin' Loo-cif-her, here?" Windy wanted to know.

"If you like," said the English detective.

The old-timer shuddered. "I can take pretty near anything the Apache think up," he said, "but when it comes to devils an' ghosts, sir, I am not your man. I guess my brain don't believe in such things, but my feet never seem to listen to my brain."

Sir Seaton clapped a friendly hand upon Windy's shoulder. "Don't worry, Mr O'Day. You shan't be called upon to deal with the supernatural. That's my business, I'm afraid."

"I ain't sure I'm much better at handling that stuff than Windy," said the Buckaroo doubtfully. "I must admit in my wildest dreams I didn't really believe old Ulrucha was a ghost!"

"He is not a ghost," Sir Seaton declared quietly. "I assure you, Tex, he is something far more powerful and terrible than that."

With a grim, distant expression, he urged his horse into a gallop and for a while raced ahead of his companions, lost in the contemplation of his own appalling knowledge.

Chapter Four
The Will of the Wolf

The three adventurers dismounted at the mouth of a towering canyon and looked in awe at the strange red limestone formations all around them. The Apache trail led relentlessly to this spot and into the depths of the canyon. What Tex and his friends had to work out now was what kind of trap it was...

Although Tex's every instinct was to ride like fury into the canyon and with both guns blazing rescue his wife, he knew that he must continue to use his brains and self-control if he was going to get Jenny free.

Suddenly there came the thin whine of an aero-engine. Glancing upward they saw the dark blue and gold hull of a Texan flying battlecruiser easing herself over a mountain peak and hovering above them.

Tex needed to see no more! While Sir Seaton took out his pocket holograph and exchanged messages with the ship, he removed his Winchester from its scabbard and checked the rifle's action.

"Are we ready, Tex?" Windy wanted to know. He squared his shoulders, ready to face the Devil himself if necessary but not looking forward to the prospect.

"We sure are, Windy," declared the young cowboy. "But you ain't comin' with us, pard. I need you here to signal."

After a quick word of explanation, the Masked Buckaroo shook hands with the old-timer, grinned his famous go-to-hell grin, loosened his twin guns in their holsters, and galloped to ride side-by-side with Sir Seaton Begg into the shadows of the vast canyon.

The silence was profound. All the men heard was the creak of their own harness, the sound of hoofs thudding rhythmically into the soft sand of the canyon bottom. Very evidently many horses had recently come this way.

"I would guess there's maybe fifty warriors," Tex suggested, when Sir Seaton questioned him. "And then there's captives, maybe loot. The waggons aren't too heavily loaded, and the horses pulling them are fresh enough. If I was readin' these signs as I usually would, I'd say it was a whole tribe, or at least a big village, on the move. Has he got his women and children with him, do you think?"

"Not his," said Sir Seaton.

Tex shuddered.

○ ○ ○

The canyon grew steeper, taller and darker, and still the two men rode steadily on until at last they came to a place where the high limestone walls widened into a rough circle and light from above poured down to give the effect of a single beam focussed on the centre of the clearing.

The shadows were full of restless shapes. Tex could smell them all around him, but he did not reveal this. He looked steadily ahead into the pool of light where three figures now moved, as if they had been waiting for him. The first was his beloved wife, Jenny, clearly unhurt and not especially frightened. The second was his wise old friend, Don Lorenzo, his sombrero brim turned down against the blazing sunshine. And the third was a thin, muscular figure in an Apache breechclout and bolero jacket, far taller than the average Indian, whose skin had a strange silvery tinge so that Tex's first thought was *the man's a leper!* From a long, tapering, handsome skull stared two dark, crimson eyes which seemed to burn with fire so ancient it had petrified. And slung over his back was a monstrous war-lance, bigger than any normal Kiowa weapon, its wide blade of black iron burned with a pattern of writhing ruby red hieroglyphs in a language neither man recognised, perhaps some ancient semitic alphabet. The man stared at them with a haughty, almost bored expression. It was as if his chief attention was elsewhere, as if those strange eyes stared into another world entirely.

Tex was immediately struck by the air of melancholy which exuded from the warrior. He had the manner of someone who had lived for ten thousand years or more and had seen nothing to confirm any faith he might ever had had in the world's improvement.

Sir Seaton Begg rested in his saddle, his arms folded over his pommel, his reins loose in his hands. "Good afternoon, your highness," he said sardonically.

The Apache leader turned his head to regard Begg, and his eyes seemed to narrow in a smile. "So you have found me, Sir Seaton. I had not expected to meet again so soon."

"Always a pleasure." Begg took his pipe and baccy from his coat and offered the pouch to Pale Wolf who shook his head, declining gracefully. As the detective filled his bowl and lit the mixture, puffing luxuriously, Tex could contain himself no longer.

"I need to know, sir," he said to the War Chief, "if my wife and friend are your prisoner."

"No longer," said the Apache chief. "They are free from this moment. They have served their turn."

"And what turn was that, sir?" demanded Jenny sharply, moving rapidly to her husband's side. Tex dismounted to embrace her. Thankfully he shook hands with Don Lorenzo. "You were never clear on the issue," Jenny continued, "even the other evening, at dinner."

Pale Wolf smiled wistfully at this. "I apologise," he said. "My problem is not that I lie, but that the truth is unacceptable to most people. Sometimes it is impossible to disguise or even modify. Everything, or almost everything, can be summed up in a brief equation: $z = z^2 + c \ldots$"

He spoke a melodic, vibrant, faintly accented English which made it immediately clear how he could lead so many young warriors by the power of his words alone. The great black war-lance was in his hands and the red engravings seemed to come alive within the metal, reflecting his blazing, ruby eyes, giving his face the sheen of a silver mask.

"Let us finish this," he said.

And then he smiled.

Chapter Five
Apache Dreams

As the strange albino lifted the war-lance to strike, the Masked Buckaroo pushed Jenny behind him and lifted one gloved hand.

From somewhere high above came the familiar notes of a Texan Cavalry cornet calling a complicated 'Alert'. The sound seemed to go on forever, and the young vigilante looked in astonishment as the silver-faced warrior threw back his long head, the white hair cascading and curling about his shoulders, to howl in sudden, impossible unison with the bugle's call.

The black blade itself now began to vibrate and moan, making that hideous, nauseating crooning many had reported. Yet gradually the pitch changed until it, too, sang in unison with the other voices.

Had Pale Wolf planned everything for this moment?

From out of the shadows came a small, crooked individual, carrying a great jewelled chalice which, once the light from above touched it, also began to vibrate in harmony with the bugle, the sword and the man.

From somewhere above a voice was calling—perhaps a warning—but those in the canyon did not hear. Their attention was on the scene taking place under that concentrated beam of sunlight where a bizarre silver-skinned warrior in the full war-gear of a Kakatanawa Apache raised his voice in unnatural, inhuman music, performing a ritual which none doubted to be of the darkest, most powerful magic. As the echo of the bugle began to fade, the albino brought the great, black blade down into the rock at his feet, his voice rising in hideous crescendo. The chalice held by the dwarf seemed to swell and shatter, and the blade bit down into the ground, splitting it wide, revealing a great opening in the darkness, a natural stairway leading into the unknown.

Out of this sudden fissure came a deep, suffering groan, as if Mother Earth herself stirred in her sleep, dreaming of all the evil her children had done. And none there dared imagine what kind of creature bore such pain or uttered such sounds.

Sir Seaton Begg took the initiative. He stepped to the opening and stared down into it, frowning.

Behind him Pale Wolf smiled. "So you have lost none of your courage, old enemy."

"Should I be afraid?" Sir Seaton looked up and met the Apache leader's strange eyes directly.

Pale Wolf shrugged. "I suppose not."

"I must credit you with excellent strategy," Begg said. "You have completely outmaneuvered us in the best traditions of Apache generals! You guessed how young Tex here would act and think. You put yourself in his shoes, imagining how he would cover all possible eventualities, leaving as little as possible to chance because his wife's very soul could be at stake. You knew he would find a way to get the army here, and that's exactly what he did . . ."

Pale Wolf reached into his breechclout and removed a compact silver case. From this he took a small, brown cigarette and placed it between his lips. He lit it with a match and drew deeply of the dark smoke. He appeared to have nothing to do in the world but listen in a relaxed, easy posture, as Sir Seaton Begg continued:

"You didn't want Jenny Brady or Don Lorenzo or even Tex himself.

You were using Tex's brains to make sure the army would be here at a certain moment. And you didn't really want the army. You wanted the army trumpeteer, that wonderful cornet which, of all the armies in the world, only the Texas Cavalry boasts. You did not really want the trumpeteer. You wanted his cornet. Or rather, you wanted a particular sequence of notes on that cornet, which occurs in the formal 'Alert' blown by Texas's bravest. And it had to sound at a particular moment, when the light fell in a certain way and when man, chalice and blade could give voice together, casting the great spell which would open the doorway you needed into Moo-Uria, the Realm Below."

At this the albino's eyes narrowed. His handsome features seem to display a strange, bitter amusement. His long-fingered hands, the colour of bone, played with the ornate red shaft of the lance. "I believe I have underestimated you, however, Seaton Begg. For I did not anticipate your presence here. Neither did I prepare for it. Neither was I aware of your knowledge."

"Acquired in the course of a long investigation," murmured the detective. "I have been seeking you and the chalice for some while. Since you stole it from Sir John Soanes' Museum in London three years ago. The Museum of which my brother-in-law is director."

The albino seemed surprised and made as if to deny the charge, then shrugged and pulled deeply on his aromatic cigarette.

"Well, Sir Seaton, you could easily have thwarted me, it seems. Yet you did not. Why so?"

Begg pursed his lips and frowned, as if he had not considered the question before. At length he said: "Curiosity, I suppose. Which is, after all, my abiding and defining vice."

"Then I am obliged to you," said the albino, swinging the now dormant blade onto his back and signalling to the people in the shadows.

As they emerged, Tex saw that they were emaciated creatures, pale from every deprivation. Tex thought one thing when he saw them: 'Reservation Indian'. Their undernourished bodies spoke of terrible hardship. Only their eyes were vital and, as they began to ride and walk slowly down the causeway into the earth, they bore themselves with a strange, new self-respect. Men, women and children, waggons and horses, moved slowly down into the darkness, their voices ringing with wonder and fresh confidence so that those above ground almost felt envious of them and what they were seeing.

"You mean, Pale Wolf, that you made such an elaborate plan simply in order to save those poor creatures?" gasped Jenny.

"I am not so altruistic, Mrs Brady," said the albino, with an ironic glint in his strange, red eyes. "But I guessed my self-interest would combine with theirs to our mutual benefit and so it proved."

"Where are they going?" Don Lorenzo asked.

"Home," said the albino tossing the remains of his cigarette into the shadows. "Home to the land of lost nations, of recollected pride and purpose. Home to the Reforgotten. Home to the Realm Below." His eyes met those of his old adversary. "Would you deny them that peace of mind, Seaton Begg? That pride?"

The English detective took an interest in his pipe. "My question has always been, your highness, whether you would deny me my peace of mind in achieving yours. It is the great fundamental debate. How do we achieve satisfactory compromise?"

"They intend you no harm," insisted the albino. "And as for myself, I believe you know how deeply uninterested I am in your kind and its ambitions. As long as I am left alone."

"Left alone to murder and steal, sir," Sir Seaton Begg reminded the strange creature. "Why, you have killed half the British parliament! Lady Ratchet herself dropped dead merely at the sight of you! While this made you something of a popular hero, you are still guilty. I made the mistake of loaning my special charge to the museum from which you stole it, threatening my brother-in-law, the curator, with shameful ruin! You have stolen that great national treasure and apparently destroyed it. You have put everyone, moreover, to a considerable outlay of time, concern and money which could have been better spent elsewhere. Sir, the rogue wolf is left alone only when he hunts in his own territory. I cannot believe you to be unaware of the fallacious nature of your arguments. You have not left us alone, sir."

At which a deep sigh escaped the albino's lips and he glared around him impatiently. "Am I to be forever plagued by dullards and fools splitting hairs in abstract arguments? I am tired of the abstract, gentlemen. How I long for the concrete!"

"I can offer you as much concrete, sir, as you please," said Sir Seaton Begg. "Her Majesty's prisons consist of little else."

The albino turned brooding eyes upward, studying the tiny figures who now rimmed the canyon. He spoke dreamily. "Did you bring the entire

Texas army here, Mr Brady? I am flattered. Please give Captain Gideon my compliments, and tell him I shall have to meet him another time."

With that he had mounted his pony and, without looking back, urged it at a rapid trot down into the fissure.

A few moments later they heard his laughter issue from the echoing depths. The caverns enlarged and expanded it, giving it a rich, eternal bitterness so that it seemed Satan himself addressed them in tones full of tormented melancholy and longing.

"Farewell, old friend! We shall meet soon enough, no doubt, in the Realm Below."

And he was gone.

A moment later a thin voice from the heights called down:

"Could someone let us know what's happening?"

Tex recognised the voice of his friend Captain James "Bible" Gideon.

"All's well down here, Captain Gideon," he shouted back, and the echo continued "giddy-on, giddy-on, giddy-on . . ." until it was spent.

Sir Seaton Begg continued to stare thoughtfully down into the fissure.

"Are you planning to follow them, Sir Seaton?" asked the young vigilante, half joking.

"Not immediately," replied the detective, "though it is my duty. I know my limitations. I lack certain fundamental equipment. I have no instinct for the underworld." He took a long pull on his pipe. "Yet that creature, that demon, as some believe him to be, can negotiate the most alien landscapes without any hesitation. You heard that equation he offered. Almost a mantra. He has that ability to sense routes and avenues which you and I could never find, even with maps. He is not the only one of his family to have that talent, of course. But it is why he can so easily pass between one realm and another. Few possess such skills."

"But what *is* he?" Jenny Brady wanted to know.

"They are sometimes called 'eternals'," the detective replied slowly, "and they are able to walk the roads between the worlds. The entire multiverse is theirs, yet some of them are still prisoners, still victims of their own stories."

"I am really not quite following this, Sir Seaton," said Jenny.

The detective gestured with his reins. "That is why, dear Mrs Brady, I make so few attempts to offer explanations. I assure you it is nothing to do with your intelligence, which is extraordinarily high. But there are some things about our realities that only a certain number of people seem to be able to comprehend. And there is no persuading them. They simply cannot see what I see or indeed what that poor white-faced creature who has just left us can see."

"I do not believe I would want to see what he sees," said Don Lorenzo, lightening the atmosphere a little. "Especially at this moment."

"Oh, my dear sir," said Seaton Begg feelingly, "you do not know the beauty he experiences as he wanders the impossible caverns of the Grey Fees where the organic and supernatural infrastructure of the planet intertwine. He will see jewelled halls so high and vast that twenty great cities stand in them, each upon a peak, high above mercury rivers and bronze mists of the valleys which draw their light from phosphorescent rain dripping steadily from the distant roofs, making fresh formations everywhere, through which move the native folk of the Grey Fees, the *Offmoo*, so tall and thin and silent, drifting like phantoms through whispering rock forests and jangling crystal gardens, practising their rituals and legalities with obsessive, mindless insistence. And you have not heard the great natural organs playing when all the cities make music at the same time, and dying travellers come from thousands of miles to spend their last ecstatic hours borne upon so many wonderfully weaving melodies. No music is more sophisticated or more moving."

"Then should we not follow him this minute?" said Don Lorenzo a little drily. "Who could resist such a paradise?"

But Seaton Begg shook his head refusing levity. "It remains, for all that," he said, "an *alien* paradise. It is an alternative. The Realm Below is a compendium of lost dreams. All the defeated people arrive there, vowing return, revenge and those other satisfactions with which we seem to perpetuate our miseries. But when they have been there for some time they become infected with a peculiar sadness. It is Pierrot's world, after all, without sunlight. That melancholy is characteristic of almost every denizen of the Realm Below. They live, they flourish, they have pride and their achievements are spectacular.

"The great American civilisations are there, as well as the African, the Indian, even the Etruscan. For the Realm Below is where the Reforgotten know triumph, where the disenfranchised and the marginalised find renewed power, where noble memory is made concrete. Where justice exists. Yet all but the *Offmoo* know that they are not native to the Realm, that they are forever exiled."

Riding back up the canyon now they could hear military voices raised in command, the busy clatter of equipment.

"Do none of them ever yearn to return?" Jenny asked the detective.

"Some dream of it. Some even make plans for conquest of the Realm Above. But that pervasive melancholy usually informs their final decisions. It is hard to make war while enjoying such emotions. They compensate for their lack of martial vigor by aspiring to a high standard of civilisation."

When they had reached the canyon's mouth again, the first person they saw was Windy O'Day, his whiskers bristling with anxiety. He sat his horse expectantly, counting the riders as they emerged and brightening as soon as he saw their faces. Behind him it was possible to see the practical magic Tex had worked, enabling Captain Gideon to get to the canyon hours ahead of the Apaches and position his men.

Nothing would have been possible, of course, without Colonel Meadley's famous "Flying Tracklayers" who had constructed a temporary bed across the prairie enabling Captain Blackgallon Jones to bring up his mighty doubledecker war-trams loaded with men and ordnance. These so-called "gun-tubs" with their electric gatlings could be of spectacular effect in plains conditions and had been employed to full effect at the Battle of El Paso against what Texas still insisted on calling The Californian Threat.

Express trams had transported the cavalry, and now Captain Gideon's battle-hardened squadrons lined every vantage point of the surrounding country! This vast display of military co-ordination brought a small smile to Sir Seaton's lips as he looked around him. He was too well-bred to observe what his companions also understood: that it had taken a great deal of organisation and a great many men to ensure that a certain cornet note sounded at a certain moment in the wilds of the New Guadalupe mountains!

Two master strategists had, for a short time, joined in a game whose rules were known only to one of them. Pale Wolf had used the Masked Buckaroo's famous strategic skills for his own purposes.

"I first smelled a rat," declared the Buckaroo, "when I felt for that dog's pulse. That animal had died of natural causes. The arrow had been shot into it much later. Did you notice that no one was killed in those 'raids'? Nobody was even seriously hurt." The Buckaroo could only admire the way in which he had been tricked.

He was not sure, however, how he was going to explain it all to Captain Gideon and his men.

As if he had had the same thought, Sir Seaton Begg leaned across in his saddle and murmured: "Remember what Pale Wolf said about not lying—that people usually refused the truth?"

The young vigilante nodded.

"Well," continued Sir Seaton, "I think we had best not explain all the details of how your dear ones were restored to you and what happened to Ulrucha and his miserable band."

Tex was inclined to agree with him.

"But first," he said, "you must tell me something about that queer fellow, Pale Wolf. He's clearly not an Indian. He's definitely a white man. But he didn't look much like an average white, either. What is he, some kind of cross?"

"He is at once the last and the first of his race," said Seaton Begg. "I should perhaps explain that he is a relative of mine. We have ancestors in common. The family is from Germany. They are the von Beks of Bek in Saxony. The family is better known, however, in neighbouring Wäldenstein. Most of its sons spent more time abroad in Mirenburg, the capital of Wäldenstein, with whom they are identified. They intermarried with the local aristocracy and share an intimate history with the place. The man you met is Ulrich, Prince of Mirenburg, who carries the ancient curse of the Bek blood..."

"Curse? More melodrama?" said Tex, almost wearily, but the Englishman ignored him.

"Every few generations they give birth to an albino. Every few centuries they give birth to identical albino twins. And about every five hundred years they give birth to albino twins who are a girl and a boy. When that occurs there is a certain stir created in the occult world. A proliferation of magical swords is one phenomenon associated with such a birth."

"What are they?" asked Don Lorenzo in some distaste. "Vampires? Werewolves? What?"

"Some of them, as I said, are called 'eternals'. They live according to different rules and conditions, but few have sinister ambitions where we are concerned. Indeed they are often fairly benign, even altruistic. No others possess the warlock's powers you saw demonstrated just now. But 'Monsieur Zenith', as that individual sometimes styles himself, is a master of magic, though his familiars are not always available to him here. His mind holds ancient secrets. His regular companions are the restlessly damned, the dispossessed, the abnormal. He consorts with criminals in the lowest dens of vice. And he plays the violin like an angel. No, Don Lorenzo, this is not an ordinary monster. Neither, in the usual sense, is he damned. I expect to meet him again. And when I do, I hope I shall have the luck to best him. Even extraordinary monsters, my dear sir, have no place in decent society."

"Which is why they deserve the freedom of the wild underworld at least," said the Masked Buckaroo with some feeling. He had been thinking over those events. "I propose we should leave them alone. Why pursue them, Sir Seaton?"

The detective sighed. "Monsieur Zenith—or Pale Wolf as you know him—is a criminal. It is my duty to bring him to justice. And that means I must follow him wherever he hides."

The Englishman rode over to have a word with Captain Gideon. The officer issued instructions and soon several saddlebags were handed to Sir Seaton. He rode back, lifting his hat to Jenny. "Goodbye, Mrs Brady. A pleasure to meet you." He shook hands with the others who were rather surprised. They had not expected the detective to leave them so soon.

None asked him where he was going. Then he turned his horse about and began to ride into the shadows of the canyon on his way to the Realm Below.

They watched until he disappeared. "A man after my own heart, that Englishman," said young Tex. "I almost wish I was going with him."

"Where he goes, he goes alone, I think," said Don Lorenzo, frowning. He murmured some sort of prayer under his breath and crossed himself. "Today is Ash Wednesday." This last remark was made to no one in particular.

"Well, I seem to be the only person looking forward to getting home," said Jenny with a grin. "After this strange experience I'll never be bored with the ordinary routines of the Circle Squared."

By now they had ridden up to where the tram tracks began. Captain Gideon stepped forward saluting.

The Masked Buckaroo thanked him for responding so rapidly and efficiently to his messages.

"I'm glad we could be of help," Gideon insisted warmly.

"You will never appreciate the full extent of your help, Captain," said young Tex dismounting. As they climbed the steps of the heavy war-tram and took their places on the mahogany bench seats, the young Buckaroo put a manly arm about his wife's shoulders. Soon the vehicle was in motion, racing back across the plains as a second machine collected track behind it, a demonstration of the skill and ingenuity of "Thunderclap" Meadley's famous "Flying Tracklayers", who had done so much for Texas's military reputation. Within a few hours they would be back at the Circle Squared.

Yet for all Jenny's talk of a return to normality, the young avenger knew that life would never be quite the same again. No matter how much he blocked it from his conscious mind, he would continue to dream of that subterranean world Sir Seaton called The Grey Fees. He would long to experience its alien wonders. And one day he knew his curiosity would get the better of him. He would give in to his impulse, saddle his horse, and retrace the trail to the Realm Below.

Something in him yearned for that day to come, but he was not to know how soon his desire would be fulfilled!

For that is another story.

Born in London, 1939, Michael Moorcock left school at 15 and by 16 was a regular contributor to *Tarzan Adventures* which published his earliest Westerns, SF/Fantasy and jungle stories.

By 18 he was working for IPC on *Sexton Blake Library* and wrote for *Kit Carson, Buck Jones, Billy the Kid* and other IPC periodicals. By 21 he edited *Current Topics*, a Liberal Party monthly, and was editor of *New Worlds* at 24, publishing his last issue in 1996 by which time he had moved from London to Austin, Texas. He has published many novels in his *Eternal Champion*/multiverse series, including *Blood* and *The War Amongst the Angels*, which featured a number of Western themes. Writing literary fiction and fiction in several genres, he was recently named by *The Times* as one of the 50 best English novelists since 1945. He now spends part of his time in Austin, Texas and part in Paris, France.

The Ghost Warriors features several of his regular characters and was conceived as an homage to all the Western stories by the likes of Clarence E Mulford and Max Brand he enjoyed as a boy.

BLUE NORTHER
Zander Shaw

Two men. Tall in the saddle. Thin men. Hungry. Driven. Long dark coats. Aged black leather. Boots patterned with the dust and clay and soil of God knew how many States. They came for us on the first proper Spring mornin of the year, the snows havin disappeared from the foothills only a week before. Nobody said anythin at first. Pa, you put your arm across Ma's chest but she did not step back. Her hand found yours: fingers interlaced feverish, like the snakes we found wrestlin in the grasses down by Rock Creek. You both looked up at their faces: dark under deep, damp brims. Sweat like churned cream frothed in the creases between leather and horse flesh. I caught a sour smell pushed before them. Ridin long, ridin hard. Many days in the saddle. Theyd ridden through the night in the lash of rain. The horses eyes were wild-lookin.

Righteous, the man at the head of that duo said. His voice was tarry and black, like the baccy he was chewin, dirtyin his teeth when he smiled, makin it look like he had a wet, empty hole in the front of his face. Couldnt see his eyes under that brim. Could been orange slits, like a cat. Could been distant, glassy, shark-black. Could been nothin there at all.

He went on: Reins tight, Morgan. We is where we mean to be. Journeys end.

Gutshot

He swung his leg over and away from the mount and dropped lightly to the ground, pattin down his coat and sendin little sprays of water away from him. The other man, Morgan, did not dismount. A rifle was restin loosely across his thighs, forearms crossed on the pommel of his saddle, as if he'd rehearsed it. His hat was well back on his head, though the rain was drummin down hard. He wore an eyepatch and his good eye didnt blink once. It gleamed like a shinin dollar.

Now then, Mr Tansey, the other man said and I heard the grin on him, though I could not see it. Why you lookin at me like I'm some kind of stranger? We know each other good as family.

Pa, I could tell he was fearin for his life, but his voice was strong. Leave Nicky out of this, Walter, he said. He's just a kid.

Walter came on. There was just the jingle-bob music of his spurs and my rabbit-frighted heartbeat. Now I saw his teeth, grinnin under his hat, and they were the colour of the fat that oozed out of the split in the raccoon I hit with my slingshot last fall.

I know you me used to bend elbows a lot back in the day, when we was bustin to grow beards, and fuck our ladies through the barn wall—excuse my mouth, Mrs Tansey—and theres times I was full as a tick you delivered me home safe and I'm grateful to you for your care, but you must be dumber'n a snake buying cowboy boots to think we wunt come lookin for you after what went down in Lucyville.

Pa didnt blink at all. He was watchin Walter with his stern eye, same eye he turned on me whenever I did somethin that warranted the whip or the belt. Walter, I was doin my duty as a law abidin citizen.

Doin your duty? The smile was slippin now. The shadow was fallin on that space beneath the brim. Doin your duty? The man you turned in—

Walter, he kilt someone in cold blood.

So you say. So the judge said. Everyone so sure about that.

He was guilty, Walter.

He was my son!

Weaker now, fear shrouded: He was guilty, Walter.

My boy was in prison for three months afore he kilt himself. Chewed his own wrists open. Imagine that. Couldnt face another day in that shit-stinkin jail, let alone the thirty years they piled on his sorry ass.

I flew out from under Ma and made to grab at Walter. I could see what was comin. I was goin to pull him off of his damned horse and pound him into the dirt. But whats a ten-year-old boy of skin n bones to a man like that? He kicked out with his boot and caught me under the chin, knocked me galley west. I lay in the shit and the dust and I did not move, even when Ma cried out. Let him think he kicked me senseless. Let him think I was dead.

I will not countenance a rattin. Not me. Comes the time of the fellin of some stout old boughs, my friend.

I aint your friend, Pa said, and his voice was all tired out. I aint your brother either. I dont share none of your dirty, poisonous blood.

Blood, Walter said, and his mouth was all thick around it like it was a treat. Lets all talk about blood for a spell, shall we? He spat a loop of brown juice into the dirt.

They were fast, the two of them. Walter with his six-shooter, his free hand blurring over the hammer, and Morgan in his saddle, his owl eye blazing as if it were on fire inside. Faster'n anythin I had seen before, and I'd seen Loke Fletcher rippin through the fenceposts in the old town backs with his Smith and Wesson once. Reloadin on the fly.

I didnt know your names till later. Thought you was always just Ma and Pa. Dont all chillun? Everyone was cleanin up, puttin your relics in white sheets and saying things like, *Aw, shit, Henry,* and *Oh God, Kate, you poor thing.* I was cawin at them: *If'n you mean Pa, whynt you say it? You talkin to Ma, then shout it out.* That's all they ever called each other when we said our good nights and good mornins. Sugar, too. A pet name for each other, even when they was bitchin.

The guns. I watched the guns blaze. I saw the fire spurt from the end of those death-dealers. I saw the holes appear in you both. I watched the blood fan out from your backs like red angel wings. They dug graves and they put us in, all together. They think I was dead? Or didnt they care? Thought the soil would see me off. I felt the dirt patter on my shoulders and back. I felt it clod in my hair and the lights growin dim. I felt the blood of my folks trickle onto me, into me, leaking into my mouth, my eyes. And still I did not cry or scream or beg. I held my breath and I waited. When the soil was coverin me, I buried my face into Ma's clothes and breathed the blood-tainted air that was trapped inside. I took solace. I took strength. Those graves werent deep enough. They could have dug for a month and it wouldnt have been enough.

Gutshot

I waited till I heard the thunder of the hooves and I started diggin my way out.

Tansey passed the needle one last time through the puckered lips of the shoulder wound and tied off the thread. His fingers were slippery with blood. The sun was sinking fast over the prairie. It had been a hot day. One of, if not *the* hottest, in living memory, full of warm, dry winds and sand flies. Forty miles east, the shape of the mountains were becoming lost to the grain of dark. Tansey was grateful that Ace, his horse, was black. Now he would not see it struggling towards death in the night. He had bought the Peruvian Paso for its smoothness of ride over rocky terrain. Long distances in the saddle, you needed comfort. Now he wondered if he should have foregone an easy life for somethin a bit faster. He heard the horse's ragged breath and wished he could put it out of his misery, but his Winchester was shot in half, lying back on the trail a couple hundred yards, and he only had one bullet left in the Colt.

His hands shook with cold and fear and hunger—he had not eaten in sixty hours, and that last meal nothing more than bread and coffee—and he was a day away, at least, from his next meal. Not that he would eat again if he couldn't find a sawbones to mend him good and proper and give him something to chase away the bad humours and spirits that would squeeze in through those tiny holes in his flesh where the needle couldn't go.

He tore a couple of strips of cloth from his shirt and wrapped them around the wound, gritting his teeth as he saw the blood move out of the fabric, red ghosts through mist. His skin was red and sore from the sun, but he no longer felt any of that. The sharp pain from the needle had gone too, overtaken by the deep ache of the injury. He was done as the shadows from the pines reached him, scrabbling for him like sooted skeletal hands, drawing the cold across him fast and lethal. He sucked his wooden fingers and tried to see from where the attack had originated. Maybe they'd just wait until he froze to death in the night.

Despite the lure of warmth, Tansey did not wrap himself deep in his old duster coat, he kept his hand firm on his Colt pistol and its pathetic chamber, and relished the icy sting of the metal handle of his sheepsfoot blade, resting snugly in his garter. But what good was a blade when your foe was a hundred yards off, or more? One bullet. He'd do himself if it looked as though the end was on him. He wouldn't stomach the dirty foreign lead from another man's shooter.

'Where'd those shots come from anyways, Ace?' he whispered. The horse wasn't going to answer, and it might be dead already, but it comforted Tansey to talk as if he was not alone. God-darn it, he loved that horse as much as he would a brother or a son. Motherfuckin' cunts would pay for that dear beast's pain, swear it. *Pardon me, Ma, but y'understand.*

He peered over the top of the scarp at the hills that were now like the crushed purple velvet dresses his mother liked to wear. Little cover up there. No clumps of trees. No rock formations. The shooter must be flat on his belly, or long gone. Tansey hoped it was just some idiot trapper maybe got lost and gave himself a dose of the heebie-jeebies as the sun went westering. Maybe Tansey had startled him and he'd shot before thinking. Some idiot with little going on north of his ears. Some hope.

Three shots there had been. One ripped through his horse's throat, another took the rifle clean off his shoulder. The third? God only knew where that one went. But why no more? Whoever had him in his sights didn't have any green in him. He knew how to handle a firearm, and then some, what with the dark coming on like that. Must have diamonds for eyes.

'What you say, Ace? We got ourselves a reg'lar hotshot? So why dint he kill me then, hmm, if he's so good? What's his problem?'

He was talking as much to try to distract him from the pain as anything else. He was not scared to die, but he didn't want to do it alone, in the dark. He didn't want to be found weeks hence, frozen into the mud, his face and fingers gnawed off by the coyotes, unrecognisable. He scanned the line of hills again and the saleratus ponds, like silver mirrors fixed into the earth, and he could feel the shock sinking into him, like cold teeth. He lay on his back and drew his knees up towards his chest. They didn't fit well, these ideas of his. *Idiot trapper. Hotshot.* Jesus Christ, this cold.

Tansey wished he'd stayed in Dewlap Falls. It wasn't as if he hadn't been given the opportunity. There was a job going at the sawmill with old Billy Boles, and Heather Colson was giving him all kinds of signals. If you saw them on the railroad you'd know the train was going to just come chuffing through without any need to stomp on the brakes. He was the eyes for his blind old Sunday school teacher, Miss Lever, a woman he had done little

errands for ever since he was old enough to carry her books or collect a jug of molasses from the store on the corner of the main street. He had still been doing them right up until the middle of last month, and happy to.
And then...

I know you.
Came a man to Dewlap and he was in all kinds of bother. His hands shook. He wore a bandage over one eye, and his other eye suffered bad from palsy. It twitched like someone was playin it with a length of fishin line. There was something haunted, or maybe hunted, in him. He wasnt wearin enough to dust a fiddle, and what he did wear was all rags and stains. He stayed at the inn and nobody saw much of him all day till the sun went down and he spent an hour or so in a far corner by himself in Maisy's bar, drinking Tarantula Juice and watchin the games of faro and grand hazard played out on the gamin tables.
I know you.
Whenever anybody drifted close enough to try to engage him in chit-chat, he would either raise his hand as if he didnt understand English, or he'd simply move to another table. Nobody knew why he'd dragged up here, but some reckoned he was wounded, or ill. He didnt look too good. His skin was like oatmeal that had dried in the pan and his hair was white and thin, a breath on a winter's morn. I would watch him ghost out of the saloon, back to his room at the inn, and that would be it for another day. It needled me so much I went lookin for Doc Logan, and asked him what the stranger's name was, and what he was sickenin for.
He wunt tell me his full name, young Nicky, he said. Just said he was Mister Kitt. And I don't discuss my patients' ailments. Not even with my wife.
No first name?
None that he tole me.
Wheres he from then? I asked. I know him.
Then whut you askin me for, y'darned knucklehead?
You know whut I mean. His face is familiar-lookin.
Said he travelled from Creede. Small silver-minin town in Colorado, I believe.
Long ways to come and get your hoss fed and your eye bandaged.

Doc Logan had laughed at that. People come to Texas from far and wide, Nicky. I know where I'd rather be.

I talked to Maisy and Mr Jeffreys, who ran the bar. I talked to Sheriff Williams, but they were all just as foggy about our quiet visitor. The sheriff said to mind my business.

I went home, I remember, and I tended to the horses and drank a cup of coffee with a little tot of rum, like Ma used to have it. And I thought of Ma and Pa, like I had pretty much every day in the fifteen years since they was kilt. Thought of the good times I had with Pa down in the valley when were shootin rabbits, or the time we waded across the shallows at Milk river and I fell in and landed on a big trout. Snapped its back. Both of us... me and Pa, not me and the trout, laughin fit to bust us new ones. We ate well that night and Ma wrapped a bandage around my skinned back, tryin not to laugh herself and her hands were so soft and careful it was like bein dressed by somethin made of smoke.

Always felt good and safe and warm when I thought of my folks. It was like they were there with me, holdin me close, like they did when I was a baby. Human contact. The best kind of warmth there is. Good skin, and strong blood beatin behind. The heat of love. Familial love. That flame, it just never goes out.

The night sky was clear and so filled up with stars that there seemed to be more light than dark. Tansey's horse had stopped breathing hours ago. A faint, childish part of him hoped that was because Ace had gone to sleep, but he knew there was no way out of this vast territory other than on foot. And the cold was increasing. He might be frozen to death by morning if the bullets didn't find him. Again he squinted into the line of deep shadow that edged the leading flank of trees. No movement. He had to try something. He had to cling to the possibility that the shooter had moved on, tired of waiting out his prey while the temperature dropped.

Painful though it was, Tansey got down on his face and snaked towards the broken Winchester. He moved slow to keep from aggravating his wound. If he got a stray rock or stick poking into it he'd cry out and that might be the end of it. It might have been an hour later he reached the splintered stock and began dragging it back with him to the shelter of the scarp. At least now he'd got a sweat on. The cold didn't feel quite so penetrating. Another look to the treeline. No change. The stars were witness to his foolishness; his desperation. He felt no fear, only a lightheadedness that he put down to hunger, and the shock of his injury. He tossed the broken stock as far as he could down the track he'd come along. It made quite a clatter on the bone-dry earth. No returning fire from the treeline. Which meant what? He was asleep? He'd moved on?

Tansey had to risk it. There was no way he would survive a night in the open. He had to find cover, and soon. He got to his feet and started shuffling back the way he'd come. Dewlap Falls would take him many hours to reach, but knowing where it was, and knowing there were people there to take care of him, made the journey seem less taxing. Dawn was already making itself known: a paler blue underlining the night. It was the colour of gunmetal. It seemed alive. Everything wore the thinnest coating of ice, including himself; his duster coat gleamed as if it contained its own source of light. He felt a pure and very deep tug of need for his dead parents and shook himself hard. Crying for people who were no longer there for you was no use to anybody. You dumb ass. Cry for the living. Cry for yourself if you have to, for all the good it will do, but leave the dead in peace.

I'll never leave you.

I tend to your graves whenever I feel myself gettin close to mopin over what happened that day. Strange. Bein near you, lookin after the stones, takin away the dead flowers and layin fresh ones, gettin everything lookin fine as cream gravy... it helps me forget the way you were taken so violently away from me. Long time ago now, but I can close my eyes and watch you die in unfair detail. Peaceful in the boneyard. Aint nobody else around generally. Cept for Hawkins, the man who digs the holes. He's got shoulders bigger'n some peoples heads. All he knows, the liftin and the plantin of that big ole spade of his. He came over to parley when he saw me there. I like Hawkins. He never came to talk at first. He just nodded and went on with his work. When I said hello one day, he held up his hands and said he didnt want to intrude upon my grief. I said it was all right, and that the worst of it was over. Not that it ever truly goes away of course. Not till you find yourself at your own finishin line, and even then, well, who knows for sure?

So now he comes over regular to shoot the shit if he sees me. Diggin graves is a lonely job, he says. But he likes it because it means he can work outside, and it keeps his body in good condition. Feels healthier now than he did when he was a kid. *Thats genuwine.*

I asked him how he could work in such heat. Every day, for the past two weeks, the sun has been high and hard, bullyin away any cloud that looks as if it might even get a sniff. The road runnin through Dewlap has shrunken and turned pale and has cracks in it like the pattern on the back of a crocodile. Its been hotter'n a whorehouse on nickel night. Hakwins shrugs and looks up at the clean blue sky, his eyes disappeared into a squint, and he tells me that it dont matter to him. He dont feel the heat. As long as you drink your fill of water mornin and night, youll be fine. Otherwise, he says, grinnin, youll dry up and turn to dust, like Old Ma Wendover's pussy. Anyway, he tells me, when he's stopped laughin, and turned to inspectin the blade of his shovel, the weather will break soon. Theres cold a'comin, bad enough to turn your bones blue, never mind your skin. *Thats genuwine.*

Now its my turn to laugh, and he looks at me as if I paid him some terrible insult. Mind what I say, young Mister Tansey. Youll go off shirtless, on shanks pony, up to the treeline maybe, maybe further'n that. Huntin possum, huntin 'coon, nary a thought, save, maybe, for young Heather Colson's fine chest—dont object, boy, I've seen yer wanderin eyes—and afore y'know it, the sky is that metallic blue, like guns, like the boilerplate on an old locomotive, and she's here, colder'n a bitch and twice as feisty and bam, you find yourself gone up the flume. And it'll be me here in this yard with my shovel, turnin your bed for you, an it'll be a cold, dirty one. A forever one. Not good. You go through the mill, you spend enough time in the fresh air, you come to learn how she behaves, the wind and the shine. I know the weather, Nicky. And it looks right pretty now, while we have this little jaw, but theres some mothercunt ice on its way. I seen it before.

When? I asked him, worried now. I never seen Hawkins like this, all tensed up and teeth grit as if his ass was bein branded.

Soon, he said. A week? Maybe two? Even now, you look at those evenin skies and they carry that colour. Gettin deeper every day. Theres death in the air, son. And I'm gonna make sure I'm inside when it comes stalkin these streets. Extra log or two on the burner, whisky in my gut, blankets and a whore to keep me toasty. Not gonna let it put its beady eye on me, no sir.

I ask him about the one-eyed guy, and he looks at me hard, as if he's judgin me, peelin me back like an old book, seein whats writ. He looks like someone with two answers, one of which is a lie. Maybe hes thinkin of spinnin me that one, but then I got a look of my own, thanks to Ma, and that gives him pause.

Okay, then, he said. I know this guy. And so do you. *That's genuwine.*

He doesnt need to say any more. Just having someone nail what I had suspected all along is enough. But he goes on, and it's like I wrote the words for him to speak: *He is one of the men that gunned down your parents.*

He listened to the wind in the trees, and its soughing was like a frail voice calling him home. Tansey had spotted the figure up ahead a little over an hour before, and had been suspicious about his halting movement, thought maybe he was bluffing, laying a trap, but the splashes of fresh blood he could see decorating the trail helped to calm his nerves. The man was maybe a mile off, but Tansey was gaining on him. The pair of them moved with the kind of overly-measured stride of someone trying to conceal drunkenness.

After another hour, the man in front became aware of Tansey, and loosed three or four shots from his rifle. He might have been a good shot when fit, but every bullet flew wide. Tansey heard the clicks of the hammer falling on air: out of ammo. That was why he hadn't heard any more shots earlier; he was saving them up to be sure of a kill. That, and this injury he'd sustained.

Some time later, the man collapsed. He hadn't followed Tansey's practice and sewn himself shut. There must have been a good quart or two of his juice all over the trail. Tansey thought of his mother flying back under the force of a point blank shot. The assault had been so great it struck whatever expression she had been wearing from her features. She died with her face ironed clear. He had never seen her like that before; she seemed utterly different, not her, and could almost believe (and kind of still did) that she had somehow escaped this awful death. Thinking of her put some spice in him. He caught up with the man not long after, on a stretch of the trail where there were five graves lined up in a row, pathetic wooden crosses trapped in the rubble covering the mounds. The man was all bent over his guts as they spooled around his forearms. He looked like a kid suffering from the flux. It was a miracle he'd come this far.

I got the bulge on you now, you fucker, Tansey said. Shit. Was gonna make you dig your own grave next to these poor bastards. What was it? Gun backfired on you? You shot yourself! Shit. You want to keep your piece clean, mister.

The man looked up at him and his face was shaking fit to throw the skin clean off of it. His lips were grey and peeled back from the teeth. His spit had collected and dried in the corners of his mouth like wads of cotton and his eye bulged in its socket as if it were jealous of its long-departed twin.

You're Morgan, aint you?

The man didn't say anything. He just continued to stare, and to quietly die, draining away into the soil.

Walter sent you, dint he? You kilt my folks and you thought youd kilt me too. But word got out, dint it? Word got back to Walter that I was alive. And what, Morgan? He shittin his britches that I am going to fetch him some retribution?

He is a old man now, Nicky. So'm I.

Tansey had to bend low to hear the words. Speak up, y'eejit. You sound like a worm fartin in the grass. You got no man left in you? Old, you say? Well, okay, but it dint stop you clip-cloppin out here to put me in a box, did it?

Tansey spat into the ground next to Morgan. Morgan flinched, despite his injuries. The spit was black there, and Tansey hoped it was just the night, nothing more.

You're a dead man, Nicky, Morgan said. You're a ghost, you just dont know it yet.

Tansey nodded. Ever since the day you took my ma and pa away from me. I guess you're right. But here, I got some news for you. He reached into the garter around his calf and slid free the knife sheathed there. He placed the silver edge against Morgan's throat. He tensed and looked away to the strange, crystallised sky, blue like a bruise to the north. Bad weather comin down, he thought.

His words were the signature on a death warrant: *Morgan, come on, come and join us ghosts.*

○ ○ ○

I had to keep checkin my knife after that, to make sure I'd done what I did. I couldnt think straight. I kept wanderin off the trail and stumblin across more and more graves. Pioneers, I reckoned, in the main. Poor bastards taken down by hunger, or arrows, as they drove West, lookin for a place to set up home, the memory of poverty and hopelessness back in Ireland or Germany or wherever the hell theyd hauled ass from puttin a fire under their heels.

Later I came across a gutted antelope and it was grinnin at me like I'd tole it a rich ole joke. There was little of it left, but whatever done this werent human: its hide was still hangin off of its bones. The eyes had been gobbled up by some lucky critter, and the flies had been at its mouth, sendin the flesh north and south, lettin us see how pretty its teeth were. I gave it a wide berth—there were wolves and bears and God knew what else and I didnt want none of its stink in me. I started thinkin about Ace then, and how the beasts would be worryin him out on the trail, and I wished I'd had the strength to dig him a hole.

I heard hooves then, scrapin and scrabblin against rock and shingle. I turned and the antelope was on its knees, tryin to draw itself upright. It couldnt raise its head—all the muscle and sinew there had been chewed out its neck—so it kind of lolloped up the trail after me with its head jouncin around against the bloodied mat of its chest. Critters that had been baskin in the darned thing's belly came tumblin out through rents in the flesh: rats and beetles and maggots. I hollered at it to go away but it ignored me, keepin its distance, following my ungainly plod with one of its own.

So you know Ace? I asked it.

Yeah, I know Ace. It had trouble speakin. Its tongue was long gone and the words were just shots of air twisted this way and that by the peculiar manglin of its vocal cords, and the gritted yellow pegs of its teeth. Ace's gone to a better place, same as we all do, eventually.

You not there yet? I asked it.

Not yet, no. Will you be joinin us?

Got somethin I need to finish first.

That business with Walter, huh? You know his fambly name? Like you, you're Nicky Tansey. Who's this Walter guy?

Don't know.

You off to kill a man, you ought to know his name.

I don't need to know his name.

He got a fambly too.

That drew me up short. I glanced at the knife I'd kilt Morgan with and it was drizzlin blood, but it could well have been my own. The wound on my shoulder had opened—stitchin was never my strong point—and fresh blood was tricklin in narrow lines down my arm, as if my veins were on the outside. The dressin was filthy, and there was a nasty green patch in the centre of the linen. Worse of all, I couldnt feel it. It didnt hurt me no more.

Morgan, he had a fambly too?

That he did, sir. A wife and two chillun. Boys. All grown up now.

And Walter?

He got a wife. She's sick. And a daughter. Pretty thing, all of ten years old.

You shunt be tellin me this. You got no right. Youre just a dumb, dead piece of long lunch.

I stuck the point of the knife into my thigh and twisted it. Pain flared up and down my leg and I laughed at it, it was good, meant I was still alive. My eyes cleared and I looked back and the antelope was just a piece of rottin meat slowly being consumed by the ants and the flies on the side of the trail. I went back and cut off its head and wedged it in the branches of a tree. I carved my initials under it and slapped a bloody palmprint next to the letters for good measure.

Comin for you Walter. Watch your back.

I reached Dewlap Falls by sundown. I'd been gone three days. Everythin had changed. The streets were empty. The kids you used to see hollerin and cussin all hours of the day and night, chasin each other round the tethered horses outside Annie's bar, well, they were nowhere to be seen. No whores hangin out the bordello windows and barin their breasts at the passersby. No songs from the barred windows of the gaol. Just a silence I hadnt known since I was a kid, burrowin into the blood-soaked dress in that grave as it filled.

I been to ghost towns before. Those end-of-the-world places where God has turned his back and the bodies lie ripe and bloated in the yards and the alleyways. Air still rich with gunpowder and the metallic reek of opened bodies. But not this place. When I left it, it was rampant with life in all its gory glory. I went lookin for Doc Logan, but there was nothin but a bunch of glass bottles and papers in his office. The Sheriff was out. The cells were empty. The bed he sometimes used in the corner of the jailhouse was a mess of blankets and suggans. The saloon was a dusty memory to song and drunkenness.

I walked on down to the boneyard. I was no longer bleedin, though my wound was open and flappin like a snitch's mouth. I had dried blood on my britches and chaps. Blood on my boots. It glazed my skin, like burnt sugar set hard. I called out for Hawkins but there was just his shovel in the dirt. Fresh grave, right next to my folks. I read the inscription on their stone and cried a little.

I turned to face the mountains and there was weather sweepin down from them that I aint never seen before. Hawkins was right. You could feel the air change. It was becoming heavier, grainier, like the air that precedes a sandstorm, but there was no sand here, only the promise of cold, and maybe nothing more for the rest of times. I felt my skin pucker up. The sky was a kind of blue I never seen before. It was like the speckled pattern in an eye, and it shifted, like an eye swimmin in and out of focus. An impossible colour, a beautiful colour. And I heard the jangle-bob music of his spurs. Lighter now, his tread, and slower too. But it was him.

I turned and he was standin there in front of me, just how I'd dreamed it over the years, and time dragged up around us as if you could look down and see it pilin against your legs like a drift of snow. He was older now, and thinner, almost gaunt, and I wondered if he was sick, and then I wondered how could he not be, with all the black that filled up inside him as time passed by. All the blood and the bodies and the shallow graves.

I became intimately aware of the world around me, saw and smelled the prickly pear and the wormwood and the chamomile. I could almost feel the larkspur petals, the china asters and roses big as fists and redder than blood. A clickin of locusts, a great cloud of them sweepin up over the hill. I thought of Ace, sunfishin on the prairie, his mane black and wild in the wind. I thought of Ma and Pa and the last hug we shared.

I watched you go into the ground. I saw the soil fallin on you, he said. I thought you was dead.

And then the cold came down like the great dresser in grandma's kitchen that time, chewed hollow by weevils. It slammed down on us and I saw the breath go out of Walter, and blue veins of frost creep across his face, despite his buffalo coat. His eyes clouded with ice in a second. I am, I said. And sent him straight to hell.

He got off a shot before he died, and I felt the bullet put a crack a foot long in my gut. Rubies and glass. The cold swept into and around us as if it had been champin at the bit for decades.

But I was warm inside. Inside, where my folks lived on for ever, I was fair burnin up.

Zander Shaw is a tattooist and a fisherman. In his spare time he takes photographs, collects raptor skulls and plays rhythm guitar for a band called Corvidae. Having studied Art in London and Durham, he now lives in a village near Dungeness, where he was born in 1984. This is his first published short story. He is currently working on a horror novel.

"As a child, the most crushing thing that I learned was that everybody dies. That my parents would one day leave me affected me profoundly, more so than the impact of my own mortality. My mother and father died within ten months of each other in 2009. I wrote this story for my five-year-old self."

IN THE SAND HILLS
Thomas Tessier

It was a long way to drive, just to kill a man who might not even be there. From Denver north up to Alliance, and then another 100-plus miles east on Highway 2, until Driscoll got to a place called Skinnerville. It was shown as a small-dot town on the outdated road map he was using, but Skinnerville had since been abandoned by its residents. Now it was nothing more than a scattering of a few dozen vacant houses, barns and other buildings in varying stages of decay and collapse. Some tilted precariously, while others had already fallen in on themselves. The former general store was built out of cinderblocks, still solid, but the large glass windows were long gone, and the metal roof and the gas pumps out front were eaten through with rust.

Driscoll pulled over for a moment. That was helpful—no one in Skinnerville. No one to see Driscoll and maybe remember his face, or the car he was driving or the license plate. No one who could even put a date on the day he passed through Skinnerville—going east at first, then later heading back west. No one with a shred of useful information to pass along to the sheriff or the state troopers, in the unlikely event that they came around later, asking about any strangers in the area recently.

Driscoll fished a crumpled piece of paper out of his jacket pocket and took another look at it. A few simple handwritten directions, along with a map that could have been drawn by a kid in kindergarten. Three to five more miles, then a dirt road off to the right, and then another mile or so. He was close now. Driscoll drove on.

A functional idiot named Walter Bopp had offended Mr. Lee, to the tune of about $100,000. Bopp had collected and delivered money for Mr. Lee for some period of time, and was considered to be a reliable, trustworthy courier. Until, that is, the day when he finally gave in to temptation and disappeared with a bag of Mr. Lee's cash—far too much of it to be written off as an expense or a minor loss.

So it fell to Driscoll to put things right. Driscoll had put many such matters right for Mr. Lee over the years. Mr. Lee's gratitude was a good thing to have. It would be very nice if Driscoll could retrieve some of the cash, in which case he would get a slice of it. But he would be paid for his efforts regardless, and it was ultimately more important that punishment be handed out. Mr. Lee was responsible for Denver, for all of Colorado, in fact. To offend and embarrass him that way was intolerable.

Mr. Lee had friends in many places, and they helped in the search for Walter Bopp. But in due course it became apparent that he was not in Vegas or Reno, living high and gambling large. Nor were there any sightings or rumors of him in Frisco, Phoenix or L.A. It began to seem more likely that Bopp had gone to ground in some place where he felt safe, where he thought he would never be found. There, he would just wait it out for a while, before making his next career move.

As if Mr. Lee would ever forget.

It took a while, but Mr. Lee was able to track down one of Bopp's former live-in lovers, Krystal Waters (now Starr). She was only too happy to tell the sorry tale of her six months with Walter, dating back several years. What a cheating, miserable rat he was, and a lot more like that. The situation got to the point where Walter was heavily involved with a married woman whose husband was a bouncer at a club, a man known to be violent and dangerous. Suddenly fearing for his life, Walter persuaded Krystal that they had to leave Denver immediately. So, they fled to his family's ranch in the Sand Hills of northwestern Nebraska. But the "ranch" turned out to be a broken-down old farmhouse out in the middle of nowhere. Walter's brother, Bob Bopp, was the only family member still living there, and he seemed a little crazy, given to long silences and occasional grunted words. He spent a lot of time staring at Krystal in a way that made her feel very uncomfortable.

IN THE SAND HILLS

They spent a month or so there before she was finally able to persuade Walter that they should return to Denver. They did, and Bopp somehow managed to avoid getting himself killed—yet. But Krystal had had enough, and dumped him.

She was very happy to draw the map and write down the few directions to the Bopp family homestead in Nebraska, and Mr. Lee was grateful to her.

The night before, Driscoll had stayed at the Palomino Motel on the outskirts of Alliance. He had breakfast at a nearby diner and was on the highway by 9 a.m. It was close to noon when he spotted the dirt road, just about where Krystal said it was. Driscoll swung the Cougar coupe onto the hard-packed surface and drove ahead slowly. He was in the Sand Hills now, not just passing through them on asphalt. It was a bizarre landscape, so arid and empty, but stitched in places with some kind of prairie grass that rippled and waved in the steady breeze. The sand itself was almost grey, kind of lunar, Driscoll thought. When a brief gust of wind blew some of it into the car, it felt granular, and it stung his cheek. He rolled up the window.

The road meandered around and through the maze of hills, which ranged from gentle, swelling rises to stark walls that towered thirty feet or more, breaking off in sharp ridges. A few looked like enormous, frozen ocean waves, carved out by the wind. It was a mystery why anyone would want to live out there.

Driscoll kept an eye on the odometer. The way the road looped and curled, it was easy to see why Krystal had been kind of vague about the distance from the highway to the farmhouse. He had driven just over two miles when he came around another bend and saw the Bopp place just ahead. The hills gave way to a wide, clear, level piece of ground, and then rose again around it. There was a very large barn, some corrals or holding pens, which suggested that at one time the Bopps had raised cattle. But the paint on the barn had peeled away, almost completely, and it looked like it was no longer in use.

The farmhouse did have something of a ranch style to it, built just a single story tall, strung out long and low to the earth, with a couple of extra rooms tacked on to the back of it. A simple frame construction job on a concrete slab that now had visible cracks in it, crumbling in places. The place was falling apart in slow motion.

More important, there was a pickup truck parked out front. Maintaining the same slow, deliberate speed, Driscoll cruised up to the house, his eyes scanning the windows and the immediate area for any signs of a person moving about. Nothing yet. He had a .38 in a shoulder holster beneath his jacket, which was half-unzipped, and he had a smaller .22 strapped under the cuff of his jeans, just above his ankle.

Before he got out of the car, he hit the horn twice, which he imagined might be the polite, neighbourly thing to do in these parts. Announce yourself, signalling good will and normal behaviour. But nobody opened the front door to greet him, no face peered out of a window to see who was there. Driscoll walked up the three wooden steps to the porch. He knocked firmly on the door, while standing just to the side of it.

"Hello. Anybody home?" he called out loudly. "Walter? Bob?"

He knocked again, but there was still no response. He listened carefully, but heard no sound of movement inside. He swung his head to glance briefly through one of the windows. Now, there was nice touch you don't see often—the front door apparently opened directly into the kitchen. Driscoll chanced a longer look, and there was no one in sight. He went to the window on the other side of the door and saw what must have passed for the living room—lumpy armchairs and other very old furniture that appeared not to have been moved or dusted in quite some time. Yeah, Krystal must have loved this place.

Driscoll went around to the back of the house, but the windows there were a little too high for him to look through. He found a shed with a generator inside, a couple of propane tanks—that would be provide electricity. But there were no telephone wires, nor a television antenna. Once you got here, you were here.

He went into the barn, which was very spacious but showed no sign of recent activity. Every flat surface was coated with a layer of sand. The milking area equipment was rusted, the hayloft above without a single bale. Driscoll took a deep breath through his nose—even the smell of cow shit had left this place.

He circled back around to the front of the house and took a closer look at the pickup truck. It was rusty in patches and generally beat up. Maybe ten years old, at a guess. The registration tag on the plate was dated AUG 83, two years and a week ago. One of the back tyres was flat, the other three were getting there. He looked inside the cab and saw a lot of empty beer and soda cans, candy and burger wrappers, a faded issue of *Hustler*.

IN THE SAND HILLS

Driscoll started to walk back to the porch, but the wind had picked up a bit and the sand was hitting his face, so he got into his car and sat for a few minutes. He had a couple of possibilities to consider now. The first, obviously, was that Walter was not hiding out there after all, and that Driscoll's trip was a waste of time. Maybe, but the remoteness of the location and the fact that it was Walter Bopp's old family home, still made it seem like the best bet, the most logical place for him to run to. Krystal's description of the house was so accurate, it only reinforced the idea.

Perhaps Walter, with or without his brother, had gone out in another vehicle earlier that morning, before Driscoll had arrived there. They might return at any time, or not until this evening. Well, Driscoll was prepared to wait. In the meantime, there was another possibility—that the money, or whatever might be left of it, was tucked away somewhere inside the house.

He got out of the car. The wind hit him hard enough to stall his movement for a second, sand peppering his cheek again. The sky was clear, but he noticed some black clouds in the distance. Driscoll hurried to the front door and had to laugh when he found it unlocked. He stepped inside with a herky-jerky motion, in case someone was lying in wait, ready to take a shot at him. But the kitchen was empty, the house still. He shut the door loudly, stamped his foot and called out another greeting, but again there was no response from within.

The room had a lingering smell of boiled food. There was a steel pot on the wooden table, containing a small heel of ham, a few chunks of potato and some cabbage. In the sink, one plastic dinner dish, with a knife and fork. Driscoll touched the food residue on the plate; it was dry but not mouldy—he judged it to be a day old, two at most. The cabinets held a few staples like salt, sugar, flour and a can of coffee, but little else. He was startled when he opened the refrigerator, because the motor rumbled into action, the light went on inside and he could hear the generator begin droning in the shed outside. The fridge held a gallon jug of milk, down about two thirds, and a couple of cans of Coors.

He quickly checked the rest of the rooms, first to make sure no one was there. A thin infiltration of sand crunched underfoot as he walked. Jesus, he would hate to live in a place like this, with its low ceilings, the long dark hallway that snaked through it, and the small, boxy rooms— most of them now cluttered with things accumulated over the course of what had to be several lifetimes.

Driscoll found one bedroom that looked as if it was still in use, or had been until very recently. The bed wasn't made, but the blanket and sheet had been thrown roughly back into place. The bureau was not dusty and there were some men's socks and underwear in the drawers, as well as a few folded shirts and pairs of jeans. In the closet, a couple of pairs of slacks and a sports jacket. Nothing special, but passable—the kind of clothing that Walter might wear in Denver.

He saw a small, portable transistor radio on the night table, next to the lamp. Driscoll picked it up and turned it on. A burst of static, followed by a pop song that faded in and out. So the batteries were still good. An AM station, most likely in Alliance. Reception would probably be better at night.

Other than the clothes, there was nothing personal in the room. No mail, no papers or documents, no photographs. Driscoll examined the floor, the walls, the ceiling and the closet very carefully, but found no sign of a hidey-hole where money or other valuables might be hidden. He gave up on the idea of searching every room thoroughly because there were just too many boxes, cartons and crates of junk in them to deal with now. It was as if the Bopps had never thrown anything away.

In the living room—maybe they called it the parlour back when— he found a clutch of old photographs, framed and mounted on a wall. History in an eyeful. It looked as if five generations of Bopps had built and run this place, each succeeding one a little smaller in number than the last, until the family gene pool finally petered out in Walter and Bob, two runty little kids standing between their forlorn parents. The kids who wouldn't even bother to try keeping the place going, who would sell off every cow, chicken and pig they had, and anything else they could get a buck for, and who would then hang on here—or, in Walter's case, return here now and then—while everything that was left slowly rotted.

Driscoll got back to the kitchen, and froze. He could smell smoke— cigarette smoke, no mistake. It was fresh, hadn't been there a few minutes ago. He reached under his jacket and pulled out the .38. The smoke hadn't penetrated the rest of the house, and he saw no butt in the sink or ground out on the floor. He spotted a clear glass ashtray off to the side on the counter, but it was empty.

Mindful of his back, Driscoll edged around the room to the front window and looked outside. No sign of anyone, just the wind whipping up the sand in short blasts. He opened the door and stepped onto the porch. No one in sight, anywhere. But he saw, at the bottom of the front steps, footprints in the sand. One set approaching the house, another one slightly overlapping the first, going away. He could tell they weren't his. Then his eyes caught something moving—a cigarette, propelled by the wind, scudding across the sand. Half a cigarette, still burning.

It was not good to be standing there, an open target. Driscoll quickly went back into the house and shut the door. He grabbed a wooden chair and pulled it around to the front window, sitting to one side of the window, so that he had a clear view if anybody approached, but without exposing himself. At the same time, he had the back door covered, as well as the hallway passage into the rest of the house. His body was tense, juiced with anticipation, but his mind was calm and in focus. These were the moments in his work that he loved and lived for—the moment of confrontation, and the inevitable crushing of the other person beneath the sheer, irresistible force of Driscoll's will.

He hefted the gun in his hand, and thought about it. Someone had come into the house, someone smoking a cigarette. That person had heard Driscoll moving about, and had apparently turned around and left. Hold on, that same person would have seen Driscoll's car first. So, why enter the house, but then immediately turn and leave? And there was no third car or truck out front, so where had that person come from—on foot? Driscoll tossed those things around in his head for a few minutes, but couldn't work any of it out.

Never mind, it didn't matter at the moment. This was their house, but now he occupied it. Sooner or later, they would have to come to him. Driscoll held the gun inside the pocket of his jacket. He was patient and ready.

An hour later, he was not so sure. In that time, he hadn't caught a glimpse of anyone outside, and the only sounds he heard were the wind whipping up and bursts of sand plinking off the window glass. It was darker now, the black clouds rolling in, and there, the first rumble of thunder. He wondered how long the storm would last and whether he should sit it out, or leave now. But Driscoll hated the idea of not finishing the job, and the fact that someone knew he was there changed everything. He could return tomorrow, but in the meantime Walter Bopp could skip off to Omaha, anywhere, just to get away. Driscoll would be all the way back to square one in that case, with no idea where Bopp was.

He was impatient now, sitting and waiting, so he decided it was time to take another, more careful look throughout the house. He went to the front door, slid the latch lock in place and, for good measure, snugged the back of a chair up under the door handle. He did the same thing with the back door. Now if somebody wanted to enter the house, they would have to make some noise to do so, and he would hear them.

Driscoll walked back down the hallway to the one bedroom that had appeared to be in recent use. This time he checked behind the bureau, under the mattress, and in the pockets of the slacks hanging in the closet. Still nothing. He tried the radio again, spinning the tuner wheel up and down, but with the storm in the air there was solid blaring static from one end of the dial to the other, all stations lost in the thicket of noise.

He sat on the bed and tried to get a sense of the life of someone living here, to feel what it was like. No telephone. No television. No useful work to be done, because it was no longer a functioning farm or ranch. No point in working on the upkeep of the house, because, really, who'd want to live here anyway? Nowhere to go, except away, forever. A transistor radio not much bigger than a pack of cigarettes—it came down to that? It spoke of a life so diminished that it barely seemed like life at all. Now Driscoll had to wonder—why would Walter Bopp come here to hide out with his loot? Of all the places in the world where he might go to escape Mr. Lee's vengeance, and start a new life. This might be Walter's old family home, it might feel safe and secure. But it was nothing, beyond nowhere.

A blast of wind shook the house, breaking Driscoll's thought. He worked his way back to the kitchen, looking through some drawers, poking through cardboard cartons and orange crates, finding nothing of value or interest. A couple of old jewellery boxes, their contents long since pawned. The same song, endless variable refrains—life devours itself to start anew, for the moment, for no other reason.

The chairs were in place, the doors still locked. But the view from the front window hit Driscoll like a kidney punch. The air outside was very dark and the sand was flying on the horizontal. Thunder continued to rumble and there were flickers of lightning, but it was not raining. Sand was accumulating around his car, already up to the bottom of the front bumper, and it was drifting higher even more quickly in the front wheel well, as he watched. He knew immediately that he wasn't going anywhere until the storm blew through and he could dig enough sand away to free his car. Tiresome thought, it took a little energy out of him. He probably wouldn't be back in a comfortable motel room tonight with a drink and a movie on TV.

Driscoll took the gun out of his jacket pocket, just to hold it for a few seconds and draw some charge from it, and it fuelled his strength and sense of purpose. Because the person with the cigarette was still somewhere in the vicinity. Sheltering from the storm in the barn, or one of the sheds Driscoll hadn't bothered to check. *In which case, good luck to you out there. I'll see you when the storm passes, and you come out.* For Driscoll to be put in this situation, there was now only one possible outcome for Walter Bopp. *He* would turn over whatever of Mr. Lee's money he had left and then *he* would dig Driscoll's car out of the sand. Then he would die. End of job. And home to Denver.

The rain kicked in then, and right away it bucketed down. Driscoll could see the sand being splattered up as gobs of grey mud on his car. A deep sense of anger began to exfoliate within him. These are what are sometimes called aggravating circumstances. You will pay for this. You, you, *you.*

Driscoll walked down the hallway on the other side of the house, room by room, kicking over boxes and crates of things, to see if anything interesting fell out, yanking out drawers and spilling their contents. Junk, junk, junk, the debris of lives that were gone and meant nothing anyway. It infuriated him—as if he had come all this way to inspect a tag-sale in which nothing would sell.

He was so angry and impatient as he stalked about, that his foot slid a bit on the throw rug at the end of the corridor. He reached out to brace himself against the wall, but it was a small door he hadn't noticed or opened before. It looked like a closet door at the end of the hallway. Driscoll turned the handle, noticing that the door opened out, not in. He found an empty cubbyhole of a room, with an open metal hook mounted in the low ceiling. Then he saw a loop-handle in the floor planks—a trapdoor. He pulled it up and secured it to the hook. The first thing he noticed was the smell of stale smoke.

Below, was darkness. But there was a length of BX cable connected to an electrical switch screwed onto the wooden frame of the opening. It must have been a root cellar, a place to store produce like potatoes and apples. Or, just as likely, it had served as a storm cellar, a place to take shelter from the massive thunderstorms and seasonal tornadoes that tracked through this part of the country. Funny, at that moment Driscoll noticed that he no longer could hear the storm outside. Maybe it had blown by and was gone already.

He examined the trapdoor again. There were three sturdy slide locks on the underside, and no locking mechanism on the top side. That was as it should be—you could secure yourself in the cellar, but you could not accidentally or intentionally be locked in down there.

Driscoll took a couple of steps down the narrow wooden stairs and flipped the switch. A light went on below. Now he could see that the stairs descended fifteen feet or more, deeper than he expected. But most of the cellar was out of sight, because the bottom of the stairs ended just a couple of feet from a concrete wall. Gun in hand, Driscoll went down the steps as quickly as he could, angling his body and head so that he could scope out the whole room immediately, his shoes clomping loudly on the boards. He went into a crouch and darted a few steps to the side as he spun away from the stairs.

He saw the body of one man lying on a mattress in the far corner. A few feet away, another mattress and a second man, who was almost in a sitting posture, his upper body propped against the wall, his legs splayed out in front of him, his head slumped down on one shoulder. Neither of them moved. Driscoll was almost certain that they were dead, but he approached them slowly and with caution, his gun moving back and forth in the cool air from one to the other.

When he got close enough to them, there was no doubt. Walter Bopp and his brother George. Not only were they dead, their grey flesh looked like dried, wrinkled fruit. Their eyes had shrunk inward and been covered over by saggy pouches of skin, leaving only thin, puckered slits as markers. How had they come to such a grotesque end? There was no sign of violence, nothing that suggested murder or suicide.

Driscoll turned to look around the cellar, but there was little else to see. A small, glass-topped coffee table. A plastic baggie with a few seeds and stem in the bottom, an empty packet of rolling papers. A dozen or so empty beer and soda cans. Cigarette butts on the floor. A box of candles, a box of wooden matches. A kerosene lantern and a gallon jug of kerosene.

Nothing else. No sack full of Mr. Lee's money. Nothing. The two nothings, Walter and George, and the nothing else they had left behind.

Driscoll heard something before he saw the movement. It was a dry, granular sound, like very fine sand sliding down a sheet of parchment. Walter had gotten up off the mattress, and George was stirring now as well. Driscoll fired one shot into Walter's chest—it made a brief *pfft* sound on impact and produced a puff of dust—but it didn't slow him at all. Walter clamped a hand on Driscoll's shoulder. Driscoll banged off five more shots directly into Walter's face, but it was like shooting into a bucket of sand—the bullets were just swallowed up without effect. Driscoll was reaching for his other gun, but George was on him too now, and the brothers dragged him to the floor. Like silent, smooth-working automatons, the dug into his body, puncturing his clothes, their fingers as sharp as blades of frozen sand. Driscoll could feel the strength flying out of him, as if in one long exhalation. Their fingers in his chest and belly and throat. They were like mindless children playing at making a mess—out of him.

Driscoll's thoughts started to fade in and out. He could not walk it back in his mind—the cellar, the stairs, the house, the storm, the drive, the purpose of his trip—none of it, and find one mistake or misperception on his part. And yet, this.

No... no... This is not what happens to me....

But it was.

Thomas Tessier was born in Connecticut and educated there and at University College, Dublin. He lived in Dublin and London for thirteen years, during which time three books of his poems were published and three of his plays were professionally staged. For several years he wrote a monthly column on music for British *Vogue*.

His short stories have appeared in numerous magazines and anthologies, including *Borderlands, Cemetery Dance, Prime Evil, Dark Terrors, The Year's Best Fantasy and Horror* and *Best New Horror*. His first collection, *Ghost Music and Other Tales*, received an International Horror Guild Award.

He is the author of several novels of terror and suspense, including *The Nightwalker, Phantom, Finishing Touches* and *Rapture*, which was made into a movie starring Karen Allen and Michael Ontkean. His novel *Fog Heart* received the International Horror Guild Award for Best Novel and was cited by *Publishers Weekly* as one of the best books of the year. His latest novel, *Wicked Things*, was published in paperback by Leisure Books and in hardcover by Cemetery Dance Publications.

Gutshot

Thomas Tessier lives in Connecticut. He is currently working on a new novel and completing his second collection of short fiction.

"One of the elements I have always liked in Westerns is the geography itself," Thomas says, "the landscape of the remote, isolated places where human beings take themselves to create their lives, and the way those locations can influence and change them. Sometimes, the middle of nowhere really is the worst place to be."

WHITE BUTTERFLIES
Stephen Volk

Before he set off into the steppe to the drop zone, Olzhan Sergeievich Sheremet'ev told his father about the beggar he'd seen in town that morning. The beggar had been holding a sign. Words scrawled on cardboard, in both Russian and in Kazakh. *Grandparents murdered by Ninjas. Need money for karate lessons.*
 His father didn't laugh.
 That beggar is a comedian. Don't give money to a comedian.
 I didn't, said Olzhan.
 He saw that the pilaf sat untouched on the tray. It didn't surprise him anymore. His father's arms getting thin as sticks but his big belly still large and round and undiminished. Full of shit and poison that refused to leave his system, just building up and building up. He'd only eat pears in sweet juice that Olzhan got from the Korean store in Ridder. Then it'd go through him and he'd panic and need to pee and Olzhan would take him waddling to the toilet and stand rubbing his back as he groaned. Nothing would come or not much and Olzhan would put a fresh diaper on him and pull up his pyjamas pants and tie the string in a bow.
 But Olzhan wasn't thinking about that as he scraped the pilaf off the plate into the pig trough.

He was thinking he needed to set off early.
He needed to get there before the others.

He spoke to the boy outside sharpening a knife on a rock.
You want to come to the junkyard?
The kid looked startled. He hadn't anticipated such a question and wasn't confident how to respond.
You want me to?
I'm asking if you want to come. Simple question.
I guess.
You got better things.
Not really.
Okay.
The older brother didn't look at him, like there were more interesting things to look at elsewhere. He said, Get a blanket and get something good on your feet. Those Nikes won't keep you warm where we're going. Hear me?
Yes, said the boy.
Truth was the older one wasn't much more than a boy himself.

The mare had a thick coat and square head, descended as it was from steeds that carried the Mongol hordes. He fitted it with its collar and crupper, strapped the girth, hooked the shafts to the front of a UAZ Bukhanka which had occupied the farm longer than anything living.
He fetched supplies. Tinned beef. Beans. Dried noodle mixes that magically bulked up with boiling water to something edible. He filled two-litre plastic bottles from the well.
The boy came back out wearing a fur hat with ear flaps and a grey and red zippered ski jacket and a black-and-white checkered scarf wrapped round his neck several times, tucked in at the front.
You're prepared, said Olzhan.
Do I need the knife?
No, leave it right there stuck in that log for a crow to sit on.
Olzhan was a master of sarcasm when he wanted to be.
He rope-bridled a second pony, younger and with a fly-swat of a tail. It had become a habit on these trips. As Papa used to say when they went out together: one horse is a necessity, the second, insurance. Olzhan didn't want to find out the hard way why that was true.

Okay, he said to no-one in particular, more an announcement of fact.

The brothers went in to tell their father they were going. Olzhan heated up some borscht but he wasn't interested. He gave him a Derbes but the old man barely pressed the O of the bottle rim to his lips and acted like that much was an effort he could hardly bear.

Olzhan kissed his cheeks. Felt the white bristles like sandpaper. Until a month ago he'd never seen his father unshaven in his life. It was a rude and brutal sign of his decline.

The room around the chair was testimony to spoils of the past; the cosmic garbage from previous expeditions. A lamp run off a pillaged electrical battery. Metal sheets of stainless alloys patching holes in the roof above. Similar fare had gone to make the outhouse, carve a water track, build the well head. A jettisoned fuel tank of ten years ago the hen house.

The old man lifted his hand but the young boy, Mirat, didn't venture close to the bed. Hadn't done so in days if he could help it.

I'm okay.

Olzhan told his father there's food, there's water to drink, there's everything you need. It's going up in two days. We'll be back in four. Maybe sooner. Look. Pears. Bottled water. The bucket. You'll be okay.

You'll be okay, echoed the boy.

Olzhan squeezed his father's shoulder.

He felt bones beneath his fingers. No muscle, no fat, just bones.

He placed down the can opener on the table beside the chair next to the little tower of cigarette packs and the disposable lighter in the shape of a naked woman.

Olzhan flicked the reins forward over the old horse's head and mounted the younger one with them in his hand. He turned and stared back at the boy in the seat of the lorry while he looped them round the horn of his saddle. The boy, head nested in his scarf, looked like he wanted to say something, then he did.

Will he be all right?

You think he's going to die.

No.

We can stay and wipe his ass cheeks or we can go and earn money.

Okay.

Are you ready? If you're not.
I am ready. Let's go.

The front horse's mane fell onto its eyes as it walked.

A woman in a field watched them with hands on her hips and wore an indigo head scarf tied at the back. With her a skinny girl wearing a baseball cap.

They passed Old Kobzhanchik's place, the crashed booster section of a Soyuz sitting in the middle of his field like modern art with grass and the thin striving lines of saplings growing through it.

They unremarked upon it.

In the newspapers it said farmers in southern Siberia were claiming compensation. One for a ten-foot slab of rocket that made a hole in his barn roof. Somebody said an Altai widow got $400 after one hit her home. The Soviets were shoddy janitors at best but now they were gone nobody tidied up after them. More and more went up though. Satellites. Spacelab add-ons. Damned millionaire space tourists. Military. Always military. And the parts they discarded on the way still fell to earth with frightening regularity.

As long as Olzhan could remember the old people were afraid they'd be hit on the head, or that the sky was falling down. Olzhan just thought it was money falling. Simple as that. It was the life he'd happened into and that was as much choice as he had in the matter.

A brown-faced man with a wide Chinese-like face rode by them on a rattling IZH-56.

Papa says you have to be careful, said the boy.
What?
Hm?
Have to be careful with what?
With them. With the Kazakhs.
He's an old man. Don't listen to him.
Why?
Because he's an old man.

To his father the good old days were the Soviet days. At least then, his father'd say, grandmothers' pensions were paid. There were schools,

factories, there were good jobs around. The only gangsters you saw were in American movies. Now what have we got? he'd say. Independence. The baby-blue Kazakhstani flag.
But it was their land long before it was ours, was Olzhan's silent opinion. Long before any Russians came to this godforsaken wilderness. Like his grandfather's family, uprooted and resettled from the Ukraine by Stalin's NKVD, dumped in a naked desert with no trees, water, houses, people. Nothing but geography.
In a drinking-hole in town there was a large mural on the wall depicting a hoard of Kazakh warriors in battle against evil. Olzhan often looked at that mural thinking of the armies long ago who rode across the steppe. Then the speakers playing schmaltzy American music would bring him back to the glass in front of him and the bar he stood in.
Once the Kremlin was in charge, his Papa said many times as he spoon-fed him. We were in charge. Now what are we? Nothing. They won't be happy till they've turned us all Kazakh or told us to fuck off home. Well this is our home. We were born here. You were born here.
Yes, Papa.
Personally Olzhan didn't care. He didn't feel Kazakh. He didn't feel Soviet. He didn't even feel Russian. He didn't feel anything.

The land opened up to reveal dry rolling grassland.
That's a kestrel.
No, it's a merlin.
I know that. I was just going to say that.

They saw men bringing sheep down from thin Alpine meadow to their lowland quarters before the winter set in. Blizzards stranded people and livestock in blinding white confusion bringing to mind the flimsy edifice of existence. The shepherds rode as if in slumber flanked by native dogs with short muzzles and curly question marks for tails.
Wind stinging him in the face, the boy considered his brother, the figure ahead with the erect backbone and the swaying lilt against the swells of his saddle, the Saiga-12 hunting rifle making a dark diagonal across his camouflage jacket. The boy watched him light a cigarette and spit out the clouds either side of him as he rode.

Gutshot

They went in the direction of the Altai Mountains heading for the line on the map the rockets took across southern Siberia. Within hours the colour green got scared away into brush. Before long the landscape grew wider than you could see without moving your head and took on a uniform palette of tan and grey.

The boy hadn't seen the heavens so extensive.

They ate cold boiled *pelmeni* in their fingers as they travelled without stopping.

Occasionally Olzhan used some kind of instrument with an air of trust or dependence but Mirat didn't understand what it was and didn't choose to enquire on the subject.

When night advertised itself Olzhan hobbled the horses front leg to back and lit a fire. They ate the brick of tinned beef bisected with a knife. Mirat drank Nescafé from granules and his brother drank vodka from the bottle. The boy watched him run a cigarette paper across his tongue.

What's wrong with Papa?

I don't know.

Why don't the doctors know?

They know. Then they change their mind.

Olzhan didn't tell the boy what he thought, that the old man's kidneys had packed in. That's why he got comfort when he got his back rubbed. And when the kidneys go that means it's near the end.

Will he always be sleepy like that?

I don't know.

He groans a lot. I don't like it.

I guess he doesn't either. That's for sure.

You don't talk to him much.

I do.

You don't.

How do you know? You don't know what happens. He took a drag off his cigarette and said, Don't go through life believing you know everything.

I don't.

Olzhan stood up. Take a piss before you go to sleep. You wake in the middle of the night out here, you won't be able to find it let alone aim it.

He turned his back on his brother and said no more.

Later he looked in at Mirat in the flatbed, cocooned in a zipped-up sleeping bag and blankets, small for a ten-year-old.

He bolted up the tailgate and sat in the cab with an eiderdown round him. The wind cut though its glassless windows, the hole of the windshield through which he had a panorama of night. He nursed the vodka bottle. His Saiga lay across his lap in preparedness for wolves. His father had told him once when they'd gone out to get a piece of debris from a launch up to Mir, a pack had closed in to get ahold of the horses and he had to keep them at bay by throwing firecrackers.

As Olzhan's eyes grew heavy he thought of his father keeping the wolves at bay.

You know what this is?
Under sunlight the boy shook his head.
Come here then. I'll teach you something. Olzhan held out the handheld GPS unit. He said, It ticks down the minutes and seconds. Not of time but of longitude and latitude. Two double-A batteries. Twenty hours.

He took it back, put fresh batteries in like cartridges in a gun, handed it to him again.

I put in the co-ordinates. It tells us which way to go. You see how it works?
Mirat nodded.
Good. You'll need to know how to do this if I'm not here.
What?
If I leave.
Leave? Where?
Go somewhere. College or something. Job or something.
Where though?
It doesn't matter, okay. You'll have to look after Papa.
You'll look after Papa. You've got to.
What if I don't? Olzhan said.

He could do something other than this and he wanted to. It wasn't a crime. He already felt old and he didn't want to feel old anymore.

His brother looked frightened as was expected. Olzhan wanted to yell at him but instead turned away. He was weary with everybody he knew looking frightened. It weighed on him like a rock and he was sick of its burden.

Gutshot

They rode past six dead cows lying bloated and stiff-legged. Liver, blood, genetic diseases, sicknesses like Papa's. All because of contaminated land soaked with liquid propellant for forty years. The old folk who worried about rockets dropping on their heads had no idea of the toxic heptyl infecting the ground under their feet. They looked at the sky instead of the ground they stood on. Death had seeped into the cycle of life while white shards of progress shot towards the stars.

He let his brother stare.

He thought he should see what death is like.

He drew marks in the arid earth with the charred stick from the second night's fire.

Each type of rocket and weight of payload needs a different launch configuration. You need an informant to tell you exactly where the crash site is going to be. Where the jettisoned sections are projected to hit the ground. Once you know that, you've got to get there and stake your claim fast or someone else'll get there before you.

The child's eyes were not to be rested on.

You'll make more in one hit out here than six months back on the farm. So it's all about who knows where and who gets there first.

The pale beads the flames spat up reminded Olzhan of when he was his brother's age, out on the steppe for the first time, excitedly watching his father's men working. Scavenging the scrap metal. Being one of them at last. Then, the weirdest thing. Sitting in the cab of the UAZ Bukhanka. Engine growling in those far off days. Thinking he saw snow but realizing in fact it was millions of white butterflies. Not like millions of animals at all but just one. Never settling long. Never able to. Somehow always restless. Always lifting, flying. Away. Moving on.

He passed the boy the vodka bottle.

The boy supped, coughed, gasped for air and took a second mouthful.

Hey. Give it back.

The boy shook his head.

Give it to me.

The boy chuckled and stood up and ran a little, looking back for his brother to chase him. He remembered when he used to do that when he was little.

But Olzhan didn't. Just sat there in the red glow of the flames. Eyes fierce.

Mirat came back with the bottle the way a hungry dog comes back to a bone when it's been scared away by a thrown stick and handed it to him so that his brother could drink and feel some of that numbness in his gut he craved. The boy felt he'd done wrong but he hadn't.

I'm cold.
Uhh.
I said I'm cold.
Go to sleep. Morning comes quicker.
I can't.
Jesus Christ. Stop whining. Did Papa bring you up to be a whining pussy?
I can't help it.
Yes you can help it. You can stop whining.
Olzhan turned over on his side, crushed himself inward.
Mirat started crying now.
Olzhan sighed. What do you want me to do? What?
That last word came out like a bark.
The boy went quiet but kept crying.
Olzhan lay and listened but could not sleep.

In the morning Olzhan woke cranky. The kid burnt his fingers on the coffee pan.
Pussy.
No.
Olzhan glared at him like an enemy.
You don't get it do you?
Get what?

By the afternoon they were in semi-desert. So dry you could snap it. Olzhan stood on the roof of the UAZ and dropped the binoculars for Mirat to catch.
What will I see?
You'll see something. Keep looking.
The boy was stripped to the waist. The sun unrelenting.

Wind came and went like God's warm breath and their footprints multiplied in the ivory dust and the sun traversed in its fashion over them.

Olzhan felt his education of the boy was sorely incomplete and sought to remedy this between bouts of chasmic silence.

The USA built its launch centre near water so they could have safe landings. Splashdowns. Hey I'm teaching you something.

I'm listening.

The Soviets in the fifties, oh no, it was all about secrecy. So they built Baikonur where it was barren, landlocked, away from the eyes of the world. Why we've got a rocket cemetery on our doorstep. Right in our back yard.

The boy tasted the bitterness in what he heard.

Hundreds of launches. Thousands of tons of scrap metal. What are we supposed to do? Scrape our fingers to the bone trying to farm this concrete or make some money out of the stuff that falls in our laps?

Olzhan looked at the vastness of the steppe.

You know what this is? It's our harvest now. Not corn and beet vegetables. Titanium alloy and high grade aluminium.

Five hours later Olzhan answered his satellite phone. The launch had been delayed. Rescheduled for 2:43 a.m. Moscow time. Mirat saw he had two watches, one on each wrist, one set to Moscow time.

There it is.

The boy sees a firefly on the horizon like a shooting star. It seems at first to be travelling in reverse. Hovers slowly, then darts straight upwards.

They see it gaining speed across the sky.

Watch for minutes in mute anticipation until the ground shakes under them like a bomb blast rattling the boy's heart in his chest.

They followed the light till they found the booster section of a Proton still burning. The smell of gasoline and smoke reminded Olzhan of his father again. The pot belly and black vest and thick hairy arms, shielding his eyes with the flat of his hand as he squinted at the sky, cursing the cloud cover. Gang-master over two trucks of hard-as-nails men. Yelling to a croak, chain-smoking, swearing, sweating. King of the dust.

It was still smouldering when Olzhan took his blowtorch and sledgehammer from the trailer to start dismantling it. He set up a work light running off a car battery it not being sun-up yet and climbed a stepladder resting on the flatbed to start slicing off pieces of the hull.

Butchering a Proton third-stage'll take a couple days and nights, he said, Depending how many pairs of hands you've got. I'll tell you about the anatomy. You've got to know the parts that are easy to cut through first. It's like slaughtering a lamb. There's the good way and there's the hard way and you do it the hard way you're some kind of fool.

Mirat watched.

First thing you take is always this. Olzhan removed a bowl-shaped part of the fuel system, twenty inches in diameter. I'll show you why.

He got a fire going. Boiled water, tossed some pasta in it like a wok.

Mirat smiled. They sat and ate as dawn threatened. No utensils, just plates and hands.

A pall of dust on the horizon. Cars.

Olzhan was atop the monolith which stood like the round turret of a fortress. He raised his goggles and squinted.

Who were they? One of the roaming bands of salvage men like him? Space-age gold-panners hunting for metal that will make them rich; or if not rich, keep them alive through another ball-breaking winter.

He hunkered down back to his work. Feeling the sweat on him. Damning it to hell if after all this effort he'd have to share the booty. Maybe they weren't even coming in his direction and he wouldn't have to think about it but they were and he knew it.

Dust settled over chrome and clothing.

A Lada Niva mini-SUV and a black Mercedes four-door.

Two got out. One stayed in the Merc.

The elder of the two that stood there squinting to keep sand out of their eyes wore a black suit and white shirt with a fur-lined parka over it and quilted body warmer over that and a black spade-shaped beard which had the pale river of a scar through it, atop all this a skull-cap like an Imam.

The younger one was jumping up and down grinning like it was his birthday. He immediately ran over to the fallen section of rocket and touched it, laughing and ululating, deep-set eyes and clipped beard like it was drawn on in black ink, denim jacket over a knee-length smock, the sort Muslims wear.

Their tongues flapped eloquently in some verbiage unknown to Olzhan. He knew they didn't look Kazakh. They looked more Asian. Uzbek or Tajik maybe, and the Uzbek and Tajik and Azerbaijani were the families who ran the heroin using the old Silk Route into Russia and from Russia into Europe and he knew the borders were wide open because someone told him that in the south it cost $5 to bribe the border guards and another twenty to ride a special "taxi" from Saragach to Tashkent through all the checkpoints. No stops.

Olzhan didn't move.

A fingertip of perspiration running down his spine, he wondered if the Merc or the SUV had the kilos in it.

Mirat looked up at his brother but his brother didn't look down.

The one in the car had his foot up against the open door so Olzhan could see without much effort he wore blue tracksuit bottoms with two white stripes running down the legs and the ankles unzipped. A burnous semi-swathed his face but that was inside the car and therefore in shadow. His toe prodded the creaking door regularly as if in some misguided way he though the motion of it might fan him.

Asselem aleykum!

Aleykum vassalam, said Olzhan, returning to his endeavours.

The blowtorch snarled.

Idiot saw shooting star, said the Imam. Said we had to follow it. Like it was star of Bethlehem or something. He and the man in the Merc laughed showing the whiteness of their teeth. He is crazy. He is crazyman!

The young one whooped and did a little dance and thereafter began to take photographs of the rocket with his cell phone cupping his hand round it to keep off the sun as he checked the image.

Hey. Government property, this one said.

They laughed.

Olzhan didn't raise his head. My property. Salvage.

The Imam gestured with open arms before their laughter faded.

He looked at the two others.

Hey.

Olzhan, head down, was thinking of the city of Osh where they say heroin is as cheap as beer and HIV is making skeletons. He considered whether they were smuggling heroin or guns or both. Did they have guns? What about the one in the car in the half-shadow whose hands he could not see?

He wondered if they were just plain bandits or Hizb-ut-Tahrirs.
He wanted them to go.
USSR. Yuri Gagarin.
No, said Olzhan. American.
Da, Ibraheem Lincoln, said the Imam smiling.
Da, Snoopy Dog, said the one in the car doing the same.
Da, 50 Cent, said the crazy one giggling. Then he saw the pony feeding from the bowl from the fuel system. Hey. Kazakh cowboy.
Olzhan hated that expression.
Hey. Montana.
Olzhan did not answer.
The Imam said, Let's go. But the young one showed him his palm.
Hey.
The crazy one with camera phone and eyes turned to Mirat.
You want to look in car? Expensive car.
Olzhan turned off the blowtorch.
He doesn't need to look in the car.
Hey. He can answer for self.
He doesn't want to look in the car.
What is name? You not seen car like this. You know how to get car like this?
The boy didn't answer.
We're done here, said Olzhan.
Let boy answer. He want to answer. Come here.
Mirat walked to the man not sure if he did it to obey him or show he was tough or just to rile his brother anyways that was what he did.
The crazy one looked at his hand which was now on the boy's shoulder and which had broken and filthy fingernails.
Olzhan felt a tightness in his throat like something was blocked there.
The brown hand squeezed his brother's skinny shoulder in a slight massaging motion and in an instant Olzhan knew what that hand had done and will do and that bad people didn't only traffic drugs. Darkness opened like a vast pestilential mouth and in the same instant he knew he had to act and he knew that act would lead where it will. Some animal part of his brain erupted free of any notion of self-preservation or concern for his own fate or wellbeing and the rest was inevitable and alacritous.

Gutshot

The crazy man with the pencil beard wrapped his forearm round the boy's throat and the man sitting in the car with the door open dropped his foot to the dust and Olzhan saw more of the Kalashnikov emerging than he needed to and the Imam swung a Glock from the back of his belt and just as Olzhan dropped and sprang erect firing his hunting rifle the shot hit him cutting a rip through sleeve and arm and the two kept firing at him as the crazy one backed away with the boy in front of him a shield, heels dragging and kicking, hand over his mouth now and Olzhan fell off the booster into the dust like a calf being born, snout-first.

His head cracked. He felt his brain go muzzy, then felt the blood from his nostrils on his lips and snapped out of it knowing he would die if he didn't.

The Imam strode towards him upside down and Olzhan bloody-handed pulled the trigger of the Saiga and smacked bullet into shoulder hearing the crack of bone kicking the Imam back a few feet reeling unsteadily like his mortality was impossible to conceive.

Behind this Olzhan could see the one with the burnous-wrapped face deadfallen out of the car into the sand, red pool forming under him, one leg still hitched up into the foot space of the vehicle and twisted.

A blow against the godless, Olzhan thought.

Pain seared through him like electricity.

Then he saw them take him.

Saw the crazy one shove Mirat towards the Imam and saw the two disappear into the blackness of the Merc.

He heard his brother's cry cut by the door slam and the crazy one coming back towards him looming with the sun radiating around him like his mother's saint and Olzhan no longer having the strength to raise the Saiga and the pistol which the young one had now shooting down at him in the body and face.

Olzhan listened to his breath in his skull as he watched the short-haired one get behind the wheel and start revving. The wheels became yellow with dust and they reversed into a thickening pall of it, vanishing.

He was alone with the torture of his continued breathing. The flies gathered on the burnous-wearing man in the dust, his treacle blood black now and the horses wandered flicking their ears and lacking bewilderment.

Night approaching he crawled into the belly of the rocket booster section figuring he might be kept warm there by the heat absorbed during the day.

The chamber multiplied his sobs and cries of his brother's name.

The orb of sky above him went from blue to black.

He thought of the astronauts up there where the payloads were going, to the ISS, the cosmonauts, even a Kazakh one up there sometimes. All floating. All waving at the camera. All the nations as one.

He wondered if, when they look out of their window, they saw the stars. Or white butterflies.

He was cold.

He had never been so cold.

Every hour into that long night he got colder like the night was telling him something.

His chapped lips wouldn't part. He tried to slow breathe but his gasps just became faster in panic.

The air in his nostrils burnt like ice.

Soon he found he could no longer open his eyes. In any case he knew it was dark and made no difference.

Gradually he lost all movement.

Toes and fingers first, then limbs altogether.

Eventually the warmest thing he could feel was his own blood leaving his body, and it comforted.

He felt its rivers and tributaries on the surface of him.

Then in time, like every human being before him, he felt nothing at all.

Stephen Volk was the creator of the TV drama series *Afterlife* and the notorious BBC 'Halloween hoax' *Ghostwatch*. His latest feature film (co-written by director Nick Murphy) is *The Awakening* starring Rebecca Hall and Dominic West, and his other movie credits include Ken Russell's *Gothic* and William Friedkin's *The Guardian*. He has also written for Channel Four's *Shockers* and won a BAFTA for *The Deadness of Dad* starring Rhys Ifans. His short stories (some of which are collected in *Dark Corners*, Gray Friar Press), have earned him nominations for the British Fantasy, Bram Stoker, and Shirley Jackson awards, and appearances in several 'best of' anthologies.

Gutshot

"The inspiration for *White Butterflies* was a series of photographs of rocket-part scavengers taken by Jonas Bendiksen: the more I researched the subject, the combination of modern cowboys and spacecraft junk struck me as hugely exciting. I knew I had my Kazakh 'Western' fully justified when I found an essay online by Kate Brown entitled 'Gridded Lives: Why Kazakhstan and Montana Are Nearly The Same Place.' Special thanks must go to Andrey Duryabin, and to Julia Melnitskaya for her invaluable notes."

EL CAMINO DE ROJO
Gary McMahon

Badge steered the mount—a skinny Appalachian mare—up the rise and along over the low plateau, his hands tight on the reins and his eyes looking dead ahead, right into the beginnings of a hellish West Texas sunset. He did not look back. He could not look back. He looked only ahead, into that shimmering, flaming line which wavered at the very edge of things.

His hands hurt. His heart hurt. Everything hurt. He was in a whole world of hurt, and nothing but death would rectify that. Not his death, no, but that of the man (if that's what he was) they called el Lobo: the wolf.

The horse whinnied and then stalled, its front hooves cracking on the hard earth, making little gunshot sounds in the gathering darkness. Badge still could not look back; he couldn't allow it.

He could not look back at the tree.

At the tree of hands.

Despite this, he could still picture it; could not rip the image from his mind. The wide-bottomed tree, its upper branches so dark and spiny, with all those human hands set amid the thin and papery leaves.

It had been a warning—a warning from el Lobo. The Mexican knew that Badge was coming, and he'd used the tree to wave at him. Used the tree and a bunch of strangers' hands to say "hello, *hombre*, "come and get me".

It was, after all, el Lobo's way: the way of red, of screams and violence and hate.

The sun slipped down past the rim of the horizon, and Badge was glad of the ensuing darkness. But it was a strange darkness—*prairie* darkness—and it held nestled within it the promise of stranger things to come. The landscape out here was fierce and unforgiving; it tore at a man's body and spat deep into his soul. He'd once known a two-dollar whore, a pretty girl with wide hips and very little facial scarring, who'd gone *loco* and set off into this same prairie, looking for God. She was found by a rancher over a week later. Her face was burned by the sun to the bone, and her hands and feet and knees were all bloody and tattered, as if she had been crawling for miles. All she would say, with her eyes staring inward, was *"I found her. I found her."* Over and over again, like a prayer.

The prairie was a haunted place, and if you rode in there with your own ghosts riding side saddle, then who knew what other phantoms might come out to meet them.

"Giddup," he said, softly, cajoling the horse to move forward. It did not have a name, this horse; he had learned long ago that to name things was to pin upon them a sense of worth, and everything of worth left you in the end.

He rode for another half hour and found a place, a good place, where he could pitch his camp and start a fire. The fire would keep the coyotes away, but it would not hold back the dreams. The dreams of the tree of hands, and of the man he was hunting; the nightmares about his dead family—his dead and raped wife, dead and raped child, dead and raped life.

Badge dismounted, wincing only slightly at the pain as he left the saddle, and began to unpack his camp. After a short while he was cooking not-too-ancient bacon at the fire, facing windward of the flames, and boiling up a pot of coffee grounds. The smell of the coffee made his mouth water; the hot fat of the bacon fell upon his hands, but he barely even felt it.

The stars were sparse, and dull; the sky was a sea of blackness. Badge had never seen a real ocean, not in his entire life, but he imagined that the sky right then looked like a quiet ocean at night, when the darkness falls across the water in a pall and nothing stirs beneath.

He sat back with his plate, and his tin cup filled with the sweet, black coffee, and he ate without tasting. Things like taste, and touch, and

EL CAMINO DE ROJO

sensation were for other men—men who were not hollow, who still possessed the ability to live. Badge had not truly lived for seasons now; he simply rode and he waited and he slowly chased down the bastard el Lobo, seeing the signs wherever he went, following the trail of blood, of meat and redness.

Just as he was about to settle in for the night, a figure approached from the west. The figure was long and tall, with scrawny legs, and as it neared Badge saw that it was a man. He tensed, sighed, and made a grab for his gun, which was under his blanket. The old Colt felt solid in his hand, more of a friend than any real friend he had ever known.

The man walked into the camp, his clothes covered in dust. His face was dust too; a mask of it, thick and white: prairie dust, the kind that gets right under the skin and stays there.

"Evenin'," said the man, pausing on the opposite side of the fire.

"Yup," said Badge, eyeing him. Waiting to see if he would make a move.

"Mind if I join you? That fire looks awful nice."

"I ain't got no vittles, but there's warm coffee in that there pot." Badge cocked his head, motioning towards the tin pot by the fire. "You're welcome to it."

The man nodded, spilling dust onto his dusty collar. "Much appreciated, brother." His voice was low but not deep; there was a quality to it that put Badge in mind of a woman.

Badge relaxed his grip on the Colt.

The man nodded and sat down, keeping his distance. He reached for the pot and took a little battered mug from his pack, which was slung across his back. He poured the coffee leavings into the mug, and then he slowly drank them.

"Travellin' far?" Badge remained where he was, on the ground, and pulled his blanket tighter around his shoulders. Prairie nights could get cold, a cold that bit right down to your bones.

"As far as I need," said the man, setting his mug aside and adjusting his pack to make a cushion. He lay down on his side, staring at Badge through the dying fire. His eyes were dark, almost black, and upon his face there appeared a slight smile that Badge could not read. "Just as far as I need, brother."

Beneath the layer of dust on the man's face, Badge could make out scars. They were not deep, those scars, but there were many, and they made a pattern across his cheeks, like stitch-marks in a knitted quilt. "You got a name, stranger?"

The man closed his eyes—his dark, dark eyes—and that smile stayed right where it was, not going anywhere just yet. "They call me Pardoner."

"Strange name," said Badge. "How'd you come by that?"

The smiled slipped, fell. The fire crackled, a cinder popping out like a Chinese firecracker on the Fourth of July. "It's a long story." And that was all he said about that.

There was a long silence then, and it stretched across the night like a skin. Distant coyotes launched into their song; the cold seeped into the blankets, searching out warm flesh to kiss.

"I believe I know where you're goin', brother." The man's voice—Pardoner's voice—hung in the air, echoing a little.

"Uh-Uhu?"

"Yup. I believe you're chasin' down the man they call el Lobo. That dirty little Mexican with a bloodlust, and his bunch o' cowardly banditos."

Badge waited, waited, and then knew that he must speak. He couldn't stand the silence, the long, twitching silence. "And how might you know about that?"

Pardoner moved suddenly, drawing himself up from out of his thin blanket. His movements were quick and twitchy, like a bird. "'Cause that's where I just been, brother. Chasin' down the bad man, dancin' with the devil." He stood; then, letting the blanket fall, he opened his shirt by the wan glow of dying firelight.

Badge sat up and pushed himself back away from the fire, his boots stirring up the dust. He brought up the Colt and aimed it at the looming figure of the other man. "Git away from me, devil. Git away from me afore I put holes in you."

The man continued to unbutton his dusty shirt, with his dusty hands. The shirt was then pulled open, pulled apart, and Badge finally saw the message that had been sent to him—sent across the miles and miles of dusty prairie, kept alive until this moment, in the waning firelight.

A string of Indian beads hung at the man's torn throat, coated in red.

Below the necklace, Pardoner's belly had been opened from gullet to beltline. The hole gaped, the two sides parting like the curtains on a tiny stage, and the dark redness seeped out. Dust had gotten inside there, mingling with his innards, and the resultant mess was clumped and clustered like porridge mixed with molasses.

The dusty guts looped and dropped to the ground, making a sound like wet clothes thrown down on a wash house floor. Steam rose from the mess. Pardoner remained standing; his feet were shoulder width apart, and his black, black eyes focussed on the lowering flames of the camp fire.

"If you go back now, he'll pardon you. If you follow, you'll be nothin' but meat."

Hands shaking, eyes watering, Badge raised the Colt. He let off two rapid shots—*bang!-bang!*—and watched as half the Pardoner's head went up in a red mist. Blood and brain and bone hissed on the fire. The man's legs went, buckling, and he fell, the dust making little tornadoes around him.

Afterwards Badge slept. No dreams came.

Come morning, he packed up his bag and untied the horse. Then he set off into the approaching sunrise, watching the sky start to blaze. Clouds of dust seemed to hang in the air for miles; layers and layers of it, tainting the morning. The distant jagged mountains reared like teeth in a gaping maw. He had travelled so far, and for so long, that even this couldn't stop him. He would go on, into the west, and never quit until he held in his hands the bloody heart of el Lobo.

Hours later he came to a little town called Bethany. It consisted of little more than a muddy main street, with a nameless saloon and a top floor bordello, and a couple of small stores. Beyond these, just outside the other end of town, were the shanty structures of a clapboard church and a once-proud but now decrepit bone yard.

Badge climbed off the horse and looked around. He tied up the horse at a watering trough and headed towards the saloon. He strode through the mud and the dirt, the hem of his long coat trailing in the filth. An open sewer ran along the edge of the road, and he stepped across it onto the wooden planks outside the saloon.

He raised his hand to the door, felt the rough wood, and then pushed on inside.

There was a battered piano in one corner but nobody was playing. The bar ran along the left wall, with a dwarf standing on a narrow coffin behind it, washing pots. A set of stairs led up to the upper floor, and the bordello. The customers sat scattered around the cramped space at the bottom of the stairs. Some of them were playing cards, and yet others were drinking in silence. All of them looked temporary; dried-out travellers like him. They had the mile-long stare of haunted men and the calloused hands and dusty clothes of those who had trod the road, and trod it long and hard.

Badge's boots were loud on the wet boards. Nobody paid him much attention, but the silence told its own story. He was being watched without them watching; they were taking the measure of his stride, of the way his hands hung heavy at his sides.

"Whisky," he said to the dwarf. The dwarf nodded and shuffled along his coffin, then poured a stiff measure into a dusty glass. Badge wondered idly if the coffin was empty.

"Come far?" asked the dwarf, setting down his drink.

"Far enough." He sipped the whisky, the awful gut-rot brew, and felt his tongue tingle. He heard footsteps pounding across the boards upstairs; then, as a door opened and closed, there came the sound of giggling females. Badge felt the muscles in his lower stomach tense. He had not had a woman in weeks, maybe even months. The slashed face of his wife flashed briefly in his mind's eye, but he pushed it away.

He killed his drink, the liquid burning a path down his throat, and headed for the stairs. Behind him, the dwarf chuckled from atop his coffin, but he let it go. He wanted no confrontation here; his fight lay elsewhere, and against a different kind of enemy.

He climbed the stairs, his boots slamming on the boards, and came to the landing. A fat woman in a tight red dress sat at a small table, counting out coins. She looked up, fluttering her ill-applied fake lashes, and smiled, showing black teeth set into thin gums. "What can I do for you, fella?"

"A woman." He stared down at her, flexing his hands into fists.

"Not much of a choice this morning, but Elena's free in the room at the end o' the hall. She's young, purdy, and keeps herself mighty clean."

Badge nodded. He counted out some coins, placing them on the table, keeping his hands as far away from the woman's podgy fingers as he possibly could. Then he turned away and headed for the door at the end.

"Being seeing you, fella." The woman's voice chased him along the landing, buzzing like a fly. "Be seeing you."

Badge knocked on the door and waited. There came from behind the door the sound of a chair being moved across the floor, followed by light footsteps, and then the door was opened. A young girl stood before him, barely out of her teens, the tawny top of her head just about level with his chest.

"I'm all paid up," he said, placing one hand on the door.

"Well come on in," said the girl, smiling without opening her lips. She pulled the door wide; he followed her in. She shut the door behind him, and locked it.

He soon found out why she had not opened her mouth when she smiled. She drew the blind and turned out the lamp, and then began to undress. She took off her over garments but left on her undies—white women, even whores, did not like to rut naked like squaws. She slid into bed next to him, and undid his pants. Her hands were rough, and up close her skin was marred by tiny lacerations, with a deep slit which had healed badly at the left side of her mouth. Her thighs were badly scarred—it was rare, or at least expensive, to attain an unmarked whore, and in a town like this one Badge doubted that it was even possible. The teeth were missing from her upper jaw—all of them, knocked out cleanly by the butt of a pistol. She told him that when he asked; she told him everything, about the beatings and the cuttings and the stinking old men who used her as a receptacle for their useless seed.

Somehow he found his way inside her, and as they thrashed on the bed the light seemed to dim. At was as if a cloud had passed overhead, coming to rest above the saloon and the bordello. Badge clutched at Elena's white-scarred thighs, at her cross-hatched buttocks. He pressed against her and into her, trying to force the length of his terror inside her narrow pelvis.

Soon it was over, and he rolled off her with a sigh. She farted quietly, and he felt the gorge rise in his throat. His desire satisfied, he felt ashamed to be lying here, with this wreck of a girl. There was barely anything left of her; she was a withered puppet, a wasted thing made of nought but sticks and hide.

He smoked a cigarette in the closeness of the room, wishing that he could burn it all down. It was dark as night, black as death, and presently he realised that a figure sat at the foot of the bed, balanced on the post like a monkey. It was thin, this figure, and limned in a darker edge than the darkness behind it. He knew it was el Lobo; it could be no-one else. But he also knew that it was a dream—a waking dream, brought on by fatigue and the terrible release of his lust.

"What do you want, devil. Why are you here?"

The figure at the end of the bed twitched, its head dipping to its chest and then rising again slowly, the mouth opening.

When it spoke its voice was flat and dead, like the sound of bodies falling into a pit.

"*Yo soy tú. Tú eres yo. Somos nosotros, Nos movemos juntos a través de este desierto interminable. Seguimos el camino de la rojez.*"

Badge blinked, and in the space between his eyes being open, closed and then open again, dusty light returned to the room and the figure of the devil el Lobo had vanished.

His Spanish was not great, but he knew enough to piece together at least the last sentence: "We follow the way of red."

He smelled blood and smoke, saw in his mind gashed flesh and legs torn redly asunder by the heaving thighs of el Lobo's men, and then his nostrils flared with the sweat-stink of his own fear. He turned to the girl, clenching his fists, keeping them tensed, and looked at her poor scarred face, her dull, flat eyes.

"What is it?" she said, pulling the bed sheets up over her heavy breasts. "What?"

Badge took the smoking cigarette from his mouth, and then stared at the fiery tip, as if it was telling him something—a great and terrible secret. He looked from the small red flare to the girl's marked skin, and then back again. She did not even struggle as he touched the live end of the cigarette to her shoulder, nor did she scream. She was used to such brutal treatment, and knew that, in the end, it would earn her a few extra coins.

The only words she spoke during the whole time where ones that he could barely fathom. "I know you," she said, her eyes shut tight. "I know you." And before long, she did.

Badge left the room in silence. He closed the door behind him, on the girl's weeping, and walked back to the fat old woman at the table. He stood before her, shaking and trying to contain his own tears—the tears shed for too many people over such a long time. Then he took from his pocket a few dollars more, and he scattered them across the desk.

"I hope you didn't mark her too badly, fella. That's prime meat in there." The fat woman began to laugh, rocking in her wooden chair. Her chins wobbled like a bucket of horse shit and her arms flapped against her sides like ragged wings of a hungry vulture.

It was all Badge could do not to shoot her in the face, to make a hole in her wet, grinning maw. So he walked away—he just walked away and bit down on his loathing, and went down the wooden stairs, across the saloon bar, and back out into the street, where his mount waited at the trough, its thirst quenched.

He untied the horse and led it at his side, not yet mounting the animal, giving it some additional rest. They had trekked a long way, and they both were very tired. Badge had scoured the land for el Lobo, and now, finally, he felt that he was drawing near to the heart of his darkness. The ghosts of his wife and daughter (never named; never called upon, even in the depths of his grief) trailed a ways behind, unwilling to stand at his side.

He headed towards the old church, not knowing what else to do. He had lost his belief along with his family, and religion was now a stale thing in the corner of his life, never handled or even looked upon. He crossed the street and went a little way beyond the official town limits, where he stood outside the clapboard structure. A welcome wind had whipped up; it blew against his face, stirring but not removing the layer of dust.

Dust everywhere, on his face and in his heart. Dust in his blood and in his bones.

"Yup," he muttered, to the horse, to nobody. "Yup." He said it again just to hear the sound of another human voice. He thought of the young whore Elena, and of what terrible things he had done to her flesh. He was less ashamed of the act itself than of the fact that he felt no regret. He doubted that she had even been real; just another washed-out phantom on his journey through the edges of el Lobo's territory. Yet another forlorn marker on the way of red.

He looked at the old timber markers on the graves, feeling a deep sadness at the way they tipped and tilted to the side, and how so many of them were missing their crossbeams, or simply falling apart. It was apparent from their condition that nobody came here to tend them; the church, and its graveyard, had been deserted by whatever citizens still dwelled within the dying town of Bethany. If once this had been a thriving little border community, then now it was but a flyblown corpse, another sorry victim of el Lobo's all-pervasive influence.

The Mexican had left deep scars across America—first in the larger towns and cities, and then in small places like this. He had arrived from nowhere, carried out his crimes, and then rode west for the border. There was neither rhyme nor reason to his atrocities; he just did them and moved on, his laughter riding the wind like the call of some terrible beast on the hunt.

The worst damage was down here, near the border; his power had increased the closer he got to his home, to Mexico. Burned-out farms and homesteads, mutilated bodies, children skinned and boiled and severed of their limbs, their torsos then used as pillows. The entire south was disfigured by his progress; he had left his awful mark across the reddened soil and the dry desert dust; his laughter was caught within the folds of prairie winds; the coyotes called his name at night: el Lobo: the Wolf. He was by now barely even a man at all.

Badge would be dead now if it were not for this odyssey. The only thing stopping him from eating a bullet was the search for his nemesis. The Mexican had come onto his farm, burning and ransacking, stealing food and dry goods, and finally tying Badge to a kitchen chair as he raped and slit his wife and two year-old daughter. Only after they were dead did he allow his men to take turns with the corpses.

The final agony—even worse than death—was that he had left Badge alive; had left him there in the ashes, weeping and wailing over the scattered and smoking body parts of the ones he had loved.

That had been a year ago. A heavy year spent in the saddle: twelve long months following the signs, sniffing the blood, and tracking the way of red. Now that his journey was almost over, and the signs had become less subtle, less sophisticated (a stunted tree filled with hands, a disembowelled cowboy, a town of battered ghosts) Badge was beginning to feel the proximity of his own death... and the feeling was a good one, a just one. He had done so many bad things along the way, killed so many people who had associated with the Mexican, he truly felt that he too deserved to die.

But not until he killed el Lobo.

Badge again tied up the horse and entered the church grounds. Closing the gate behind him, he walked towards the tired looking building. The stones were stained, the windows broken. The door, when he got there, was ajar, and he pushed it open and walked on in. The pews were all upturned and shattered; the floor was broken up, as if attacked by heavy hammers.

The altar, at the front of the church, had been vandalised. As he approached the stone slab, Badge saw that it had been defecated upon, and that fires had been set across its pitted surface. The religious artefacts were scattered; most of them broken, and the rest had been picked clean of any gold or jewels. Lit candles flickered from niches in the walls, casting ugly shadows. A man was kneeling by the altar, off to the side. Badge had not at first noticed him, but now he realised that the man was praying.

"Excuse me," he said, keeping his voice low so that he did not scare or unnerve the man.

The man—who was a priest; a man of worship, another of el Lobo's crude symbols—turned to face Badge. In the wavering candlelight, his face was a mosaic of pain. The scars across his cheeks were in cruciform shapes, and he had been messily scalped. White skin showed through the gaps in his hair, with dry red patches scattered throughout. "Good day, my son.Badge stepped back, going for the Colt. As the priest's head turned around, and he spoke the greeting, Badge saw that the man's eyes had been gouged out, and the sockets were badly scarred over.

"Who did this?" he knew the answer; it was always the same.

"The devil did this. The devil from Mexico." The priest got to his feet, stumbling slightly. Badge went to his aid and helped him to a pew that was just about intact. "Thank you," said the priest, clutching Badge's hand.

Badge stiffened at the contact. He did not know why, but there was something repellent about the touch of the priest.

"Son . . . my son. Do I know you? Have we met before?"

"We've not met afore," said Badge, standing. "Never afore."

"I . . . I'm sorry. I didn't mean to offend. It's just that . . . no, it's nothing."

Badge stood before the seated priest, staring at the mess of tissue over his eye sockets. He passed a hand before the man's face, moving it close to those ruined eyes.

"He blinded me only after they ransacked the church. He wanted me to see what he'd done, and then to live with it afterwards. They...they raped me and beat me and used me as a toilet. They are devils, my son. Wolves and devils." The priest began to make a strange whining sound in his throat, and Badge finally realised the man was crying. He was crying without tears—for he could produce no tears from those scar-sealed eye sockets.

"Why are they doing this?" He glanced around the church, at the old stone walls and the shattered windows. "Why?"

The priest stopped crying. He coughed and shuffled in his seat. "Because they can; because we let them. This is a new age, my son. We are gradually taking over this land, stealing it from those who have lived upon it for centuries, and ripping out its heart. Men like him—men like el Lobo—are the direct result of these actions." He paused, swallowed, and then continued: "We made him. He is ours. I am you. You are me. I am us. *Seguimos el camino de la rojez.*"

Badge staggered backwards, his boots crunching on the holy debris and one arm catching a candle in a hole in the wall. He brushed his sleeve, sparks flashing in the gloom, and finally managed to get his fear under control. "Why did you say that? Where did you hear them words, preacher?"

The priest turned to him. Turned to him with his blind eyes, and yet Badge still felt that he could be seen. "Those are the words he said to me, just before he took my eyes."

He spent the night in a tiny room out back of the church, with the mangled priest's blessing. Cold and damp seeped through the stone, but it was better than the bitter, biting night of the prairie. It was better to be under cover than out there, in the desert dark, and at the mercy of the elements.

The priest was called Nathan, and he was kind and careful. He left Badge alone until morning, and then fed him a meagre breakfast of jerky and coffee. But it was better than nothing, and when he rode off he waved at the blind priest, who waved back, as if for a moment he could see.

He was nearing the end now, getting closer to the heart of things. He could smell el Lobo on the wind and taste him in the tainted water of the streams he drank from along the way.

The Mexican was nearby; even the animals knew that, and they were silent, as if they either feared or respected his presence on the land.

He rode all day, south of El Paso and along towards the border, traversing gorges and narrow switchback trails, passing through empty camps and stopping at burned-out homes and corrals. The distant mountains formed a spine along the horizon, its vertebrae fractured and bent out of shape. The sky lowered, drawing in close and forming a roof over his head. At dusk he came upon a row of dead horses, all lined up in middle of the dirt road. Their bellies had been opened and small fires set within. The smell of cooked offal hung heavy in the air, and there was a yellowish pall of grease everywhere, even on rocks and the trunks of trees.

By twilight he came to a spot where there was a small mound of rocks. He glanced at the cairn as he rode on by, and then looked swiftly away. Human heads, their hair carefully removed, had been set like nightmare gems between the stones. There were hundreds of them, each one lovingly barbered, and their eyes were open and staring.

Then, still early in the reddening evening, he arrived at a place of no roads, just flat scrubland and jagged outcroppings of rock, all hemmed in by dead and darkening trees.

Just as night fell proper, he completed his journey. Not far from the banks of the Rio Grande, on the far side of which lay the temptations of Chihuahua City. The moment was bittersweet, and filled with a sense of dread. A man stood up ahead, his hands on his hips, and he was flanked by an intricate latticework of human body parts—arms and legs, split torsos and severed genitals all laced together to form a gore-streaked framework within which the man stood.

Badge dismounted and tapped the horse on its behind. It trotted off, into the trees, heading for a safer place. He would not need it again; the horse had carried him far enough—too far—into this hellish interior.

Badge walked slowly towards the Mexican. The man was naked; his flesh shone in the moonlight, shimmering like polished coffee beans. Fresh scalps hung from his wrists and were tied about his waist. He did not move, just stood there, hands on hips, and waited. He waited within his cage of blood and bone and gristle, with a fine drapery of yanked veins forming a purplish skein above his unmoving head.

"El Lobo," said Badge, drawing near. "We meet again at last." He took out his Colt, cocked it, aimed, and fired. There would be no long, drawn out climax here; he aimed to end it quickly and brutally, and then bathe in the Mexican's blood. He fired again. Black blood flew in the black night. Flesh came off in large chunks. But still the Mexican did not move. He did not move and he did not speak; he did not scream.

Badge stopped before the man for whom he had travelled so far, the enemy whose name had been fire at his lips, whose eyes had stared back into his own each night. He stopped and he looked into the face of death, examining the features of his own darkest desire. On this shivering borderline between countries, between states of being, he stared down the source of his own horror.

His own face stared back at him, limp and unmoving. His own eyes stared back at him, unblinking. Those rigid lips twitched, coming apart. They spoke:

"*Yo soy tú. Tú eres yo. Somos nosotros, Nos movemos juntos a través de este desierto interminable. Seguimos el camino de la rojez.*"

I am you. You are me. I am us. We move together through this endless desert. We follow the way of red.

Somehow the barrel of the Colt had made its way into his mouth, squeezing gently between his teeth.

Do I know you? Have we met before?

His finger tautened against the trigger, pulling, pulling... squeezing.

I know you.

We follow...

He could not speak with the steel between his teeth so he thought the words instead. Wading with difficulty through the blood of his family, and then standing to face himself from within a frail structure constructed from the brutalised corpses of his men, his murderous banditos, the Mexican let it all flood through him.

And just before he pulled the trigger, it all made terrible sense.

Seguimos el camino de la rojez.

Gary McMahon's fiction has appeared in various magazines and anthologies in the U.K. and the U.S. and his stories have been reprinted in The Mammoth Book of Best New Horror, The Year's Best Fantasy & Horror and The Year's Best Dark Fantasy & Horror. He is the British Fantasy Award-nominated author of the novels *Hungry Hearts* (Abaddon), *Pretty Little Dead Things* and *Dead Bad Things* (Angry Robot/Osprey), and *The Concrete Grove* trilogy (Solaris). You can find out more about Gary at his website: www.garymcmahon.com

"This story came to me when elements of Cormac McCarthy's *Blood Meridian* and Christopher Nolan's *Memento* collided with memories of *El Topo* and Leone's spaghetti westerns. And I had a dream: a Mexican, a demon, a cage of flesh and bone, a red road, and the endless arid desert that sometimes lies deep within the human heart. I figured that if I was going to tackle a western story, I had no choice but to take on the classic mythical tropes of the genre: a nameless man, a mysterious quest, whores and drunks, and a final confrontation at some kind of frontier—be it geographical, psychological or metaphysical. In *El Camino de Rojo*, it's all three."

THE BONES THAT WALK
Joe R. Lansdale

I could see the rope was fraying above me, unraveling as my weight pulled it tight and the sharp rock cut into it. The moon hung above me like a great golden platter, and I feared I had come all this way for nothing, and feared even more that the rope would snap and I would fall, going down quickly, my last sight of this life being the big gold moon and the bright gathering of the constellations, a glimpse of the red planet mars, but mostly all that blackness stretched between.

Taking a deep breath, I went at it again, started climbing. I didn't look at the rope. That didn't do any good. It would either break or it wouldn't. The way I was hung over the edge of the cliff didn't offer me a lot of second chances. I either had to climb to the top or swing back down onto the ledge in front of the cavern.

But there were ways to die better than others, and what was waiting for me on the ledge wasn't the way I wanted to go.

Because they were there.

It began with a map. The Dutchman's Gold.

It's an old legend. The Dutchman, a miner, kept coming in from the Superstition Mountains with a load of gold nuggets. And, like so many miners and gamblers, in a short time he lost it, used it up. Drank it up or wasted it on prostitutes. Bottom line is the Dutchman died broke.

But he left a map.

Of course, he did.

There's always the map.

There's always those who follow it and say: I've got it. No one else has got it, but me, I got it and I understand it.

I should have known better.

Not that I was wrong. There was a treasure. I found it. But there were other problems. Really bad problems. I would have been better to have kept wrangling cattle, even if that way of life is dying out. It wasn't much, but it was my profession and I should have stuck to it.

But not me.

You see, I knew a man who knew a man who knew a man that had the map. There were plenty of stories that explained the map. That a certain woman had it. That a relative had it. That he had no relatives and he sold the map when he was on his death bed.

Whatever the case, I got the map.

I got it like this.

A man who worked for the Dutchman, a former slave named George, claimed to have the real map. Said in the process of moving the Dutchman's body from the room where he died, he bumped a place on the floor with the toe of his boot. A loose board. Through a crack he saw something shiny.

After stowing the dead Dutchman away, he went back and pulled up the board and took a look. Sitting on the ground beneath the gap in the floor was a fruit jar. Inside of it was a single nugget of gold. The Dutchman hadn't been broke. Just sick, and if rumors are right, out of his mind. On his death bed he kept talking about the mine and the bones that walked.

Bones that walked.

I know what that means now.

But then, no idea. Thought maybe it was just part of a delirious dream from a dying man, or part of the story the way George wanted to tell it.

George not only claimed he found the nugget in the jar, but also inside, folded tight, was a map.

That's the story.

Over the years the former slave tried to find the mine. No luck. He got old and he sold the map. No one knew what happened to him after that. He seemed to have melted away.

Others tried to find the treasure. Others had different maps. There was even a joke around New Mexico that the Dutchman sold a dozen maps himself, and that's how he made his money.

Maybe that was true.

But this map, this was the right map. I didn't know it when I first saw it, but I know it now.

An old man named Turner died about two years back, and he owed quite a bit of money, so all his belongings were sold, same as the Dutchman. That's why they say the mine and the map just bring bad luck. No one gets the treasure and their lives go great.

At the Turner estate, or what was left of it, I bought a copy of Shakespeare. Having been an actor before my wrangling days, I was attracted to it. I loved the bard. I loved the stage. But I delivered lines worse than Wild Bill Hickok. I had seen him on the stage some twenty-five years before when he was in frontier plays with Buffalo Bill. Hickok knew he was bad and quit. I knew it, and I quit. But the love for the bard, for plays, for the stage was still there. That's what led me to the book, and you guessed it. Inside the book was the map. Folded up and so thin from age it hardly made a lump in the book. It fell out as I turned to the play Julius Caesar.

The map had writing on the back. Notes.

I had heard the story of the Dutchman and of the former slave. The territory is full of those stories. So, I knew what it was supposed to be, because on the back of the map were notations written by Turner. If that wasn't enough, the Shakespeare book had been worked over and pages cut out and replaced with glued in diary pages. All of them written by Turner.

I studied the map. Unlike a map designed to make it easy on the follower, this one was written with some directions, drawings and ciphers. It was like trying to figure out Egyptian hieroglyphics.

And though the diary contained notes to help me better understand the map, they were the sort of notes that were only clear to the man who had figured it out and had been there. They really were not designed to help someone else.

In a nutshell, Turner claimed he had found the mine.
There was gold.
There was something else there too.
The diary said: Beware the Bones that Walk.
There was no explanation. The last few pages of the diary were torn out. Either by Turner at some point, or a relative.

I researched around the area best I could, found out that Turner had been quite well off for a time, but then, the wealth played out. He always said he got his money from gold he had found in the mine.

Few believed him. Some even thought he was a bank robber.

His story was he bought the map from George, The Dutchman's servant.

I wondered why he hadn't mined the treasure out. Why he had only taken a bit of it. That's what the diary claimed.

Possibly he hadn't found any of it and the map and the diary were all a hoax, and like so many associated with the story of The Dutchman's Mine, he was a con man.

Still, I couldn't resist.

At the time I bought the Shakespeare book with the map in it, I was a cattle owner, a rancher. I became a wrangler later. Nothing wrong with the profession, but once upon a time I was on top of the world.

I had failed at acting, but at ranching I had done fine. I had a lot of money. I thought with my money I could find the mine. I began trying to decipher the map.

I might also add that I had a wife when I started my search for the Dutchman's gold. I had a family. A boy and a girl.

But the draw of the map, the search for the mine took up more and more of my time. It seemed as if one day I was thick with money and a fine wife and family, and then I looked up and they were gone. Much of the ranch had gone to ruin. I had been cheated and rustled and lied to, and I hadn't even noticed. I was preoccupied with that damn mine.

And then I lost the ranch.

Now, I'm a wrangler on the ranch I once owned.

It gnaws at the gut.

Then, one day, I was looking at the map for no telling how many times. Looking over the symbols, and all the places on the map I had searched, and it hit me.

There was a great rise of rock on the land, and on the map, it said the rock makes a long pointed shadow. I thought this meant that I should follow the shadow to its tip, to where it was pointing, as the sun rose. But suddenly, I saw it a different way. It only said the rock made a shadow. It was to be identified by the kind of shadow it made, due to its shape. That way the reader of the map could recognise the rock, for there were many rocks that made a shadow. But instead of the tip of the shadow pointing the way, I decided it meant that if you stood on the tip of the shadow and looked back, you could see the opening of the mine.

This struck me so strongly I became convinced that this was the secret.

Leaving my job as a wrangler, taking the last of my savings, I bought rope and tools, food supplies, and a mule. I led the mule by rope from my horse. I had all that was left of my goods on that mule, plus all the equipment I would need to finally dig into the Dutchman's mine.

It was all or nothing.

I felt giddy. Weak, and yet invigorated.

I had Gold Fever.

The rope creaks. I keep climbing. I am near the lip of the overhang. I feel the rope shift.

Don't look up.

Keep climbing.

Faster.

Faster.

Faster.

The rope drops and so do I.

But no. It hangs.

I can't help but look.

It is unraveling and I am hanging by strands.

I am still twenty feet from the top.

Below me is a long, long fall.

Hot days.

Cold nights.

The moon and stars as my roof, blankets for my bed.

I made small fires early evening, ate, and then travelled. It was too hot to travel in the day time.

During the day I made a tent of one blanket, lay on another and slept. I killed rattlesnakes. I shot a rabbits. I ate them both. Rabbit is good. Rattlesnake isn't bad. It supplemented my beans and jerky.

When I wasn't sleeping during the day, I was studying the map, or reading the plays that survived in the book that contained the diary. I also had a book of poetry by Byron.

But I could never totally delve into the beautiful prose of those writers. My thoughts were always on the mine.

The gold.

Touching it.

Digging it out of the rock.

I had risked everything for this map, for this mine, and I knew that even though I was not exactly an old man at forty, this would be my last hurrah. When I was done, the money I had saved was gone. I had spent it on the mule and the supplies. After this, the best I could hope for was to go back to wrangling cows. Doing that at my age, look at the probability of that for the rest of my life was another motivation. That and the fact that once upon a time I had been rich and had liked it. I wanted to like it again. But mostly, I wanted to find that mine. It always seemed to be just out of reach. Now, with my new interpretation of the map, I felt I was so close that all that remained was for me to dig it out and put it in a sack.

On an night turning into morning, as I rode and led the mule, I saw in the distance the great tower of rock, and my heart began to beat faster.

I had been here before, of course.

But it never ceased to excite me. And now I was looking at it in a new way. It was as if I were seeing it clearly for the first time. I was certain I understood the map.

It looked near. But it was not.

That thick finger of rock was still a half day's ride.

As morning cracked open the sky and laid its flames across the tower, it gleamed orange, and yellow, red and gold. The night was sucked away, except for pieces of it that hung in the rocks like velvet curtains. The tower's shadow stretched out like a pointing finger, more dark blue than black.

I rode on with greater enthusiasm, forcing myself not to ride the horse too hard. Out here, without a horse and mule, I would be doomed. Walking out of this was not a reasonable option unless you were an Apache.

THE BONES THAT WALK

It was near past mid day by the time I arrived at the base of the great rock. I paused in a shade from an overhang, took care of the animals with grain from the supplies, and let them drink moderately from a trickle of water that flowed out from some place within the rock.

I sat beneath the tower of stone in the shade of a boulder, rested my back against it, and drank from my canteen, chewed jerky and looked at the map. Though I felt certain I had figured it out, there were still things that confused me. Drawn on the map was an eye. The way it was sketched, it was positioned against the centre of the tower.

That confused me. I felt certain, from the written directions on the back of the map that I had figured out the bit about the great shadow. But the eye... Not entirely sure there.

This much I was certain of. The treasure was near the area where the eye was drawn. It had confused me before, and I had thought, since it was above the shadow, that it was telling me to look toward the shadow, where the tip of it first hit the ground in the morning.

In the past, when that hadn't worked, I changed different times of day, following the tip of it around. It was a tedious and fruitless search, and it had taken all my time and money. But now... Now I was certain that the base of the shadow, in line with where the eye was drawn, was my best bet.

There was another thing that confused me.
The bones that walked.
What could that mean?

The rope snapped again.
But hung by a single strand.
The snapping made the rope and me spin.
All I could think was: this isn't fair.

I hobbled the mule and the horse and climbed up the rock and went to where I could best judge where the eye was positioned on the map. I stood below where I thought it should be, but could see nothing that resembled an eye. What I concluded, was if I walked to the end of the shadow, and looked back, I would perhaps see something about the rock that I had not noticed before.

I walked out to the tip of the shadow. It was a long walk in that hot, dry desert. I looked back at the base of the tower. I started walking back within the shadow toward the base of the tower.

When I was nearly two thirds of the way there, my eye caught something, and that something sparkled brightly. I took another step. Saw nothing. I stepped back. I could see the sparkle again. The sun was striking something up there, and I figured out that the sparkle was representative of the eye. It could only be seen walking down the length of the shadow, watching carefully for a spot the sun was striking, halfway up the tower, exactly where the eye was drawn on the map.

I went back to my little camp and got my pick and shovel and few other items, my canteen and some jerky, my pistol for snakes and such, and what I thought at the time was a very good rope. I started winding my way up through the narrow path toward the eye. I had been up this way before, so I was a little baffled as to why I could have been here many times in the past and not seen this eye, this sparkle, this clue.

When I was almost even with what I estimated to be the spot, there was nothing there, just a solid wall. There was a pretty good ledge that stuck out from the wall, but the wall itself was as smooth as a Bible thumper's tongue. I walked out on the ledge and carefully looked down.

Nothing.

Just the ground.

And then a bird flew out from under the ledge.

Where had it been sitting? The tower dropped straight down.

I lay on my belly and hung my head over and saw that the ledge I was on stuck out about six feet over a rise in the rock. From below, the rise would look to be connected to the ledge, but it was an optical illusion. From this vantage, I could see that if I swung off the ledge, I could slip down between the rise of rock and the ledge, and down to where I could see a cave with a ledge that jutted out from it. I also realised that the thin slit that was the eye was not easily visible from below, but the sunlight was striking down between the walls and into the cave, and that's where the gleam was coming from, and it was so bright it threw a beam up and out of the cave and against the far wall, and if it was the right time of day, early morning, it sent a reflection upwards. That was the eye.

And, besides the sunlight, what made it sparkle was simple.

Gold from the cave, from The Lost Dutchman's mine.

THE BONES THAT WALK

Besides the gold in the cave, the rise of rock across the way was littered with it. Some of the ore that stuck out of the outcrop was as big as eggs.

I slung my strapped canteen over my shoulder. I attached a little pack containing matches, a pocket knife, a few strips of jerky, and my book of Byron's poetry, to my belt.

Fastening the rope around a boulder, then binding my pick and shovel in the bag, I secured it to my back, and slung myself over the edge.

Way I had to do it was I had to get between the rise and the ledge, and that was a narrow gap. I could see that once I got through the gap, that it was wider.

It was a long drop to the cave, and there was gold on the rock rise, but it was near impossible to mine, positioned the way it was. Maybe closer to the bottom would work. But what I decided was the dark cave below was my destination, and if I pushed off backward with my feet against the rise when I was about thirty feet down, I could swing onto the ledge that served as a kind of porch to the cave.

If I lost my grip on the rope, there was just enough space between the rise and the tower wall for me to fall through, narrow enough I could get stuck and not manage to get out.

As I eased between the rock wall and the tower, the bag of tools and supplies got caught and I had to wriggle a bit to get it free. When I was a little lower, where it was wider, I pushed off with my feet against the wall. That caused me to swing. I eased down the rope as I did, and though I was good at it, and had made a slip loop in the rope for my foot so I could slide down and the loop would slide with me, it was still scary business.

When I got even with the cave, because the gap got wider there before it got narrow again below, I would have to swing out again, kicking really hard against the wall so that I would swing back. Then I hoped to drop down on the ledge without breaking any part of me or losing my gear.

Normally, I would have been frightened, but that Gold Fever had me.

It was a little difficult packed up like I was, but I shoved off with my feet and swung out over the narrow crack that went all the way to the ground inside a dark drop, a kind of sleeve between the outer and inner wall. I guess my kick drove me about halfway between wall and cave, and when

I came back to the wall again, I tucked my feet and placed them firmly against the wall and kicked off with all my might.

Judging when I was where I wanted to be, I slipped my foot from the loop, let go of the rope for support, but kept my arm encircled around it. That way I was able to land on the ledge in front of the cave, and still have control of the rope.

I took off my pack with the pick and shovel fastened to it, and laid it on the ledge. I tied the rope off to the pack so it wouldn't drift out too far for me to get hold of it. I got candles out of the pack, and one of the two torches I had prepared from rags and pitch, and took the paper covering I had over one of them off. I put the candles in my coat pocket. I put a match to the torch and it flared to life. I knew the pitch would burn slow and last a long time, the way the torch was made, but it wasn't going to last so long I wanted to waste time.

I looked back at the wall across the drop and studied the gold imbedded in it. Never had I seen gold like that, coating the rock like a coat of paint. I didn't know it could even be that way.

But as amazing as that was, I was certain that the map was indicating this cave, showing that it was in fact a mine. Holding the torch before me, I went inside.

The first thing the light of the torch picked out was the gold.

The walls of the cave were lined with it.

They were lined with other things as well.

Bones.

Lots of them. Skulls and pieces of leg bones and arm bones and hands and fingers. They were scattered about the floor of the cave like the remains of a chicken dinner. But the bones didn't belong to chickens.

And there were other things there as well.

There was armor, like that worn by the conquistadores. I picked up one of the rusted helmets. It was said they had looked through the New World for Gold, and this indicated clearly that they had discovered it, but they hadn't lived to spend it. There were several pieces of armor lying about. Maybe a half dozen Conquistadores had died.

But how?

There were other bones. Some had enough clothes remaining for me to determine they were white men. There were some bones with Apache ornaments, fragments of weathered moccasins.

I waved the torch around and moved deeper into the cave.
I turned to my right—
—and jumped.
A Negro, who at first appeared recently dead, was sitting with his back against the wall, his head turned toward me. Though he was more recent than the others, he was not as fresh as he first appeared. His skull was empty of eyes. His lips were gone. But the rest of him, though withered, had survived. Even his clothes still hung on him. A red shirt and grey pants. Only the soles of his boots remained, and his feet were nothing but bone. For some peculiar reason, his body had not rotted away, but had partially mummified in the desert air. As I brought the torch close to his face, I couldn't even be certain if he was in fact a Negro. Now that I looked at him, I determined that like all dead men, the colour of the skin didn't matter. I gently touched his shirt, and it slid off of him like dirt. I noticed that the top of his head was hollow, like something had dug out his brains.

I turned back to the other skulls, flared the torch over them.

They were the same. A feeling like ants with icy feet crawled up my back.

I thought, what's going on here?

When I looked back at the dead man, I noticed a leather pouch near his side. I found a place in the wall, just over the dead man's head that would hold the torch in place. I picked up the leather pouch. It had turned green, but was still sturdy. I opened it and looked inside. There was still a piece of tobacco twist inside, a chunk of something that might once have been a strip of jerky, and a folded piece of paper.

Carefully, I removed the paper, and was startled to discover it was intact. It was a map. The same as my map. Or almost.

Suddenly, I got it. This was George, the ex-slave who had worked for the Dutchman. He had gotten the map, and maybe to finance his trip here he made copies of it to sell. Strangely, he hadn't made false copies. Or at least the one I bought wasn't false. Maybe it wasn't George who made the second map. Perhaps the Dutchman had made two maps.

No way of knowing.

George's map was the same as mine. Except it was more detailed. It had arrows and circles that defined the location better, pointed out that there was gap in the wall where the Dutchman had originally drawn the eye. His version of the map was more sharply drawn, and time had been good to it. No insects had bothered it. Had I had this map, I could have saved myself years of research.

But my man here had followed the map, and had found the gold, and here he laid, the top of his head torn open, like a possum cracking an egg to suck the insides out.

I began to feel more than a little nervous. I put the dead man's map in my pocket and took the torch and stuck it in the direction of the rear of the cave. The light didn't act as if it wanted to go there. A wind from back there blew at the flames and made them flicker. I could smell something sour too, and I thought I heard movement, like the scuttling of a million thumb-sized roaches.

I got my pistol out from under my coat and put it in my right hand, and held the torch in my left. Moving close to the wall, I went back a distance to see what might be making the noise. Bats. Birds. Animals. I doubted a bear could be in this location. It wasn't easy enough to get to. Bears were only industrious when it came to food.

As I moved into the depths of the cavern, the gold in the walls glittered in the torch light. There were also paintings on the wall. I had heard of such. Ancient Indians had painted on walls in ancient times. Pictographs they were called.

I held the torch close to them. They were painted in a variety of colours, and the dry air had kept the paint, whatever its source, in tact. There were all manner of stick figures. Hordes of them. They were small, and were often shown in battle with more defined drawings of people. In some paintings there were black spots, and the little stick men were by the spots. The stick men were attacking the more defined paintings of people.

Studying the paintings more closely, I saw that the small figures, though skeletal in appearance, had oversized heads, and they were always drawn with an assortment of very nasty, large teeth that seemed out of contrast with the rest of their bodies. There was some kind of story being told by the drawings, but I wasn't sure what it was.

I had heard Indian legends about Little People who lived in the ground and did mischief, or worse. But I assumed it was only a legend, and that these drawing depicted that myth.

After studying the paintings for a long time, I walked farther back, my torch still burning well. There were more skeletons there, skulls with their heads split open. They were all over the place. It looked as if there had been a war. They were very old bones. They were not big people. Not as big as the conquistadors, who were not all that big either, but bigger than I thought the paintings had suggested for the stick men.

The smell was really strong back there. It reminded me of something dead, rotting under a house's floor boards. Once, when I was a child, a skunk and our hound had gotten into a fracas and the hound and skunk had ended up under the house. The hound got sprayed. The skunk got bit. The hound, after several washings and letting him roll in the dirt, got over the smell, though we made sure he stayed off the porch for a week or two. The skunk didn't get over its bite. It died under the house, mixing its skunk spray with its rotting corpse. It was a terrible odor, and it finally got so bad, my father made me crawl under after it, pull it out with a stick.

This odor was akin to that.

I saw a dark spot in the floor. I moved toward it. The stench was stronger. The torch flared as cold air came up and out of that hole. It was like the hole painted on the walls. I leaned over the hole and held the torch down there. The sides of the hole were smooth. The sides of the shaft, as it descended were smooth. Nothing larger than a foot across could come of that hole. But on the sides, smeared on the slick rock walls, were the damp shapes of fingers. Long fingers. Something had been in that shaft, and since the damp outline of fingers had yet to fade, it hadn't been that long ago.

The last strand popped.
I fell.

I pushed deeper inside the cave, saw there were other holes. All of them the same. The smell was near overwhelming. It made me gag and cough. I turned and went back to the front of the cave.

I walked out on the ledge. The day was starting to fade away. I thought of my horse and mule. I thought of the gold. I thought of a lot of things. But mostly what I thought about were those holes and those wet imprints of fingers, those drawings on the wall.

When I said earlier it looked like a war, I began to suspect it was just that. A war between what lived here, down in those holes, and the men who came here hunting for gold, and the Indians who came here to rid themselves, unsuccessfully, of what was down in those holes.

The Dutchman may have chipped some easy nuggets from the front of the mine, but it was doubtful he had really mined the place. Or anyone had. It didn't have that look.

Now and again The Dutchman would come back to civilization, spend up his gold, and then go back. I began to suspect that he knew what was in that mine and that was the reason that in his latter days he ceased to go back. Too many close calls with . . . Well, I was uncertain.

Instead, he contented himself selling copies of the map. Giving his old servant the best copy. Maybe there were only two real copies. The one that belonged to the servant, and one that the servant, or someone, drew for someone else.

I stood out there on the ledge, standing in such a way I could look back into the cave. And then I thought of something else. My map and notes from Turner. He had seen these paintings too. Because now that I thought about it, those stick figures looked like bones, and Turner had talked about The Bones That Walked.

In that moment I had a chance to escape. I could have given it all up and gone up the rope, then walked down and back to my horse and mule. That seemed like the right thing to do. I could, without going to too much trouble, do what the Dutchman had done. Carve me out enough gold to be well off for some time. Later, I could come back, same as the Dutchman and probably Turner. Take what I needed, and no more.

In quick.

Out quick.

A shadow, like the shape of a great bird wing fell over the canyon and moments after my torch went out. I didn't need it out there on the ledge, but soon I would. The day was about to go completely dark.

I was burning daylight.

I got the pick out of the bag and the spare torch, lit it up, and went back inside the cave. I had the pistol in my belt. By this time I was nervous and a little more than certain there was something here with me, and not something I should be anxious to see.

My plan was simple. I would use the pick to knock some of the ore out of the wall. I would pack up a little to take down with me, and later I would come back and get more.

Gold Fever is an odd thing. It takes the best laid plans, the finer thinking of man, and turns them to mush. Once I lit candles and placed them about, and began to pick the gold from the wall, I couldn't stop. I had the torch in a spot above me, and when I had enough gold to take with me without it being too heavy, I altered my plans slightly. I thought, since I had the mule, I could take down some, and them come back tomorrow morning and take down more. I knew that I had to go up the rope before I could go down on foot, but it I took a light enough collection of ore, I'd be okay. I could even leave some of the supplies here, the pick and shovel, and tomorrow I could get one of my other ropes, fasten it to the supply bag, fill it to where it was light enough to move, and pull it up with the spare rope when I got to the top.

In a few days' time, I could pack up the mule with ore, and maybe some on the horse as well. I could go out of here a wealthy man for the rest of my life.

And if I needed to return, I knew where the gold was.

It seemed like a good plan.

I was thinking on all of this, piling ore at me feet, when I smelled that smell again. It had been in the air all along, but now it was stronger, and I heard again that scuttling sound, like a bunch of roaches.

I turned and leaned the pick against the wall and grabbed up the torch, poked it toward the rear of the cave.

And then I saw them.

Sticks, that's what they looked like. With some kind of parchment pulled over them. And there were those great melon heads and dark holes instead of eyes. Their mouths stretched from ear to ear, though they didn't really have ears, just holes where ears should have been. Those mouths were full of teeth. Teeth like that I had seen in drawings of sharks. There hands were tipped by over-long fingers with sharp nails.

They were easing toward me, and as they came closer, into the light, they put their arms up over their hollow eyes. I knew then they were not in fact blind, but sensitive to light. Their eyes were down deep in their sockets, like buckets at the bottom of wells. When they moved, their little feet, tipped with three thick claws, made a noise on the stone that I recognised as the sounds I had heard before. The sounds like cockroaches.

They were closing in.

I waved the torch and they drew back, hissing like snakes.

But there were so many. When I moved the torch to the left, they came from the right, when I moved it to the right, they came from the left.

I grabbed the pick and tried to back out of the darkness. But, as I backed out of the cave, onto the ledge, I realised it was solid dark.

They made noises like pigs slobbering at trough. I backed until I knew I could back no more. The rope, tied to my pack was to my left. And behind me, less than three feet away, the dark sleeve between the rocks.

Pausing momentarily, as if to gather themselves against the light of the torch, they attacked.

There's no way to explain how it felt as they came.

They were like a wave of bones and stench. They snapped their teeth at me, slung their claws, and leaped up, as if trying to bite out the top of my head and feast on my brain.

I fought back with the torch until it went out, and there was only the moon and the light glow of the candles burning inside the cave.

I swung the pick. I brought down several, and slung several out into the void between the cave and the rock wall.

Still they came, and finally I was swinging the pick so hard and so often, it became as heavy as an anvil and dropped from my hands.

I kicked one back, pulled the pistol from my belt and began to fire. The six shots were soon gone, and I had only killed three.

At the mouth of the cave, in the light of the fading candles, I saw they were still coming, flowing out of the cavern like a dark river of sticks.

I was hit across my thighs with their nails. I was bit on the arms by their teeth. One of them leaped up with a screech and crunched his teeth into my shoulder. I knocked him off.

Still they came.

I knew I had one chance.

I jumped for the rope, jerked it free of the pack. Clutching it tightly, I ran toward the drop-off and leaped.

I went way out and down. The rope swung back against the wall of the tower. I braced myself with my feet and that bounced me back so that I was swinging in the middle of the gap, the rope hanging from the high ledge from which I had first descended.

As I climbed, I could see them.

They were all along the ledge. The wave of creatures washed up and over the lip of the abyss and they began to fall. Some, frenzied, foaming at the mouth, leaped out into the darkness, trying to grab me where I hung on my rope.

THE BONES THAT WALK

One of them came close enough to touch my boot, then slipped, and fell.
I took a deep breath, and kept climbing.
Up, up, past them, almost to the top where I had lowered myself down. But then, that rope broke, and I fell.
I fell.
I fell.

That would have been the end of it, but the dark sleeve of rocks narrowed below me and my body was too wide to go through. I was jammed in there tight as a bullet in a chamber—tighter.
The impact snapped something inside of me.
Ribs, other bones.
I heard them crack like peanuts under a hammer.
The pain was tremendous.
I blacked out.

When I awoke, my eyes had adjusted.
A blade of moonlight was falling down into the drop.
I was wounded from the fall, and from the attack of The Bones That Walked.
I was bleeding.
I was weak.
I looked up.
They were on the ledge, looking down.
One of them, overzealous, leaped down after me, missing me by a foot, passing through a wider split in the rocks to crash like a china dish on the rock floor below.
I had a little pack at my waist. I still had my canteen. I was able to lift it on its strap and open the lid and take a drink. The water felt good and cold going down.
I screwed the lid back on.
I got out of the little pack a piece of jerky. I chewed it. It gave me a bit of strength.
But I knew it wouldn't be enough.
I thought about my situation, decided I didn't want to die like this.
I tried to wriggle loose, so that I might fall and finish it.
But no luck there. I was wedged in good.

After awhile, I took the little book of Byron out of my belt pack, a pencil. I found that I could rest my elbows on a rough ledge of rock that held me. I could rest the book there. There was plenty of light from the moon.

On that book's pages, written across the words of Byron, I am recording these events.

It probably doesn't matter. But when I finish, I'm going to put the book inside the pack and rest it on this shelf. Before I seal up the pack, though, I'm going take out the little and very sharp pocket knife, and I'm going to quickly as possible, cut my throat.

Maybe someday someone will find the book, and my story. Know what happened to me. Know what waits up there in that cave, in the Lost Dutchman's mine.

Feeling weak.

Have to finish up.

The moon.

That rope.

I feel as if I'm still clinging to it sometimes.

I take my pocket knife out of the pack.

Now I'm writing my last words before I seal it up and use the knife.

Above me, on the ledge, those things, whatever they are, hang over and look down at me, chattering, frothing, rolling over each other like monkeys in a circus.

I wonder about the horse. The mule.

Perhaps they'll get free of their hobbles.

I hope so.

Oh, Lord.

Can hardly hold the pencil now.

Weak.

So very weak.

Damn that Dutchman.

Damn that glittering gold.

Joe R. Lansdale is the author of over thirty novels, and two hundred short articles and short stories. Joe says: "My love of Western fiction and films along with my interest in folklore, including American Indian folklore, combined to become this story."

GHOSTS
Amanda Hemingway

We came to the West when the world was young, and we found Paradise. A wild, raw paradise with forests of giant trees and rivers of foaming rapids and plains of wind-rippled grass where the great herds roamed in numbers beyond count. There were red desert mountains where the rain never fell and white winter mountains where the snow never thawed, a coastline of yellow sands and hollow coves, of mists and echoes and secrets, and then the sea, rolling in endless waves towards the setting sun. We were the first Men to come there; only the animals were before us, the wolf and the bear and the mountain lion, and we worshipped them and hunted them and wore their skins in honour of their prowess. We were the first Men, and we took forest and river, mountain and valley and made them our own, we were born and died and were buried there, and our spirits danced in the snowflakes and sang in the windsong and drew close round the campfire at night, whispering the mysteries to those with ears to hear.

Sometimes we gathered on desert crag and mountain top to watch over the land, and we saw the fires from far off, like tiny star-clusters in the vast midnight of the plains, and we knew all was well with our people. Tribe fought with tribe, as must happen, and made peace, and fought again, and our warriors grew fierce and strong, and our women were beautiful and our infants healthy, daughters of the moon, children of the sun. So the ages passed unrecorded, and the smoke of the fires was lost in the wind's breath, and the fallen years lay thicker than the leaves on the forest floor. Ah, the good days, the great days! Who now will remember them? The good days, the great days—we thought they would last forever.

Until the White Men came.

We called them white but they were not white: they were every shade of pale, sallow-pale and plucked-chicken-pale and pinkish-pale like blossoms that wither in an hour. They named us Redskins but they were the ones who turned red in the western sun, sore and red so they had to cover themselves with cloth, shading even their faces. Some were dark-haired and dark-eyed like us but others had eyes the colour of stone and fair hair which they cropped as if they were ashamed of it. They did not revere the many animal and nature spirits; instead, they had one god who sought to banish all rivals and rule alone, a tyrant among deities. He did not dwell on mountain top or in forest grove: they built wooden houses for him, and planted the cross that was his emblem on every burial mound.

But the White Men brought more than their god. They brought unknown weapons and cruel magic, weapons of hard metal which spat death and sicknesses which devoured us while leaving them unharmed. They brought a drink which tasted like liquid fire, searing the throat, souring the stomach, curdling the brain. They travelled in huge lumbering machines, drawn by beasts we had never seen before, beasts they would also ride—nimble as deer but larger and stronger, cloud-dappled and shadow-blotched, with a mane and tail that flowed in the wind like the plume of a warrior's hair. When we defeated them—in those days we still thought we could defeat them, we thought our little victories would make a difference—we handled their death-spitting guns with fear, and vomited their fire drink, but we took the horses and learned to ride them more skilfully than their former masters, and we hunted our enemies on their own steeds.

The White Men were few at first but more came and always more, a little, a trickle, an army, a swarm. No matter how many we slew, others came to take their place. They were greedy for things we did not understand, for the paper notes and coins they liked to hoard and the yellow gold they could sift from the rivers and dig from the ground. The gold sent them mad, the gold and the firewater and the sight of a woman. Their spitting guns were swifter than arrows and more deadly: they slaughtered the buffalo herds, they slaughtered our people, from the youngest child to the most venerable elder, then they began to slaughter each other, and the stink of death rolled like a mist across the plains. Now, we were fighting not to win but to survive. They took the empty plains and the mountains of ice and stone and gave us a few barren acres of the lands that had once been ours, penning us there like cattle, those of us they had not killed, and like cattle leaving us to die. We stole their guns to use against them, and we drank their firewater to ease our troubles and rot our brains, and our sacred places were befouled with the blood of strangers, and our shamans prayed for an omen, a prophecy, a promise.

"He is coming," we told them, "the Chosen One, the child of destiny. He is coming to save our people."

He came. Tall he stood among the warriors, tall as a god, his body copper-brown in the sunlight, and the sweat-gloss rippled over the flex-and-swell of his muscles. But a leader needs more than sweat and muscle, and the look in his eyes was as cunning as a coyote and as reckless as a maddened bull. "We will defy the invaders!" he told the people. "We will abandon this desert hole where they have impounded us, and ride out in force, and take back what was ours. Are we not the true children of the West? The White Men shrivel in the sun and walk blind in the dark—they are slow and fearful and fear makes them cruel—they worship a god who is deaf and dumb and lives in a heaven too high to reach. They have butchered your brothers, your fathers, your wives and your sons. It is enough. The time has come for us to reclaim our heritage. We will hunt them without mercy until all are slain or fled and their very bones crumble into the earth and are forgotten. To war! To war!" And so we rode out, fierce and proud in the dawn light, and fought and killed and died, and when our arrows were spent and our stolen guns were empty our enemies drove us back to the prison lands, and the Chosen One threw down his weapons, and bowed his head to the White Man's god.

The years passed, numbered now after the custom of our rulers, who sought to order even Time. They carved the plains into wheatfields and piped water into the deserts and gouged tunnels through the great mountains, and their roads and railroads tracked the trackless places, and the steam from their engines rose higher into the sky than the smoke of our camp fires long ago. They built houses, with thick walls to keep out winter cold and summer sun, and roots that went deep into our earth. And the houses clustered together into towns and cities, and grew taller than the tallest tree, touching the clouds. Then at last they delved into the very heart of the planet, and out gushed the black blood more precious than gold, and the burning of it tainted the air and lit the city lights—so many lights that the stars could not match them, and hid their eyes, and the mystery of the night was gone forever.

Many of our spirits faded in the brightness of this new world and were lost, but some of us remained, deep in the wilderness, on ground that was still sacred, still secret, too arid for farming, too distant to steal. We spoke to our people, those that remembered, as a murmur in the heart, a whisper in the soul. One day, we told them, the Chosen One will come again, and this time he will not fail. His muscles will ripple, and his weapons will gleam, and he will be touched with destiny, whatever our destiny may be. But our voices had grown faint, like a dream which vanishes on awakening; few listened, and fewer heard. Our people filled their heads with the music of the new century, and our children sang unfamiliar songs, and played unfamiliar games on machines that hummed and clicked, and the sound of our call was drowned out in the din of another world.

But he came, the Chosen One. He came again. We knew him by his eyes, which were as cunning as a coyote and as patient as a lizard on a rock. He did not stand tall because he had no need, and the sun gleamed on the steely sheen of his business suit. If his muscles rippled, they rippled unseen. He did not hunt, nor sweat, nor rouse our people with passionate words. He read books, and studied the White Man's laws, and smiled a secret smile all to himself.

He came to the elders of our tribe and spoke to them, though not of war. "The land they gave us is infertile," he said, "desert or near-desert, and what gold there was they took, and there is little water and no oil. Yet we have something that they do not, and because of that we may yet reap a harvest richer than gold or oil, and take payment for all that they stole from us, with interest and compound interest. We will fill our coffers with the White Man's wealth, with coins and paper money and numbers on a balance sheet, until the bank vaults are overflowing and the golden zeros are sifting through our fingers like sand in the desert. Does that sound good to you? Is that not a vengeance sweeter than blood or war?"

The elders were silent, unbelieving, save for one who said: "We do not want the White Man's wealth, which corrupts all that it touches. We want things to be the way they were."

But Time does not run backward, not for us or any man, and Paradise once lost is lost forever. The other elders paid no attention, and the Chosen One in his chosen suit spoke on.

"These lands were given to us absolutely, an empty gift perhaps, or so the giver intended, but they are ours, and the only law that rules here is the law we have made. In most of their own country our enemies banned all games of chance, the flick of a card, the fall of the dice, the spin of the wheel, but such games may still be played here, by all who wish to come. We will build a palace of games, and they will come here to play, and gamble, and lose, and so we will reclaim the blood money for our brothers of long ago."

The elders agreed, and followed him, for the tribe always follow One who is Chosen. They built temples to the goddess of fortune, who is more fickle than any god or spirit of nature, but she smiles on those who pander to her whims and bend the rules in her favour. And the White Men came, though they were no longer merely white: the plucked-chicken-paleface had gathered into the West other races, of other shades, chocolate-brown and coffee-brown, ebony and ivory. They turned the cards and rolled the dice and whirled the wheel of fate round and round, and the money came pouring back, a little, a trickle, a torrent, a tide—paper money and copper money and plastic money, blood money and gold money and invisible money, in numbers too large ever to leave the balance sheet. Our people took the White Man's money and bought the things White Men value: gleaming cars and gleaming television sets, sailing yachts and psychotherapy and small countries. They built houses with double-glazing to keep out the sun and wind, and artificial light and air conditioning inside. The elders sat on Boards and shook handshakes, owned hedge funds and trust funds and stocks and bonds. And our young men went to college, and drank firewater until they vomited, and made love to girls with skin like milk and eyes as grey as rain.

But they do not hear us any more. There are a few who remember, and tell the old stories, name the old gods, and sing of the days that are gone. Yet only a few, and some not even of our people, and they do not listen for our voices in the wind, nor read our messages in the mist-patterns and the smoke-patterns and the smoulder of a dying fire. They do not give thanks for the season's turning, nor the success of hunt or tribal raid, nor the overflowing bank vaults and the paper notes that they gather in a harvest without end, till they lie thicker than the leaves of a thousand winters. The dreams we send them are undreamed and our whispers to heart and soul sound less than the buzzing of insects and the fretting of a spring breeze. And so we are gone, to the places still wild and lonely, the desert where no water runs, the mountains still peaked with unmelting snow, though not for long, they say. Not for long. One day, the deserts will vanish under wheat and chaff, and the snows will melt, and the bare bones of the mountains will be left naked to the sky. The last ghosts will be blown away on the free wind, our voices stilled, our memories withered, and the West that was will be forgotten.

We came to the West when the world was young, and we found Paradise. There were animals that had never been hunted, rivers that had never been fished, forests that had never been logged. The city smokes, the reek of cesspits and drains and horsedung, the drawing-room tea and polite conversation were left behind; here, the air was so pure you could get drunk just breathing. And there was space: great plains where only the buffalo walked, cloud-capped mountain-ranges none had yet climbed, desert canyons where the sun's rays stretched paths and shadows still untrodden by the White Man. A few tribes of savages lived here, but they were few indeed, and their tented camps melded with the wilderness, relics of a more primitive past. In a strange way we felt akin to them, closer to the hunters and warriors with their warpaint and their crude weapons than our tea-sipping, social chit-chatting cousins back East. We were the people of the wild, steering our canoes past rock and rapid, sleeping under the moon. Red Man or White, it was our place: the Wild belonged to us alone.

But we were wrong. The Wild belongs to no man, since once belonging, it is no longer wild. The wide open spaces where we hunted wolf and beaver and camped out, leaving no trace, were colonised by those who came after us, the pioneer farmers who built their little townships, with house and chapel and homestead, fencing the fenceless meadows, bringing cattle where there had been only buffalo. We found gold, flowing free in the mountain streams, running in deep veins under the earth. The prospectors followed, burrowing into the virgin rock, digging the gold and drinking it, losing it at the poker table or in a woman's arms. For the women came too, the desperate and daring and down-on-their-luck, looking for a new love, a new life, a new way to live. The men fought over the gold and the women, over a careless insult, a hasty word, and the makeshift wooden crosses leaned drunkenly on their graves.

Then came the war, a cause more terrible than gold—a war of politics and principle, of lust for this new country and hatred as old as Cain. The casual killings and the tribal skirmishes were swallowed up in blood-soaked battlefields, ambushes and massacres and last stands, and the dead were too many for tombstone or graveyard, and our own flesh enriched the earth where the corn would grow tall.

After four bitter years the war was over, but in the West there was no peace. The homeless and the hungry roamed the land, deserters and outlaws, by need or choice, stealing, killing, raping, more cruel than any savage. Following the hungry came the greedy, land-grabbers and carpetbaggers, men with measuring tapes to measure the wilderness and dynamite to blow it up and train-tracks and telegraph-wires so it could be captured and tamed. Folk fought over grazing rights and water rights, over every yard of railroad, every acre of the once-empty land. Little towns were dominated by little emperors who hired gunmen to gun down their opponents and lawmen to make it legal. And out of all this came the stories, the legends, the nameless heroes chosen by fate or chance, caught up in the battles too small for history to remember—the ones who were brave enough to stand up for what they thought was right, or just too obstinate to run away.

He rode into town, the chosen one, a tall, dark, deadpan stranger on a tall, dark, deadpan horse. He chewed a stunted cheroot which he would re-light from time to time, striking the match on his boot, or on the stubbled jaw of a casual enemy. Under his hat-brim his narrowed eyes were sea-grey and sea-cold, eyes of the north from where his ancestors had come long before.

Sometimes they were waiting for him, lurking in doorways, on rooftops, behind shattered windows. He would catch the glint of gun-barrel in the shadows, or hear the creak of a floorboard in an empty saloon. They were fast but he was faster, always faster, and bullets would fly and bodies would hit the dust, and when the hired guns had shot themselves out then at last the emperor would walk into the street to face him—the little emperor in his little empire. He might be an outlaw who had butchered friend and foe to be leader of his gang, or a businessman who did business from the trigger-end of a gun. He might be a smooth-talker, a sharp-shooter, with a Smith and Wesson on his hip that glittered with the chill glitter of steel, and somewhere there would be a girl who stayed with him because she was afraid to leave. But he would stand there in the end, with his surviving henchmen skulking at his back, and the sun beating down on the street from which the townspeople had fled. Hot yellow sun on the hot yellow dust. High noon. And the chosen one would be weary from the fight, dirt-smeared and blood-smeared, save for his eyes, which stayed cold and tireless. Maybe one of the townsfolk would return to take the henchmen down, or it would be the girl who would forget her fear and pick up a rifle. Then it would be just man against man, gun against gun.

Time stretched out. The sun glared. The men glared. A clock struck, a pin dropped, a glance flinched or shifted—and the guns spoke. Two guns firing as one. Almost. The little emperor went down, seeing the lifeblood run from his chest, realising in surprise that he could die like other men. And the chosen one still stood, alone on the empty street.

When it was over he would kiss the girl and ride away, leaving not even a name behind him. Sometimes there was blood on his clothes too, but they never saw him die, the people who made a hero of him. The chosen one could not die. Town after town, fight after fight, he would be there. And as the years passed they gave him a tin star, and a name to keep, and a home to call his own, and the West was wild no longer.

A new century came, a new age. The mines were mined out, the horses replaced by automobiles, and the people left the little townships to live in cities like their Eastern kin, becoming tea-drinkers and churchgoers and society chatterers, settling down and living safe, enclosed lives, out of sight of the stars. The smoke of their engines hung above the city sprawls in a haze so thick the sky was bleared and the once-pure air was poisoned for good. Many of the more isolated places are abandoned altogether, and the saloons where we once drank and laughed are empty, and only the wind rides into town, rolling the tumbleweed down the deserted street, rattling the shutters and swinging the saloon door to and fro, to and fro, as if the ghosts of gold-diggers and gunslingers long dead are striding into the bar.

Maybe those ghosts are among us now, for the memories seem to get all mixed up, the memories of solitude and space, of recklessness and lawlessness and war, of hunting the beaver for his pelt and the buffalo for his meat and man for his pride and the hell of it. And there are other echoes from long before, far-off visions of a Paradise still untainted, where we were the first humans to pitch our tents and sing our songs. For ghosts have no colour, no kind; memories are our only substance. Memories of a world that is gone, a dream dreamed out, riding our spirit-horses, or maybe only riding the wind, over plateau and meadow, snowfield and wheatfield, a Wild Hunt without hoofbeat or cry, riding, riding into Forever.

Amanda Hemingway was "born, grew up, and is still going strong despite an erratic lifestyle, low income and high alcohol intake". Of *Ghosts*, she says: "This story came to me when I was trying to think of a Wild West parody with a shoot-out between vampires and gunslingers and a heroine with a dodgy German accent (ref. Madeline Kahn). Instead, I found myself writing a pocket history of the West from the viewpoint of all its ghosts . . ."

THE BOY THUG
Christopher Fowler

G iddens had been riding with the two grain merchants for four days before he cut their throats. It never took less time than this. The pair had come out of Bismarck with fat saddlebags, but Giddens could not be sure what was in them. The tall one, name of Sweeney, had arranged to visit a bank before they set off, that much was sure, and his horse was heavier when he left. There was a story that the merchants were quietly moving gold across the state, travelling without protection so as not to draw attention to themselves. They weren't too smart; Giddens liked that.

His method was a tried and tested one.

At first he rode silently behind them, waiting for an opportunity to be useful. He did not have to wait long. The track was bad, and Sweeney's pot-bellied horse soon threw a shoe. Giddens palmed a thick briar thorn and appeared to extract it from the nag's hoof. The merchants were grateful, but wary of strangers. He rode beside them for three hours, jawing about the weather, the troublesome tribes further South, anything he thought might interest them, but they gave nothing away.

So he left, knowing they would get suspicious if he befriended them too quickly. Same thing next day, three hours of riding, then gone. Finally it got so they were expecting him, and then he knew he had won their trust. That was when they were as good as dead.

The rest of the gang had been running a parallel trail, and now moved in so swiftly that they were able to take the merchants' guns before they so much as looked up. Giddens took care of the killing. He buried the merchants side-by-side in the creek at the end of the red clay ravine, then emptied out their saddlebags.

He found a brick of bills thick enough to keep them warm through the winter. He allowed his best men to send small amounts of money home. There was also a cloth filled with gemstones, blood-red crystals the size of coat buttons, but they had no way of fencing such rarities, so Parson emptied fist after glittering fist into the river.

That was four years ago, when things were still good. A lot had changed since then.

The gang led by Parson and Giddens was made up of men who had lived with them in the Dakota Territories, and loyalties ran strong. They were uncles, cousins, brothers, and they had joined because they needed money, or needed to stay on the move, and preferred the nomadic life to breaking their backs on the hardscrabble dirt of their homelands.

Some of them had been soldiers who had left the military in bad circumstances. Others would not be drawn to their reasons for joining; they had stolen, or killed, or abandoned their families. Anything was better than slowing starving to death in townships that had failed to take root.

As the frontier moved westward the military followed it in, so the gang was forced to live between two shifting barriers of settlers and lawmen. There were too many people around now. The garrisons served as troop bases, from where attacks could be launched on Indians, and once they were in place it was time to get out. The settlers caused almost as much trouble. They kept a cold eye on strangers, and winning them over took a great deal of effort and patience.

In 1873, there were three memorable events that were to have repercussions for the gang. The territorial officials decided to harvest Black Hills timber and float it downriver to Missouri for new settlements. The first Colt Peacemakers got sold out of Connecticut by mail order for $17 apiece. And Sam Henry Ezekiel Franks joined the gang at the age of eight, making him its youngest-ever member.

The gang never took women or children as a rule. A few years earlier at the end of a bad winter, they had stopped a party of five men, four women and two little girls, tracking them through an overgrown route to the Cheyenne River. It had taken Heck Giddens six days to convince the party of his good nature and honest intentions, but at last he had persuaded them to let him travel with them as a scout. Parson was waiting with the others down near the shoreline, and when the first two travellers appeared on the path he shot them both dead. The third he blinded, but the other two got back in time to warn their families. It turned into an unholy mess; Giddens cut the throats of the two little girls and stuck the most beautiful of the women with his knife because she kept screaming, although she took a long time to die and still made a hell of a fuss.

It took another two days and nights to round up the remaining survivors. The men were rabbity little things and gave in easily when cornered, but their wives were hard, and had thin brittle bodies like boys. Parson and Giddens built them a shack in the woods, and kept them there for sexual purposes—the women could not leave because they had no horses or supplies—but the arrangement was to no-one's satisfaction, and at the end of the summer they were killed and buried in the woods.

As a consequence, the ban on women and children stayed in force as the gang went about its business. It was a strange time to be surviving as they did. It was hard to tell who to trust anymore; the prospectors, the railroad officials and the land developers were all arriving to stake their claims. The Sioux were being pushed into reservations, the remaining buffalo hunting grounds were under threat, tribes and militiamen were fighting among themselves, and nobody except a few men in the East knew what the government was planning to do next.

The gang—it had no name—had been working in a loose figure-eight for several years, cutting down from the grey shale below the treeline to hit the old expedition routes and settlers' paths. The winter of '72 had been harsh, and the numbers of travelling parties were down. The longest it had ever taken to win the trust of a party was almost three weeks. Each time it grew a little harder.

They were careful in their choice of victims. The risk was always weighed against the prize. They paid off their members in instalments, usually when they were far from any town, to prevent them from heading for the nearest bar and whorehouse, where they might talk to the wrong people. It was, Parson said, like a family, although here he was only guessing at the idea because his folks had thrown him into the forest at the age of two, and he had been raised by a fat little Yapa Comanche who had lost his own parents.

"We got to get a good haul in before spring ends," said Parson one night, as the gang settled back into their old camp at Twelvetree Point. Only Giddens and his sidekick, a young halfbreed Arikara named Blue Star, were still awake.

"There's talk of a party coming down from Fort Gray end of the month," said Giddens. "You know what that means."

Parson did not need to be reminded. The fort held military gold reserves, and in the past had sent out interest payments with settling parties in the form of reshaped bullion. According to the prison warden, a gurning halfwit the Arikara had befriended, the bars were melted and pressed into leaves that were stitched into the floors of the ladies' saratogas, but nobody knew for certain if this was true.

"Gives us three weeks to prepare," said Giddens, "should be enough." He was eight years younger than Parson, and took care of the planning. Over the past decade, he had perfected the art of inveigling himself into companies of suspicious strangers, but it never got any easier. The uncertainty of the times meant that men who were by inclination friendly now studied new companions with cold distance in their eyes.

"Get your Indian back up to that fort," said Parson, "and get that stupid old drunk jailer talking. We need to know how many they gone be."

Parson told him little he did not already know. He and Blue Star had already made plans of their own. A schoolteacher and his wife, they'd heard, an old man, probably his father, two outriders with a cart, not a riding carriage but something to haul a weighty object—what were they carrying, and why would they be making the journey? There was no settlement this side of the river, and no way across for a cart. He went to the ridge and looked down into the blue night, thinking. It was logical to assume they were headed for one of the new Wyoming settlements, but the schoolteacher was travelling with two escorts, and that smelled bad. No-one could afford to waste men on accompanying a civilian couple unless they were carrying something special with them.

Giddens kicked over the fire and lay awake for the next hour, feeling the earth cool beneath him. The mystery of the schoolteacher had dug into him now, and would not easily be released.

The weather turned foul in the last week of the month. Sun and moon both vanished, and rains turned the old settler's route into a mudslide. The gang resolved to set camp at Twelvetrees until Giddens brought in the party. None of them was deterred by thoughts of jail or hanging. They worked from necessity, knowing that each party they robbed might be their last, because each was smarter than the one before, and would not be gulled by a pleasant stranger with a helpful smile. Giddens knew it would come to an end some day, but not quite yet—there was talk of uprisings and a coming war with the red men, so minds were preoccupied and treasure parties grew reckless, risking plunder. Until the train arrived there would be no easy way through this route, and at least the gang killed quickly when they could, which was more than could be said for the half-starved bastards to their North.

Blue Star returned from Fort Gray to tell them he had seen the party setting off for a settlement downriver. The teacher was 'birdsmall', the wife was 'driedleaves', the old man a 'gravewalker'. Their carriage was little more than a wood platform on cartwheels and there was only one outrider. To anyone else this would have come as bad news, but Giddens still felt confident that they were delivering something important. To be given a scout at all was a luxury. The group would pass close to Twelvetrees Ridge in two days' time. Their outrider would arrive three or four hours ahead of them. The ridge formed a bottleneck through the tail of the forest, where the land opened out into flat brown earth. It was exposed but tightly contained. Even so, there was danger in an ambush. Better to befriend the teacher and win him over. Giddens was a man of some learning, and could exert considerable charm. It was his chief advantage over Parson, who was roughly born and branded through with it like a birthmark. He was bandy from riding and lack of greens, and had once received a knife in the eye, which had left it glazed. He did not look naturally trustworthy.

The others, who this year numbered about fifteen in total, were no better. None could read or write, and few spoke above a cuss. They were hungry and dirty and stank, and got sick from wiping their shit-stained hands on their breeches before eating with their fingers, and when they fucked their women they often left them dead. Mostly they were like mean children, even Shug, who was the oldest and reckoned he was probably about fifty, although he could not rightly be sure—he'd seen too much to stay in kindly disposed spirits.

So Giddens rode out to greet them. He had an advantage; the path had washed out some half-mile South and he knew better than any guide how they could circumnavigate it. He sighted the party moving from the seagreen shadows of the pines, and drew in alongside. Within seconds the outrider, a soft-chinned, bug-eyed young man who looked like he'd never seen sunlight, had drawn close and was resting his hand on the rifle in his saddle.

"I hope your boy here knows the safest passage through these woods, sir," he said, doffing his hat. "Hector Giddens, at your service."

The schoolteacher was indeed small, a bundle of female bones reshaped into a bookish man. He observed Giddens with a still eye. "He knows the way well enough."

He's been warned, thought Giddens. *I've seen that look before.*

"You know him well, then." He indicated the outrider without glancing at him.

"We were introduced by Captain Mallory at the fort," called the old man at the back of the party.

His father is the weakness. He's already given too much away. "I should perhaps warn you, sir, that the path ahead will unseat your horses. We've had bad rains, and the road has been washed out in a number of places."

"Thank you. I shall be wary of that." There was a movement under the tarp on the cart. The teacher called back sharply, "Stay down, Sam." So there was another riding with them.

"Then I wish you well enough," said Giddens. "You need have no fear in these parts, although it never pays to drop your guard. 'Covert enmity under the smile of safety wounds the world."

'You know your Shakespeare, sir.' The schoolteacher tried not to look impressed. He held out a cautious hand. The outrider flinched. 'Lemuel Franks, and this is my wife, Mayla.' He indicated a stony-faced woman with centre-parted dark hair. She was dressed in a stiff, high-collar and grey silk skirts unsuited for the terrain. "Back there is my father, Abel, and my boy. Come out, son."

Samuel Franks emerged from beneath the tarp, maybe eight years old, small for his age. He looked feverish.

"He has not been well," said the teacher's wife. "His stomach."

"Well I'm sorry to hear that. See the big green leaves at the base of the pine brush? Tear them up and boil them to broth, they'll improve his bowels. Pleased to meet your family, Mrs Franks. I feel I am in good Christian company." Giddens knew she would appreciate the formality. He ignored the outrider, but kept a carefully respectful distance. He deliberately avoided looking at the cart behind them.

The first and most important thing was to give Franks a reason for trusting him, and to do that he needed to produce a reason for riding with them. To offer an immediate explanation would sound wrong, so he let Franks fish for answers. Giddens explained that he'd been living out here alone since his dear wife died of pneumonia. That he was lonely, a former marshal turned trapper waiting to be relieved of his post by Captain Mallory's men. These days he made a living scouting out forests for the logging companies. Sometimes he was glad of educated company—not too many of the fellows he ran into had any learning to speak of. It made a man hungry for good conversation. He allowed droplets of information to fall from him like thawing branches.

Blue Star's knowledge of the group's departure stood him in good stead. He was able to display his knowledge of the fort, its men and even its jail. They joked lightly together about mutual acquaintances.

Franks, in his turn, explained that he and his wife were to set up a school for the militia to teach them map-reading, for he was a geography teacher. As Giddens suspected, his wife was a bible-wringer and had been placed in charge of the new chapel. The outrider's name was Billy; he was Captain Mallory's grandson. That night, Giddens took his leave and promised to return early the next morning. Only Billy was displeased, because his authority had been usurped.

This charade carried on for five days and nights. Giddens was beginning to despair, because the party was moving further and further away from camp. He promised to ride with them one more day, but knew he was running out of time. If Franks was really the guardian of a treasure, it had to be in the trunk they kept under the tarpaulin, but there was no way to it.

The boy's health and spirits improved. He asked to ride with Giddens, but Mayla Franks would not let him out of her sight. Lemuel knew about the land's geography, but had little experience of it. He rode badly, and more than once risked overturning the carriage when the path proved too steep. The outrider remained wary—hell, that was his job—and Giddens plotted a way to get rid of him.

He prearranged a meet-point with Parson and three others. If he failed to show, they would ride on ahead and stake the outrider's figure-eight, hoping to waylay him. Billy rode out early each morning, returning before noon to report. On the sixth morning, he did not return. Giddens went to see what had happened, and returned with bad news.

"I'm afraid your rider is dead," he told them. "He's in a glade about three miles West of here. Looks like his horse lamed itself and threw him. His neck broke when he landed, I don't suppose he felt any pain." That much was true, although Parson had tortured him a while, trying to find out what the schoolteacher was delivering. When he went too far and Billy left them for another sphere, Parson realised the outrider had died without giving them a clue.

Giddens offered his services, and they were readily accepted. A fine blue mist was settling into the valley ahead; the pines were laced together by a sheen of dew-filled spiderwebs, and even the birds had fallen silent. They rode without talking, but Giddens felt a tension building in his gut. Parson and his men arrived without sound. They fell in around the convoy and calmly, quietly strangled Abel Franks with a rope. Giddens cut Lemuel's throat from behind with a straight razor. Mrs Franks was too ugly even for them, so they twisted her neck and pulled her from her horse without so much as a pudgy hand raised in protest. These acts were not undertaken out of malice but from a sense of practicality; no-one could be left to report back. Lately the militia had been behaving in an excessively violent manner, and none of the gang would have reached trial after capture, so it was better this way. One of the horses grew frightened at the sight of blood and bolted. The others accepted their new owners.

Parson and Shug would have killed the boy but Giddens stayed their hand. It was agreed that Sam was young enough to be trained for a different future, and two of the men took him back to camp. Giddens and Parson uncovered the tarp and broke open the chest on the cart. Inside were damp-riddled schoolbooks and clothes, nothing more. It made no sense until Giddens set to wondering if the treasure Lemuel Franks had been carrying was not gold but information. And what if it was the boy who held such knowledge? It would explain why they had kept him hidden under the tarp.

Giddens buried the boy's parents below the cottonwoods in the river bed and brought the old trunk along. When they reached camp he emptied the schoolbooks and bibles into Sam Frank's space, a hide they had stretched across the bushes for him. Giddens burned the clothes because they were evidence. Inside Myla Franks' Sunday dress he found around thirty dollars, two small gold coins and a small stash of jewellry, obviously paste and easily identifiable. The necklaces went into the river. More and more, he became convinced that the boy must know something of greater importance. So he waited.

In the same way that Giddens showed a stoical, infuriating patience with his victims, he now resolved to do the same with the child. He could see from studying the boy's still brown eyes that threats would provoke little response. He was his father's son, except for his jet hair and the tougher fibre within him. The only way was to win his trust. He was careful right from the outset, making sure that Samuel did not actually witness his father's bloody death, or his mother's strangulation. Sure, the boy would realise they had gone and that he had been adopted by a very different family, but in time Giddens hoped that he would become reconciled to his fate. The young were pliable. Giddens had seen it before; angry twin brothers had joined the gang on their eleventh birthday. He had never asked why they had run away from what seemed like a pleasant settlement, but had accepted them, fed them, taught them how to kill. They were gone now, in tragic circumstances, and he missed them.

Sam rode with them and did not look back. He never asked questions and he never complained. He took to riding with his arms around Giddens's waist, and rarely spoke about the past. One older man in the gang began to show a lively interest in the boy when he was washing himself in the creek, so Giddens stayed by his side at night, sleeping at the edge of the hide.

It was only a matter of time before Captain Marshall sent some men after them. Word had reached him that the Franks family had never arrived, but this news upset him less than discovering that his grandson Billy had gone missing. Giddens heard troops from the fort combing the forest on four separate occasions, but by now the trail had grown over, and besides, they never thought of searching the riverbed. Eventually the loss was written off, in that curious way the old West had of dealing with unforeseen tragedies.

One night the gang camped out in a wide Southern plain of rock and stubble where no fire could be kindled without being seen for miles, but it was warm enough for them to stay without. The stars had come down to brush the earth. Giddens hunched himself into his jacket and looked over at the boy, who was watching for comets.

"Did your father ever say why he was moving the family?" he asked.

The boy remained motionless, his large head tilted up at the spilled-out sky. "We had relatives in Wyoming," he said finally. "We were going to meet them halfway and set up a mission. It was my Ma's idea."

"But your old man was gone teach geography."
"Only 'cause they was nothing else he could do."
Giddens knew that a man like that was useless out here.
"And your grandpappy came."
"Couldn't leave him behind."
"Captain Marshall sent a rider along with you."
"We heard about the scalping party." There had been reprisals for an attack on a reservation, but that had been some three years ago.
"That the only reason?"
"My pappy didn't know the way." He pointed at a silver streak in the heavens. "There's one."

Jesus, thought Giddens, *what the hell is wrong with the folk in this country? They deserve to be taken advantage of.* "You want to ride with us the next time we go out?" he asked.

"Sure. My hands are cold." He put his right fist into Giddens' jacket and they stayed in place, side-by-side, watching the stars drop from their orbits.

The next day they went looking for a party that was headed West, taking mail and supplies to a settlement known as Cricktown. The boy proved useful in gaining the trust of the waggoner. Giddens introduced him as his son, and found that smiles soon appeared. The boy was damned cute, and knew how to sell it. He won the women over first. Suspicions quickly lessened, so that they were able to surprise the party and take it in half the usual time. He remembered the look of shocked betrayal on a ranch-hand's face as he cut his throat and thought *Hell, we haven't had a reaction like that in years.*

Sam got better. Soon he was clinging to Giddens and hitting their victims with so much bull about travelling with his daddy that there was hardly any more work to be done. He learned the trade real fast. It was difficult not to feel proud of a boy who figured things out like that. The rest of the gang adopted Sam as a mascot, sending him to check the trail ahead of them because he could get through low brush without making a sound. Only Blue Star kept away from him, because he had lost his standing in the gang.

But life was still hard. The winter of '74 was meaner than the last, and two of their men died of the cold. One was rock-solid and dead on his horse, which meant that Parson had been talking to a corpse for a morning without realising it.

The pickings were mixed at best. One party headed for Yankton was carrying banknotes intended as a kickback for the mayor, which meant that the loss couldn't be reported, but too many setters travelled with just their bedrolls and the clothes on their backs. Old Shug was heard to complain that they'd have made more money as pirates. Then Parson got sick to his stomach and died of something wrongly cooked. They shovelled aside pine needles and dug him a pit, covering it with brush. "Ain't nobody going to say a few words for him?" Giddens asked, and Sam stepped forward with a short speech he had written, which cheered everyone.

But losing the gang's first partner lowered their spirits. Nothing was quite the same for the next two years. New settlements were springing up in the sheltered valleys, where the worst of the weather passed overhead and there was plenty of game to be caught, and they regarded all strangers as enemies. Giddens knew that the days when he could charm the women out of their britches was coming to a close.

One day, watching the halfbreed slowly dismounting from his horse, he realised that even Blue Star was getting old. The gang got by on stragglers and fools who had taken routes they had no right to be on, but it was a poor way to make a living. The only advantage they had was the boy; there was an innocence about Sam that could pull the wool so far over folks' eyes that they didn't feel the blade going in. Giddens would not let him take part in the kills. He needed to keep the boy fresh. In turn, Sam kept the gang on its toes, so that they learned from one another.

Giddens always knew when Sam was about to come up with some new idea. His brown pupils dilated and he would gaze into the distance, his lips pressed tight together. Then he would say "How about if..." or "What would you think..." and suddenly he would run off at the mouth with some scheme that got less crazy the more you worked it out.

On one of their increasingly rare trips into town he persuaded Giddens to purchase a great iron pot, which they dragged back to their new camp at the ravine and filled with water, keeping it boiling through the dark winter months, adding meat and bitter root vegetables that could cook for weeks and still taste good. They built several small bases deep in the hills and kept a cow for milk, so that they could stay healthy. As the boy grew, there was just one bone of contention between them. He didn't like what they did with the women. He didn't understand it exactly, he just knew it was wrong, and wanted them to stop it. Giddens said he would see what he could do, but could not promise that the men would easily change their ways.

The composition of the gang altered from time to time. Men went back to their wives or decided to chance their luck in another state, but around twelve of them stayed, a sufficient number to attack a band of travelers without mishap. During one miserable summer the gang was forced to steal clothes and kitchen utensils from a settlement as it moved upstream. When it seemed they could no longer scrape a living from their trade, more members drifted away, under oath never to mention what they had seen or participated in, upon pain of death. They had no romantic notion of being outlaws. They were of a criminal class far below the admired rebels of the time, and no townsfolk would ever welcome their arrival. Sometimes Giddens looked at the boy and was shamed by the way he made his living. He had grown up in the East, and been educated to appreciate the value of the classics. Now he hankered for the erudition to express himself, to somehow pass on what he had learned about the world to Sam. A hole had opened up inside him like the gnawing of a rat, but it was too late to find a way of changing for the better.

Without realizing it, Giddens started to call the boy his son, and the sentiment had been quietly reciprocated. Newcomers to the gang assumed he was Sam's father, and neither of them did anything to challenge the notion. But there was something unspoken standing between them. Sooner or later it would be time for Sam to earn his keep by killing, and Giddens did not know if the boy would be up to it. He knew the subject needed to be discussed, but in the long and easy stretches of silence that passed between them on the forest slopes, he realised that he was afraid of losing his boy. Everyone treated Sam as the gang's natural heir, and even Blue Star had fallen into a kind of truce with him.

One evening the boy returned from hunting with the Arikara, and saw his adopted father dashing out a man's brains at the base of a tree. Giddens' face was badly slashed. The broken body yielded just a handful of coins, and was buried beneath the scrub. Nothing Sam saw affected him, for he had retained the blankness of his childhood. The gang's business made no difference to him; they might have been selling rabbit skins instead of fencing stolen goods.

Giddens had been keeping a mark on the boy's birthday, and understood with something of a shock that he was to be sixteen the coming week.

The men had gone across the ravine to Fort Redcliffe, where they had a nice little trade going in dead men's weapons, and were not expected back until the next day. He tried to think of something special he could do for the lad, but as always the suggestion came from Sam.

"We could go to the buffalo plain," he said.

"You won't see any, son," said Giddens. "They've all been driven out. The railroad has staked the land as far as you can see. Soon, when the fencing starts, the travelling parties will have to travel the long way around to go South, and they won't come past here no more."

"Then we should hunt," said Sam, who enjoyed the thrill of stalking an animal and killing it. "Tonight we should stew venison, which is deer meat."

He was always surprised when Sam sprang new words on him, and marveled at his memory. He realized now that he loved the boy more than he had ever loved anyone; no woman had come this close. They found a small doe grazing in the bracken and clipped it, but it was the boy who brought it down. He was lithe, fleet and silent, and could get close without a creature suspecting a thing. They skinned the carcass and set the hide aside to be seasoned and dried, then carved the bony young animal into joints, although it would easily have fitted whole inside the pot. They added beans and roots and pilotbread.

Giddens had been saving the bottle for over three years now, and decided the time was right to uncork it. He poured brandy for the both of them. The boy coughed and punched his chest when he drank. A sooty cloud of bats rose in the red dusk light.

"You never hear wolves out here," he said, listening intently.

"Not for years," Giddens replied. "They moved back to the deep timber."

It was nearly dark now. The pot popped and boiled. A butterfly flickered about the boy, as white as phosphorus, and settled on his knee. He stared hard at it. "I'm sixteen," he said. "Leastwise, in a few days. I'm ready."

Giddens knew what he meant, but needed to disguise it for a moment more. "What you mean, son?"

"I'm ready to do what you do."

"I didn't want to speak of it before it was your time," said Giddens softly.

"I just wanted you to know."

Nothing else needed to be said. They sat by the pot and drank. Some while later, they heard a trap snap closed. An animal released a high cry of pain. "You got something," said Giddens, "sounds like a hare."

He turned to find the boy holding a Colt Peacemaker to his temple. "I had to wait for the trap to shut," said Sam blankly. "You'd have heard the gun cocked." He fired at close range, blowing out the rear left quadrant of Giddens' skull. The forced threw Giddens onto his back. The boy climbed to his feet and disappeared for a moment, returning with a Bowie knife and a logging saw.

He cut off Giddens' legs at the knees first, then severed his arms at the elbows and shoulders. It was hard work and he was soon sweating violently. Surprisingly, Giddens was not dead. He tried to speak, but after a while he just stared up at the sky and squeezed out tears, which the boy was careful to catch in a tin cup.

In an act of mercy, he cut off Giddens' head. Then he slowly added the old cowboy to the pot, piece by bloody piece.

When the gang arrived back next day they were starving hungry, and he was able to feed them all. He sat with them and drank his adopted father's tears from the tin cup. Then, once the gang had eaten their fill and had fallen into drunken stupors on their bedrolls, he quietly rose and returned to his hide. Digging beneath his blankets, he sorted through the old books Giddens had dumped from Lemuel's trunk. He gently removed and rewrapped the Shakespeare first folio. Then he slipped it into his saddlebag, mounted Giddens' horse and rode out of the camp, into the waiting night.

Christopher Fowler was born in Greenwich, London. He is the award-winning author of thirty novels and twelve short story collections, and creator of the popular Bryant & May mysteries. He worked in film and fulfilled several schoolboy fantasies, releasing a terrible Christmas pop single, becoming a male model, appearing as the villain in a Batman comic, running a night club, writing in the Pan Books of Horror and standing in for James Bond. He has written comedy and drama for the BBC, has a regular column in the *Independent on Sunday* and is the Crime Reviewer for the *Financial Times*. He lives in King's Cross, London. When asked about his story, Christopher admits: "This is an odd one. I wanted to write a story with the stark tone of Cormac McCarthy but couldn't get the voice. Then I went on an extended jaunt around Northern India and found some frontier-like towns where people seemed to have a clear correlation to the wild West. By melding the two attitudes, the story came in one clear run without a single word change, and was one of my most satisfying writing experiences."

KISS THE WOLF
Simon Bestwick

Halfway up the Crag, winded and tired, I stopped for breath and looked back.
Bad idea. Always is. Just ask Lot's wife.
But, for the record, I saw this:
This was, had been, north-west Lancashire. Farm country. Now the farms were blackened craters. Long black scorch marks trailed across the land. A fat bright orange glow burned a mile off; somewhere they'd missed before.
Only one thing moved on the ruined plain, or more precisely three grouped so closely as to be one: long black shapes in long black coats and wide-brimmed hats, on long, black horses.
Riders.
They'd have guns, of course—they always did. But they liked using their long knives much more.
I had a gun too, but it was useless against them. I knew because I'd tried. I'd shot one of them three times, chest and face—if you can call a slitted helmet beneath a wide-brimmed hat a face—and knocked it to the ground, but it'd only shaken itself and stood again, then come for me. Now the only chance I had was a rumour I'd heard in the days and weeks of roaming the wastelands looking for food. The kind of rumour you had to be mad or desperate to believe.

Still, if all else failed, there were three shots left in the gun. I'd only need one.

We sat in the front room. The clock ticked. No other sound. Nobody wanted to speak first. A pot of tea and a plate of fishpaste sandwiches stood on a trolley in the middle of the room. The TV burbled faintly in the background. Mum sat in one corner, glaring at the back of Dad's head as he fiddled with his pipe, packing tiny pinches of tobacco into the bowl with the precision of a bomb-disposal expert. *Say something, David,* she was thinking. But he didn't.

Hannah and I sat on the sofa and held hands. I wore a suit. I didn't know why. It wasn't the first time Mum and Dad had met Hannah; just the first since they'd heard she was pregnant. "We'd better get it over with," Hannah'd said, with the wry, resigned smile she met all life's absurdities with, one those artless things a lover does that melts you in an instant. Then she'd ruffled my hair and added "... and if you're a brave little soldier and get through it without any trouble..." Well, I won't repeat what she whispered in my ear, but it would've made anyone promise to behave.

So that's how we were. A tableau. In a neat little living room facing a trim front garden, a driveway, a row of suburban semis each side of the road. A grass verge along the pavement, planted with saplings. That's the scene.

The TV stopped, cut off. Dead.

Dad looked over at it.

The glass vase on the windowsill thrummed. Vibration. Then I heard the sound, even through the double-glazing.

The thunder of hooves.

I can hear the clatter of horse's hooves, so start running again. It's faint, like the smell of burning. Distant. But gaining.

The Riders don't kill you directly, unless you're in the way—they'll ride you down without a thought—or try to fight. I don't know why—I've seen them shrug off everything up to and including artillery shells. I'm not even sure a nuclear bomb would finish them. But attack them and you'll be hunted down and killed. Slowly. That's their idea of fun.

No, they don't usually *kill* you. Just take away all you need to live. Food, transport, tools, shelter, medicines. Death takes care of itself. It has so many ways to try—starvation, exposure, hypothermia, disease—and then of course there's the cannibalism.

I probably shouldn't think about that.

No, actually I *should*. Not for the grief. For what comes after. The *rage*. The rage will keep me going, get me to the top.

Because if I can get that far...

Twilight's coming, and the sky and the mountain blur together. But somewhere, up above me, I can see a faint light shine.

Hoofbeats. And then the loud sharp crack of gunfire.

Mum yelped and dropped her tea. The cup bounced on the thick pile carpet, turning it dark as the spillage soaked in.

An orange flash. A thunderclap. The glassware rattled.

Shouts and screams. A teenager ran past our drive. Tracksuit bottoms, Kappa top, baseball cap—the kind of kids everyone feared. What scared them?

The answer came soon enough; men on horseback thundered by. Black horses. Long black coat. Wide-brimmed hats shadowed their faces.

The shots, the explosions—they'd made me jump, made Hannah nearly break my hand, but I wasn't scared. It wasn't real; couldn't be. Any minute now we'd see the camera crew, a director would shout *Cut*-

One of them raised a gun as he rode past us. It was a massive thing, the size of a sawn-off shotgun, but he held it easily in one hand. The Rider pointed it at the Ford Focus Dad washed and waxed with loving care every Sunday morning without fail. Then he fired, again and again. The barrel belched smoke, thunderclap noise, and bright, livid fire. The car's windows shattered. Its doors flew open. It sagged like a dying wildebeest as the tyres blew out.

And then it exploded.

Something like a big hand seemed to grab me and fling me across Hannah and the sofa. Not the blast; this got here first. It was something I didn't have a name for, that knew, that always knew, what had to be done in order to survive. I'm not always proud of it; it keeps me going even when the decent thing would be to lie down and die.

There was a flash I caught even through squeezed-shut eyelids. And then a dull, deafening thump, and the room shook.

Dimly, through the roaring in my ears, I heard Hannah scream.

The high, brittle noise of shattered glass; the roar of a rushing wind. Glass fell on my back; wet warmth trickled down my neck.

Distant screaming. Wailing sirens.

And the thunder of hooves.

All fading, drowned out by the shrill whining in my ears.

I got up. The curtains were on fire. Mum and Dad both lay on the floor. The sofa had been against the wall, to one side of the windows. Their chairs had lain right in front of it.

For a second I saw and didn't believe. Then I screamed. Mum's face was gone. Just blood. A hand with all the fingers sliced off. Nearly all the clothes gone, and half the skin. She was, had to be—please god—dead.

Dad was trying to hold her, but he couldn't keep a grip and she slid to the carpet. He moaned and fell on top of her, blood hosing out of him in a dozen places.

Holidays. First day at school. Plasters and TCP on grazes and cuts. Stories at bedtime. Songs at night. All of these came back and I stepped towards them.

"Come on!"

Hannah had my wrist in both hands and was pulling, hauling me towards the door as the wallpaper caught fire and the room filled with smoke. "Come on!"

I fought for a moment; then that cold thing I had no name for took hold of me and pushed me through the door. I looked back once. The flames roared across the ceiling. The sofa erupted. Dad's trouser legs were on fire. He didn't move.

They're the past. Hannah is the future. They're beyond help. She's carrying your child. GO.

In the hallway, Hannah made for the front door, but now it was my turn to do the dragging—it led to a burning driveway and galloping Riders. I pulled her into the kitchen, to the back door. My eyes were streaming and my throat burned.

Down the drive, the Focus was a black, twisted bundle amid roaring flames. More smoke, thick and black, billowed out to engulf us. Screams. Sirens. Thundering hooves.

Running up the back garden. Cold, clean air, but still the taste of smoke. Sometimes it seems it'll never go away. Climb the fence, drop into next door's backyard. Stumbling into their front drive.

And there's a Rider.

He sat in the saddle, looking down at us. Beneath the hat, a steel helm with slits like gills. Rank, steaming breath hissed out of them. A single, horizontal slit at eye level; a yellow bandanna knotted beneath the steel face. Under that, a plain shirt, trousers made of hide. Possibly human. The hide, not the Rider. His gun was half-raised.

A long moment passed.

I somehow managed not to piss myself.

The Rider lowered his gun. Then turned his horse and spurred it on, while the house began to burn. I touched the wet warmth on my neck, and traced it to an earlobe sliced almost clean off by flying glass.

It's there. A glow, right, at the top of the Crag. Not natural light. Has to be man—or woman—made.

Keep climbing. Can't hear the horse's hooves anymore. As I get closer I see a cave. There's a fire in it.

I was told she lives in a cave on top of the Crag.

Please let it be true. *She can kill the Riders. She can teach you how.* It seems stupid to think so now. If she could, why didn't she? Most likely, it was just some half-crazed loner peddling witchcraft stories to scare off unwanted guests.

But what if it's true? And what if she doesn't like intruders? Will she burn me to ashes or turn me into a frog?

Hooves clatter. Burning to ash or going *ribbit, ribbit* seem comparatively pleasant just now.

I dive into the cave.

The witch, if that's what she is—looks up from a fire burning low in a pit and smiles.

She's not what I'd expected. Small, for a start. Tiny. Barely five foot, petite, but big-chested. Strawberry-blonde hair, a light-olive-skinned face. Quick brown eyes. She wears a grimy, but otherwise presentable trouser suit. Let out around the belly, obviously.

Because—oh, yes—she's pregnant. Looks about eight months gone.

"You took your bloody time, didn't you?" Her voice is high, bright and chirpy, with a Salford accent. "Well, come on in then. Park your arse."

"You OK?" I whispered.

Hannah nodded, leaning into me. My spine ached, but I held on, supported her, propped her up. My feet ached. The sole on one shoe flapped loose.

We kept walking.

We'd joined the dazed and the desperate, the forlorn, the ones who'd had the rug pulled out from under, stumbling along the A-roads and the motorways with shuffling steps and slack, empty faces and eyes like scuffed glass, like a procession of the dead, searching for rest, for a home. But there was none to be found.

A fire engine on its side, windows gone, spattered with bullet holes, the crew's bodies strewn nearby.

We all have our dead, by now. Parents, spouses, lovers, siblings, children, dead in burning houses, exploding cars, trampled to a muddy pulp beneath the Riders' hooves. But that's just the start. The real slaughter starts here.

Cars, transport—destroyed. Power stations crippled or blown up. Homes burnt down. Food supplies destroyed, farms burned and ransacked, water mains blasted...

Once there was a dull chatter of rotors above, and we saw two military helicopters passing overhead. We watched them go. A little later, there was gunfire, a scream of tortured metal, and something fell from the sky to erupt in a soaring bubble of flame.

The columns start thinning out. People fall and don't get up, dead or too weak to rise. And Hannah and I staggering on like Siamese twins, joined at the hip. The baby is weighing her down, devouring every scrap of nourishment she took in.

This can't go on.

Then the other disappearances from the column began. You'd wake up in the morning, and someone would be gone, but lo and behold, there'd be a rich cooking smell, a pot of stew bubbling over a fire.

There was a third category of people who vanished, and we chose to join them before either of the first two could claim us. They were the ones who slipped away by night in twos and threes to go their own, lonely way, realising that now there was less to fear from the Riders than from their own kind.

"Sit down," said the—witch?—again. "Before you fall down."

"The Riders are after me," I said. "There's not much time."

She grinned. Her teeth were clean and white, with a gap between the top front ones. Mine were thickly furred and, last time I'd seen my reflection, a truly disgusting shade of yellow and brown. With a hint of green. Three had fallen out. "Don't worry about that, mate. I've a few tricks up me sleeve. You must've known that if you've come all the way up here."

I still stayed standing.

"Look," she said, "in here we're safe. No-one finds this place unless I let them."

I blinked at her.

"Never mind," she said kindly. "Anyway..." She hung a kettle over the fire. "We haven't got all day, but you can catch your breath before we get down to it. Want a brew?"

Was she serious, or just mad? What the hell; after coming this far, I might as well play along. "Please."

"Tea or coffee?"

"Coffee, please." I kept a tight grip on the revolver.

"Hope you're not thinking of using that on me," she said, spooning Mellow Birds into a thick china mug.

"N-no."

"It's sod-all good against the Riders anyway."

"I know," I said, "It's for me. In case..."

"They can't get in here," she said. "By the way, I'm Louisa. Louisa Bardillo."

"Mike." I didn't give my last name. It sounded like something dead, part of a lost age, a vanished way of life. Which, I suppose, it was.

"Milk and sugar?"

We didn't stay long in one place. The only danger from the Riders now was if they caught you trying to establish anything. To build a house, anything like that. We were like a man who couldn't swim who'd fallen in a deep pool. The Riders were the man who stands on the bank kicking the first man's hands away whenever he tries to get a grip. Besides, you had to keep going constantly, in search of food.

Sometimes, if you were lucky, you'd find an old can of beans or a packet soup—once we'd found a bar of chocolate—or you'd catch a fish, a rabbit, a bird. There were plenty of crows about. Hannah thought that probably counted as cannibalism once removed, but it didn't stop us eating them; it beat starvation.

I was half-afraid, half-hopeful that Hannah would miscarry; there was so little food to keep her going, never mind the kid. But it continued to grow. And Hannah faded; she grow thin and gaunt, and the spark I'd loved her for disappeared.

I made us a place to stay. A sort of bivouac; I'd learned something from my Cub Scout days. It kept out the wind and the rain and it was fairly well-hidden and hard to spot, in case any Riders passed through.

I took time and care making it because by then Hannah was getting close to term. She was permanently hungry and exhausted. Her bloated belly looked like some horrible parasite clamped to her, draining her dry. Her hair was matted; her teeth were nearly as bad as mine. Kissing had become rare if not extinct—although we no longer tasted quite so bad to each other, the state of our lips, gums and teeth was downright off-putting.

"It's going to be soon," she said. An autumn afternoon, and the sun dipping. A few hours of light left for hunting. I nodded and kept sharpening the spear I'd improvised from a length of birch wood and a chipped flint and tried not to think about keeping a baby alive too. It wasn't hard. No-one thought farther ahead than the day's end now. None of us would live long. To call it a mediaeval level of existence was too kind—Neolithic was probably closer to it.

I kissed her forehead, stroked her belly. That cold thing I'd never named urged me to leave her, or kill the baby at its birth. Survival. I'd live longer, move faster. I tried to hate myself for thinking it, but hadn't the strength.

But still, we were together, even if it was only out of habit now. You took what comfort you could find.

"I'll be back before dark," I said.

But when I did, with a small dog I'd managed to kill, she was gone.

"So," said Louisa at last. "What've you come to ask us for?"

I put down my coffee cup and I took a deep breath. "They say you know how to kill the Riders."

"Yeah?" Louisa looked amused. She'd taken out needles and wool and started knitting.

I tried again. "Can you show me how to kill them?"

She looked up. "Serious?"

"Yes."

"You want to fight them, do you? Kill them?"

"*Yes.*"

"Yeah, you and everyone else who's still alive. You're not the first and you won't be the last. There've been a dozen before you already. They all went back empty-handed, and I'll tell you something else—they were glad to."

"Why?"

"Oh, nothing I did." She put down her knitting. "I had what they were after, yeah, and I was willing to give it them, but I'm honest. I had to tell them about the price."

"What price?"

She pointed at her belly. "It's different each time. I was eight months pregnant when I called on it. That was five or six years back."

I stared at her. She nodded. "Yes," she said kindly, in case I was slow picking it up. "*This pregnancy.* I'm not joking. Wish I bloody was."

"That was the price?"

"My price. Part of it. Other part was keeping the wolf's head safe."

"The what?"

Louisa unwrapped a bundle of rags. Inside was a life-size wolf's head, worked in some dull metal like pewter. It looked old. The wolf was snarling, eyes slitted and dark.

"This is where it all comes from. The power, the gift, whatever you want to call it. I've got to keep it safe. Give it to other people if they want. But, there's always a price, and you don't know what it is till after. No-one does."

"I wouldn't have thought anything could be worse than this."

"No?" She turned the wolf's head in her hands. "One man got changed into a wolf. Forever. 'Nother one went mad, ended his days running round on all fours, eating raw meat and screaming. Another got his face changed. Got stoned to death as a demon. Then there was another one—got something like leprosy, only worse. Didn't affect *him*, just gave it to anyone *he* touched. And there's worse, a lot worse. Course, it's not *always* that bad. Might be something small, something you can live with. You don't know. Sometimes it's a small price for a big gift. But it could just as well be a big price for something small. Only one way to find out."

"What's that?"

She proffered the head. "Kiss the wolf." Firelight danced over its contours, flickered in its empty eyes. "Your choice."

○ ○ ○

I knew it wasn't the Riders. The bivouac was torn and trampled, but it hadn't been burned.

I had the spear and a knife. They weren't hard to track. Hunger made them stupid. If I'd been there, I might have fought them off, even on my own. But a pregnant woman, tired, malnourished, without help...

I saw the smoke of their fire, and made for it.

They were in a clearing in the woods. Five of them. Mum, Dad, two teenage boys and a girl of six or seven. An iron pot hung over the fire. They were all eating. Bowls of stew.

I could smell it cooking and saliva rushed into my mouth even though I knew what—*who*—it was.

Hannah lay on the edge of the clearing. Her eyes and mouth gaped. Her arms and legs were gone. Her belly was open and empty.

I think I screamed as I ran at them. The father rose, lifting an axe. I rammed the spear into his throat. The flint snapped off as he fell back.

The boys were on their feet, snarling. I kicked the big iron cooking pot over, and they leapt back, hissing and yelling. The wife lunged at me with a knife, scored a line of pain across my ribs; I rammed the broken spear into her left eye and she fell screaming. The girl clawed my legs as I picked up the axe. I knocked her to the ground and stamped on her head.

Yes and yes and yes. I did those things.

I'd seen something, you see, in the stuff that'd spilled out of the iron pot. A very tiny, but very distinct hand.

I went after the boys. One had a spear of his own and jabbed it at me. I knocked it aside and caved in his head with the axe.

The other ran away, into the woods. I went after him and knocked him down.

He died slowly.

Yes and yes and yes. I did those things.

And yes and yes and yes, I ate their flesh. I'd crossed the line. I no longer cared.

But I didn't eat my wife and child.

I didn't eat my wife and child.

I didn't eat my wife and child.

I buried them deep.

KISS THE WOLF

○ ○ ○

But killing the family changed nothing. It was what the Riders wanted. It was the Riders I had to hurt.

I found the mutilated bodies of three police officers. Nearby, I found the gun. The Riders had missed it.

Found, too, later on, how useless it was.

Heard, as I fled, of the cave on the mountain they now called the Crag. Where else could I go?

It was dark when I came out of the cave. The night skies were clear and full of stars—no more light pollution. The slopes were clear and empty.

For about three seconds.

Then the thump of hooves, the rattle of metal, and they were all around me, the three of them, their long chase at an end.

Their laughter hissed and steamed out through the slits in their helmets.

Until I started laughing too.

I looked up at the moon and raised my arms and-

My one regret is that I hardly remember it. I remember the howl that tore my throat, the prickle of fur in my arms, and foul-tasting inhuman blood in my mouth. That's all.

Dawn had come. I gathered my torn clothes and put them back on. I took the Riders' knives and guns and one of their horses, which stood by, cropping the grass. Last of all I took their severed heads, still helmed, and hung them from the saddle horn.

I donned one of their hats, to keep the sun out of my eyes. Then I mounted up and rode.

Perhaps the guns and blades could be used against them, perhaps not. It didn't matter. I could pass on my gift, extend my brotherhood, with a single bite, to any who wanted it. I knew the rules and limits of the gift already, without being told.

The price was another matter. But I'd pay it when it came. And when it did, I'd worry then about what I'd lost and left behind.

Till then, blood would be enough.

Simon Bestwick lives in the wilds of Lancashire (well, Swinton) and is the author of two short story collections, *A Hazy Shade of Winter* and *Pictures of the Dark*, a chapbook, *Angels of*

Gutshot

the Silences and a novel, *Tide of Souls*. His novella *The Narrows* was shortlisted for the British Fantasy Award and reprinted in Ellen Datlow's *Best Horror of the Year*. His second novel, *The Faceless*, will be published next year by Solaris Books, and another chapbook, *Cold Havens*, is forthcoming from Spectral Press. When not pursuing the delights of wine (well, single malt whisky), women and song, he can be found with his nose in a book, watching a good film, listening to music or hiking. He's also threatening to learn to play guitar. Ideally he'd like to con somebody into paying him to write for a living, as it's so much better than a proper job.

"*Kiss the Wolf* developed through my reading about the 'Harrying of the North', which took place during the Norman Conquests; the Normans crushed a rebellion in the North of England by systematically razing villages, slaughtering livestock, burning crops, tools and weapons—basically by destroying anything the rebels needed to survive. They defeated the rebels, but over 100,000 people starved to death, many resorting to cannibalism to survive. The idea of a lone survivor seeking (supernatural) revenge came out of that, but I hadn't the time or energy for all the research required, so I transferred the concept to the present day. Luisa Bardillo wandered in from another story of mine, *Salvaje*, which will appear in the *Black Book of Horror*. I rather like her, and I have a feeling she'll be back."

WAITING FOR THE BULLET
Mark Morris

The first thing we saw was the smoke. It curled into the air from fuck knew how many barbecues and burger vans, giving a dirty grey underbelly to the fluffy white clouds. Before then the sky had been nothing but pure, pigeon-egg blue, the sun high and hot and blinding, like a permanent camera flash reflected off a steel plate. The roads were baking blacktop layered with white dust from the surrounding desert, which kicked up in clouds behind us. Whenever we found ourselves behind a slow-moving truck—it hadn't happened often, maybe twenty-thirty times on the entire four-hundred-mile drive—we had had to close the windows to avoid choking to death, though that had trapped the stink of Jed's skunk in with us. It was the lesser of two evils. Just.

Couple of minutes after the smoke the Frisco site became visible on the horizon. All we saw at first, appearing and disappearing as the ground rose and fell, was a random selection of roofs—spikes and jags and domes. But then we crested a rise and suddenly we saw the whole panorama laid out before us.

"Fuck me," Abi muttered from the back seat.

I touched the brake of the camper van, slowing the vehicle to a crawl, so we could take it all in. Within the vast circle of the high perimeter fence a bizarre shanty town had formed, composed of pre-fabs and marquees and the multi-coloured triangles of thousands of tents. We could hear music playing, see people milling like insects over a corpse.

"Bullet time!" Jed announced gleefully, his pink-eyed, bearded face appearing between the front seats.

Fran, sitting beside me, asked anxiously, "Where are you going to park, Chris?"

I thought that was pretty obvious. On the right-hand side of the road, before the Frisco site itself, a quarter-mile square of desert had been transformed into one huge parking lot. Some of the vehicles were so caked with dust they looked as though they had been there for years. People were sitting on lawn chairs beside their mobile homes, reading or eating or praying. I could see kids playing ball or Frisbee. There was even one guy with a beard down to his navel, who had painted himself blue, doing some kind of tai-chi.

I cranked the van into gear and cruised down the hill. Just before we came parallel with the first of the parked vehicles, a guy in a sweat-stained grey T-shirt and khaki shorts stepped up on to the verge and started gesturing to us. His left arm was stuck out at a right angle and his right arm was windmilling, in the familiar gesture of a traffic cop ordering a vehicle to pull over. I slowed to an idling halt and instructed Fran to wind down her window.

"Hi," I called, leaning across.

The guy stepped up, put his hand on the window frame and peered in at us. He was maybe twenty-five, tall and tanned, his tousled hair bleached by the sun. He grinned, though the grin was intended mostly for Fran. I felt a brief stab of ownership as he ran his gaze over her tight, salmon-pink top and white shorts.

"Hi," he said. "How long you folks here for?"

"We got a four-day pass with an option to extend," I told him.

"Care to show me?"

I shrugged. "No offence, but we have no idea who you are."

The guy held up a finger as if I'd made a good point and produced a grubby laminated card from the pocket of his shorts. Beneath the words OFFICIAL FRISCO STEWARD was a picture of him with darker hair and his name, Brad Chesuik. His steward number, some eight or nine-digit affair, was on there too, but I couldn't be bothered to read it.

I handed the card back and dug our pass out of the glove compartment. I had a moment where I wondered whether the ID he'd showed me was fake, and whether I'd be able to catch him if he took off, but he barely glanced at the pass before giving it back to me.

"That's cool," he said. "Follow the channel through there. Someone'll show you where to park."

"Can't we park inside?" asked Fran.

"Not without a thirty-day pass."

"But all our stuff's in the van. Are we supposed to walk all the way back to it when we want something?"

"Sorry," Brad said, but he didn't look as though he was sorry and I couldn't really blame him.

"It's okay," I said, putting a hand on Fran's knee, "we'll manage."

"Yeah," said Abi from the back. "What're we gonna need anyway? Money and water. It's no big deal."

Fran and Abi had started this trip as best friends, but their relationship had begun to fray almost from the off. Me and Fran had been together almost two years, and I had always known that Fran was more uptight than she usually let on, especially when she was outside her comfort zone. It was one of the things I found endearing about her; it brought out the protective male in me. What surprised me, though, was that Abi, who had known Fran since they were both five, seemed to be finding all this out for the first time. Had their relationship really been so shallow before? Or maybe Abi had changed? She certainly didn't seem the easy-going, fun-loving girl I'd always taken her to be. She was more moody and self-obsessed than I'd expected—she got angry and irritable at the slightest thing. One night we'd got pissed in a bar in Texas and Abi had disappeared. I thought she'd staggered out to be sick and went to see if she was okay. I found her in the front seat of the camper van, sobbing. But when I asked her what was wrong, she just said she was 'homesick'.

Anyway. We'd been in the States nearly four weeks now and this was our last major stop-off before flying home next Thursday. Once we'd spent a few days at the Frisco site we'd drive the camper van back to San Fran and that'd be it.

What 'it' actually was I wasn't entirely sure, but it felt like . . . I dunno . . . the end of innocence; the end of the adventure. I know that sounds a bit wanky, but the thing was, all four of us had finished Uni in the late spring and had worked our butts off in menial jobs through June and July so that we could afford this trip. We hadn't actually said as much, but I think we all saw this as our last big blow-out before settling down. On August 2nd we'd flown out in a state of near-delirious excitement, and back then the days stretching ahead of us had seemed endless, a glorious buffer between ourselves and real life.

But those days were now nearly all gone. It was hard to believe. Before heading off, Fran and I had talked about this being a life-changing experience, but had it been? I honestly don't know. I think we thought we'd arrive home with a fresher, more focussed, more mature perspective on our individual futures—but at that moment all I was really sure about was that I was knackered from all the driving, and the nightly drinking, and the lack of sleep. And as for the others, well, it didn't seem to me as if any of them had undergone any great epiphany. Fran had spent most of the last four weeks worrying; Abi had spent it lurching from one foul mood to another; and Jed had spent it stoned out of his skull.

It felt good to finally get out of the camper van and stretch my legs and back. Abi was right—we didn't need much. Some water, some sun-block, my wallet and my green Oakland Athletics baseball cap to prevent me getting sunstroke.

It was weird to finally be here, to be walking up to the Frisco site, past all the parked-up vehicles and the reinforced food vans and the opportunists selling shitty souvenirs. We'd seen these places on TV. In the early days especially they'd been all over the news. Atmosphere-wise, I hadn't known what to expect, but now that I was actually here, I felt the same kind of eager anticipation I felt at somewhere like Glastonbury. I didn't feel scared, or even apprehensive, probably because out here hardly anyone was wearing protective gear. There were a few family groups—mum, dad, kids—sweltering in bullet-proof vests, but that was about it. Maybe there'd be more inside, I thought. Or maybe, after seven years, people had just become blasé.

Jed, typically, was a sucker for all the souvenir shit. He bought a bullet on a key-chain (it wasn't even a genuine replica) and a Stetson whose hatband was imprinted with the slogan: *I Survived the Frisco Shootout.*

"Don't count your chickens," Abi said. "We're here for four days, remember."

"Yeah, well, if I do take a bullet I won't really care, will I?" he grinned.

We arrived at the main gates, above which a big sun-bleached sign proclaimed: *Welcome to Frisco*. The main site was ringed with police vehicles, behind which a chain-link fence topped with razor wire stretched away on both sides. Armed cops in helmets and flak jackets were patrolling bad-temperedly, their faces red and sweating, eyeballing the steady dribble of people going inside. I suppose, when you thought about it, it was pretty amazing that even seven years after the first fatality these sites were still so popular. In fact, they had grown and expanded over the years; the whole thing was a social phenomenon, crazy and inexplicable, but undeniable all the same. The reason why people continued to flock to these places had been written about and analysed in newspapers, magazines and academic theses throughout the world. Psychologists had a phrase for what motivated the permanent residents, those who had become addicted to the idea of being constantly in the firing line: 'Shootout Syndrome', they called it.

At first we had planned to go to the OK Corral site in Tombstone, Arizona, but when I went online to book tickets I found that there was a three-year waiting list. Some of the other sites had waiting lists too—the Wild Bill Hickok site in Springfield, Missouri, for example—so in the end we had opted for the Frisco site, mainly because it would be a relatively short drive to the airport afterwards.

As we stood in the queue, Fran sidled up to me. "Why are we doing this, Chris?"

It was a question she'd asked several times before, except then it had always been: 'Why would we want to do that?'

'It'll be a laugh,' I'd always told her, but now that we were actually here, I felt something more considered was called for.

"Because... it's an experience," I said. "Nothing like this has ever happened before, and people still don't really understand how it works. And it's historically fascinating. And it's just... well, it's a thrill, isn't it?"

"Is it?" she said.

"Course it is. Isn't it a buzz to tempt fate? Doesn't it make you feel alive?"

She shook her head. "Not really. I don't see the point of putting ourselves at risk."

Fran had never understood my predilection for tomb stoning and bungee jumping and body boarding. She'd never been an adrenaline junkie. But I needed it. It was my drug, my high—though, unlike Jed, I didn't feel the need to be out of my fucking tree twenty four hours a day.

"We're not really at risk, though, are we?" I said. "There've only been— what?—twenty fatalities in the past seven years? Statistically we're more likely to die in a plane crash."

She winced. "Don't remind me." She was not a good flyer either, and was hardly relishing the flight home.

I smiled. Fran was like the yin to my yang. Or the yang to my yin. Whatever. I put my arm round her.

"Don't worry, I'll look after you," I said.

Getting into the Frisco site was like passing through the security check at an airport. You put all your money and belts and shit in a plastic tray, then walked through a metal detector. Then, once you were through, you were frisked to make doubly sure you weren't carrying any concealed weapons.

The reason for the security was because when the sites had first started up, some nutters had seen them as a kind of weird invitation to bring along their own guns and let fly. Random murders had been committed on the twisted premise, submitted by several killers in their defence, that anyone who visited a site was presumed to have a death-wish and were therefore fair game.

Of course, not all the murders were random. Some were more calculated. In one famous case some guy bought an original 1873 Peacemaker, had some bullets made for it and then used it to kill his wife at the Blazer's Mills site in Lincoln County. He was only caught because a ballistics expert realised that the killing bullet was made from an alloy that wasn't around in the nineteenth century.

Once we were inside, we just stood for a few minutes, taking it all in. It was like a cross between some massive bazaar and a kind of warped, ramshackle Disneyland. The shootout sites attracted all sorts of people— thrill-seekers; tourists in helmets and protective vests; research scientists; religious weirdos; opportunists out to make a fast buck; the reckless; the suicidal. There were street entertainers—acrobats and jugglers, fire-eaters and magicians. And there were Wild West enthusiasts, strutting around in their Stetsons and their waistcoats and their cowboy boots, looking a bit pathetic because their holsters were empty of the replica pistols they'd had confiscated at the gate.

"So what do you wanna do?" I asked.

Abi shrugged. "Get hammered."

"Score some dope," said Jed.

Fran, who was clutching my hand tightly, sighed. "Let's just look around," she suggested and pointed at a wooden street sign. "The main street's that way. Let's start there."

We started walking, stopping now and again to see the sights. A bored-looking Chinese girl in a pink and white cowgirl outfit that was all sequins and tassels thrust a leaflet at me. The leaflet was advertising the Frisco Museum and gave a brief history of the Frisco Shootout. I whistled.

"Hey, listen to this. Around one thousand rounds of open fire were expended during the Frisco Shootout, which lasted for approximately thirty-three hours."

"How can a shootout last thirty-three hours?" asked Abi scathingly.

"It was actually more of a siege," I said. "A bloke called Elfego Baca was wanted for questioning about the murder of a ranch foreman, but holed himself up in a house, which was then attacked by around eighty cowboys. It says here that the cowboys fired over four thousand shots into the house, but Baca wasn't hit once. During the siege, Baca killed four of his attackers and injured eight others. In the end a friend of Baca's convinced him to surrender and he walked out of the house unarmed."

Abi shrugged as if this was the most boring thing she had ever heard, but Jed raised his eyebrows, impressed.

"Four thousand shots," he said. "Fuck, man. If those bullets show up, we are gonna be Swiss cheese."

I felt Fran tense beside me.

"They won't," I said.

"They might," said Jed, grinning as if he relished the idea.

"Not while we're here," I said. "The chances are infinitesimal."

"Isn't that what everyone thinks?" said Fran tersely.

"What?" I said.

"That they'll be all right? That the chances of them being here when the bullets show up are so small it isn't even worth thinking about? But it's going to happen one day, isn't it? Somebody's going to get hurt?"

"Not necessarily," I said. "This thing's pretty random. The Frisco bullets might never show up."

Jed nodded. "Yeah, those scientist guys might find a way to, like, close the wormhole or whatever."

"Or they just might never show up anyway," I said. "It hasn't happened everywhere."

"It's happened in enough places," Fran said.

"Eleven," I said. "Eleven sites in seven years."

"God, you are such a geek," muttered Abi.

I frowned. "I knew we were coming here, so I Googled the information. Isn't that understandable?"

"For you maybe."

I felt my temper rising. I'd done all the fucking driving, I'd booked the tickets, and all Abi could do was behave like a twat.

"What's your fucking problem?" I snapped. "Why do you always give everyone such a hard time?"

Abi glared at me. Unlike Fran, who was small and blonde and pretty, Abi was stocky and a bit... well, butch, I suppose. And just before the trip she had dyed her hair a deep, almost-black maroon. It didn't suit her.

"Maybe it's the company," she said. "Maybe it's having to hang around with Mr Pointless Trivia and Mrs Oh-I've-Got-Nothing-To-Worry-About-So-I'd-Better-Invent-Something."

She said that last bit in a simpering falsetto.

"Oh, fuck off," I snarled.

"Ooh, how articulate," she sneered back at me.

I felt myself starting to shake with anger. My ears felt as though they were burning and melting on the sides of my head.

Aware that I was spitting and starting to lose control, I said, "No, tell me, really, what is your fucking problem? Are you just angry because you're too fat and ugly to get laid? Are you blaming everyone else for the fact that you look like a fucking bull dyke?"

As soon as the words were out of my mouth, I regretted them. I felt awful, not least because Abi looked at me with an expression of utter desolation and burst into tears.

"Hey, look, I'm sorry..." I mumbled, reaching towards her.

"Fuck off!" she screamed, flinching back so violently that she stumbled, almost losing her balance. "Don't fucking touch me!"

Then she turned and ran. I made to go after her, but Fran pulled me back.

"I'll go."

She hurried after Abi.

"But I won't know where you are," I called.

"I'll text you."

The girls disappeared into the crowd, leaving me and Jed standing there. Jed patted me on the shoulder. He looked genuinely amused.

"Nice one, mate."

"Fuck off," I replied.

We walked on. I felt miserable now, ashamed of what I had said.

"Why does Abi have to be such hard work?" I asked Jed.

He shrugged. "Like you said, maybe she just needs to get laid."

"No, but seriously, Jed, has she said anything to you?"

"Why should she say anything to me?"

I sighed. I didn't need this shit. Why didn't people just talk to each other, get stuff out in the open, air their grievances if they had any? Why did everyone have to be so fucking uptight?

"So what do you wanna do?" I said.

Jed gestured off to the left. The muffled throb of music was coming from a red-and-white-striped marquee, the top of which towered over the huts and vans thronging the streets. "Head towards the sound of salvation, man," he said. "Sex and drugs and rock n'roll. The only real truth."

"You talk some utter shit sometimes," I said.

Jed grinned, as if I'd paid him the highest possible compliment, and led the way.

More sights: kids in bullet-proof vests queuing up for a Wild West Ghost Train, the outside emblazoned with skeletal gunslingers; a bunch of drunken guys wearing comically huge foam Stetsons; a Yogi-type guy wearing nothing but a turban and a loincloth, sitting cross-legged on the dusty ground, a yellow snake coiling around him. It was a colourful mish-mash of styles and cultures, a vast melting pot of humanity. The shootout sites were unique in that people were drawn to them for a variety of reasons—celebration, introspection, historical curiosity, scientific research. But that wasn't the strangest thing. The strangest thing was that all of this—this whole amazing, ludicrous, terrifying phenomenon—had blossomed from the death of just one woman.

Minnie LaChance. A forty-nine year old housewife from Trinidad, Colorado. Seven years ago, Minnie's husband, Earl, had arrived home from his engineering job at a local gas drilling company to find Minnie lying dead in their back yard. It seemed that she had been hanging out washing when someone had shot her in the thigh, shattering her femur and severing her femoral artery. She might still have survived if she had received prompt medical treatment, but she had lain undiscovered for over seven hours, during which time she had bled to death.

At first it was thought that there might have been a racial motive for the killing—Minnie and Earl were black in a town where only 0.5% of the population were African American—but further investigation revealed a curious fact. The bullet that had killed Minnie had been fired from an 1866 Derringer. This was not especially unusual in itself—there were still plenty of old guns around in full working order—but what was unusual was that it had not merely been the murder weapon which was vintage but the actual bullet. The bloodied slug extracted from Minnie LaChance's thigh was found to be an original .41 Rimfire Cartridge, a 130 grain lead bullet propelled by 13 grains of black powder. The Trinidad PD worked hard on the case for several months, determined to bring the killer to justice, and yet, despite the oddity of the bullet, forensic evidence proved to be frustratingly non-existent and Minnie LaChance's killer was never found.

Eight months later in Coffeyville, Kansas, during the annual October celebration in remembrance of the 1892 Dalton Raid, four of the town's citizens, including one eleven-year-old girl, suffered fatal gunshot wounds. A further nine victims received hospital treatment for injuries sustained by what at first was thought to be a lone gunman on a killing spree. However, events took a turn for the strange when it transpired that not a single witness to the shootings could actually recall seeing a man with a gun. Indeed, those citizens who had been in the vicinity of the killings all claimed more or less the same thing—that the bullets had not only seemed to come from nowhere, but from several directions at once.

As in the LaChance case, the murderer (or murderers) of the Coffeyville Four, as they became known, was never found. Also as in the LaChance case, it was subsequently discovered that the victims had been struck by a variety of vintage bullets from vintage guns. Perhaps not surprisingly, rumours began to circulate that a group of unknown and unseen psychos had decided to celebrate the anniversary of the Coffeyville Shootout in their own unique way—by re-enacting the incident as accurately as they could.

It took two similar incidents, however—in Hunnewell, Kansas, nine months after the Coffeyville killings, and in San Antonio, Texas, just three weeks later—in which a total of five more people were either killed or wounded by vintage bullets, for someone to finally stumble upon the truth.

That 'someone' was a freelance journalist called William Marby, who, seven months after the San Antonio killings, sold an article to *The Fortean Times* entitled: *Bullets From The Past?* In his article, Marby postulated the outrageous theory that the murder victims of the four seemingly random incidents had in fact all been killed by stray bullets fired by various gunmen back in the late nineteenth century—bullets which had, in effect, moved forward through time. There was a lot of nonsense in the article about 'time ricochets' and 'temporal pockets', but for the first time Marby pointed out what no one had previously noticed—that all four incidents had occurred on the sites of significant Old West shootouts. At the end of the article, Marby included a map of the US, supplemented by a list, pinpointing where future incidents might possibly occur. Of course, neither he nor his article was taken seriously—until his predictions began to come true.

Now, of course, Marby was world famous. He had five best-selling books to his name and travelled the world, talking about his various researches into the unknown. Sometimes he even gave lectures at the shootout sites themselves—those, like Frisco, where the bullets had yet to fly. The American public loved him for this, his willingness to put his life of fame and riches on the line by tempting fate via the very phenomenon he had identified, and through which he had made his fortune. There was a neatness about it, a braggadocio which appealed to them. And if, in the course of one of his lectures, he should ever actually be killed by one of his famous 'bullets from the past', well then, that would be the neatest trick of all, one for which he would most likely be made a national hero.

The inside of the marquee was like an oven. I hadn't taken more than three steps through its arched entrance when sweat started to pour from my skin. The place stank of hot rubber and unwashed flesh and cannabis smoke. I took off my baseball cap and swiped an arm across my forehead, and wondered whether maybe Fran hadn't been right, after all: why the fuck were we here?

Jed put a hand on my shoulder and leaned in. "Off to see a man about a dog," he yelled above the music, before disappearing into the crowd.

Alone, I began half-heartedly pushing my way through the dripping, stinking audience towards the stage. The band was a punky country-and-western outfit, all manic fiddles and scything guitars. The lead singer had a shaved head tattooed with Celtic symbols and a thick handlebar moustache which curled up to the lobes of his multi-pierced ears. As the swirling wail of the song came to an end, he frenziedly ripped off his sweat-sodden shirt and hurled it into the crowd. Beating his gleaming, muscular, tattooed chest with his fists like a depilated King Kong, he screamed, "Come on, fucking bullets, I fucking dare you!"

The crowd whooped like fanatical supporters at a political rally.

I stood just behind the mosh pit and watched the band rip the fuck out of another song as the crowd surged and heaved in front of me. Despite the energy and the noise, I felt miserable and isolated and bored. I checked my phone to see whether Fran had texted me, but there was nothing.

My clothes were so wet it felt like I'd jumped into a swimming pool full of warm, barely-set jelly. I looked around, trying to spot Jed, but in the red-tinted gloom it was impossible. I decided to head towards the exit, and shivered as I stepped outside the marquee, even though it was thirty degrees out there. I squinted into the sun and, although my hair was matted and drenched with sweat, put my cap back on. A line of shaven-headed Buddhists wearing white robes went by, chanting softly and clashing little finger-cymbals.

I texted Jed: *Where r u?* Then I texted Fran: *Whats going on? U ok?* Then I began to walk, heading in the vague direction of the main street, thinking about the future.

Did I want to settle down, get a job? The prospect frightened and depressed me. I had talked to Fran about running my own business, starting up a company selling adventure holidays to thrill-seekers like myself. She'd been encouraging, enthusiastic even, but the truth was, I hadn't really thought it through. I liked the idea of doing the research, checking places out, experiencing the holidays myself, but I didn't know the first thing about business. Paperwork, tax, advertising, getting premises, building up a client base—all that stuff seemed beyond me, a crushing, daunting weight of toil and responsibility.

Whenever I'd expressed doubts, Fran had said, 'You can go on a business course,' or 'You can do book-keeping at night school,' or 'You can get a bank loan to start you off.' I'd nodded, but inside I'd been horrified; she might as well have suggested I wrap heavy chains around myself and jump in the river.

Thing is, I knew I was being immature, I knew I had to face up to real life sooner or later, but... I dunno; I just didn't feel ready for it yet.

Another thing: Fran was assuming we'd get a flat together when we got back, start life as an 'official' couple. To be honest, though, I wasn't sure I wanted that either. I mean, Fran was brilliant and we got on really well, but did I actually love her? Was she the one? I'm not sure I knew what true love was, what it was supposed to feel like. Isn't it all tingly excitement and choirs of angels and never wanting to be parted from the other person?

I found a bar en route to the main street and went inside. I ordered a beer and sat down at a spare table and texted Jed again: *Am in Red Eye Bar. Just head towards Main St. C u soon?*

The bar, all dark wood and green-and-white-checked tablecloths on round tables, was about a quarter full. A family—Mum, Dad, two small boys—were sitting by the front window beneath a flashing neon sign advertising Budweiser. They were eating burgers and drinking sarsaparilla in tall glasses; the boys had curly plastic drinking straws in theirs. A balding middle-aged man was sitting alone, staring sadly into space, nursing a beer. In the shadows at the back of the room, beside a small stage, was a quartet of what I can only describe as good ole boys in lumberjack shirts with the sleeves cut off to reveal their brawny arms.

I stared out of the window and drank my beer. My phone remained silent. It was almost four in the afternoon. The smell of burgers reminded me that I hadn't had lunch. Draining the last of my beer, I walked up to the bar and perused one of the laminated menus.

"Get you, buddy?" said the barman.

"I'll have a cheeseburger and fries with a side order of coleslaw. And another Coors," I said.

"You got it."

When I lowered the menu, one of the good ole boys was standing at the bar, about three feet away, looking at me. He had a crew cut and a thick sandy moustache. His hairy upper arms were thicker than my thighs. Sweat glistened like tiny diamonds on the velvety side of his head where the sun hit it.

"Hi," I said with a half-smile. He didn't smile back.

"English, huh?" he said.

"Yeah."

"So what part of England you from?"

"Sheffield," I said.

"That in London?"

"No, it's about a hundred and fifty miles north."

He continued to regard me, his eyes half-closed, as if I was some exotic creature. I felt uncomfortable. I paid the barman, took my beer and half-turned away.

"Nice speaking to you," I said.

"Well, now, ain't that rude," replied the man loudly.

I turned back. "Pardon?"

The man had been leaning on the bar, but now he straightened up, rotating his head so that his neck muscles crackled. He was a good seven inches taller than me.

"Here we are in the middle of a nice little chat, and you just up and leave. I call that rude."

I sensed violence thrumming off him. It hit me like a wave, drying out my mouth, making my guts ripple.

"Sorry," I said, trying to keep my voice steady. "I didn't mean to cause offence."

"Oh, you didn't mean to cause offence, huh?" said the man quietly.

"No," I said. "I'm here for a quiet drink and something to eat, that's all."

"You just a little English fag, is that it?" said the man.

I couldn't see the correlation between my comment and his. I felt a bead of sweat ooze from under the brim of my baseball cap and trickle down my face. "Sorry?" I said.

"What you sorry for?" he demanded, as if I'd bad-mouthed him.

"I mean... pardon?" I said, and licked my lips. I was still holding my beer. My mouth was so dry I was desperate to take a sip, but was afraid that if I made any move he would see that as provocation enough to hit me. Trying again, I said, "Look, I'm sorry if I've offended you. I don't want any trouble."

"You don't, huh?" said the man.

"No."

I could sense that the good ole boy was about to go for me. I had already decided to throw the beer in his face and run like hell when the barman appeared from nowhere.

"You okay, gents?" he asked.

The good ole boy looked at him, as if sizing him up too. "Oh yeah, we're just fine. My little English buddy and me, we're just shooting the breeze."

The barman's gaze flickered from the good ole boy to me. I could see he had taken in the situation at a glance.

"Your burger'll be ready in just a moment, sir," he said. "If you'd like to take a seat I'll bring it right over."

"Thanks," I said.

"And what can I get for you, sir? Four more Buds, is it?"

I slipped away while the good ole boy was distracted. I considered heading right out of the door, but I'd just spent fifteen bucks on a burger and a beer, so fuck that—why should I be intimidated? I caught the eye of the mum sitting by the window and she gave me a sympathetic smile. I smiled back, though my lips felt as dry as old rubber bands.

I gulped my beer and kept my head down. I didn't want to look up and find that the good ole boy was still staring at me. I didn't want to give him an excuse to come over.

I jumped when I heard footsteps approaching my table, but it was only the barman with my food. He had put it in a takeaway box. He leaned forward conspiratorially.

"Entirely up to you, friend, but I thought I'd give you the choice of eating here or elsewhere," he murmured.

I nodded gratefully. "Thanks."

"My pleasure. You take care now."

I risked a glance over at the good ole boys. They were refreshing their glasses from a jug on the table. I picked up my box of food and headed for the door. I didn't look back.

Outside I began to walk away from the Red Eye Bar at a brisk pace. Every instinct urged me to break into a run, but I resisted, knowing that that would only draw attention. I was just beginning to relax when I heard a shout behind me:

"Hey!"

My heart lurched and my muscles tensed. I was getting ready to leg it when the voice came again:

"Chris! Wait!"

It was Jed. Relief shuddered through me. I waited for him to catch me up.

"You okay, man," he said. "You look like shit."

I barked a laugh. "Yeah, I'm fine. Just met a guy in a bar who took a dislike to my face."

"Well, that's understandable. What's that? Food? It smells like food."

"Burger and fries. You want some?"

"Do I? I got the munchies like you wouldn't believe."

We found a bench and sat down, me still keeping a wary eye out for the good ole boys. My run-in with them had ruined my appetite, so Jed ate most of the food, wolfing down the burger like it was the first thing he'd eaten in days. He was polishing off the fries when my phone chimed. It was from Fran:

In Frisco Tavern on Main St. Everything ok. Join us? xx

I texted back: *C u there in 5 xx*

The Frisco Tavern was like a big Wild West saloon, with swing doors, sawdust on the floors, a guy playing honky-tonk piano. A wide wooden staircase led to an upper balcony, where ample-breasted women in low-cut velvet gowns winked and catcalled to the clientele below. I think they were just window dressing. If they weren't, they would surely have been pissed off at the big Mohawk standing at the bottom of the stairs with his massive arms crossed, forbidding access to all and sundry. As Jed and I walked in, I spotted Fran near the back of the room waving frantically.

She and Abi were sitting at a table in an alcove beyond the end of the bar. I mimed lifting a glass to my mouth. She nodded and raised an almost-empty wine glass. With her other hand she made a V sign. I gave her the thumbs-up, then headed to the bar.

The place was busy, the atmosphere relaxed, convivial. The staff was in period costume. The barman had oil-slick hair in a centre parting and a small waxed moustache. Behind the bar was a huge mirror, the name of the place engraved across it in gold leaf. Optics held bottles of brightly-coloured liquid, each of which was stamped with a black skull-and-crossbones. Above the bottles was a sign: Dare you try the Frisco Fire-Water Cocktail? $9.50

I leaned closer to the barman so he could hear me above the clamour. "What's in the Frisco Cocktail?"

He grinned. "State secret. Tell you this, though—it's good."

I turned to Jed. "Wanna try?"

"Go for it," he said.

We took the drinks across to the girls. Fran gave me a wide-eyed look which could have meant anything.

"Hey," I said.

"Hey," she replied.

Abi avoided eye-contact.

"You okay, Abi?" I asked.

She glanced at me, her face unreadable. "Yeah," she said, and took the wine I held out to her. "Thanks."

Fran was still giving me the look, though how she expected me to interpret it I have no idea. She waggled her eyebrows and swivelled her eyes meaningfully.

Clearing my throat, I said, "Hey, Abi, sorry about earlier. I was totally out of order. I behaved like an utter cunt."

Abi shrugged, took a sip of her drink. "S'okay," she muttered.

"No," I said, "it's not. I said some bad things. Things I didn't mean. I'm really sorry."

Abi sighed, and this time when she looked at me she held my gaze. "You're forgiven," she said. "And I'm sorry too. I've been a right mardy cow these past few weeks."

"No, you haven't," I said automatically.

"Yeah, I have. And I know I have." She raised her glass, and her voice. "Now let's forget about it—and get totally pissed!"

"Yeah!" Jed yelled, downing his cocktail in one.

The next few hours were the best we'd spent together since arriving in the States. That might just have been my interpretation based on the immensely efficacious effects of several Frisco Fire-Water Cocktails, but somehow it felt as if the air had been suddenly and magically cleared, as if for the first time in weeks there was no hidden agenda, and that the only reason we were there was to have fun.

And we did have fun. We were on a high, all four of us. It was one of those nights where you start laughing at stupid stuff and then find that you can't stop; where the stars seem in perfect alignment and you're absolutely certain of your place in the universe and the people you're with; where it seems completely feasible that you might live forever, and that if you did, forever would continue to be as amazing and brilliant as it was right then.

I have no idea what time it was when the shadow fell over our table. That's how I remember it—something large and dark, blotting out the light.

"Well, lookee here," said a voice. "If it ain't the little English fag and his fag friends."

It was the good ole boy from the Red Eye Bar. All I could see through my booze-goggles was the glint of his eyes and the porcupine-like quills of his moustache. I was aware, in an intense slow-motion kind of way, of Abi peering up and saying in a slurring, sniggering voice, "Who the fuck are you?"

Then Jed began to laugh and point. "I am the walrus," he said, "coo-coo cachoo."

As he and Abi exploded into giggles, the good ole boy seem to swell, to get bigger.

"What did you say, boy?" he muttered.

Realising he was being addressed, Jed blinked at the good ole boy. He seemed to have no inkling of the guy's mood. Or if he did, he just didn't care.

"Are you in the Village People?" he said. "Are you the–"

The good ole boy's fist exploded into the centre of Jed's face. In my drunken state it seemed so massive that it appeared to obliterate Jed's features. Then Jed fell back, his eyes already glassy with unconsciousness, his nose a mangled, bloody mess.

That was when it all turned bad. Suddenly I no longer felt indestructible, merely incapable. I tried to stand, but my legs wouldn't respond, and I ended up sprawling across the table, scattering glasses. All at once there was uproar. Fran crying. Abi screaming obscenities. Glass smashing and furniture breaking. Things being overturned.

I felt hands on me. I pinwheeled, flailed, fought them off. Other people were yelling. I had a confused impression of wrestling bodies, flying fists.

I slipped, or maybe I was pushed; I don't remember. All I know is that suddenly I was under the table, sitting in something wet. Then Fran was with me, her tear-stained face close to mine.

"You okay?" I asked.

She nodded, but she was upset, shaking so much her teeth were chattering. "Who are those people?"

"Bunch of pissed-up muscle heads," I said. "They had a go at me earlier. Don't think they like the English."

Someone crashed against the table we were sheltering beneath. It sounded like there was a full-on bar brawl happening above us.

"I don't like it here," Fran said.

I put my arms round her. "It is a bit lively," I agreed.

"I want to go home."

"We will," I said. "In a few days."

"I want to go home now."

I frowned, irritated. "We can't," I said. "Our flights are in four days. We've got tickets."

"I want to go now. Abi needs to go now."

"What's Abi got to do with it?"

Fran paused, then said, "She's got cancer."

"Cancer?"

"Ovarian cancer. She needs an operation. She found out just before we came away."

"But... why did she come then?"

Fran gave a wan smile. "Last fling. Last big adventure before going home to face it all."

"Last?" I said. "You don't mean... I mean, she is going to be all right, isn't she?"

Before Fran could answer, the table we were sheltering beneath was lifted up and away from us. I thought the good ole boys had found us, but it was the huge Mohawk who had been guarding the stairs.

"You," he said. "Out."

I scrambled to my feet. "What? I didn't do anything."

"Everybody out," he said.

I looked around. The place was wrecked. Furniture broken, smashed glass all over the floor. The big mirror behind the bar had black zig-zag lines radiating out from a central crater of shattered glass. People were flowing towards the exit, herded by armed cops. Some were limping, others bloodied and bruised.

"Where're Jed and Abi?" I said.

The Mohawk just looked at me.

"We were attacked," I said. "My friend Jed was the first to get punched."

Fran put a hand on my arm. "They're probably outside, Chris," she said. "Come on."

We went outside. It was dark now, getting cold. Instead of reviving me, the air hit me like a fist in the guts and I reeled away to throw up. Suddenly I felt wretched. I just wanted to lie down, slip into unconsciousness. Fran tugged on my arm.

"Come on."

"Where?"

"Let's find Abi and Jed and go."

I allowed myself to be led. I had no idea where we were going. My head was swimming. I didn't ask questions. I concentrated purely on putting one foot in front of the other.

For a while we were in a crowd, bodies ebbing and flowing around us. I was vaguely aware of people sitting around camp fires, singing and laughing. We passed various establishments lit up like beacons, belching with music. The smell of food from street-vendors made my stomach roil. We passed someone who was fire-eating, attracting oohs and ahhs as he breathed flames into the night sky. We passed patrolling cops, armed and armoured. Then the noise and people slipped away and we were somewhere else. Somewhere dark.

"Where are we?" I said.

Fran put a finger to her lips. "Shh. People are sleeping."

"Where are we?" I asked again, whispering this time.

"Campsite," Fran murmured. "Thirty-day pass area."

"Why are we here?"

"This is where Abi said she'd meet us. Look."

She held her phone up. There was a text, presumably from Abi, but it just looked like little black insects jittering on a tiny light box. It made me feel sick again. I looked away.

"Where?" I said.

Instead of answering, she took my hand and dragged me along. I felt limp and rubbery, my head bobbing. I just wanted to sleep.

"Abi," Fran was whispering, "Abi."

Then something slammed into my back.

I felt for a moment as though my spine and ribs had exploded. I fell forward and something landed on top of me. I had a confused impression that I'd been attacked by a bear, a big grizzly. This was America, after all.

My head was crushed into the ground, my face turned to the side. I saw Fran's feet kicking. I saw her phone drop to the floor. Then I heard muffled voices, grunts. Fran was forced forward, onto her knees.

Suddenly I realised what was happening. An ambush. The good ole boys had ambushed us. In a flash of sobriety I realised they must have taken Abi's phone. The text hadn't been from her at all. It had been bait.

They made me watch while they raped Fran over and over. They used her like she was nothing, an object, a series of holes for them to abuse. They slapped and punched her until her face was unrecognisable. They made her say she loved it, made her ask for more. They used a beer bottle on her, a splintered branch. They giggled and joked as they tore her open. I tried to scream for help, to beg them to stop, but they shoved rocks and dirt into my mouth. I wept and struggled, but I could do nothing. I could do nothing.

It reached a point where I knew it would never be over. Even when it was, I knew it never would be. They went eventually, those good ole boys. They left us lying in the dirt. They left Fran, my beautiful, gentle Fran who had never hurt anybody, broken and torn and lying in the dirt.

I crawled to her. I was crying. Empty. I told her I was sorry over and over. I don't know if she heard me.

Before coming here I had thought: *Even if the bullets do come they probably won't hit us. The chances of any of us getting hurt are infinitesimal.*

But what I hadn't considered was that bullets are personal, individual, that they come in all shapes and sizes. Each of us has a bullet out there somewhere with our name on it. And when it hits, no amount of statistics or rational argument or magical thinking or any of the other bullshit we wrap around ourselves and convince us will keep us safe is going to make a blind bit of difference.

The bullet hits, we're gone.

End of story.

Mark Morris became a full-time writer in 1988 on the Enterprise Allowance Scheme, and a year later saw the release of his first novel, *Toady*. He has since published a further sixteen novels, among which are *Stitch*, *The Immaculate*, *The Secret of Anatomy*, *Fiddleback*, *The Deluge* and four books in the popular *Doctor Who* range. His short stories, novellas, articles and reviews have appeared in a wide variety of anthologies and magazines, and he is editor of the highly-acclaimed *Cinema Macabre*, a book of fifty horror movie essays by genre luminaries, for which he won the 2007 British Fantasy Award. His most recently published or forthcoming work includes a novella entitled *It Sustains* for Earthling Publications, a *Torchwood* novel entitled

Gutshot

Bay of the Dead, several *Doctor Who* audios for Big Finish Productions, a follow-up volume to *Cinema Macabre* entitled *Cinema Futura* and a new short story collection, *Long Shadows, Nightmare Light*.

Mark says, "The idea for this story came to me while watching the Glastonbury Festival last year, and from simultaneously musing on why people tend to flock to/are attracted to sites of danger/tragedy/devastation. I was interested in exploring that whole notion of human beings feeling more alive by flirting with, or getting closer to, death, and how different people would respond to that in different ways—some would see it as a bit of a laugh (like going on a roller coaster ride), whereas others would regard it as a spiritual or religious pilgrimage."

CARRION COWBOY
Paul Meloy

Iktomi meets the North Dakota cowboy where the streambed is wide and dry. It is nearly dark and Iktomi has just kindled a fire using green willow sticks. A young moon draws its way across the prairie sky like the tip of a duck feather.

Iktomi is a spider fairy. His face is pinched and very brown. He wears deerskin leggings with tiny beaded moccasins. He paints his face red and yellow and draws black rings around his eyes. His long black hair is parted in the middle and is wrapped with red bands. Iktomi dresses like a Dakota brave.

He looks up at the North Dakota cowboy who sways in the saddle. The cowboy is dead. Iktomi can smell the rich, red rot. He can see the dark skin of the cowboy's face in the shadow beneath the wide brim of his hat. It hangs like a dirty cloth mask. The North Dakota cowboy has one eye, his left eye. His right eye is gone all but a rim of gristle.

Iktomi is a wily imp. He cannot find a friend to help him when he is in trouble. No one really loves him. He lives alone in a cone-shaped wigwam upon the plain. He hops and scuttles around the dusty feet of the North Dakota cowboy's worn out horse like a hungry bird.

Iktomi claps his hands and the North Dakota cowboy slides from his saddle and falls to the streambed. Iktomi shouts, "Hin, hin!" and the horse bolts away. Iktomi hoots and capers, his red and yellow face with its big dark ringed eyes shining with mischief.

Iktomi begins to chant his charm words. His fire crackles and glows with a bright green flame. In the glow of that wicked fire, Iktomi casts his scuttling shadow. The North Dakota cowboy begins to rise.

I will have fun with this, thinks Iktomi. He spins a web and with these strings he makes the cowboy dance a puppet's dance around the fire.

In his filthy bloodied shirt and ragged pants, the North Dakota cowboy topples to and fro. Iktomi laughs and throws his arms about and leads the corpse around the fire. "Ha! Ha!" laughs the wayward imp and does not see the shadow that draws to the edge of his camp while he frolics and spins.

Drawn to the fire, and to the smell of red, rotting meat, proud Coyote comes. Coyote narrows his eyes. "My my," he says to himself, "Who among us has not been tricked by that crafty fellow Iktomi before? Now we shall have some fun of our own."

Iktomi jumps upon the cowboy's back and hoots and hollers as they jolt about on the dry streambed. As they spin towards the edge of the circle of light, Coyote speaks, "Iktomi," he says, "I see you have found a friend. Will you introduce us?"

Iktomi is startled. The North Dakota cowboy stops his dance and stands at the edge of the fire. His arms hang at his sides and his head nods as Iktomi climbs onto his shoulders and peers over the crown of his hat. "Come out where we can see you," says Iktomi.

Coyote pads out of the shadows. His pelt is yellow-green and his eyes glow like minerals in the firelight.

Iktomi watches as Coyote circles the North Dakota cowboy. Coyote is grinning, his big, dark tongue hanging over his teeth.

Coyote stands on his hind legs and puts his claws on the cowboy's shoulders. He breathes on the cowboy's dropsied face, puts the tip of his thick tongue into the abandoned socket and tastes the salt-blood-gristle. Coyote feels a great hunger and wants to eat this thing. Coyote's narrow belly rumbles like a cart full of stones.

Iktomi scrambles down the cowboy's back. He jumps into the dust. He knows Coyote of old and knows his hungers and his pride.

"Vain Coyote," Iktomi chides. "My friend would like to dance. Have you the patience to indulge before you feed?"

Coyote gapes and rolls his moon-drenched eyes.

Iktomi folds his arms. The North Dakota cowboy does the same and pulls Coyote to his breast. Iktomi begins his dance. With flying hands and jumps and shuffles, Iktomi spins a web. He wraps Coyote in the cowboy's arms.

Coyote howls, a-stumble in that bitter clasp. Together they spin around the fire. Coyote smells his partner's high decay. He cannot move against these bonds Iktomi weaves.

"Dance, vain Coyote!" Iktomi shrieks beneath a night of wheeling stars.

Coyote, cunning spirit and ancient rival, trickster, sometimes wise and sometimes cruel, is helpless in these mystic ropes. He knows Iktomi has him fast; he curses his stupidity. What can he do to free himself from this dreadful carousel?

Coyote bites away the cowboy's throat. He shoves his muzzle in the rent and bores it down towards the heart. His tail whirls, a bouquet of prairie grass, and he claws the bloody shirt and flesh beneath until they flutter like red ribbons in a Wi An's hair.

Iktomi skips and plays his webs. The North Dakota cowboy twirls like a bobbin across the shadows of the streambed.

Coyote can do but one thing against the trick and trap of this potent imp; he climbs inside the North Dakota cowboy and wears the corpse like a fresh-skinned hide. The stink of meat and the wet-slip-slurry of putrid guts drives Coyote's fury, hunger and his pride.

Iktomi claps his hands and the webs break free. The North Dakota cowboy reels across Iktomi's camp and into darkness beyond the rim. Coyote cannot break his bonds; in fury his spirit seeps into the bones of the North Dakota cowboy and, now trapped inside this shambling thing, Coyote's rage and hunger does not dim. It grows, consuming him.

Iktomi, fickle, bored and weary, waves his arms and sends the North Dakota cowboy home. He sighs and throws earth upon the embers of his fire. Soon this mischief will be forgotten and Iktomi will find other tricks and traps to work.

And so it is that when the dead arise, their first hunger and their craving is for flesh, to feed the vain Coyote's raging at Iktomi's insolent arrest.

With foul, wet tread, towards his lighted town of shacks and bars, the North Dakota cowboy starts to lurch, his hunger great, and his belly growling.

Gutshot

Paul Meloy was born in 1966. He works as a Charge Nurse for a Mental Health Crisis Team in Bury St. Edmunds. He is the author of the collection *Islington Crocodiles* and a novella, *Dogs With Their Eyes Shut*, forthcoming from PS Publishing.

"Wanting to write something for *Gutshot* which avoided standard western tropes," explains Paul, "I started reading about Native American folklore and found myself intrigued and charmed by the myth of Iktomi. So I thought I'd have a crack at creating my own little story about him."

SOME KIND OF LIGHT SHINES FROM YOUR FACE
Gemma Files

'It is immediately obvious that the Gorgons are not really three but one plus two. The two unslain sisters are mere appendages due to custom; the real Gorgon is Medusa.'
—Jane Ellen Harrison

Cooch's the one thing always plays, Miz Forza told me, right from the start. And damn if I didn't come pretty quick to believe her 'bout that, just like I did 'bout so much else: Better than freaks, better than tricks, safer and more sure by far than creatures that required twice the feed of a grown man, not to mention a whole heap of mother-lorn care lest they catch ill and shit 'emselves to death, run wild and kill the rubes, or just bite at their own bellies 'til their guts fell out on the road.

Not that anything was really safe back then, in them dustbowl days of endless dirt and roaming; it was our stock in trade to hook folks in and get 'em riled up, after all, then see how much money we could pull from between their starving teeth before the inevitable backlash. The whole damn world was a half-stuffed firecracker, just as like to fizzle as it was to take your face off, and waiting on the spark—or maybe a mine dug deep in the mud of La Belle France of the kind Half-Face Joe used to tell tales on, a-whistling into Skinless Jenny's ear and flapping his flippered hands along for accompaniment, as though he was making shadow-dogs bark on Hell's own wall. After which Jenny would translate, her own uncertain voice sweet and slow as stoppered honey, while the lamplight flickered so bad it looked like every one of her Thousand and Ten Tattoos was dancing the low-down shimmy with each other.

Joe'd been a handsome young man once, 'fore them Europe kings and such got to squabbling with each other. Now he took tickets with a bag over his head 'til it was time to stump up on-stage and exhibit himself, making women and kids squeal and grown-ass men half-faint with his flesh's horrid ruin. In an odd way, he made a perfect palate-cleanser for the cooch show, too... always boiled the crowd off a bit, sent the ladies scurrying, leaving their menfolk ready to pay big for a bit of sweet after all that sour.

Them gaiety-gals was the real stars of the show, though, for all they came and went right quick—got picked up in one shit-hole town, dropped off again three more over, and never seen since. I didn't ever tend to look too hard at their faces, myself—why bother? Be it on-stage or off-, wasn't a one of us didn't know how with them, all true interest began to build strictly beneath the neck.

Five gals on either side, one in the middle. Ones on either side did their Little Egypt harem dance, the classic shake and grind, in outfits that flashed their hips, thighs, the fake jewels in their belly-cups, 'fore popping their front-closed brassieres apart to let their boobies sway free. One in the middle, though, whoever she might be that week—she was the real deal, the star attraction. The one who risked the full blow-off and lifted her split skirt high, let the rubes gape at the hidden-most part of herself while up above the Mask of Fear nodded and grinned, all pallid skin and bruisy eyes and dead snake hair hung in clusters like poison vine, adding a very particular sting indeed to her all-too-naked tail.

"I don't suppose you even know what this is," Miz Forza said to me, the first night I turned up shivering at their campfire with my hand half out, half not, just in case they took a notion to whip me for it. She had it hung up on a stand, like for wigs, and was stroking it all over with some foul-smelling stuff meant to keep it supple; the other gals all just sort of looked 'round it, shoving Miz Farwander's stew inside as fast as it'd go, like they was trying to forget how one of 'em would have to stick her head inside 'fore the next work-a-day was done.

What the Mask was made of I didn't know then, and didn't want to—but I sure did want me some of what else they had. So I squinted hard, then back up at the caravan's walls, which were covered in similar figures, their paint weather-worn yet still somehow bright, like fever.

"Looks like the Medusa, to me," I said, finally. "That old hag-lady with hissers for locks, who could turn men t'stone with one look-over. Some Greek fella cut her head off for her, hung it on his shield, an' used it to get him a princess t'marry. And then a horse with wings come out her neck, if I don't misremember."

The Mizes exchanged a glance at that, near to surprised as I'd ever seen 'em come. From the start, they read like sisters to me, though their names was different: Miz Forza was the smaller, dressed like a fortune-teller in a hundred trailing skirts and scarves, all a-riot with colour; Miz Farwander was tall as some men and tougher than most, never wore nothing more elaborate than a pair of bib overalls and a greasy pair of cowboy boots, with her hair crammed down inside an old newsboy's cap so tight she might as well be bald. Come to think, they neither of 'em liked to show their hair none—Miz Forza's was wrapped like rest of her in a scarf the colour of money, wound 'round with a string of old pewter coins. And she wore gloves, too, right up to her elbows, while Miz Farwander's hands were covered so deep in grime and such it was like they'd been dyed—black and grey, with no easy way to tell their fronts from their backs, except by what she was doing at the time.

And: "That's good," she said, approvingly, and grinned at me wide, so's I could see her teeth were all capped and shod in metal from east to west—metal of every sort: Silver, tin, steel, bronze, and even a hint or two of gold. "Ain't it? Most don't know the old tales, not anymore."

Miz Forza nodded back. "That's right, that's right; they do not, sad to say." To me: "And who was it taught you the right way of things, dear? Your mother, maybe? Grandmother?"

"That'd be my Ma. She loved all that old stuff."

"But you don't have no true Greek in you, do you, even so? Not by the shape of your face, or the colour of your eyes . . ."

I blushed a bit at that, though I tried not to, for I'd been twitted over these things often enough, in previous days.

"Don't rightly know," I said, shortly. "Don't rightly care too much, either . . . not 'less it'll get me a job, or some of that stew you're ladlin' out there. 'Cause if it will—"

Miz Farwander laughed. "If it will, then you're Greek through and through, ain't you—both sides for a hundred generations, all the way back to Deucalion's mother's bones? Aw, you don't have to answer, child; I can see you need feedin', sure as sin. And the storm-bringer Himself knows we got enough to go 'round."

Miz Forza cast eyes at her, sidelong, as though to warn her not to speak so free. But Miz Farwander just shrugged, so she turned back to me instead, asking—

"And what might your name be, gal? If you don't mind me askin'."

"Persia," I said. "Persia Leitner."

"That German?"

"For all's I know."

"Your Ma might be able to tell us."

"Might, if she was here," I allowed, the pain of that old wound seeping up through me once more. "But..."

Miz Forza nodded as though she'd heard all this before, which she probably had. "And you don't know your Pa either, I s'pose," she suggested, without any malice.

I grit my teeth. "S'pose not," I answered. "But I sure ain't the only one like that, 'round these parts."

"Oh, no, no, no. No, Persia... you surely ain't." A pause. "Sounds a bit like 'lightning', though, that name. Don't it?"

I'd never thought so, but that smell was making my mouth water hard, so I nodded. The gals all murmured amongst 'emselves, like a flock of cooing doves. And:

"It does, yes, now you mention," Miz Farwander told Miz Forza, musingly, as she passed the last cup they had on over—and even as I sunk my face in it, threw one more glance back and forth again right overtop me, like I wasn't even there. "It certainly does, at that."

You'll recall the pictures, no doubt—migrant mothers, carts jam-packed with Okies bound to pick or beg, Hoover camps in every mud-field and vacant lot. Houses buried window-deep in sand and milk-starved babies buried shameful shallow, or not even buried at all. They look like a bad dream now, or even lies, but they sure wasn't; I saw it all. Hell, I lived it.

When the crops dried and the dust come down to scour us clear, it was like every drop of colour just went out of the world—drained slow, way a man can die from one little cut alone, he only gets caught the exact wrong way. Like we was all of us being poisoned by coal-dust, or tin, or cheap nickel coating boiled off of pot-bottoms along with our daily mush, and didn't even know it. Oh, there was symptoms and that, which we mainly put down to hunger, a powerful thing; hunger will make your head ache and give you double vision, sure enough, under any circumstances.

But I can't think it was hunger alone that drove my Ma stark crazy, always following things from the corners of her eyes that simply weren't there to any other person's reckoning—not that, nor having no money, doing things with all manner of men that weren't none of 'em my Pa, always living hand to mouth, chased from town to town like dogs and thrown rocks at for grappling at scraps.

My Ma said my Pa was some gangster in Kansas City, and she'd had to run from him—or maybe it was *her* Pa she'd run from, who'd paid men to cram her in a car's trunk and dump her far from her home, to fend off the shame of her falling to ruin. But then again, sometimes she said my Pa was a wolf, or a burst of lightning, or the wind. Said he'd come winding through sunlight-wise under her window-shade one day, and fell headlong into her lap like a shower of gold.

He made me shiver, she told me. *Made me bow down, like Heaven's king himself. Persia, don't ever forget . . . he made you.*

I learned to hate just about every person I saw, during those days. While my Ma grew more and more tired, more and more silent, 'til the morning came she wouldn't say nothing at all, wouldn't even open her eyes. Wouldn't even call after me when I left her there by the roadside, sleeping under a tree like King Minos' daughter after the wine-god told old Theseus he wanted her for himself, so's he and his had better cut and run 'fore she woke up to complain about it.

I was glad she'd told me stories like that one, eventually; they gave me different ways to look at things and bright scenes to play out inside my head when I sore needed 'em—like radio-music to most, I guess, or those Motion Picture shows I never had a coin worth wasting on. Helped me make my mind up, and told me how one day I'd know I was right to do her like I did. But the further I got from her side, I found, they didn't give me no damn comfort at all.

It was on down that same road a spell I first met with the two Mizes, though, once Momma's face had faded into the same dust as everything else that ever fell behind me. And it was only 'cause of them yarns of hers I knew what-all tale them paintings on their caravan's side spelled out, which (like I told you) soon proved to at least count for something, in their eyes. With that one conversation, I gained what few keys to the kingdom they ever seemed like to dole out: The knowledge while this was their show, in the end, we at least had open invitation to try and keep up with it, for exactly so long as it suited them both that we should.

Miz Forza and Miz Farwander offered an open hand and a shut mouth, which was a hell of a lot more'n most; they didn't care where you'd been or where you was bound for, and they neither of 'em seemed to count the straight law as a friend. Hard work spent setting up and tearing down got you a share in whatever food might come their way, a part of the day's take and the right to sling your bed-roll near their fire.

"Depression", they called it, and that was the God's own truth. You felt it in your empty gut, your equal-empty chest, as though it was you who'd died instead of everybody else and all this living on you'd done was only a cruel trick, a walking ghost's delusion. Made your days so bone-weary it was like you was still dreaming—and not a good dream, either, nor yet a bad; nothing so easy. Most like them awful dreams you have where you work all day, then muse on doing the exact same thing all night, back-aching and useless: Ones you wake up from spent as ever, but with nothing to show for all your toil.

So the cooch, with its tinsel and soft light, its sway, its trailing crinolines... the curve of a woman's flesh barely wrapped, then peeled free by stages... that was a show worth the seeking out, for most men. And at the end of it all they went knees-down for a glimpse of that ultimate holy mystery, some girl's secretest parts shining like a rose on fire, exposed at the tangle crook of two thighs and framed in stocking-tops and musk.

Under the Mask or not, working cooch was fast cash that left almost no taste of sin behind. Unlikely as hell any of 'em would find herself recognised once she chose to move on, and we didn't truck with private viewing parties after the lights went down, either—not like most others did. Not unless someone pressed too hard for Half-Face Joe to handle, wouldn't resign himself to take "no" for an answer. And even then—

—well, we didn't tend to see those men again, no matter how short a time 'fore we swung back by their town, in future. And nobody, to my knowledge, ever did ask the two Mizes why.

Yeah, I saw how the cooch made fools and kings of men both at the same time, how it drew one common sigh wept out from twenty different mouths at once. Saw how it made 'em throw down pennies they couldn't afford, or stuff worn-soft bills they should've fed their kids with into the girls' garters with lust-shaking hands.

And I ain't too proud to admit it, either: After so much toil and sorrow, I wanted me a piece of that, cut big and steaming. Wanted it bad.

Lewis Boll I met in Miz Forza and Miz Farwander's service, too. He was twice my height but a third of my weight, lanky as a giraffe's colt, with squint blue eyes and a lick of too-long black hair that always fell down to brush his brows by noon, no matter how hard he slicked it back of a morning. He had stubble on his stubble, a shadow that started well before four o'clock and ran 'til right you could see exactly where his beard would go, if he just let it. And half-grown or not, he was the first boyfriend I ever had that seemed like a man. Lewis was a genuine Okie from way back in the Bowl, last left standing in a clan that'd once been thirty or so strong; he liked money far more'n he liked his liquor, so we had that in common. Right now he worked roustabout, wrangling ropes and poles for the cooch show tent, but his grand ambition was to either rob banks like Pretty Boy Floyd or get himself in my pants, whichever came first; sounded a deal nicer, the way he used to say it. But fine talk or not, he did get a tad nasty when I told him straight out which one it wasn't likeliest to be.

"What you savin' it for, Persia?" he demanded. "I'm gonna be rich— hell, we both are. What's mine'll be your'n, you just wait a while..."

"Uh huh. Well, holler back at me when you already got somethin' to swap me for it—'cause right now, what you 'n' me both got's 'bout the exact same amount of nothin' much. And that ain't enough to make me drop my drawers on-stage, let alone off—."

Lewis coloured a bit the choice of words, since he well knew where my ambitions lay: Up on that same podium with the rubes all panting up at me like begging dogs, and the Mask of Fear stuck fast to my kisser.

But: "You got your blood yet, Persia?" was all Miz Farwander asked me, back when I made my first play for the position. "No? Then you'll just have to wait, my darlin'. 'Cause we won't take no gal ain't bled yet."

"No indeed," Miz Forza chimed in from her crocheting in the caravan's corner, nodding right along. "No gal ain't bled can wear Her face, for us, or elsewise."

"She" was what they both called the Mask, though damn if I knew why—what everyone called it, even the gals who'd put it on, none of whom got to keep it for long. Like I said, they came and went; went faster than came, if I'd stopped to think on it. And the one time I collared one to quiz her on how it felt to be inside, she'd only shook her head, as though there weren't words enough to answer my question in the short span of time she had 'fore the next show rolled out.

"You just sort of have to be there," she said, finally. "Be in it. That then... that's when you'll know."

But being hungry makes a gal apt to stay maiden far longer than if she's well-fed, as I'd long since found out and hitherto been grateful for, seeing how it meant no matter what-all might occur along the road, I wasn't too like to catch myself a child from it. So all I could do 'til my courses came was sit there and watch Miz Forza handle the Mask of nights, curing its slack white face like leather with delicate strokes of that awful-stinking salve. Sometimes she'd raise it up so they was eye-to-eye and contemplate it a spell, mouth pursed and sad-set, like she ached to kiss it. Then Miz Farwander might brush by and pat Miz Forza's dainty-gloved fingers with her own grease-black ones, delicate enough to not even leave a smudge behind.

"Courage, my dear one," she'd murmur. "Her time will come again, and ours with it."

And: "I don't see how," Lewis said, from the other side of the fire. "That Greek fella of Persia's did for her way back when, ain't that so? Took a sword to her, and sawed her neck right through. Cut the head off a snake, what the body does after don't matter none; it's dead 'nough from then on, all the same."

Miz Farwander shot him a dark look. But Miz Forza just give a light little laugh, suitable to polite dining-room conversation.

"Oh, men do like to think that," she replied, to no one in particular. "But a woman like Her—She's right hard to kill, just like that serpent with a hundred heads: Strike off one, two grow back out, twice as poisonous. Cut off the head, more monsters just leak out; new monsters, maybe. Maybe even worse."

Agreed Miz Farwander: "A woman like that can strike every man alive blind, deaf and dumb without even tryin', root him to the spot and make him stand stock-still forever. That's why cooch plays so well, in the end; they say all's we are is pussy, but what comes from pussy, exactly? Blood, and dirt, and salt, and wet... poison like wine, fit to turn both heads on any man ain't queer. Any man, at all."

Lewis give a disgusted look, and spit hard.

"You bitches is somethin' else," he announced, probably aiming it my way, as much as theirs. But I'd still been following that last thought along, which was why I suddenly heard myself come out with —

"Well... everything does, don't it? Everything."

Miz Farwander grinned her too-sharp grin at that, all those metal fangs a-glint in the firelight, like scales on a skittering lizard.

"Reckon you got the right of it there, Persia. So don't you let no one tell you you ain't smart enough to keep up, not when it really counts."

That night Lewis took me up into the midst of a fallow corn-field to show me the gun he'd won in a card-game two nights back, and I let him kiss me 'til I was wet and panting, slip my shirt off my shoulders so's my titties could feel the night on 'em while up above a storm came rolling in, fast as Noah's Deluge. Don't rightly know why myself, but I wanted to, even if it wouldn't go no further; good enough reason for that night, at the very least.

But then ball-lightning started to roll back and forth 'cross the sky, snapping at the clouds like some big invisible body was riled near to bursting by the idea of what we were doing—and when he pushed his hand down under my skirt it come up dark red, copper-smelling, with proof of my sin come upon me at last smeared all the way up his palm to the wrist.

"Finally!" I blurted out. "Very first chance I get to run Miz Forza down, that damn-almighty Mask is mine!"

Lewis looked at me like I'd grew another head, then, and that made me angry—angry so much, I hardly couldn't speak.

"Don't want that for you," was all he said, shaking his head.

"What should I care what you want, Lewis Boll, 'for' me or elsewise? You ain't my damn Pa."

His eyes sparked. "That's 'cause you ain't got no Pa, Persia Leitner, nor no Ma neither; you did, maybe you wouldn't be 'spirin' to flash your trim at every Jack Henry got the fare. That stuff leaves a stain, gal, deep and deeper. Just 'cause it don't show on the face—"

"Oh, go on and shout it, preacher's boy! I'll have Her head to hide me, you fool; won't no one know me from Adam's house-cat, once that thing's fit on."

"'That 'thing' is right. Horrible goddamned . . ."

"It's a mask, is all. All of it! All of this. It's just a damn mask."

A mask. The Mask. Both, and neither.

I guess he thought we'd made promises to each other; he'd made 'em to me, anyways, that was true enough. But I never said a thing of the same sort back to him, and that's the fact, 'cause going by my Ma's experience alone I already knew better than to trust some snake-in-pants with my one and only future, no matter how much I liked him or how good his lips felt on mine. Any man made me shiver or want to bow down, that wasn't exactly a recommendation; quite the opposite.

So I left him there with his pecker out and I walked away stiff-backed, buttoning up my front again as I went, straight to the two Mizes' caravan. And when I made 'em my offer again, this time—

—they took it.

I remembered what my Ma said about that old hag-woman, Medusa. How she'd been young and pretty once, and her sisters alongside of her. How she'd been took up and played rough with by yet one more of them horny old god-Devils—the one who ruled the seas, might be? Him with his trident? And because he'd made sport of her in the temple of some goddess she served, it was her who had to bear the brunt of things when the goddess got angry, though only on her own behalf . . . Medusa who ended up getting cursed to monsterhood while the one who'd stole her virtue swum free, and the goddess she'd vowed her life to left her to weep in the ashes.

It was her sisters who stood by her then, and them only—they who were immortal, while she could be killed. They who took on the same monstrous form, and spun a spell so's that she could protect herself by turning any man fool enough to try and approach her to lifeless rock with her naked eyes alone, a human statue fit only to crack and crumble into dust.

But that one Greek fella who cut her down, he used a trick to 'scape her wrath—taught to him by the same goddess who'd took against her for all time, back when the sea-god had his way. He was a god's son himself, the cause of much unhappiness on his Ma's part, when her Pa saw what'd come to pass. And his name, his name . . .

. . . damn if his name wasn't almost same as mine, now I come to think.

But it took me a long time to recall that, afterwards. And by the time I did, at last . . . it truly didn't matter none.

No God but the one, down here where I was raised. And not too much of Him, neither, when things really counted.

Skinless Jenny helped me fit the Mask of Fear on that very night while the two Mizes watched, holding hands, and Half-Face Joe extolled my charms out front, racking up the take. I hadn't seen Lewis Boll all day, though the tent sure got itself up on time; thought maybe he'd finally run off to find himself a bank to knock over, and told myself I didn't much care.

I'd worried over my state, too, knowing what-all I was going to have to do in order to earn my money that night. But Miz Forza simply smiled, and called that last gal over—she gave me her Dutch Cap, all fresh-boiled and cleanly, to cram up inside myself. "Works just as well t'keep things in as it does t'keep 'em out," she confided, and I chose to believe her.

I barely recognised my own body in the dim bronze mirror hung up at the back, to make the tent seem bigger—so smoothed and plucked and powdered, legs shaved and wild half-whatever hair tamed to a fare-thee-well, pinned up under the Mask's slippery cap. I was a creature of myth, of legend, and where I moved I cast a net far wider than my gauze and crinolines alone could swing. My high heels clicked onto the stage like talons.

"Oh, you're a demigoddess like that, my sweet Persia," Miz Forza told me, admiring. "I always knew it, always. Didn't we, dear?"

"Yes indeed," Miz Farwander chimed back, nodding her head, her grin curling up on either side to show even more teeth than was usual. "Always. Right from when she told us what they called her."

And I saw her tongue poke out to touch her bottom lip, a bit too quick to notice, 'less you were looking at her straight-on—so long and red, so thin, a flickering spear. Almost as though it'd been sharpened.

Up above, the dregs of last night's storm still roiled, and the Mask felt hot and heavy against my sweating face. Behind one curtain, Skinless Jenny struck up on her dulcimer, hammers flying, skittering out trails of extra music while the gramophone ground on: Some mean old moanin' blues tune I half-remembered from earlier days when I'd heard my Ma humming it, leant up 'gainst the sill in some lousy little coal-town hostel—

Black mountain people, bad as they can be
I said black mountain people, they bad as they can be
They even uses gunpowder... to sweeten they tea...

While out from behind the other, meanwhile, my fellow cooch-gal handmaidens come trooping heel-to-toe, white arms waving languid as twister-shucked branches after the real wind's already blown by. Their palms were stained with henna and lip-rouge, a kiss pressed full-on at the centre of every one right where those lines that are supposed to map out love and marriage split apart—like they split apart now, so's the rubes (who were standing ass-to-elbow by that point) could catch their first glimpse of me in full regalia, with everything I had 'neath my jawline hanging out on display.

Oh, and I heard 'em make that single almighty gasp, too, as they did; Jesus, if it wasn't enough to make my own head swim same's if I'd been punched, under the Mask's brutal weight. Like a shot of that same rotgut I'd been proud to never touch a drop of, sped straight through 'tween my breasts and into my beating heart.

I let my own arms drift up, slow as parting black water. Let my own hot hands cup together 'neath Her face and made with a vampish pose, like I was Theda Bara. There in the spot's single bright column, I shook back both our heads together, and let them snaky locks fall where they may—up, down, to either side, so's my nipples rose up and peeped out like two new red eyes through a dreadful forest's wall of vines. Took my cue from Miz Farwander and stuck my tongue through Her slack mouth—far as it'd go and farther still, 'til it ached right to the root—to lick Her bluish-purple lips.

And as I thrust the Mask open 'round me, forcing myself inside, it was as though I felt myself crack open too, somehow. Felt Her enter into me, through every pore, at the very same time...

Which, of course, was right about the moment I finally noticed Lewis Boll standing in the third row back, with that gun of his already drawn and cocked the Two Mizes' raptly attendant way.

They can't see him, I thought. *Light's in their eyes—no way, no-how. Oh, goddamn him and goddamn me too. He's gonna go 'head and ruin every damn thing.*

"Gun!" one of the rubes yelled out, which let loose with a general backstumble, a crash and rip and the racket of thirty men with two feet apiece set off running flat-out, not caring who they might plough into, so long's they ended up out of range. The gals did much the same, scattering like mice when the kitchen door slams open. I saw Joe grab Jenny by the arm and haul her clear in mid hammer-fall, putting paid to half the music; one kick did for the other, as the gramophone needle skipped and tore 'cross the whole of the record at once.

An empty tent with the back half tore down and rain falling in—just me, Lewis and the Mizes, with me froze in place mother-naked and masked, sweat drying on my goose-pimpled everything. As he looked me right in the eye, or close enough, with his finger never straying from the trigger—stood there with his hat-brim dripping into his collar and told me, like it was some sorta damn foregone conclusion —

"Persia...you're comin' with me now, gal. Gonna leaves these two witches to their own damnation. We'll git married, have us some young'uns, live high; Law won't never catch us, not if we start out runnin' fast enough. Won't that be fine?"

And: Might have been, for some, was what I thought, but didn't say; *might still be, for you, with someone else. 'Cause... I just ain't that gal you're thinkin' of, Lewis Boll. Never was. Never will be.*

I looked at him, past him. Saw the dim bronze shadow of myself in Miz Farwander's mirror, looming over Lewis like an angry spectre, for all you could see the full range and extent of my shame. And as I kept on looking, I saw one of Her snakes—my snakes—start to move its slick green head, to rise and keep on rising like it planned to strike, flickering its impossible tongue out like a kindling flame.

And Lewis...

(oh, Lewis)

...for all he didn't see it too—for all he couldn't've—he went rigid, went grey, went heavy, went dead. Stood there while the stone spread fast all over him like mould does on cheese or a blush follows a slap, 'til Miz Forza stepped forward lightsome as always, took him by the elbow and pushed him off-balance, to shatter on impact with the raw dirt floor.

"There," she said, clapping her gloved hands. "That's that. And now we're alone again at last—just the three of us."

Upstairs, the thunder crashed, like God Himself was breaking rocks. But Miz Farwander simply shrugged her shoulders at it with a brisk little tut-tut noise, flicking her too-long tongue against her metal teeth, and told the sky above her:

"Oh, go on and howl all you want to, father-killer—you had your chance 'fore you let yourself get old, let the white Christ take half the whole world over and some host of no-name one-gods take the rest, with barely even a fight. But you still had to keep spillin' your seed hither and yon, didn't you, where we could get to it? And now it's done. We're three once more, whole and perfect, with nothing at all left to stop us."

She put one hand on my right arm as Miz Forza took my left, and the two of 'em drew me away—cooed at me, stroked me, told me to keep my eyes down 'til we was inside the caravan itself, for fear of any further accidents. And when we got inside they sat me down easy with my feet up, to give me some time to settle in and come to terms with what had happened; Miz Farwander made tea, while Miz Forza tipped a bottle of something into it—that salve she'd used to keep the Mask good-looking? I hoped not, but it sure to hell did stink almost the same —

I was shaking as I sipped, watching her slip off her gloves, so's I could see her hands clear for the first time ever: Black like Miz Farwander's, from tips to wrist. Exactly like.

They knit their four black hands together tight and rocked together, like they was almost about to cry. And I saw—

—I realised—

—remembering those sisters of Hers, who lived forever and took on Her ugliness, who made monsters of 'emselves even though they didn't have to, just so's She'd never have to be alone —

—that all their fingers were nails, and all those nails were claws. That their tongues were equal long and sharp, just as their teeth (metal or no) were fangs. That their hair was snakes too, come seeking out now from under cap and scarves alike, to say hello to mine.

For it was like Miz Farwander'd told my no-'count Pa, that ranting lightning-strike voice lost behind the thunder: We was all the same again, all three, at long last. Just like 'fore my head was cut off, and my spilt blood birthed out a horse with wings, in and amongst so many other equal-awful creatures.

I wear the Mask of Fear at all times now, shows notwithstanding, and am worn in turn: She is my face, I her body. To even try taking it off would rip us both apart and force the two Mizes to start over—something I could never countenance, even for my own comfort; I owe them so much, after all. And thus together we hold pride of place while Miz Forza sets at my right hand, Miz Farwander at my left, looking up at me with a swoony mutual love that I can't feel, startling-keen as any knife slid fast and sure 'tween the ribs.

We eat well, and plenty. I freeze 'em in their tracks, they knock 'em down. And the caravan moves on, moves on, through this new world with its ancient tides, the ebb and flow of inhumanity. Dustbowl's just a word to most, near nine decades gone, all but forgotten. Yet you only fool yourselves to think it's over, for though hunger may be better-hid, it is never far behind.

That's why cooch still plays, now as ever. Like it always did.

I take the stage nightly, hard and proud and cold, a dead light shining from my rigid face; I live always in company but always alone, obdurate, untouched, imperturbable. As though I too was turned to stone that night, so long past—me, Persia Leitner, who am now called by many other names: Sister, Dread Lady, Queen of Snakes, Mask of Fear. Poseidon's whore, Athena's injustice, Perseus's victim. Zeus's bane.

Medusa.

Next show starts right soon, rubes. C'mon inside, look up. Look hard. No, harder.

And now...

...let me show you somethin'.

Gemma Files' first novel, the self-described "blood-soaked gay porno black magic horse opera" *A Book of Tongues* (volume one of the *Hexslinger* series) (ChiZine Publications), won the 2011 *DarkScribe* Magazine Small Press Chill Black Quill award, in both the Editors' and Reader's Choice categories, and was also nominated for a Bram Stoker Award. Its sequel, *A Rope of Thorns*, was published in 2011, and will be followed in 2012 by a final book, *A Tree of Bones*.

"*Some Kind of Light Shines From Your Face* was inspired in equal parts by Greek mythology, HBO's *Carnivale*, and the Barbra Streisand-sung theme from the movie *Eyes of Laura Mars*," explains Gemma. "Most people forget that Medusa even had sisters, which seems a bit sad; I just wanted to give the Gorgonae their due, while also grubbing around for a while in dustbowl carnie Americana. Hope the result proves bleak enough for everyone's tastes."

SPLINTERS
Peter Crowther and Rio Youers

Gus rode into Retribution like he had the devil on his back. His oul' hoss ain't never been up to much ('that bindy-legged oul' bastage' is what he calls it), and Gus hisself ain't no ranny, but he threw a charge up its oul' ass and held on. For a time he even kept level with the linehumper out of La Junta, or so he tells me, but I can't rightly say if that's true, seeing as I was back at the homestead, adrift in tears. "She was rattlin' all aside me like a boxful of sins," Gus told me later, when all was done and the only sound was Aunt Maude in the kitchen, praying atween tears. "You shoulda seen me on that bindy-legged oul' bastage, Clementine. I was burnin' the breeze." I had an idea Gus was stretchin' the blanket, but I didn't say nothing. I just nodded and kindly smiled. God knows I was all out of words.

So Gus rode into town, fairly choking the horn, and I know he was at sixes and sevens but at least he had the good sense to make Saul Staenzer's Saloon his first stop. He figured that's where the men would be, and he figured right. "That doggery fell rightly silent when I walked in," he said, wanting me to believe he was all square-shouldered and big in his dustins, but I heard from Farren Landers that Gus was wide-eyed and close to crying. I can't hold that against him, given he's barely fifteen years old—still atween hay and grass, by God. And asides, we all cried that day. Even Farren (who *is* big in his dustins, make no mistake) shed a tear or two.

"I need help," Gus said. "As many men as can ride out. And come heeled. We got some God almighty disturbance afoot."

Farren told me that some of the men got to laughing, prob'ly at the sight of Gus all slack-jawed and knees knocking. Oul' Saul shook his head, poured a hit of firewater, and slid it on down the bar.

"Tame your tongue, boy," he said. "Get that on down, now. It'll steady your nerves, and maybe put some hair on your sack."

Now I seen Gus nipping at Grandma Zippity's bottle of firewater afore now, and always with a face turned inside-up. But he fairly bent his elbow at Saul's and took the hit in one. I'm not sure why and I never asked him, but I think it's 'cause he wanted to show them big guns that he was more than a shaver, no matter how his knees was knocking. Must've worked, too, 'cause the laughter smart dried up, and it was Farren hisself that stood up and said:

"What's got you all out of fix, boy?"

"An ungodly bag of nails," he answered in a hurry, and took off his hat so he could knock the sweat from his brow. "I ain't lyin', Mr. Landers, you got to cut dirt to the Willow place. Bring anyone as can shoot straight. Hell . . . bring anyone as can't."

He had the attention of near everyone in that doggery, including them that was fairly roostered. It was the look in his eyes, I think, more than the craziness spilling from atween his lips. Sort of intense but vulnerable at the same time; the eyes of a man (in this case a boy) that has seen something he shouldn't have. It had folks ascairt, I'd say. Even Slim McFarlane, who could talk a rattlesnake into sleep, was silent as a winter night.

Oul' Saul took hisself a hit of firewater. Some of the men stirred uneasy-like, just the sound of their leather creaking, and their steel on the dirty wooden floor. Farren stepped forward, opened his mouth to say something, then closed it again.

"It's an oul' shitstorm," Gus said, and bright tears spilled from his haunted eyes. He wiped them away and left dirt on his cheek.

Farren nodded, drew a circle in the air with his trigger finger, and whistled through his teeth. This got the fellers moving. They put on their hats and checked their irons set for fighting.

"Let's see what's got you tremblin', boy," Farren said.

Fifteen men left Retribution that afternoon, all dead-eye gunslingers, fire in their eyes and grit in their souls. Less than half would ride back, and them that did would never be the same. They saw bad and did worse, and something inside them broke forever. They spilled bullets and tears, and left their faith burning on the badlands.

I never thought you could kill a man's soul, but now I know different.

This oul' shitstorm started when Uncle Jack came back.

It had been raining all week. Devil-black storm clouds rumbled across the sky and brought their anger. Some of the trees on Big Horn Point lost their hold and came down heavy, and Brotherly River split its banks—fairly flooded-out oul' Josephine Byrd's place and she had to go live with her sourpuss sister east of Retribution. I never seen so much rain, I swear. Uncle Jack would've called it a regular toad strangler (Gus said as much and that got Aunt Maude all teary-eyed; there are times when I think Gus must have hoss-shit atween his ears). We didn't think it would let up, but by Friday afternoon most of the clouds had rolled northeast, and it had stopped raining by the time we went to bed. Saturday morning brought blue skies and sunshine. The world never looked so pretty, with everything green and clear, birds singing. We took breakfast on the porch, full of smiles, watching the water wash from the high pastures, down the steep hillside, and across the oul' dirt track.

That was when we saw Uncle Jack.

He stepped out from the woods and started down toward us, kind of shuffle-walking, as if he was learning from new. Gus jumped back so quick that he forgot he was sitting down—spilled backward over his chair and hit the porch so hard that I thought he might stay there a while. Any other time I would have laughed fit to piss my britches, but all I had inside me was a kind of hollow sound, like when you drop a pebble down the well. Grandma Zippity was solemn-faced as always, but she was rocking fast in her chair and I guessed that, under all them skirts, her oul' legs was fairly trembling. Aunt Maude wept and whispered prayers and clutched that cross around her neck. When I saw the palm of her hand some moments later, I noticed a bright red X set into the skin, deep as a boot print in wet dirt.

Uncle Jack shuffled closer and we could smell him now, carried on a breeze, like spoiled vegetables and turned earth. Baby Ellen wrinkled her nose.

"Don't be ascairt now," Grandma Zippity said. She stopped rocking and looked at each of us in turn. "It's your Uncle Jack and you know him well. Ain't no need for fearin'."

I can't rightly say that I was fearin'. I was too numb to feel much of anything. Gus had picked hisself up and taken my hand—as much for his comfort as mine—but I couldn't feel that, either. It was like I was floating in a bubble, drifting away and looking at a world that was suddenly out of true.

"I ain't sleepin' tonight," Gus whispered to me. I wondered if I'd ever sleep again, and opened my mouth to say as much but no sound came out.

Uncle Jack reached the porch steps and tried to get up 'em. He held the rail and his right leg trembled in the air, doing nothing, reminding me of the way Rufus, our oul' bloodhound, would lift his paw for a treat. He had three steps to get up, but couldn't make but one of 'em. It was Aunt Maude that got out of her seat to help him, tears spilling down her face. She held out her hand and that was when I saw the shape of the holy cross embedded in her palm. Uncle Jack took it and his lips quivered in what might have been a smile but I couldn't rightly tell.

"I think he done pooped his pants," Baby Ellen said, waving a hand in front of her nose a couple of times, and that made Grandma Zippity crack a smile. Just a little one, though, and then she tightened up again, right smart.

"Hush, child," she said.

Aunt Maude led Uncle Jack across the porch, hand in hand, and I imagined them on their wedding day, all those years ago, with the world's joy cooped in their hearts and those same hands tightly clasped. The first of many tears I would cry that day welled in my eyes and I blinked them away afore anybody could see.

"Sit down, Jack," Aunt Maude said, trying to keep her voice steady but not doing so good. She'd led him to the wicker chair by the door and pushed lightly on his shoulders. "Sit down afore you fall down."

Uncle Jack just stood there and made like he wanted to speak though it didn't seem to work. All that came out was air, rasping and wheezing like an oul' bellows, and I could see that Baby Ellen wanted to laugh but she didn't dare.

"Sit down, honey." Aunt Maude pushed on his shoulders again and he flopped into the chair with a sloppy thud. Grandma nodded and started rocking again, as if having Uncle Jack back was the most natural thing in all God's world. Aunt Maude didn't look so sure. She wiped her eyes and brushed loose hair from her forehead. One hand was on Uncle Jack's knee. The other was back clutching that holy cross, as if it was the only thing she could believe in.

I thought I should say something, being the oldest child 'n' all (and Uncle Jack's favourite, though I never told Gus and Ellen that), but I could hardly breathe, let alone speak. In the end I reached deep and found something. They was words—just four of 'em—spoken soft . . . but *loud*, somehow. I can't rightly explain that, except to say that I think it's 'cause I spoke with my heart, and not my mouth.

"Welcome home, Uncle Jack," I said.

He looked at me and smiled, and that set the tears rolling again. It was his eyes, you see. His lips barely twitched but his eyes fell wide and they was filled with love, and for just a moment it was the *old* Uncle Jack sitting there . . . the man that had bounced me on his knee when I was a little girl—bounced until I couldn't laugh no harder; the man that had lifted me on his shoulders and run around the yard, making them chickens scatter 'n' flurry, with me flapping my arms and pretending to be a bird. *You got the prettiest feathers in all the land, Clementine,* he'd say, and that always made me happy. And the feel of his strong hands around my ankles, holding gentle, but firm-like. That made me happy, too, 'cause I knew he'd never drop me.

He smiled, and I saw him again. Uncle Jack. He reached out his hand and I took it. And he was cold. *So* cold. I knew he would be, but it still made me sad.

We all looked at him for a moment, not saying nothing. Only sounds was the squeak of Grandma's rocker, the morning birds singing their happy little hearts out, and—down the path apiece—Pa working in his shed, hitting something with a hammer. I wondered what Pa would say when he came in to take lunch and saw Uncle Jack sitting at the kitchen table, rightly helping hisself to bread and soup. I ain't never seen Pa at a loss for words, but I reckoned I would afore the day was done.

That said, Uncle Jack wasn't sitting at no kitchen table in his present getup. Grandma Zippity wouldn't have none of it. He hadn't smelled too good when he'd arrived and he smelled a whole lot worse having set around a few minutes, and sure as shootin' nobody wanted to be *eating* around him. Even outside, in the fresh air, the stench was settling like graveyard mist, so thick you could almost see it . . . like the heat haze on one of them macadamed roads, or the shimmering comes up from fresh-laid manure (I favour the second of them comparisons, mainly 'cause of the smell and all). Also, he was covered in mud and sludge, all stuck in his hair and clotted in his ears, and that handsome suit he wore to church every Sunday morning was rightly ruined—all torn up, with mould in the seams and buttons missing. And there was something else, too. It took me a while to place it (I was rightly out of fix, after all), but when I did I guess Baby Ellen noticed it at the same time, 'cause she upped and said:

"Hey, Unca . . . you got a piece of wood through your nose."

And he had! A long piece—some kind of splinter, like a needle. And then I noticed his right hand (still held in mine, but it was the first time I really looked at it) and saw the nails all broke, with more wood shards going through the soft flesh of his fingertips. His left hand was the same. Split nails and full of splinters.

"Where you been, Unca?" Baby Ellen asked, but she was only five years old and didn't understand. Uncle Jack just shook his head, waving his splintered hand nevermind, not saying nothing.

"He's been over," is what Grandma Zippity said. Her rocker squeaked and her face was cast like stone.

"Hush, Serendipity," Aunt Maude said.

There was noises coming from Uncle Jack's stomach. I imagined storm clouds in there, boiling and raining. Worse rumblings was coming from the seat of his muddy oul' pants and I think Baby Ellen was set to shout out, *'Hoo-eeey!'* but Aunt Maude made a face and she stayed quiet.

"Been over," Grandma Zippity said again, chair rocking. "And he's got to go back."

"Not yet." Aunt Maude's words was whispered but firm. "He came to say hello. Least we can do is give him a moment."

"It ain't right."

"Just hush."

Uncle Jack kindly sat there, almost smiling, his head moving in little jerks as if it was attached to his neck by a rusty joint. I got to thinking that he was trying to fit back in—sitting there like he was, as if the world was all-level, nothing amiss. But them rumbling noises from his belly and ass—not to mention the smell—said mighty different.

I dropped his hand with a little squeal when an earwiggy crawled out from under his cuff and skitter-clicked across my fingers.

"I know why he's here," Grandma Zippity said. She pointed at the splinter in her son's nose and said, "It's the wood." And the wind lifted up a piece of her hair and set it to tumbling across her forehead.

We all knew the story of the wood, right enough.

Grandma had bought it from one of them traveling fellers, come to town on the saddle of a dust-wind, selling tonics and lotions, pills and potions. She bought it along with a remedy for leg cramps, a jar of Abe Lincoln's breath (still unopened in the cellar, its label all mildewed and the edges sticking up), and a pocketbook that would never be empty. "As sure as God Hisownself is my judge," the feller had added.

It wasn't a big piece of wood. Not much bigger than Pa's thumb, I'd say, and not cut from any tree we recognised. Too dark to be maple. Not hard enough to be hickory. *Ain't from these woods,* Uncle Jack had said, and Pa—who has sawed down more than a few trees in his time—rightly agreed. This all satisfied Grandma Zippity, 'cause it tied in with what the snake-eyed salesman had told her. With hand on heart he'd declared that the wood was come from the Cross itself, a splinter from the very pieces that they'd nailed up the good Lord on all them years ago. Hearing this, Grandma Zippity handed over two not-so-crisp dollar bills, and used the wood as kind of a 'tallies-man'—her word—against stuff. (By stuff, Grandma meant pretty much everything from preventing a rainstorm when she'd just hung out a yard of washing, all the way to making the blood in her poops and the marble-sized hard lump in her left tit just fade away to nothing.)

Like everyone else (except Grandma, of course), I didn't much hold on with the notion of this piece of wood being nothing special but we went along.

Well, over the years, the wood got itself smoothed down with everyone touching it—sometimes just a finger or two, whisper-like, and other times gripping all white-knuckled, like it was all that kept them from dropping off the edge of the world.

And, to be fair, Grandma Zippity had herself a good life... leastways as good a one as a body should reasonably expect. She'd been married for near-forty years to Arnold Chisholm, and together they'd brought six healthy children into the world—five girls and a boy. Grandpa Arnold lived long and died of the yellow fever twelve years ago (the only thing I remember about him is the wispy cloud of white hair atop his head). But this past July their only son, Jacob—my Uncle Jack—went and got hisself bushwacked by a bunch of Injuns over to the woods. It was quite a talking point, seeing as how most redskins kept to the reservation over to Cheyenne or the boardwalk out front of Saul Staenzer's Saloon.

I remember seeing Uncle Jack in his coffin, dressed fine in his Sunday suit, fresh and clean, as if he was going to meet the President, rather than being put in a hole in the ground. My Uncle Jack, with his strong hands and broad shoulders, made to nothing by a bunch of thieving redskins that didn't care how big his heart was, or that he sometimes brought Aunt Maude flowers just 'cause he liked to see her smile.

I recall watching Grandma Zippity step to her son's pine box, her oul' face wet with tears. She kissed her boy (Uncle Jack was touching forty years old, but he was still her boy), opened her left hand, and there was the piece of wood—the splinter—kindly sitting in the middle of her palm. Then she lifted one of Uncle Jack's hands from where it was crossed atop his chest, and placed that holy splinter inside, curling his fingers tight around it. She kissed him again and stepped away. The lid went on the box, and the box—with Uncle Jack and the splinter inside—went in the boneyard on Sanctuary Hill.

And that was that. Or so we thought.

"Guh," Uncle Jack said. Not a word so much as the sound of his tongue clicking off the roof of his mouth. "Guh . . . *guh*."

"What is it, honey?" Aunt Maude asked.

"Guh."

More thundering sounds broke from his oul' ass and this time Gus waved a hand in front of his face and took a few steps back. "God's Teeth!" he said.

"God's Teeth!" Baby Ellen rightly echoed, giggling and flapping a hand of her own. "*Hooo-eeey*, Unca Jack. God's Teeth!"

Grandma Zippity, face like bark, whipped out her hand and cuffed Baby Ellen's ear. "You apologise to your Uncle Jack, child. And apologise to God in your prayers."

Her eyes got big with surprised tears. She nodded. "Sorry, Unca Jack."

"Guh."

"Sorry, God," she added.

"In your prayers, I said."

"He can still hear me, Grandma."

"That He can. Alrighty, then." And then Grandma Zippity fixed her attention on Gus, with him standing too far away to whack. "I'll deal with you later, cuss boy! Taking God's good name, like so."

"Yes, Grandma."

"Long-leggedy strip o' piss, ain't ya?"

"Yes, Grandma."

"Guh."

Aunt Maude was fretting with Uncle Jack during this exchange. "He's wanting something," she said, and looked at me, as if I understood what-all 'Guh' meant.

"I'm sure I don't know, Aunt Maude," I said.

She shook her head, all harried and desperate, and turned back to Uncle Jack. "What is it, honey? You tell me what you want."

He dragged his eyes to her all too slowly. "Guh."

"I can't rightly—"

"*Guh.*" I guess Uncle Jack knew he wasn't making no sense 'cause he started making motions with his hands. He held the left'n out to his side, them splintered fingers curled inward, and the right'n he moved up and down over his chest, like he was strumming an invisible—

"Guitar," I said. "Uncle Jack done wants his guitar, Aunt Maude."

He looked at me and smiled again, and I thought of him telling me that I had the prettiest feathers in all the land, and I kindly smiled back.

"Gus," Grandma snapped. "Go on and fetch your Uncle Jack's guitar. And put some grease on them heels, by God."

"Yes, Grandma."

"Y'oul' leggedy strip o' piss."

"Yes, Grandma."

So Gus shot off to fetch Uncle Jack's guitar, leaving us on the porch to listen to the sweet morning birdsong, the almost rhythmic squeaking of Grandma's rocker, and the not-so-fair sounds of Uncle Jack's nasty oul' ass (cuffed ear or not, Baby Ellen was grinning again, and I wished I had her flower-like innocence). Every now and then we'd hear the clang of Pa's hammer, and I was about to suggest that someone oughta go down and tell him about the happ'nings, when Gus came back with the guitar and Uncle Jack, all excited, fair leapt up and shouted:

"*Guh!*"

Gus grinned and handed Uncle Jack the guitar. "Here you go, Uncle Jack. Play us a sweet oul' song now, just like you used to when you was... well, you know... afore you..." He nodded at Uncle Jack, sat down, and rightly shut up.

Uncle Jack set the guitar across one knee, placed his splintered fingers on them strings, and played a bone-rattling chord. We all smiled and nodded, as if it was the prettiest sound we'd ever heard, but Uncle Jack knew different. He shook his head, farted twice, and tried again. Another bone-rattler that shook the birds from the trees. "Nuh," he said, and his bottom lip kindly pooched out. He tried a third time, his fingers trembling on the fretboard, and it made my heart bleed to see him struggling so. I could be mistaken, but I think Uncle Jack was using that guitar as a kind of test. If he could play it again—play us a sweet oul' song, just like he used to—then he'd be proving to us, and hisself, that he was ready to live with us again. Sure, he might be a little slow in learning how to do everything from new, but he'd get there in the end.

It all came down to the guitar, though. And that's why he was trying so hard. If he could play... he could stay.

We sat listening to him for what seemed like three hours but was prob'ly only five minutes, maybe ten. Uncle Jack moaned, all poochy-lipped and anxious. The guitar made plinkin' and plunkin' sounds, and every now and then he'd strike something that sounded roundabout decent, maybe by accident, and his eyes would light up all happy-like, and the next time he tried there'd be that bone-jarring sound again and I thought he'd cry.

"It's okay, Uncle Jack," I said. "You take your time, now. It's okay."

But I wasn't sure he had much time. Grandma Zippity got out of her rocker with a grunt and said to Aunt Maude, "We need to talk. In the kitchen."

"But, Serendipity, I just—"

"*Now*, Maude." She hobbled along the porch boards, her joints squeaking like the rocker. "Y'all stay out here with your Uncle Jack. And you—" She pointed at Gus, who shrank back as if her finger could bite him. "Keep that pie-hole closed. The Baby Jesus is listenin'."

"Yes, Grandma."

"Clementine, look out for Baby Ellen, now."

"Yes, Grandma."

She squeaked back into the house and Aunt Maude followed, her eyes dark and downcast. Uncle Jack watched her go. His jaw trembled and his fingers still tried to make something good come out of that guitar. I gave him the warmest smile I could find, but I was nearest the door and half my attention was on the conversation atween Grandma Zippity and Aunt Maude. I didn't hear it all, but I heard enough.

"Can't he just stay a while?" Aunt Maude asked. "He ain't hurtin' no one."

"He's hurtin' his pride, Maude. His memory."

"I don't see how."

"He's got a piece of wood jammed up his nose and there's bugs a-crawlin' out of his clothes," Grandma said. There was a thud that I thought was prob'ly her heel coming down on the floor. "And in case you didn't notice, he's shittin' his pants like his oul' ass has fallen out. God in Heaven, Maude, how much more pride can a man lose?"

Aunt Maude muttered something that I didn't catch and Uncle Jack continued to 'play' the guitar, his splintered fingers scratching along the fretboard, making it sound like a cat was pawing up and down the strings. Gus and Baby Ellen sat all quiet, lost in their own thoughts. I looked at them, then out at the woods that Uncle Jack had shuffled from, where the shadows were deep and the birds was complaining. Something caught my eye. Something moving in there. I blinked hard and looked again, but didn't see it no more. Prob'ly just the shadows, I thought.

"—get Thomas to build him a new box," Aunt Maude was saying now. "Then we can say our goodbyes and put him back."

"Won't do no good," Grandma said, trying to keep her voice hushed but I still heard her. "Leastways not until we settle him down some."

"Settle him down?" Aunt Maude asked. "How are we going to do that?"

My heart was already running at a goodly clip, but I felt it fairly gallop when I trained my ear closer to the door and heard Grandma Zippity say:

"Thomas has got tools. Axes and saws. Sharp as the devil's wit."

"Oh no!" Aunt Maude said, and I felt sick inside. I think even Uncle Jack had a sense of what his wife and ma was jawin' about, 'cause he said, "Nuh-*nuuuuh*," and ran his fingers over the strings, trying to find even a single note that didn't sound all broken.

"It's the only way," Grandma Zippity said, and I heard the thud of her heel again.

"No, Serendipity. *Please.*"

"He ain't got no rights being here with us now," Grandma said. "You don't have to watch, Maude. I wouldn't expect you to, neither. Just take him on down to Thomas, kiss him goodbye, and come on back."

"I can't, Serendipity. Lord and Jesus please. I *can't.*"

They continued to jaw but I couldn't hear nothing 'cause of Uncle Jack's guitar—that and the thump of my heartbeat in my head, as if one of them oul' boys from the Retribution Marching Band was banging his drum up there, and rightly stomping his dustins at the same time. I thought of grabbing Uncle Jack and riding someplace distant...just keep going until I found him a nice little patch in the wilds where he could play his guitar and sleep under the stars. But I knew in my fiercely aching heart that Grandma Zippity was right. Uncle Jack had been over, and he had to go back. It was God's will. And I know he wanted to stay with us, 'cause he loved us, but I also know that he didn't want to be in such a wretchedly state. He was rotted through and coming apart at the seams, same as that suit he was wearing. As much as it pained me to admit it, Grandma Zippity was shooting straight: Uncle Jack had to go back in the ground, but first he had to be settled.

I caught the back-end of Grandma saying. "—can't get down that path. Not with my oul' hips."

"But, Serendipity...you *can't* expect me to take him."

"Someone got to," Grandma said, and I knew who that someone would be. Sure enough, the door opened and out squeaked Grandma Zippity, followed by Aunt Maude, wiping her eyes. They was so red I thought she could see in the dark. Uncle Jack reached for her hand and she took it and squeezed.

"Clementine," Grandma said, dropping back into her rocker. "Take Uncle Jack down the path to your pa. Tell him he needs to be settled."

"Nuh." Uncle Jack made desperate sounds on the guitar.

"Settled?" I asked. I glanced up at the woods and thought I saw movement again. Wasn't no shadows, neither. Something was up there. Or someone.

"You heard me," Grandma said firmly. "Your pa will know what to do. Then you hurry your britches back here, girl. Right smart. You hearin' me?"

SPLINTERS

I looked away from the woods and nodded. "I'm hearing you, Grandma."

So I took Uncle Jack down the path, but not afore he and Aunt Maude said their goodbyes, and that was just a heartbreaker—can't hardly bring myself to think of it again. Of course, they didn't get to say goodbye afore, so this time made up for all. Uncle Jack pulled her close and wrapped his arms around her waist, and Aunt Maude didn't care that he was smelling like an oul' bag of hoss-feed, or that his skin was fair-slewing off'n his bones like a cooked turkey. He kissed her and his face made all the crying motions, but no tears came from his eyes, and I guess that was just fine 'cause Aunt Maude had tears for them both.

"Goodbye, honey," she said.

"Guh-eeeeeh." His bottom lip had pooched out again.

Grandma Zippity stepped toward him, grabbed that splinter in his nose, and pulled it out. Black sludge poured from the hole it left behind and trickled over his lips.

"I pray you find peace, son," she said.

"Eeesh," Uncle Jack said.

Later on I heard Grandma tell Pa that she buried that piece o' the Cross with Uncle Jack 'cause she thought it would bring him closer to the Lord. And Pa shouted at her: "Damn fool woman." And she done wailed back about his foul cussin' mouth and didn't he know the Baby Jesus was listenin' (though she didn't mention the Baby Ellen), and he called her a crazed oul' coot and didn't *she* know that with her precious 'tallies-man' and all that rain, that she had done made Resurrection Soup.

For all this, I don't know how Grandma's piece o' the Cross got from Uncle Jack's hand into his left nostril, but I know for a fact that the heavy rains washed through Sanctuary Hill and dislodged more than a few boxes—Uncle Jack's being one of 'em. I can see in my head (though I wish I couldn't) Uncle Jack's co'pse slumping sideways, and his hand flopping up and jabbing that holy splinter right through his nose. Then his eyes open in the wet darkness and he starts scratching at the lid of that box... and all this time the rain is washing through, and the juju that done woke him up (and I can only imagine that a piece of the holy Cross would be some mighty potent juju) is kindly trickling downhill, mixing with the mud 'n' sludge and rightly pouring into all them other boxes.

Resurrection Soup.

Anyways, Grandma Zippity and Aunt Maude went inside, with Gus and Baby Ellen close behind, leaving me and Uncle Jack on the porch. He grabbed his guitar, looked at me, but couldn't find a smile.

"Let's go, Uncle Jack," I said.

We walked down the path together. The sky was dusty blue and the birds was singing again. Uncle Jack carried his guitar and held out his hand for me to take. And I did. I held his hand tight and it didn't feel right but I didn't care.

Thomas Flynn—my pa—got his nickname, the Irish Bear, 'cause he stands clear over six feet tall and is covered, back 'n' all, in thick black hair. His arms are as thick as most men's legs and he knows how to work, by God. He'll build a table, a barn, sling hay, fell trees, break hosses, shovel cowshit...whatever it takes to earn a greenback. My pa ain't afraid of no work. Never has been. Ma was struck dead by consumption three years ago and he does a fine job of making sure that me, Gus, and Baby Ellen are taken care of. Not only that, but he provides for Aunt Maude and Grandma Zippity, too—them being widowed 'n' all. Uncle Jack brought us all into his house just after Ma—his sister—died, and Pa has always made sure there's clothes on our backs and food on the table.

I remember Gus being little—Baby Ellen's age—and asking Pa if bullets bounced off'n him. Pa had smiled and scooped Baby Gus into one arm and told him that bullets don't bounce off'n nobody, and that he'd do well to remember that. But I know why Gus asked that question. Pa gives off that powerful quality...like when you see one of them big machines running, all gears and cogs oiled and turning, and you think that it'll run forever. I ain't never seen Pa hurting (not even when he whacks his thumb with that oul' hammer). I ain't never seen his tears. I think maybe he *does* cry, but he keeps them from us. I think maybe God cries sometimes, too. I really do.

And there are times when I think Pa *is* God. I saw him carrying a tree once. A *whole* tree. And it wasn't no small tree, neither.

Anyways, I ain't never seen him ruffled, but when I walked down the path holding Uncle Jack's hand, Pa done cried out and staggered back, rightly dropping his hammer so as he could make the Sign of the Cross.

"Lord and God-Jaysus," he said, and fell on his ass. Pa cusses with an Irish accent, even though he was born and bred here in Steel County—the seventh son of Patrick and Brenda Flynn, who crossed the mighty ocean from Galway some fifty years ago.

"Darh," Uncle Jack said. I think he was trying to say *Tom*, and figured that if he stuck around much longer I'd be able to understand him, the way you can sometimes understand a baby's burbles and half-words. Anyways, I didn't say nothing, on account of being some amazed at seeing Pa so flustered he done fell on his ass.

"Jack...Jack, by God, what...?" Pa's eyes was bug-wide and he picked hisself up (perhaps a little embarrassed that he'd fallen down in front of me), smearing mud from the seat of his pants, his mouth moving silently. I remember thinking earlier that I might see him at a loss for words, and sure enough here it was, but it didn't give me no satisfaction.

"Hi, Pa," I said.

"What...Jack...?"

"He came back this morning," I said.

"What...?" Pa looked from Jack to me, beads of sweat shining on the few parts of his face that wasn't growing hair. Then I saw his eyes fix on our clasped hands, and thought they was going to pop out of his skull and fall in the mud.

"It's fine," I said.

"Clemmie, Jaysus," he said, and he grabbed my arm and pulled me away from Uncle Jack—pulled so hard that my feet left the ground.

"It's fine," I said again, rubbing my arm.

"It's ungodly," Pa said, pointing at Uncle Jack. "It's... it's *unholy*, by Christ."

"Well, that it ain't," I said. "On account as it was Grandma's piece o' the Cross that brought him back."

Uncle Jack said, "Guh," and held up his guitar.

"That's right, Uncle Jack," I said. "Guitar. That's good." And then I said to Pa, "I'm sure it's lots of things, Pa, but unholy ain't one of them."

"Piece o' the Cross?" Pa said. His face was screwed up but his eyes was still wide. "What...that *splinter*?"

"Yes, sir," I said.

"She done *buried* him with it?"

"It was done stuck up his nose," I said.

Pa shook his head and pushed his big hands through his hair. "I swear that oul' bitch is as crazy as a bag of hammers." And he gave me a look that said I'd better not repeat that.

Uncle Jack let rip a couple of loud farts—what Pa hisself would have called crack-splitters, under more befitting circumstances—and gave his guitar a peg-shakin' strum. Pa winced and shook his head again.

"Did the world stop spinnin', Clemmie?" he asked.

"Not that I know of, sir."

"Mayhap all that rain brought up the deuce, like a big oul' worm."

"It ain't the devil's doin's, Pa," I said.

"I ain't so sure."

"Guh," Uncle Jack said, and strummed again.

"Grandma says he's got to go back," I said to Pa, and my eyes kindly flicked to the handsaw hanging in his shed. Its blade shone like the Brotherly on a June morning. "But first, she says, you got to settle him down some."

"Settle him . . . ?" Pa followed my eyes to the handsaw and said, "Oh."

I nodded and looked at him, my insides all twisted with emotion, my heart still drumming. There was so much to say but it all bottlenecked trying to get out, and in the end all I could do was smile all sad and squeeze his arm.

"Right," he said, scratching his bearded chin, sawdust flaking out of it. "Best you run along, Clemmie, leave me and Uncle—"

His words was cut off by a scream from the direction of the house, and I ain't lying when I say it was blood-curdling. Everything inside me turned cold and my golden hair lifted at the roots. Pa grabbed his saw from the shed and started running. I was only a step or two behind, but no sooner had we started up the path than a shot let out.

"Who the sweet Jaysus they shootin' at up there?" Pa asked. He stopped and looked at me like I was going to be able to tell him, but I couldn't. We was in the dip behind the crest of the hill leading up to the house so we couldn't see but the roof. We could hear, though . . . a whole lot of crying and shouting. Then another shot.

Pa was running again. "You stay down here, Clemmie. Understand?"

In that brief moment I realized with sure-fire certainty that we're none of us going to live forever, and I got a wave of pride for my daddy, hi-tailin' it up that path to who knew what, with only a handsaw to protect hisself.

"No, sir, I surely *don't* understand," I shouted to him. "I's a-comin' with you."

Pa disappeared over the brow of the hill and I wasn't far behind (we'd left Uncle Jack back at the shed, strumming and farting in unmelodious harmony—settling him down would have to wait). Another shot rang out and I shuddered. As it died away I heard Pa shout out, "Great Jaysus!" A few seconds later, as I followed him over the brow, I saw why.

I'm only seventeen years old. Barely a woman. Until that morning the most exciting—and upsetting—thing I ever saw was Rusty 'Coldeye' Slater and his nefarious gang take a necktie social behind the Marshall's office in Retribution (hearing five necks crack at the same time can colour a girl's dreams, believe me). But what I saw when I came over the brow made that five-man hemp party look like chicken feed. Now, I might live another fifty-some years, but I know as sure as God made little green apples that I won't never see the likes of it again.

Leastways, I *hope* not.

Dead folk was shuffling out of the woods, crossing the pasture toward our house, and all of them rag-torn and rightly stinking. I saw Mean Joe Wallace (who took a necktie social of his own two years ago), walking kind of sideways on account of his neck being broke and he couldn't turn it straightways. Another oul' moss-back was trying to keep his rotted guts from falling out of the hole in his belly. I saw something long and dark slip through his fingers and coil in the grass like a hisser. He left it there and kept walking.

I counted two dozen co'pses, shambling slow but sure across the field, and there was more coming... fairly pouring through the woods, some slipping in the wet mud but picking themselves up and shuffling on.

I think my heart done stop beating. I really do. I remember Pa asking if all that rain had brought up the deuce, and thought he might be right, after all.

"Jesus help us," I said, and then gunshot cracked the sky. I screamed and staggered back, looking in the direction of the blast. Grandma Zippity stood solid on the porch with her trusty Winchester socked into one shoulder. She called for Gus and then squeezed off another shot, hitting Yancy Morlins—who taught me to read when I was six years old—plum in the chest and knocking him clean out of his stogies.

Yancy hopped right back up and carried on walking... even though you could see the trees behind him through the hole in his chest.

They *all* carried on walking. Cold as waggon tyres, all of 'em, yet on they walked.

Pa had froze on the spot, his saw flashing sunlight and making a wobbly sound. I was right behind him.

"Jaysus wept," I heard him say.

"*GUS!*" Grandma screamed.

"I'm right here, Grandma," Gus said.

"Ride into town, y'oul' leggedy strip o' piss," Grandma squealed. She loosed another shot that took off'n the top of Jenny Ripley's head. "Ride like the wind and fetch help. The whole dang bone orchard is a-walkin'."

I remember the good days: Pa cradling me in the palm of his hand as if I was no bigger than a pear; me and Ma picking flowers in Dreaming Field—so many flowers, until I could see their petals even when I closed my eyes; Grandma Zippity telling tall tales by the fire, and I wanted to believe them just 'cause her face looked so lovely in the flickering light; Uncle Jack flying me on his shoulders and getting the chickens all-overish, with me laughing fit to split seams. Good oul' Uncle Jack. What I remember most is how he would play his guitar in the barn. He liked the barn, he said, 'cause of what he called the koo-sticks. *Them koo-sticks are right fine in that oul' barn,* he'd say. *It's like there's three guitars a-playin'.* You'd often find him out there of an afternoon, sitting on a bundle of hay with his guitar on one knee, playing such sweet melodies. The birds would come to him, too. Doves and pigeons. Even bluebirds. They'd line the rafters in the loft and softly sing along. It was pretty to see, and even prettier to hear. Sometimes Aunt Maude would sit cross-legged on the barn floor and listen to him play, kindly swaying, flowers in her hair.

Yes, sir... I remember the good days.

Uncle Jack bought this oul' farm some ten years ago. It was full-running back then, even though it was small—less than ten acres, end to end, given to crops and cattle. Uncle Jack sold off a goodly chunk of that land and most of the cows, too. He kept the barn (how he loved that barn), a small cornfield, and a lucky-seven head of cattle. Uncle Jack was a blacksmith and he didn't take to farming—kept just enough to manage; he bought this place 'cause he liked the farmhouse. It was a good size and it caught the sunlight. He liked the location even more. Two miles east of Retribution and surrounded by the bright drips of God's paintbrush: pastures that turn from green to yellow; the reddish peaks of the Copperhead Mountains to the north; the blue drift of Brotherly River; the brown and green of towering trees.

Beyond these trees—called Chiming Woods by townsfolk, on account of the sound the wind makes blowing through 'em—the ground rises steady afore falling away into a valley where Black Eyed Susan grows in broad yellow waves. Beyond this the ground climbs again to a plateau crested with spruce and ridges of sandstone, poking from the earth like knuckles. The eastern slope of this plateau is Sanctuary Hill—Retribution's one and only cemetery, and the final resting place for so many folk, ne'er-do-wells and loved ones alike.

Except—thanks to Grandma's piece o' the Cross—they didn't rest so final.

The rain turned Sanctuary Hill into one big mudslick. Stones toppled and boxes was coughed from the ground, all slewing downhill in muddy drifts. Some of them boxes was already rotted through and the co'pses spilled out all slick and pale, like fish from a creel. I don't know at what point they all upped and started walking around, but Grandma's piece o' the Cross added some spice to that muddy oul' pot, powerful enough to stir even the deadest of the dead. (I saw more than a few skelingtons, less meat on 'em than a chicken leg, kindly strolling through the pastures as if they had eyes in their skulls and lips for whistling.) I'm guessing they wandered aimlessly to begin with, except for Uncle Jack, who was fresh-dead and had enough brains to remember home. And so he shuffled... through the valley of Black Eyed Susan, up the hill (stumbling 'n' farting), through Chiming Woods, and then down across the pasture to where we was all sitting on the porch.

The rest of 'em followed when they heard the sound of his guitar.

This I know.

Everything from then on happened quickly, and for this, if nothing else, I thank the Lord.

Farren's boys rode in like another storm, their hosses snorting and splashing up mud. I heard Grandma Zippity cry out, lungs fairly booming: "Here comes the goddam cavalry, you dead sumbitches." (She must've forgotten that the Baby Jesus was listenin'.) I only *heard* her 'cause I was back in the house by this time—fairly carried in by Pa who told me to stay put and not come outside no matter what. "What if one of them dead folks gets in?" I asked, thinking mostly of Ennis Jenkins, who I saw carrying his own head like a bag of coins. Pa didn't answer. He just glared at me and I saw another reason why they call him the Irish Bear, showing his teeth and seeming twice as big. "Look out for Baby Ellen," he stormed, and walked out with his saw on one shoulder. Well, Aunt Maude was looking out for Baby Ellen—they was rightly cowering in the cellar—so I ran upstairs to watch the happ'nings from my bedroom window.

    I couldn't see it all, but I saw enough. Farren ordered his boys to ride around the co'pses and herd 'em together, cattle-like. It might have worked, too, if they *was* cattle, but some of them deaduns was buried with their shooters as well as their boots, and they chose to make a fight of it. Stony Landers—Farren's little brother—put two bullets through the chest of some raggedy carcass, knocking him back among the trees. Only that deadun got up and used bone-hands to draw his irons. He aimed for Stony and yanked both triggers. The hammers fell on dud rounds (I could almost hear 'em clicking from up here) and then caught a live one. It hit Stony in the left side of the face and he flew off'n his hoss— but one boot got caught in the stirrup and the hoss, rightly spooked, cut dirt, dragging Stony along and spilling his brains all over the pasture.

    This set the carnage in motion.

    Farren screamed and started unloading, firing a full chamber into the co'pse that had shot his little brother. He blew four holes through his guts, shot off his arm and most of his head, but that co'pse kept ticking... and shooting, too (even the arm that was shot off kept shooting). The rest of the posse was just as trigger-happy, and for a time all you could hear was guns cracking and hosses braying. Ennis Jenkins's head was shot clean out of his hand and he walked in stupid circles until Grandma Zippity fair cut him in half with a blast of double-ought. Mean Joe Wallace shot a hoss dead (he was surely aiming for the feller on the hoss, but his aim was off, prob'ly 'cause his neck was broke and his eyes was all eaten out). The feller jumped up, unshucked his carbine, and blew off Joe's right leg. This didn't stop Joe; he picked up his leg, tucked it under one arm, and carried on shooting. I watched as Slim McFarlane was gunned down by Edward Topper III, whose heart had stopped beating while in the company of a wag-tail. His co'pse was rightly grinning, until his face was shot sideways by a bullet from Farren's Peacemaker.

"That'll knock the smile off, y'oul' dawg," he said.

It was hellfire, and the only co'pses that stayed dead was the ones that wasn't in the bone orchard to begin with. Most of these got caught in the crossfire. Their bullets was hitting targets . . . only them targets was mostly rotted out and the bullets passed right through, hitting whatever was on the other side. I saw Rowdy Bright shot dead in just this way. It was a bullet from his best friend's gun (having passed through the skull of something that was mostly rags) that killed him. Then his best friend turned-tail and rode from the fight—south, toward Mexico—and I'd bet all the money in Steel County that he's still riding.

Another of Farren's posse rode around the side of the house where no one could see him (he didn't reckon on me watching from the bedroom window). He was a young man, maybe twenty, crying and pale afeared. He wiped his tears, though I can't think why, 'cause the next thing he done was put a shooter in his mouth and pulled the trigger—shot hisself from one hell to another. I saw the back of his head open like a split tomato.

More gunshots, like thunder all over again. The air was oil-coloured and smoky.

"Farren, what do we do?" one of his boys asked. "God's sakes, we can't stop 'em."

"Pray," Farren shouted back. "But don't stop shootin'."

So they kept shooting, and them co'pses kept coming. One of them skelingtons got blown to pieces—and I mean to *pieces*. But them bones, scattered in the grass, kept jumping and moving just the same. Even its skull kindly hopped along, teeth chompin'.

Meanwhile, Grandma Zippity was doing a fine job of keeping the deaduns from the house. They'd get to within ten paces and—*BOOM!*—she'd blast 'em back fifteen, cracking that Winchester over her knee to reload. "Get on some o' that, y'oul' sumbitch," she'd cry, and then—*BOOM!*—she'd loose another shell. "You want some, Henry Sherman? I never liked you when you was above snakes, you wily oul' cocksucker!" *BOOM! BOOM!* They'd all jump right back up, of course, but Grandma had a bucketful of shells and she seemed to be having a gay oul' time.

Pa was doing more damage with his saw than all them bullets put together. It was long and curved like a grin, with a handle at each end (Pa and Uncle

Jack would grab a handle each and use it to fell trees), and he got among the deaduns, using every muscle in his bear-like body to whip it from side to side. Them co'pses never stood a chance, most of 'em being dried out and rotted through. It was like hitting dead wood with an ax. Heads was flying. Arms and legs, too. Pa done tore through Wolfie Frye like he was a sheet of wet paper. His top half turned twice in the air and landed facedown, while his legs skiddled around like one of them first-time skaters on oul' man Willoughby's pond come December. They ran on apiece, then tripped on Slim McFarlane's sprawled body and struggled to get back up.

Pa swung that saw and it flashed in the sunlight, meeting deaduns and slicing them like baked ham—men and women that he'd known and prayed with, worked and laughed with. I was sure he'd be caught in the crossfire. Bullets was raining every which way and he was sure to catch one of 'em. But he never did... and I'm wondering now if bullets really *do* bounce off'n him.

He stopped eventually, but not 'cause he was tired, and not 'cause the deaduns had been settled. His big body sagged and he dropped the saw, looking toward Chiming Woods, where a woman with golden hair was moving among the trees, shuffling toward him.

"No," I said, and cried bigger than any storm.

I saw Pa hold out his strong arms. I heard him say my mother's name. My heart was thunder.

It occurred to me later that—except for a few lonesome outlaws—Sanctuary Hill had been filled with loved ones, and that Pa wasn't alone in coming face to face with someone he'd lost. Farren's boys had family buried there, and no doubt saw 'em staggering out of the woods with their skull-eyes wide and the breeze blowing their rags. Were they forced to shoot their loved ones? Did they even recognise 'em? I recalled the young man that had shot hisself at the side of the house. Had he just fired a bullet through his pa's head, or his sister's, and when they hopped back up couldn't bear to do it again? Did Farren Landers shoot his Aunt Meredith, who'd raised him from a boy and died five years ago? Did he shoot her again and again?

And again?

Grandma Zippity had buried more than most in that boneyard. Parents and children, uncles, aunts, brothers and sisters. Did they all come back to say hello? We know Uncle Jack did... but was that rickety skelington with a little crown of snowy white hair atop its skull my Grandpa Arnold? Did Grandma whisper a prayer afore she loaded her 'Chester with double-ought and blew his creaking bones all over the pasture? I'll never know.

But I saw my ma—this I *do* know. I saw her through my tears. She was three years in the ground and her golden hair was thick with mud and her skin was stretched tight across her bones, split in places, and that burying dress was hanging off her in dirty streamers. Her lips and eyelids had clean rotted off, and I noticed that her right ankle was broken, her foot kinked proper sideways. She must've done that walking through the woods—maybe tripped on a stone, or something. But she got up and carried on walking... walking.

It all blurred with tears. I wiped them away and it blurred again.

Pa lowered his shaggy head, then he wrapped his arms around Ma and pulled her close—lifted her off'n the ground, which wasn't hard given she little more than a bag o' bones. I wondered what she'd do. Would she hug him back, or maybe turn feral and take a bite out of his throat? I wiped away my tears and watched, one hand on my angry heart... but Ma didn't do nothing. She just hung in his arms all limp, with only her hair and raggedy dress moving in the breeze. Then my eyes blurred over again and by the time I could see clear Pa had let go of Ma and was holding the saw.

"Oh no," I said, one hand pressed against the glass. "No, Pa... you can't."

Pa raised that saw. He pulled it back over one shoulder, both hands wrapped around one handle.

"No... please *no!*"

The shooting had died down some; the deaduns had run dry of bullets and Farren's boys realised that bullets was doing no good. In the near-silence most everyone was watching Pa (the living and dead alike)... watching as the thick muscles in his arms tightened and he got ready to bring that saw down.

Ma looked at him. She reached forward, touched his barrel chest, and nodded.

No... I couldn't even speak. I left the ghost of my hand on the window and fell into the corner, covering my eyes, not wanting to see, not wanting to *think*. I cried hard and my shoulders jumped and I stomped my feet

on the floor like Baby Ellen throwing a tantrum. I ain't never seen the ocean, but I think that's what my tears was like: a great swell of furious blue, drowning me... drowning everything.
I'll never cry so hard again. My poor heart is full of splinters. This I know.
I stayed in the corner with my eyes closed, drowning in my ocean, and I didn't move until I heard the sweet strumming of Uncle Jack's guitar.
It was coming from the barn.

The birds would listen to him. I told you that. Sometimes you'd hear the flurry of their wings and look up and see 'em all colouring the sky—a fair stream of birds fluttering from the trees to the barn, where they'd bustle for space in the loft. I can't rightly say why. Something in the guitar's tuning, perhaps, or the way Uncle Jack would strum a certain chord. Whatever the reason, he played and them birds listened. Every time.
It was the same with the deaduns.
I ran into Pa's bedroom, on account of his window having a better view of the barn. The doors was open and I could see Uncle Jack inside, sitting on his regular bundle of hay with the guitar on one knee. And he was *playing* it, I swear. Them sweet melodies I remember so well. *You did it, Uncle Jack,* I thought. *Now you can stay.* He looked up and kindly smiled as the first birds swooped in through the doors. Then I looked and saw the deaduns was shuffling from the pasture, drawn toward the sound of Uncle Jack's guitar. All of 'em—even the ones that was shot through or cut into pieces by Pa's saw... they stepped or hopped or dragged themselves along, through the pasture and up onto the dirt track. Grandma Zippity watched from behind a cloud of shotgun mist. Pa threw his saw into the grass and stepped back. Farren's boys (what was left of 'em) looked at each other, wild-eyed and bullshit-ascairt. One of 'em—I don't know his name, nor care to—shot a young co'pse in the back as she shuffled by. Her chest blew open and she went down, but got up quickly and carried on toward the barn, not even glancing at the man that shot her.
Uncle Jack's splintered fingers danced along the strings. Sweet sounding. And it hurt my heart to realise that he wasn't playing 'cause he was hoping to stay with us (this may have been his thinking to begin with, but not

anymore). No ... he strummed that guitar 'cause he knew that whatever brought them birds (the koo-sticks, maybe) would bring the dead, too.

He was drawing 'em into that oul' barn so as we could have a settling. And that we did.

They slumped in, bullet-torn and decayed, most of 'em in pieces. I saw a pair of legs (I think they was Wolfie Frye's) strolling along without no upper-half, and something in the way those legs strolled told me that if they'd had an upper-half, it would be whistling. I saw bones jumping and severed hands crawling like spiders ... all of 'em following the path to the barn. Uncle Jack kept playing, and when the last of the deaduns was in (a gap-toothed skull, springing along on its jaw, and Farren done helped it along with his boot), Pa closed and barricaded the doors.

"Let's burn this box o' co'pses to the ground," he said.

It was ashes less than thirty minutes later.

Gus missed it all, and that can only be a good thing. His hoss—that bindy-legged oul' bastage—clopped tiredly back to the homestead, blowing out of its ass, and by the time he jumped down from the saddle the barn was blazing. I stood in the yard and watched black smoke lift into the blue sky. We all did, saying nothing. Some of Farren's boys had tears in their eyes. It might have been the smoke, but I don't think so.

I never told Gus about Ma. He doesn't need to know. It's bad enough that Ma's limp co'pse is the last thing I see afore I close my eyes at night—that the flash of Pa's saw chokes my dreams. Gus doesn't need that in his head ... couldn't *take* it, neither. He's a sweet boy, but he'll never be strong.

The praying started soon after, and it hasn't stopped yet. Even now I can hear Aunt Maude in the kitchen, and Grandma Zippity in her bedroom. Pa hasn't cried, and he hasn't prayed, neither. Not that I've seen or heard, at least. Perhaps—after Ma 'n' all—he isn't ready to talk to God as yet.

I can't say I blame him.

There's another storm coming.

This I know.

I just looked out the window and the sky went all bright for just an instant while, out toward Retribution, a clap of thunder let out and then mumbled away like an oul' dog that is just a little tired of life.

I hope it's a hard storm. I want God to come with His rain and lightning and wash everything away. Until then I have to listen to the constant prayers and tears... to the coyotes howling on the plains, sounding heartbroken. They're all such sad sounds. But sometimes, if I close my eyes and if the wind is blowing just right, I can hear Uncle Jack playing his guitar. I'm *sure* I can. It's such a sweet, tempting melody and I can feel myself lifted high... flying like one of them birds and singing along, my wings outstretched as I soar over the pastures and woods and the clear blue belt of the Brotherly.
Flying... listening to him play.
You did it, Uncle Jack.
Prettiest feathers in all the land.

Pete Crowther fell in love with the Wild West for two reasons: one was the movie *Drum Beat* (1954)—"My first ever visit to the cinema: I was six years old!"—and the other was Oliver Strange's *Sudden* novels, most of which he read before he was 10 years old. "When Conrad pitched his 'weird west' anthology idea to me as a PS title, I couldn't resist," Crowther recalls. "And the same goes for when he asked me if I wanted to try him with something. But I knew that, with it being under my imprint, it needed to be extra special..."

"So I get this telephone call from Pete one evening," says Rio Youers, "asking me if I'd like to collaborate on a western tale filled with zombies. It took me a few minutes to convince myself I wasn't dreaming and then arrangements were made... and Pete sent the opening across." Less than one week later, after a couple of bats of the ball across the net for fine-tuning, the pair had themselves the answer to an age-old question: what would it be like if the dead came back to life on Walton's Mountain?

Pete is the author of the offbeat witches tome *By Wizard Oak*, the *Forever Twilight* cycle and, with James Lovegrove, *Escardy Gap*. He has produced six volumes of short stories and his work has been adapted for TV on both sides of the Atlantic. Rio is the British Fantasy Award-nominated author of *Old Man Scratch* and *End Times*. His first short story collection, *Dark Dreams, Pale Horses*, was released by PS Publishing in 2011. He lives in Canada with his wife Emily.

ALL OUR HEARTS ARE GHOSTS
Peter Atkins

Los Angeles, 1934

First time Henry Burgess saw Addison Steele, the guy was getting himself shot.

Henry, first day on the job and excited to be sent from the production office on Melrose out to the Placerita Canyon studio ranch, parked his Austin Roadster—tiny amongst the big Plymouths and Fleetwoods favoured by the cast and crew—and made his way across to where everybody was working hard on bringing *Outlaws of Calico Creek* to life.

People and equipment were gathered in front of one of the ranch's standing sets: a segment of an old west's main street; a general store, a corral, and a one-storey chapel. Henry walked toward them, glancing beyond the fragment of a town to where the canyon stretched plain and clear between its low hills and offered a view in the far distance of the Sierra Nevada, still snow-topped in late April.

"Quiet on set!" a voice yelled, and Henry froze in place like everyone else not actively involved in the shot. From a few yards behind the director's chair he watched as, up on the chapel roof and on the shout of *action*, an older man—lean, wiry, wearing a black coat and black hat—jerked his hand to his chest and staggered like he'd just taken a bullet between the ribs. Henry turned to see who'd shot him and felt like a rube when he saw that the actor playing the good guy, knowing he was out of frame, was simply standing and watching like everybody else.

The older man's body went limp and he fell from the roof, playing dead all the way down until hitting the bunched mattresses piled below the camera line.

At a nod from the director, an assistant yelled, "Cut! Moving on," and Henry waited for applause from the crew for the stunt but none came; they were all already busy shifting the camera and the other equipment across to where the next set-up was to be.

Henry moved after them in the direction of a scrub-covered hill with a narrow cave mouth at its base, waving the batch of revised script pages at the assistant director to get his attention.

The AD hung back to let Henry catch up. "Who are you?" he said, glancing at the pages but not taking them—Henry wondering if he was used to dodging process servers or something—and turned to wave the camera crew on.

"Henry Burgess," Henry said. "From the production office. New revisions." He fluttered the pages again. "From the writers."

"Oh, yeah," the AD said, and then turned again to shout across to the crew. "Grant! Get the damn horse inside!"

Outside the cave mouth, a wrangler, presumably Grant—a big guy in his early thirties, ruddy-faced, with scowl-lines permanently etched in his brow—was standing tugging at the reins of a roan horse which was refusing to be led into the narrow darkness of the cave.

Even Henry—no farm-boy, Boston born and bred, and fresh out of Princeton—could see that the horse was afraid. Could see too that Grant wasn't helping; taking a tighter grip on the reins, jerking them, trying to get the horse's head down as if he could simply drag its thousand pounds inside.

"God damn it," Grant shouted. "Get in there!" He reached out his other hand and swished a tight leather riding crop hard against the roan's flank. The horse reared and he cut at it again.

"While there's still daylight, Grant!" the AD shouted.

The older man Henry had watched make the fall from the chapel roof walked out and around the crew to stand in front of the horse. "Mind if I try?" he said to Grant, holding his hand out for the crop.

Grant gave it to him, and the man held it low and loose at his side, Henry wondering if he was letting the horse see it was no longer any immediate threat. "Let go the reins," the man said to Grant, though his eyes stayed on the horse.

"Don't be crazy, Addison," Grant said.

"Let go the reins," the man, Addison, repeated, with only a shade more emphasis.

As Grant dropped the reins, the horse shivered and flexed as if ready to buck again. Grant stepped back sharply but Addison moved closer to the roan and breathed out through his nose into its flaring nostrils, murmuring softly and reaching a confident hand to stroke the animal's brow. A few seconds later, he'd walked the calmed horse into the cave and come back out to rejoin Grant.

The wrangler nodded a slightly resentful acknowledgement. "Shoot," he said. "You didn't even need the crop." He held out his hand for its return.

"Sure I did," said Addison, and slashed it across the younger man's face—once, twice, left, right—before dropping it to the ground. "But I'm all done with it now."

Henry was as silent and still as everyone else as Grant stepped forward, the welts already forming on each of his cheeks. Addison stood perfectly still, letting the man come ahead if he was going to.

But he wasn't, Henry found himself realizing, and wondered why—the wrangler had fifty pounds on Addison and was half his age. The director stood up from his chair and shouted, "Save it for wrap, both of you. We've got work to do."

"I'll let it go, old man," Grant said to Addison. "You're lucky we're on a tight schedule."

"Right," said Addison. "That's why." He turned to look at the director, gave him a wink, and walked away, Henry turning his head to watch him go until the AD's voice brought him back to business.

"Pages?" the guy said, with a show of impatience, like he hadn't been just as fascinated as Henry. Henry placed the revisions in his outstretched hand and asked if he could stay to watch a couple more shots.

"Don't you have phones to answer back at the office?" the AD said, and Henry wished he had a riding crop.

Second time Henry saw him, he was getting quietly and elegantly drunk.

Gutshot

The residential hotel on the eastern reaches of Wilshire was hardly the Waldorf Astoria but Henry liked it enough. He'd been there four days now, the cute redhead in the production office having found it for him after he'd spent a few minutes whining to her about how the apartment he'd been promised—hell, put down a deposit on—had fallen through. She'd said that several members of the company were rooming there. "Including you?" he'd asked—you know, taking a shot—but she'd wiggled her engagement ring at him with a seasoned efficiency and he'd retired gracefully.

The hotel's bar looked like it had never heard of the Volstead act nor its repeal, like it had been quietly open for business all through prohibition, though Henry assumed that that couldn't actually be true. He hadn't given it his custom yet but on this fourth night decided to treat himself to a beer. He'd got his first week's wages earlier that morning and had had a long day.

Addison Steele was standing there, in the same black outfit he'd worn on set, one booted foot on the bar's brass rail. There was a shot glass full of whiskey in front of him, and two empty beside it.

"I'd like to pay for that, if you'd let me," Henry said, walking up to stand beside the older man and gesturing at his glass.

Addison gave him a look. "Man's a fool to refuse a free drink," he said. "But a bigger one if he doesn't ask the reason."

"I liked the way you looked out for that horse," Henry said, and saw a slow recognition come into Addison's eyes.

"Right," he said. "You were over to the Canyon Monday last."

"Henry Burgess," Henry said, putting out his hand. "From the production office."

"Henry," Addison said, after he'd shaken his hand. Not addressing Henry, simply weighing the word in his mouth and finding it not entirely to his taste. "Anybody ever call you Hank?"

Henry told him that no, nobody ever had, and Addison nodded like that was perfectly understandable. "I'd like to call you Hank," he said. "Unless you have any objection to that?"

"No," Henry said, amused, kind of pleased, but keeping it to himself. "None that I can think of."

"Well, alright," Addison said, and raised the shot glass in Henry's direction before throwing the whiskey down in one and flicking an upraised finger at the bartender to bring him another.

"My friend Hank will be paying for that one," Addison said to the bartender, "but I don't want him held accountable for the several more with which I intend to chase it."

The bartender nodded, and Henry waited till he'd walked away. "Talking about names..." he said, letting it hang.

"Yeah?"

"Addison Steele?"

"What about it?"

"It's a stage name, right?"

"A *stage* name?" Addison said, like the very idea of such a thing was bizarre. "No, Hank. It's not a stage name. I've worn it close to forty years now."

"So you weren't born with it?" *Born* with it? Henry being polite. If the guy'd worn it for forty years, he must've been twenty-five when he first tried it on.

Addison cocked his head. "Full of questions, aren't you, Hank?" he said.

"I don't mean any offence."

"None taken, son." Addison took a sip of his next shot, staring at the mirror behind the bar. Staring *through* it, Henry thought, to somewhere very far away in time. He'd just about given up on getting an answer when Addison turned back to him.

"It was given to me by a friend," he said. "At a time when I had sufficient reason to let go of the one my people had christened me with."

"Oh," Henry said, wondering what *that* story was but not ready to ask. "Because it's a...well, not a pun, exactly...a play on words, I guess." Desperately avoiding the word joke. "A literary *jeu d'esprit*." Jesus Christ.

"A *jeu d'esprit*, huh?" Addison said, a little glint in his eye. Amused by the words but pronouncing them perfectly.

"It's the names of two eighteenth century writers. Addison and Steele. Editors of *The Tatler*. And *The Spectator*."

"Is that right?"

"It is."

"Huh," Addison said, and was silent for a moment, looking through Henry like he'd looked through the mirror. "Well, the friend in question was an educated lady," he finally said. "And her sense of humor always favoured the sly."

"It's a good name," Henry said. "Must read well on the posters."

Addison smiled, kind of. "I don't get my name on movie posters, son. I'm just another bad guy in black. Someone for the hero to pick off. I get shot for a goddam living, Hank. Been doing it a long time. Been shot by Bill Hart and Bronco Anderson, been doing it since before the movies learned to talk."

Henry was eager to ask him about his life before Hollywood started paying him to die, because he could smell real western history on the man, but Addison—perhaps mindful of his manners, perhaps for reasons of his own—turned the conversation to Henry's own story and how a kid with a degree from a fancy school back east could think it a good idea to come out and work as a glorified errand boy for the hacks at a B-movie factory, a move Addison plainly, albeit politely indirect about it, thought of as a symptom of a sadly undiagnosed mental illness.

They continued to talk, and Addison continued to drink—the impressiveness of his intake matched only by the impressiveness of how little it seemed to affect him—and Henry thought he'd heard the last of the man's secret history until they were almost done for the night.

"Know what she said to me once?" Addison suddenly said, out of nowhere, out of a conversation about gunfights and wasted bullets—*you do it right, it only takes one*, he'd thrilled Henry by saying—and the other ways in which the movies got it wrong.

"Your friend, you mean? The educated lady?"

Addison nodded, and Henry asked him what it was she'd said.

"She said, 'All our hearts are ghosts'."

Way he said it, it sounded like a quote from something, Henry thought. Thought too that it sounded like the saddest thing in the world, but he was, after all, a little drunk himself. "What does it mean?" he said.

Addison paused before replying, covering it by throwing down his last shot. "Damned if I know, Hank," he said, slamming his emptied glass down onto the bar like an unseen director had told him it was a good way to end the scene.

Henry was damned if he knew either, but he watched Addison stare again into the bar's mirror after he said it and figured it for the first lie his new friend had told him.

Third time he saw him, he drove him upstate to kill the richest man in Houghton County.

Henry'd been taking sandwich orders in the office when he was urgently re-assigned. It was the last day of the *Outlaws of Calico Creek* shoot and Addison Steele had ruined everybody's morning by not showing up for work at the ranch location. Henry was told to drive back to their hotel and get him out to Placerita as fast as he could.

There was no answer to Henry's repeated knocking on Addison's door but—a phone call from an enraged studio executive overcoming any scruples the hotel management felt about letting anyone short of a cop into the room—a bellman eventually unlocked it for Henry.

The room wasn't empty, but clearly deserted. The belongings were few, but were all tied in neat and ready-to-be-disposed-of bundles in a way that suggested Addison had no intention of ever returning for them.

On a circular occasional table, two items had been bound together with a thin red ribbon and stood beside a newspaper clipping and the envelope it had been mailed in, the envelope bearing the previous day's postmark. The clipping itself was from a Lake Tahoe daily and was an obituary notice for a woman, a Mrs. Lester Cutter, who had died in Northern California's Houghton County the previous week at the age of sixty-three. Survived by her husband, it said, the founder of Cutter township and three times its Mayor.

Untying the bundle beside the clipping, Henry looked at the two things Addison had thought worthy of a red ribbon rather than the twine with which he'd bound everything else he'd left behind. The first was an old photograph—so old that it was not on paper but on tin, its silvered image seeming so fragile that Henry feared his fingers could wipe it clean—and was a formally posed portrait of a beautiful young woman. Hardly more than a girl when the picture was made, Henry saw but knew—if only from the fierce and eager intelligence glowing from her dark eyes—that he was looking at an educated lady.

The other item was a book—published, Henry saw from the title page, back in 1894 and by an author with the unlikely name of Lafcadio Hearn. It was called *Shadows in Running Water; tales and verse from the Japanese,* and there was an inscription on its fly-page in a beautifully neat copperplate. *To my dear friend Addison Steele,* it read, *who knew me well when both our hearts were alive. In affectionate remembrance, Marianne Cutter (nee Ryan).*

A worn leather bookmark protruded from the text-block and, at a gentle touch from Henry's hand, the book fell naturally open there, as if the bookmarked page had been looked at many times over the years. There were four three-line verses on the page and the last line of the third haiku, underlined long ago in pencil, read; *all our hearts are ghosts.*

"Let me spare you the suspense, Hank," Addison said, when Henry's roadster pulled up at the bench outside the Pasadena train station. "You are not going to succeed in your mission."

"You're not going to come back?"

"The prospect seems unlikely."

"I gathered that when I saw your room. Even though you left everything behind."

"Not everything," Addison said, and Henry knew at once what he meant, though Addison's coat was roomy enough to conceal whatever he might have been wearing at his waist.

"At least let me give you a ride," Henry said. "Train to Tahoe stops every damn half hour. And you'll still be twenty miles from Cutter when you get off."

Addison looked almost impressed. "Well, Hank," he said. "You've been busy with your research. And quick, too. You know, once you've got this picture business crap out your system, you should head up to San Francisco; I believe Pinkerton's still hiring."

Henry didn't say anything, just leant across to spring the passenger door. Addison didn't say anything either, just got in, and Henry let him stay silent for almost the first hour of the long drive, before opening with what he figured was his best way in.

"The book and the picture," he said. "Everything else, sure. But I don't get leaving them behind."

"I didn't want them buried with me," Addison said, and let that sink in for a minute. Then, in a gentler voice, "Besides, I figured it'd be you that found them."

Henry felt a rush of sentiment, but didn't surrender to it. "They're in the trunk," he said.

"Well, you look after them then."

"I'm hoping I won't need to," Henry said. "I don't know how this story's going to end."

"Oh, you know how it's going to end, Hank," Addison said.

"I do?"

Addison looked at him like he was stupid. "I thought you liked those western pictures," he said.

"Sure, but—"

"Then you know they all end the same way. Two guys pull down on each other and one of them dies."

"*One* of them dies," Henry said.

"That's something else the movies get wrong," Addison said. "Real life, both those idiots usually wound up dead. Unless one of them got real fucking lucky."

Henry waited another half-mile or so before saying, "Okay, enough about the ending. I want to know the beginning."

Addison looked out to the side of the road for a moment or two, to where the Southern California topography was slowly giving way to the harsher and less forgiving look of the north, and then back to Henry.

"Price of the ride?"

"Price of the ride."

So Henry heard a story from the tail-end of the boomtown days, from when tiny communities would grow a hundredfold in three years when the gold was leaping out of the hills and dwindle back to nothing in two when the seams were exhausted. But truth was this particular story could have happened almost anywhere because it was a story about people, about a young girl and her dreams and the young hothead who loved her for them and how she was lost to him and became another man's wife.

"Rich guy from the big city?" Henry said, thinking he knew how this part went. "Turned her head with fancy jewellery and fine manners?"

"Big city? Fine manners?" Addison said and Henry, ashamed, heard the older man struggle to keep the contempt out of his voice. "Jesus Christ, Hank, maybe you are dumb enough to be in the goddam movie business. I believe he may have been born back east, yes, but Lester Cutter had killed three men before he was twenty-one. And enjoyed it. Poor as dirt, mean as they come, and fast enough to back it up."

"So why did she—"

"She didn't," Addison said, and his voice got very flat and very cold and he told it quickly lest the scars of the ancient wounds start bleeding anew. "He raped her. Got her pregnant. And I'd've killed him the day I found out if her people hadn't forced a wedding the previous night."

"My God, Addison," Henry said, not knowing what else to say.

"God wasn't paying much attention," Addison said. "I've found that to be the case more often than not."

Henry gave him a moment. "And the child?" he finally asked.

"Lost almost at full term, along with the chance of others," Addison said. "But I was long gone by then. It was my last promise to her, that I'd pay no visit to her husband while she was still alive."

"And now, what, you're just going to *kill* him? Just find him and kill him?"

"We've been over this, Hank. I'm not going to *bushwhack* the guy. I'm doing her memory the courtesy of facing him down properly."

"You're going to knock on his damn door or something?"

"No need," Addison said. "He knows I'm coming."

"He *knows*? That's ridiculous. How does he *know*? Some old gunfighter instinct?"

Addison just looked at him, letting him start to believe that that was in fact exactly right, before giving a little snort of amusement. "The modern world has its conveniences," he said. "I called him up on the telephone. Made a date."

"Christ almighty. And he *agreed*?"

"Of course he did, Hank," Addison said. "Lester always appreciated the opportunity to kill someone. And it don't matter how much money he's made, how sleek he's got. Guys don't change. Not guys like me and him."

Henry had nothing to say, just shook his head and stared out at the road ahead. Who the hell were these people, he thought. He knew the wild ones were still out there, of course. Papers were full of them. Pretty Boy Floyd, Baby Face Nelson. Dillinger. And it was they, Henry thought, with a stab of something lost, who were the true heirs to the men of the old west, not the shiny-suited heroes of the silver screen with their guitars and good manners. They were just pretty lies made for boys like him. He had a wild animal in his car, he realised. A wild animal, no matter its charm and elegance. He really didn't have much to say for the rest of the drive.

They could as well have been back on the *Outlaws of Calico Creek* set, Henry thought. They were more than a mile from the modern township with its stoplights and paved streets and Woolworths and, yes, movie theatre. This was the slowly decaying old town, long abandoned, a ruined thing left to rot out of sight of all those people with their eyes on the glittering American future and no mind for its past. Chroniclers of his country's recent history had already coined a phrase for places like this, Henry knew; *Ghost towns*, they called them. And, standing here, he knew that they'd named them well.

Lester Cutter, though, was fully alive. Unlike Addison, he'd grown fatter with the years and the fedora hat he wore, unlike Addison's, paid no homage to the days of their youth. But his eyes were feral and excited and Henry was instinctively afraid of him on sight.

"This is Hank Burgess," Addison said, before Cutter could ask. "He's got no dog in this fight and I trust you'll respect that. He's just here to take me home. You know, one way or another."

Cutter's half nod was unpleasantly amused. "Appreciate your thoughtfulness, Addison," he said. "I'd hate to have to call out the fire station boys to clean up my mess."

Henry wondered if there'd be some kind of formal countdown, some kind of etiquette and stated rules of engagement, but they both slipped into it like old boxers back in the ring, old gladiators back in the arena, pausing instinctively about fifteen feet from each other on the dry neglected dirt that used to be a Main Street. There was no right or wrong left in their scenario, Henry realised. No good or evil, no black hats or white hats, nothing but mutual appetite and excitement. They both waited a second or two, their atavistic clocks perfectly synchronised. Savouring it, Henry realised. Jesus Christ. *Savouring* it.

And then—without a word, without a gesture—it happened.

Cutter was fast, just as fast as Addison had said, fast on the draw and fast to fire, and his eye was as good as if the years between had never happened. Three bullets had slammed into his opponent before Addison's Colt had even cleared the holster. All in the chest. At least one in the heart.

Henry's own heart lurched in despair as if he, not Addison, had been the target. No, not despair. A terrible sadness, perhaps, but not despair. Because Henry knew something that Cutter didn't; Addison Steele got shot for a goddam living.

Addison didn't fall, didn't falter, taking Cutter's bullets like they were no more real than the many he'd mimed taking in the movies. His gun was in his hand, his arm was up and straight, and his aim was cold and true.

The man in the black suit may have already been dead, already been as much of a ghost as the town he'd come back to, but this ghost had its finger on the trigger of its colt and enough will—or its memory—to squeeze it.

You do it right, it only takes one, he'd said to Henry. And, one last time, Addison Steele did it right.

The entrance wound was nothing, Henry saw, through eyes already wet with tears—a small, elegantly centred hole in Cutter's forehead—but the exit tore half the fucker's skull off and Henry watched Addison's old enemy hit the dirt before he did. Whether Addison's eyes saw it or not, though, was something Henry was never able to say.

Peter Atkins was born in Liverpool and now lives in Los Angeles. He is the author of the novels *Morningstar*, *Big Thunder*, and *Moontown* and the screenplays *Hellraiser II*, *Hellraiser III*, *Hellraiser IV*, and *Wishmaster*. *Spook City* was a three-author collection featuring him alongside fellow Liverpudlians Clive Barker and Ramsey Campbell. *Rumours of the Marvellous*, a new collection of his short fiction, has just been published by Alchemy Press.

"I was driving with the car radio on and trying to work out the story when a misheard lyric gave me the title," Peter explains. "How the hell I heard *All our hearts are ghosts* when the line Pink actually sang was *All my underdogs* I have no idea, but I thank the gods of serendipity and partial-hearing-loss for their assistance."

BEASTS OF BURDEN
Sarah Langan

When they first discovered it, the New World was a dark, unforgiving place. The winters were hungry, and the woods adorned with dried human scalps. The winds whispered ancient words, and those who travelled across those verdant fields of madness, trod alone. But after a time, an idea called civility took root and chewed up the darkness. It burned the witches into silence, and wiped out the buffalo, and Indians, too. Angels and ghosts turned translucent in bright lamplight. The noises of mankind drowned out the magic, like infants paddling in an ocean at high tide. In savagery's place came houses, and flower beds. Weddings and children who nursed to sleep. But in the Old West, there were folds of land that civility did not grow, where outlaws and the desolate took refuge.

It was July 4, 1876, when Master Brown opened his door to the foundling swaddled in wet rags. They'd frozen to his backside and chest like stuck lettuce leaves. Brown carried the infant inside, and fed him mare's milk while warming him by a fire until his blue skin returned to pink. The birthmark at the small of the child's neck was overlapping triple 6's. These Brown hid with mud until his thick, black hair grew in.

The town was Elko, a tiny dot of a place on route to nowhere. The trees were short and thirsty, the men rugged and wrinkled beyond their years. They'd lived so long without word from outside that they came to believe everything that happened there, from the gnawing locusts to the restless spirits in the cemetery, was normal.

Master Brown guessed, but could not know for sure, that the child came from an old whore at Smith's Tavern named Inez, who kept her cheer in a bottle. Growing up, Inez and Brown used to fish the creek and draw ant mazes in the dirt. She'd had an innocence about her, pure as snow. When Brown turned fifteen, he'd arranged to build his fortune in Carson City, so he could marry her. But by then it was too late; her father had sold her. Brown watched her go, cursing his own lazy courage. If he hadn't waited so long, they'd have run away. They'd have set-up house, and lived like people with something to lose.

At Smith's Tavern, Inez got broke like a horse. The spark left her eyes. Her spirit became a pale thing, crippled but still shining, like bent tin. After learning his trade, Brown ought have stayed in Carson City, but he came back to Elko and built his cabin and horse stable across the street from Inez' captivity, to let her know, though he never spoke to her again, that he was with her.

The world spun. A quarter century passed. From passers-through, he learned that the brave Yavapai and Apache had gotten boxed into reservations. Fences went up across the free range. Sitting Bull and Crazy Horse surrendered. A man called Edison invented a machine that played dead sounds. The East got educated, the West got rich from dug gold, and the middle fought wars. The transcontinental Rail Road at last kissed San Francisco.

Elko stayed the same, except for Master Brown, whose farrier skills were the best in 500 square miles. Riders with ailing animals made special trips, bringing a new wave of stranger into the small, strange town. Some characters were good, some bad. Brown attended them all. The shoes he made were determined by the horse's spirit, which he claimed he could see. Some got copper amalgams, some iron, some silver. He spoke to them while he worked, and salved their sore hooves. They came in limping, and left in full sprints. Cowboys, ranchers, lawmen, and murderers dropped their horses off at Brown's, then took rooms at Smith's, and bought Inez or one of her daughters for the price of a beer. At night Brown watched Inez' kerosene lamp through her window. He focussed on that light, and how she never turned it off, just let it burn until it was gone.

Then Inez got sick. Brown saw her through her attic window, slugging back a glass of dirt-coloured whisky. As if she'd had a terrible fright, overnight, her hair turned white, and she coughed red into a ratty swath cut from her own dress. In Brown's heart, he blamed himself for her infirmity, because there is no greater crime than wasted love. He knew then, that he should have run away with her long ago. Even now, he should go to her. He did not go. Nine months later, the foundling arrived. He swaddled the unholy thing and carried it to her funeral. Neither cried.

Brown took pity on the strange foundling, because it was the last that remained of Inez, so he gave it shelter, despite the way it giggled at invisible jokes told by what Brown could only hope were saints. As the boy grew, Brown taught him the equine shoe-making and veterinary business. In return the boy cooked and cleaned and slept in the stable. Because Brown had only ever known cruelty, and because he both resented and loved the child, whom he believed the devil had sired, he did not touch it with gentleness, or name it.

Times got worse in Elko. Some blamed the foundling. The wind whispered harder, and the ghosts became more audible. Men stopped falling in love. Women lost hope for salvation, and instead washed their privates with diluted lye, to keep children from grabbing purchase. The civilised, or those who wanted to be, left. Those townspeople who remained grew lonely and strange. They talked to themselves, and at the church in the back of Smith's Tavern, were taught that the written word was damnation.

Elko seemed like an island, floating father and father away in time and space from the rest of America. In the East, Coca-Cola was invented, and men rich in leisure discovered football. Blacks got freed, and occasionally replaced by Chinamen and Irish. But in Elko, the creek where Brown and Inez had once fished, gushed blood. On dark nights, heading home from errands, men heard the whispers of a deep-throated thing. *Make ready my horse*, it told them, and though they never articulated it, they knew somehow, that this referred to Master Brown's apprentice.

The foundling grew tall, with a reedy voice like a plucked fiddle's string. His birthmark turned black with age, its edges sharp as whittled wood. "You can have all this one day," Brown told him, after drinking too much whiskey, and feeling maudlin.

The foundling, sensing his Master's loose lips, spoke freely. "Do you know my father?" he asked. "I hear him at night, scratching at the stable door. He frightens the horses. He wants me to know he's there, but he won't show himself. I think he's waiting."

In his fear and lonely rage, Brown beat the child, who peered silently back at him with Inez' innocent eyes.

When the child turned fourteen, a carnage happened in Smith's Tavern. Brown had been there drinking when Inez' ghost appeared behind the bar, looking sullen and thick-middled. She drew three words in salt along the bar that read, "KILL MY SUN."

The other patrons did not see her, but they must have felt something amiss, because they began to fight, first with words, and then guns. Brown hid under his stool, his ears ringing from stray bullets, while the blood drained from nine men and Elko's last whore. It leaked so far and wide that all of Smith's Tavern turned crimson.

The carnage orphaned six horses, all with broken nerves and wills. Together, Brown and the foundling healed the animals, then wrought them new shoes of iron and copper, which they preened for passersby, like shiny new hats. Three weeks later, the foundling was shaken awake by an old soul, and told to hurry. The soul smelled like mare's milk, which reminded him of the mother he'd never met. He crept out from his straw bed stall, and discovered a parade of ghosts setting lose their former horses, and reclaiming them. The foundling held his breath.

"Shout. Help them!" the old soul cried out. "If you don't save them, you deserve the fate your father intends."

The foundling curled himself small, covered his ears, and tried not to weep. The old soul left him in disgust, and never returned. He felt that absence keenly, because all children miss their mothers. As the ghosts rode off, one after the next through the stable doors, each rider broke his horses' back. The sound was worse than any human lament, and for a moment, it clotted the blood in the foundling's heart, like milk mixed with vinegar.

In the morning, Master Brown found the carcasses of six horses in a line outside the stable. When he heard what happened, he lashed the foundling for his cowardice. Ever after, the ghost riders and their murdered horses raced through Elko, swarming Main Street like lost, hungry wolves. Their dead masters beat them while, on broken backs, they screamed.

After all he had seen, and the handicap of absent parents with which he'd been born, the foundling had a hole in his heart. He did not love anyone, and no one loved him. Even the horses seemed like obligation. When he turned fifteen, he told Brown, "I need to strike out on my own. I want to see something of the world that is good. I know it probably does not exist, but I have to find out for myself."

Brown was a reasoned man, and from travelers, knew that the West had changed. If you rode 100 miles in any direction, you'd find a different, modern place where none but the destitute believed in magic, and the law was not always corrupt. "Good," he said. "Go and find something better."

He made the boy a pair of metal shoes wrapped in leather, so that they might last the rest of his life, and saddled up his prized stallion. At dawn the foundling struck out with two other young men, the last of the Elko's children, in a population that now numbered less than ten. They headed West.

The three made it as far as San Francisco, where in their thirst, they stopped at a saloon. Six weeks later they'd lost all their money, and developed a taste for the pipe. When the boy exhaled that opiate, the smoke formed the shape of his father, looking back at him. A tall, dark man who shared his black hair. A man who knew his name, and did not call him foundling. He'd have stayed forever in the den, but the hole in his heart cried out for a different sort of filling; he missed Master Brown.

The foundling rode back East, through wilderness. He passed junk men and starving Indians, and winter storms that trapped families of pioneers. The wind blew through the rocks like whispers, or the commands of Gods. He got lost, and found, and lost again. His father followed him, always standing behind trees, or watching with angry eyes. By the time he came home three years had passed. The town of Elko was abandoned. Even Smith's Tavern was termite-rotted. All that remained was the blood-red floor, and its sign, which now read:

Foundling—Your Father came looking. Prepare his horse.

The foundling searched for days before discovering Master Brown's corpse under an apple tree. He still wore his old coat of brushed buffalo hide, but his skin had gone tight and sunken-in. The Foundling buried him, along with the horses from the stables, that had starved to death.

He took residence in Brown's house, and stabled his stallion. While hunting deer in the woods, he came across two more sick horses, which he nursed to health. He took pleasure in this, now that Brown was no longer looking over his shoulder, passing judgment. He realised he had a talent for offering comfort.

In the storm cellar below Browns house, he found a safe which held the shoe metal, including copper, silver, and heavy, priceless bars of gold. Along with this came a note, written in misshapen letters:

Of Sound Mind, I Will all My Worldly Possessions to the Foundling Boy, Whom I Believe to be the Only Son of Inez Erendira, fathered by the devil himself, whom we invited, because we ate our hearts like bitter castor oil. I loved the boy the way I loved his mother. Like a coward. And Now They are Both Gone and My Regret is the Sky.

At these words, the foundling wept. For nights, and weeks, and months, and a full year, sorrow weighted his blood like lead. He did not sleep, and forgot meals, and trudged through that empty town half-naked even in winter. When that year ended, he came out the other side with a heavy but mended heart. Though he had not known it at the time, he had been loved, and had given love, too.

He was twenty-one years old by the time he finished the cabin and mended the stables, so that they stood strong on that broken Main Street. His hearth fires burned thick winter smoke, which travelers, seeking shelter, surrounded like moths. They stopped, asking for a meal or bed. He always provided, and for a fee, attended their horses, whose souls appeared like shrunken shadows alongside their bodies, that only he could see. News soon travelled of the farrier with the magic hands, under whose care all horses emerged faster, more steady, and more calm, even under gunshots. It was worth staying with the strange man with black eyes, and the disembodied whispers they heard in the stables; a good horse was a man's kingdom, out here in the wilds.

The sheriffs, new to the West, and often assigned by the US Marshall's Department, came first. Like their masters, their horses were well-fed and slow, but distrustful, because they'd been beaten. The foundling housed them for weeks and months, and forged shoes that were u-shaped, blocked, or riveted. Some copper, some silver, some gold. His shoes were works of art, more ornate even, than Master Brown's. When he brushed down the beasts, he explained to them their lots in life, and the work expected of them. Once they knew these things, they accepted them, and returned to their masters with new leases.

Enough customers came, that enterprising men rebuilt Elko's Main Street. Smith's Tavern became a restaurant and Inn. Beside that, Farrier's Laundry, Steph's Bar, and Heinrich's General Store appeared. Cheer invaded the town like climbing morning glories birthed from a windswept seed. The ghosts had no old haunts to inhabit. It was 1900, and Elko, like the rest of the Old West, had reinvented itself in a way that hewed more closely to modern life.

After the sheriffs came the bounty hunters, always in twos or alone. Their horses were skinnier, and often mouth-foaming, gunshot deaf, or bullet-scarred in their hinds. The foundling salved their wounds, and bathed them in fine salts as if they were princes. He fed them fresh barley, eggs, and root vegetables to fatten them, and explained to them that their lots were badly drawn. Their masters wasted their money on liquor, and would one day get them killed by outlaws. Once they accepted this, they behaved. Their shoes were sharp, jagged things, that cut into the earth and left a mark, to remind them that while they would soon die, at least a part of them was eternal.

The world spun. The Foundling slept in Brown's old bed, because it served as protection from his father, who preferred the stable. Innovation seeped into Elko, like tiny drops of ink through water. Texas oilmen passed through. Women started talking about the vote. Kid Curry Logan finally got what he had coming. Henry Ford found a new way to turn men into animals.

With the drought, the Idaho root farmers arrived. Four and six starving horses dragged carts crammed with shoddy pine tables, wives' silver and lace dowries, and preserved beet jam as payment. The foundling took them in, too. He fed them like he fed their horses, and fattened them for weeks and even seasons at a time, until they were strong. *You are loved and respected, he told the horses. But your masters have no money, and you will be worked so hard you might die. Still, what you do is honourable, and you should take solace.* He crafted their shoes with swirls and intricate arcs made from majestic iron. Once they knew their lot, they accepted it, and carried their masters home on proud backs.

On the darkest night of December, 1908, came a man with wild eyes. His knock sounded like bricks, and they smashed the wood on the door that had once belonged to Brown. The foundling leaned into the opening. "What do you want?" he asked.

The man wore chaps, a bloody bandana, and coal black hair. For the first time, the Foundling saw a human soul. It was crinkled and black, and inside it, small creatures squirmed.

"I need you to fix my horse," the man said.

"I see no horse," the foundling answered.

"This," the man said, pointing at himself. "It fights me. I need you to break it, so it rides."

"I only take human customers, not devils," the foundling said.

The thing wearing human skin swore at him. "You bear His mark, but you don't even know what you are," he said. "You'll die unloved and alone. Just like your whore mother and coward guardian. You father will come for his horse, because he is the eater of souls." Then he turned, and started back down the empty road. He walked in jerking motions, because his human horse was fighting him.

The foundling did not know whether he believed this. But it weighed heavy in his heart, and be began to question the value of his work. Why did he soothe so many wretched horses, and make them pliant to a fate they didn't deserve? Why was life such cheap misery?

His joy leaked like sap from a tree. Less customers came, because they had less need, in a world of cars. Elko fell back into the past, as if it had been hurled there. The foundling watched it happen from his window, just like Brown had watched Inez. With regret and helplessness, and terror in his heart. His father would come soon; he could feel it.

The next to come were the robbers and murders. They pointed their revolvers, and left Brown no choice. He housed the horses, and the men who brought women to rape, and grudges to settle. Brown fed the animals, all sored with lesions, and hungry. It's useless to fight, he told them. You are unloved, and you carry monsters who will shoot you today or tomorrow, so make your peace. He gave them shoes of tin, that were too soft to protect them, because he did not like to lie. These animals could not be repaired in body or soul, and kept working in the same way they'd always worked. Except for the one, that ran away.

The nights in Elko got worse. Ghosts paraded. The horses he'd seen murdered so many years before stared at him through his windows. He thought about the girl who'd lit his pipe in San Francisco. Had she survived the earthquake? Was she thinking of him? He hadn't loved her then, but he believed now that he did, because every thought for him had become regret.

It happened one night during a blizzard in 1919, that he heard the loud neighing of a horse, and its hoof-beats, above the spinning wind. It came closer and closer, and he knew at the very core of him that the reaper had come. And it seemed sad to him, because the visit was a relief. His lot was not a good one, but he'd worked his best, and at forty-four, was tired, and so lonely it physically hurt.

The knock was hard. He opened the door. A man on horseback entered his home. The small table and chairs and pretty oak things he'd been given as payment went crashing. "Can I make you some soup?" he asked the rider, whose horse was pale as snow. The rider got down, and pulled off his hood. His hair was wild mange, and his teeth missing. His skin pocked. The foundling was sorry, for this was no angel of death, but an ordinary beast.

"Soup?" he asked.

The man nodded. They ate. The horse waited outside. He set out a bed for the man, but the man shook his head. "I need you to fix my horse," he said.

The Foundling nodded. "Of course. In the barn. My payment is what you can afford."

The man pointed at himself. "My horse fights me. I need you to break its spirit."

The foundling sighed. He knew he should shun the thing, but instead, he led the man out to the barn, and kept him in a stall next to his favourite stallion, and cleaned him, and spoke to him. In the morning, two more men arrived, both with chewed-out teeth and sunken eyes. He put these in the stalls, too.

"Your lot is the worst imaginable," he told them. "You house devils in your skin. But I'm no exorcist, and I cannot save you. I can only tell you to give up, and stop fighting. You are not human anymore; only beasts of burden."

And inside each man, he saw a tiny, withered soul, riddled with worms. He made them shoes of soft clay, so at least one place in their bodies did not hurt.

That night, eating dinner, gunshots rang out from Smith's Tavern, Farrier's Laundry, Steph's Bar, and Heinrich's General Store. He went to his window and witnessed the savagery. The town was littered with bodies. The year was influenza. The outside world was ashes and mustard gas. For once, Elko was no different than the rest.

The foundling walked into the street strewn with bodies. The thing that had shot all these men slouched forward. He was tall, and rotten. His body was a heap of broken bones upon which, he somehow still walked. He had no teeth. A mark on his arm was triple 6s.

"Father," the foundling said.

"Son," the monster answered. "You bare my mark, and now that I've used this one up, your are destined to be my horse, for that is your lot. Accept it."

The foundling let him into Master Brown's house where the trappings of comfort distracted him. They sat at the table and ate potatoes and deer. "When?" the foundling asked.

"Tonight," the devil answered. "I've got work to do. Darkness is a cancer, that spreads easily in times and places such as these. You will be my best horse yet."

The foundling looked down at his shoes, that Master Brown had made for him. They were leather on the outside, and gold on the inside, like a secret king's. "Let me sleep first, my last sleep," he said.

The monster agreed. The foundling could see his soul. It was worms, and worms alone.

That night, the foundling sneaked out into the stable. Six possessed men waited. Their devils teased and laughed, while the men inside them moaned. The foundling fired his pistol, one stall after the next. Because there are some burdens no man or beast should endure.

"I am the foundling, and I take the name Brown Erendira," he said out loud. "After the life that could have been." Once he said this, he knew that he was this man, born of love unconsummated, of loyalty that never once wavered, of work that had value.

In the morning, the devil tried to enter the foundling, but could not. The foundling raised his pistol and shot him, so that he had no body, save that of a donkey. This, the foundling locked in a stall, and made the most beautiful of the shoes he'd ever crafted with the last of all his metal. He fed the animal oats and apples and fine cakes, until it was fat and content, though its master, locked inside it, simmered.

Along Main Street, he cleaned and buried the last bodies of Elko. When he was done, he was an old man of fifty-five. The town began to fill again, but would never be the same. The cowboys and Indians were gone, and the range fenced in. Farriers served no purpose. And neither did men without learning. The devil from long ago had been right: he would die alone and unloved. But the devil had not known this: the potential of a thing has value. Even unexpressed, that value is palpable, and can change the world.

"The stories I could tell you," Brown Erendira announced like a crazy old fool at the new incarnation of Smith's Tavern five years later, when the year turned 1936, and Oakies and bankers alike were starving, except in Elko, where Brown Erendira had saved everything he'd ever earned, and shared it. "This place was a ghost town, haunted and full of devils. I shot six or seven of them, at least!"

Because he was kind, and in civilised places such as these, old men deserved respect, the patrons listened.

Sarah Langan is the author of the novels *The Keeper* and *The Missing*, and her most recent novel, *Audrey's Door*, which won the 2009 Stoker for best novel and was optioned by The Weinstein Company for film. Her short fiction has appeared in the magazines and anthologies *Fantasy & Science Fiction*, *Lightspeed*, *Brave New Worlds*, *The Year's Best Horror and Dark Fantasy 2011*, *The Living Dead 2*, and *Unspeakable Horror*. She is currently working on a post-apocalyptic young adult series called *Kids* and two adult novels: *Empty Houses*, and *My Father's Ghost*.

"The title *Tell it to my Horse*, a book by Zora Neale Hurston, refers to demonic possession: a spirit mounts a human, and when the human is asked a question, the spirit answers, "Tell it to my horse." I think that's pretty cool, and at the time I was asked to write this story, my husband was directing a movie about demonic possession. I was thinking of the old west, and the ways in which mankind, with its dubious gift of self-awareness, is necessarily a horse to fate and God or whatever you believe runs this show. That's how *Beasts of Burden* was born."

WHAT GOD HATH WROUGHT?
Adam Nevill

1848. Utah.

And in the darkness the soldier came upon the old man. Five miles out the dragoon had seen the red spark of the camp fire, down in the desert, like it was the last ember in hell yet to wink out and leave only the abyss behind; the black void that was there before all of this, and before hell too.

And the soldier came upon that old man as silently as a Comanche upon his pony comes with ease into an enemy's camp to leave more widows in this world than it ever wanted. Came out of nothing with not so much as a jingle of spurs or a jangle of sabre against his saddle; like he'd been showed by the Apache scouts down on the Rio Grande, when he rode for "Old Rough and Ready" General Zachary Taylor against the Mexican Army of the North.

When the old man saw the dragoon come out of the night air just like he was some kind of avenging angel with an hour glass and scythe in each celestial hand, it was too late to reach for the musket he had laid out on his bed roll.

Around the fire the soldier spied a mule, a pick, a shovel, some pans. Smelled coffee, a mess of beans in a skillet. A prospector, heading for the Barbary Coast of San Francisco. Another fool.

Since the news broke in New York about the gold out west, the soldier had been coming across these men and their desperate dreams all along the trails through Iowa, Nebraska, Wyoming. Men would suffer for their greed more than they would suffer for anything else. Give them snow and road agents and Indians and starvation and every disease that rolled your eyes up inside your head, and all the privations of hell on top of that, and they would still suffer and make others suffer for a mere rumour of gold.

"Easy," he said to the old man, whose yellow eyes had gone wider than billiard balls, and his skittery honking mule now seemed to be transmitting a crazy terror into its owner; who might yet reach for the musket, or snatch at the Bowie knife stuck in the sand, and end up getting himself shot dead.

From up high in his dragoon saddle, the soldier holstered the pistol in plain sight. Then flashed all forty four inches and six pounds of his sabre through the reaching red light of the camp fire, before sinking "Old Wristbreaker" back into its scabbard, real smooth. "You ain't the one," he said, without even looking at the prospector, who was just sat on his ass, all wide of eye and open of mouth before his skillet.

The soldier dismounted.

"Well I sho' is pleased to hear it, sir," The old man said. "Had all the fear a man can git for one day."

"Mind sharin' that fire a time?"

Out of instinct for self preservation, and a relief that he'd live a little longer, maybe even long enough to see some of that gold up near San Francisco, the old man said, "Sure. Got a mess of beans and some biscuit I'm willing to part with." The old man would refuse him nothing; the soldier knew that. There was a time when he'd have felt bad for scaring some old boy in the night, but that time was hard to even remember now.

"Coffee be appreciated. Few words. Then I be pulling out."

The old man nodded back at him. His beard was filthy with tobacco juice; his face creased like dried fruit in a store jar, the skin brown as molasses. He smelled of mule, years of sweat, bear grease, pipe tobacco, and shit.

The soldier fed his horse; talked to her in a soft voice, touched her ears. She nuzzled him like an obedient daughter. Then he pulled his cape of navy blue wool round his neck and squatted opposite the prospector.

The fire snapped between them, blinded them to the greater darkness of the desert, a whole universe of it with no edges, out there.

"Where ye headed, fella?" The old man asked, jittery in his hands that were busy with the pouring of his guest's coffee, black as oil, into a tin cup from the jug sat among the embers.

The soldier never answered or moved his pale blue eyes from staring into the fire, right into the red ashes. "Yer beans burnin'. Go ahead. Eat," he eventually said.

The old man complied. Straight from the hissing skillet and piled onto a long spoon, he shovelled beans into the dark hole within that dirty beard; all the time wary of moving his big veiny eyes from the soldier, who removed his leather gloves and held the metal mug of coffee between both hands.

They sat in silence for a while, until the soldier broke his stare from the fire and looked at the old man's meagre provisions; a few sacks tied with rope, two large canteens, probably already empty first day out of the mountains. He'd seen others, foot sore and half-mad with thirst, carrying twice as much. "You still got five hundred miles of desert to ride. Think you can make it?"

The old man laid aside the skillet. He took a pipe from a shirt pocket as dark and greasy as the flakes he stuffed into the little clay bowl with fingers thick as corn cobs and nails dirty like they'd been blacking boots. "Aimin' to resupply from them Saints."

The soldier's face tensed; his blue eyes narrowed hard and the old man couldn't look into them for long. "Don't call 'em that. Saints. They ain't no such thing."

The old boy nodded. "Them sons a bitches with Brigham Young been shakin' everyone down passes through here, I hears," the old man said, wary all over again, but eager to be conspiratorial. "But there ain't nowhere else to get feed. Supplies. Not this far out."

The soldier stayed quiet. Remembered the cup in his hand, sipped at the coffee. Winced. "You come across any of them today?"

The old man looked down. "Ain't rightly sure."

"Either you come across them, or you ain't. Which is it?"

"Easy fella. I see all kinds. Mind my own business mostly. I got no beef with no one. Them Mormon Saints neither." He looked at the insignia on the soldier's cap, swallowed. "You one of them Grey's militia, from Missouri way? If you are, I ain't no Mormon. I swear on the Lord, sir. Just aimin' to buy some vittels from them so I can get to the ocean. I —"

"I ain't ridin' with no militia."

The prospector relaxed, sucked on his unlit pipe. "Them Mormon's all out at the dead water. Timpanogos. Since '47 I heard. New settlement.

Gods own kingdom they callin' it. The Saints Zion. You got a beef with them, then that's where they is at."

The Dragoon spat. "They ain't all out there with Brigham Young. There's others of a similar creed. Settin' up on their own. Nearby."

The old man sucked too hard at the pipe stem; a shake had come into his shoulders. The soldier looked hard at the old man. "You ain't never asked my name."

The prospector's hands shook too now. He cleared his throat and his voice wasn't much when it came out. "I learned a long time ago to mind my own."

"You never asked on account of you just guessing at who I am. That right?"

"Man hears things."

"What they calling me now?"

The prospector started to look like his skin was full of sand. "Look, sir. I'd as soon as share a pipe with you and get my head down —"

"I ain't gonna hurt you, old man. Long as you're straight with me."

"Yessir." The old man dared to look up at him. "Some talk about a man out here. Cavalry. The Devil's right hand, they been sayin'. Man I hear about's goin' to chase Brigham Young and his polygamist sinners right back into hell. Others be callin' him the Destroying Angel. Like it's the Lord's work he be doin'." He finished with a swipe of one grubby hand across the appalling beard.

Under the brim of his cap, the old man saw the soldier smile. "They's work to be done, whether it be the devil's or the Lord's, who can say? But looks like I been chosen for it. And it ain't Brigham Young and his congregation I'm here for. It's them others that came this way too, and the preacher they follow."

The fire seemed to shrink then, all of its own, and take away its glare and heat from them, as if the mere mention of a certain man was enough to even put out the light of the stars. And all the blood suddenly seemed to flow out of the old man, leaving his tanned face pale as a dressmaker's dummy.

"Have you seen the black horse? Have you seen the black carriage?" the soldier asked the old man, who started to shake again, like the night time cold suddenly dropped a few degrees further at the mention of these things of black. He pulled his bedroll around his shoulders. It had once been grey, but was now just grubby with no particular colour around the holes in it. The old man nodded. "And I'm fixin' to forget it."

The soldier leaned his face further into the firelight. "To have seen it and still be breathin' is somethin'."

"I never got close enough to parlay. No, sir. That be who you lookin' for?" The soldier said nothing.

The old man reached out a hand, pointed a finger at the dragoon. "They say an angel put a curse on them, and only an angel can take it off again. You an angel, soldier?"

"Who I was and who I am ain't the same things no more. One time, I was Sergeant Ephraim Lisle. Dragoon. US Cavalry. Now, you could say I truly am an instrument of vengeance. But I ain't no angel."

"He took yer wife?" The old man said, his voice not yet put back together, but his curiosity was overriding his fear.

The soldier mused that the story of their meeting and what passed between them would be told again, by other old men at the foot of mountains older than them, older than time, and the tale would change with every telling, until no one would ever know who that soldier ever was. It mattered little what he said. The only truth in the world was what you saw with your own eyes and that truth never came from another man's fool mouth. But maybe some of his purpose that had its business with death, should be put in the wind. Tonight. Here. He was close; and this might be his last night on earth. Ought to be, considering the odds that would be stacked high against him in the morning. Maybe a last testament was called for at these times.

"Sister." And just that word in his mouth and in the air around him, seized him up inside and he had to dip his head so the old man could not see the tears that shone in his eyes; eyes that had been open for twenty five years but had seen things no man should ever see in all of ten thousand.

And then he spoke for himself as much as he spoke for the old bearded fool in the desert. So that there was a chance it might be known that when all of the black blood was let, it was shed for a purpose pure and righteous. He began by telling the old prospector that the thing that rode the black horse, with the black carriage rolling behind it, was no longer a man.

"Sho' didn't look much like one neither," the old man said to himself, and now seemed uncertain about his appetite for such stories in this lonesome part of the earth. "I ain't sure they's any damn thing a man can do to hurt them more than they is already sufferin'. I heard they all had the black pox and was out here to do some dyin'. Sure looked like it this mornin'."

"You heard of the Second Great Awakening?" The soldier asked the night. "And of the con man known as Joseph Smith?"

"The martyr."

"He weren't no martyr. He was a bum. A trickster who sold himself as a seer and a prophet to them with shit for brains in Missouri, and then Illinois once Missouri come to its senses. A dabbler in peep stones, scrying, witchery. Plenty a fool and his money were soon parted, old man, when Joseph Smith was around. As they was soon parted from their wives and daughters and . . . sisters too."

The prospector nodded. "They say he got gold tablets straight from the lord by way of an angel Moroni in a cave? On the hill Cumorah."

"Horse shit."

"No doubt."

"But Smith got something he weren't bargaining for, sho' enough. He and his friend in black you saw out ridin'. In an old Indian cave in the hill they call Cumorah."

"Fella that went inside with Joseph Smith was a man named Lemuel Hawkins. Man just as crooked as Smith. Was a time old Lemuel Hawkins and Joseph Smith claimed they could find treasure with their black magic and peep stones. But it weren't no angel of the lord who they mixed it with inside that cave in Cumorah."

"How you come by way of this?"

"When I come back from the war in Mexico, my sister was missing from home, as well as the damn fool aunt and uncle I left her with. And most every other woman an' girl in my home town was gone too. Cuz they were all wedded to the Prophet and on the great Exodus to find the Kingdom of God, out in this desert. Following the man once known as Lemuel Hawkins. Who claimed he was given instructions like Moses, in some cave, by an angel Moroni."

"Before I lit out to fetch my sister back, I went and stood in that cave, looking for the divine message. And all I saw was drawin's up on them walls. What the Indians and them before the Indians, had put up there. A warning. Any fool could see it. Ain't no angel of the lord was ever in that place before or since. I reckon that cave went all the way down to hell. Sure smelled like it. I seen brigs, I seen jails plenty. And that's what that cave was. A prison with no bars. Made to keep something inside it for a long time, old man, with something stronger than bars. What them fools found in that cave, was nothing I reckon they were bargaining to find neither. But those fools broke it out of there."

And the soldier remembered the place because he could not ever forget the terrible black fear that frosted his wits, like he was walking in the devil's own foot prints. It could have been a child that made those markings on the brown stone of the long low cave in the Hill Cumorah. But the pictures in the damp and the dark were all the worse to look upon because of their rough nature; and what the unschooled style of the artists had scratched on stone, when viewed by lamplight, a mind given to figuring would not easily forget.

The soldier guessed it was the thing that traded under the name the Angel Moroni. So tall and thin and tatty about the head. Etched over and over again, onto the walls and the ceiling. Striding at the little figures of the Indian braves who pointed their bows upwards. In its talons it often held the bodies of men. Into its spiky mouth it shoved them, like they were corn dollies to a dog. It was able to fly like an eagle in some of the drawings too, and all the animals and men of the earth would flee beneath it.

And the longer the soldier stood in that cave and moved his lantern here and there, he got to figuring that the thing the Indians had taken to drawing with such frequency and desperation, might nary have been a single deity after all; it had been drawn many times by them, because there had been more than one.

In one corner of the low dark cave that still stank of sulphur and the meat of a dead man left in the sun, he determined another clear message being imparted to him, as if those warriors of old were telling another warrior in another time that such things that preyed upon the flesh of men, and had to be shut up in caves, could be beaten. Because the little figures of the braves on the far walls of the long low cave were using bone and flint axes to take off the angels' heads, one by one.

But why the Indians had left one behind, alive, sealed inside a cave in the dark, was still a mystery. Because judging by the way it had dug at that floor, and thrown itself against the walls with stones in its long fingers, and then just ended up waiting and dreaming and reaching out for the minds of the men who came nearest to it, the soldier guessed it had been inside the cave for a very long time. And it had left its bones behind. Because no man walked upright on legs like that. But whatever black spirit those legs and bones had once carried, must have still been deep inside that hill Cumorah when Joseph Smith and Lemuel Hawkins found the cave and opened it up like two greedy lecherin' fools all out of better ideas.

The dragoon sighed. "I reckon what folks say was the angel Moroni, promised ole Smith and Hawkins it could make them gods among men. God men. And they could take as many wives as there were cattle in the field, and as much wealth as was in all the world. So them pair of hustlers with nothing left to lose, who wanted to clean up in the Second Great Awakening, made some kind of bargain."

The soldier paused, spat into the fire. "Seems they had it all too, for a while. Over twenty wives each and a parish of six thousand fools, who handed over all their worldly goods, victuals and assets to them. People who were ready to die for their prophets.

"When Smith was murdered in Carthage by the militia, Brigham Young took up Smith's believers and lit out here from Illinois. Seen his own opportunity there, I reckon. But the other one who was in that cave with Smith, Lemuel Hawkins, goes by the name of Brother Lehi now. He broke away from Smith early. Started sayin' he was the true leader of a lost Hebrew tribe, not Joseph Smith. Pronounced himself true king of the Fair-skinned Nephrites. Maybe he thinks he is, but whatever he is, it sure ain't Lemuel Hawkins no more. I reckon whatever was in that cave got hisself into old Hawkins. And it was Hawkins took my sister, and took the whole damn town too. Aimed to bring his congregation out here. One hundred and forty men, women and children, ever' one, came with Hawkins. Ain't but a few left breathin' now. I been finding and dealing with them . . . all the way in here from Illinois."

"'Bout your sister?"

"Ain't seen her since '46. I'm guess she's still be followin' the black carriage, and the black horse."

"I sure hope she ain't, soldier," the old man said, and looked into the palms of old hands as worn and beaten as boot leather.

The soldier swallowed another mouthful of the bitter coffee. "Would had been a mercy for me to find her back aways with all them others. She was not yet fourteen years old when Lehi took her for his bride. What she is now only the Lord can say."

"They's sayin' you's shootin' Saints dead soon as you look at 'em. Running them to ground. Burnin' farms."

The soldier nodded. "Some. Sure. Them's that used to be neighbours. Family too. Kill't my old school teacher last week in Bear Creek. But it's only them's that Lehi made into Nephrites I got dealin's with." The soldier looked hard at the old man. "I be doing them a favour. And this world too. You truly seen Lehi and his tribe of Fair-skinned Nephrites, you'd know it too, old man. Devil in that cave already took 'em for his own."

The old man wiped at his mouth. Produced a small metal flask. Uncapped it, offered it. "They was down yonder. South of the dead sea."

The soldier shook his head at the offer. "It truly there, the great dead sea?" he asked.

The old prospector nodded. "Seen it with my own eyes jus' this mornin' while lookin' for Brigham Young's place. I heard of Timpanagos back east. Nary believed a word of it. But it's right there, just as sho' as you is, sir. White sand of salt. A dead ocean in the middle of it. Godforsaken. A place damned in the Lord's eyes, where the damned will surely congregate with impious ways."

"Where was Lehi's place?"

"Half a day's ride due south. They got up a few buildings. Some tents too. I took it for Brigham Young's Zion. Thought I was lost and all turned around from the Wasatch mountains. But I never was, and it weren't Brigham Young's new town I found neither. That's north a' here. This place must be Lehi's. It ain't on any map. Nor should it be. But I see's a bunch of his people comin' through the desert this morning, out of them buildings they got up like I told you. I saw 'em through a spy glass from back aways, then lit out up here, real quick."

"What you see?"

"Was like you said. Black horse. Black carriage."

"How they lookin' to you?"

The old prospector stared at the embers. Studied his pipe like he was surprised to suddenly find it in his hand. Then looked at the soldier, and shrank further down inside his blanket. "What's the worse thing you ever seen?"

In the shadows under the peak of his cap, the dragoon's eyes narrowed. "Same thing as you I'm bettin'."

The old man nodded. "Seen my younguns get took by cholera in '35. Wife a year later. But hard as that was to see, least ways doctors say it's the way of things. But them Nephrites down there ain't part of any way of things I ever seen afore this mornin'."

The soldier nodded. Took out his tobacco pouch and a thin sheet of paper. Spat into the fire once he had it rolled and lit. "At Palo Alto a gunner in Ringgold's artillery fired a single shell, full with shot, and it took down a whole Mexican band. They was playing to rally their side against our artillery. Nary one of them stood up agin. Not even the saviour could a' put all them pieces back together." He shook his head. "Never thought I'd see a thing as bad as that agin. But I was wrong. How many you see out yonder this mornin'?"

"Didn't look long enough to count. But there was him, Preacher Lehi, on his horse. And . . . and his wives in the carriage behind. Some chillun too. Six, seven maybe. Maybe more. An' all lookin' like the dead that rise on Judgement Day, but what's come early."

The trooper nodded. "That's them."

"If they the devil's own, soldier. How can a man cut them down?"

Thumbing a hand back at his horse, the soldier said, "1843 breechloading carbine does some mean work at distance. That's how I started the cullin'. Take 'em down, then get in close for the disarticulatin'. Afore they's got wise anyway, and started hidin' like Injuns. Waitin' for me. When things get close, I got a smoothbore pistol back there too. Fires a 230-grain ball. Clusters up twelve inches wide on fifty yards. Long as it's about they's heads, she be fine." He nodded at his sabre. "Wrist Breaker come out swift when we get eye-to-eye. The head on a Fair-skinned Nephrite got to come away from the shoulders, so old Wrist Breaker done most of them so far."

The old man was impressed and afraid; his dark mouth hung open like he was some kind of imbecile. "Shee-it." He snapped out of his gaping. "You gonna do 'em all, soldier?"

"Ever' last one."

The old man swallowed and his eyes went wide again. "What about your sister?"

The soldier stared right into the black heavens. "She ain't my sister no more. She ain't like you and me. No, she ain't. When the time comes, the time comes." He pinched his fingers into his eye sockets and the old man looked away to let him have his moment.

"Aw heck," the dragoon said, shaking his head. "That's how it spread. Folk wanted to hold onto their own, even though they was bit by Lehi. Then they got bit too by their own folks. Pretty soon, the whole town was on its way out here. All bit. Converted. All of them Fair-skinned Nephrites."

And when the soldier rode away from the old man, who he left with a gift of three hundred Yankee dollars, and his campaign medal, and his story, he remembered too the time he rode away from his sister. All white in the face with her bottom lip trembling she was, as the last person she knew enough to love, rode away. He remembered every moment of their parting. Not only because it was the last time he saw her. But he remembered every moment of their parting because it was wrong of him to have left her alone in the world at his Uncle's dirt farm. Consumption took their daddy and small pox killed their ma. And they was all each other ever had after. Two orphans with a dour aunt who knew more scripture than she did kindness, and an uncle who thought the young should get whipped like mules. And he left little Mercy Lisle with them because she wasn't old enough to lit out and run herself, like he did by joining the army to get into the scrape down in Texas. He left her cryin' on that porch. And only after he was gone from sight did he let himself feel the cold unbearable anguish that he had left behind in that child's little heart. And it burst inside him like canister round and the hurting never faded like the scars of old wounds are supposed to do.

But he kept himself alive through every charge at the Mexican lines, and kept his head down and under every one of General Mariano Arista's cannon balls, that pounded out of those big brass guns and came down at the dragoons like the fists of giants thumping the earth all about their mounts. He kept his head and his blood all in one place through that war, because his memory of the abandoned child on that porch kept him eaten by guilt so strong, that not even his recriminations about what his sabre did to the hatless heads of routed Mexican infantry could ever be the equal of.

There was nothing left of her when he returned from the war to his uncle's patch in Illinois; none of her trinkets, or any of the three little grey dresses she wore, or the dolly his pa had made her. Nothing in her bare room in that ramshackle house sat at a slouch on a few acres of miserable dust. Every farmhouse was the same for ten miles; left dismal and swept empty of life on account of the little settlement's vigour to be part of Prophet Lehi's lost Hebrew tribe of Fair-skinned Nephrites.

Some Gentiles across the wash told him of the town's exodus following their suffering a plague that past winter, from which many of them miraculously arose from their sick beds, but changed. Ravaged bone-thin by disease, but somehow brighter of eye, and quicker on foot than any survivor of the black pox had a right to be.

And the Nephrites had organised themselves but four months before his return from war, to travel in a long waggon train to the promised land as the Day of Judgement was all but nigh. Because Lehi's congregation needed to be in place at the Great Dead Sea to escape the persecution of the apostates, the gentiles and the already damned, who comprised a multitude so vast that it included anyone who was not a devoted and servile follower of the Prophet Lehi.

And the soldier learned from the first few Fair-skinned Nephrites he came across, as they snapped up at him with their dry mouths, around the sole of his boot that pressed their necks into the dust, that his sister had been wed to his uncle soon as he left for the war. Then taken from his uncle, along with his aunt, and married to Lehi after the Prophet's final engagement with the angel Moroni on the Hill Cumoreh.

Lehi had branded his uncle an apostate, the fate of many simple men in that town; men who atoned for their lack of faith by parting company with their wives and children and goods and chattels, and finally with the very blood in their veins if the prophet so wished. It was the only favour the Prophet Lehi had ever done him; saving him the trouble of shooting down the dog that was his uncle.

But this act of mass witlessness and self-trickery perpetrated by an entire community, the soldier began to see as an act of the most grievous wrongdoing against his sister; the little girl he left behind, defenceless and alone. And an act that demanded retribution. A swift and violent end to any and all who stood by and watched as his sister was married to those two sons of bitches, so full of low animal cunning they may as well have been prairie dogs and run to the Great Dead Sea on all fours.

And his first opportunity, after leaving the old prospector, to settle matters, or to find the very end of his own dealings on this earth, came in a long thin ravine made of red rock and floored with shadows and dust, south of the Great Dead Sea.

The soldier rode slowly through it, his carbine resting across the saddle, and his eyes moved beneath the peak of his cap from his horse's ears to the steep sides of the ravine. He'd ridden all morning on the prospector's directions, and guessed this was the last of the canyons before he came across the settlement that the Nephrites had hidden here.

He could see it was a strategic location. Far enough away from Brigham's Mormon Saints to not compete, but close enough to both lay the blame on them for its nefarious actions, and to attract its share of the sun-beaten, thirsty California gold rush traffic, that could be waylaid in these ravines and gathered like rich pickings.

Toward the end of the ravine, his horse began to pull her head away from whatever scent she'd caught on a cool morning breeze. The soldier calmed her by whispering into her ear like he always did, and stroking her fine chestnut neck with one hand.

She cantered to one side of the ravine and they waited until her master could also hear the squeak of the axles and the rolling creak of the carriage's wheels across the rocky floor.

The Dragoon dismounted and crouched, not more than two feet from the stirrup of his saddle, aiming the carbine straight ahead. When the carriage came rattling and shaking around the bend in the ravine, he was disappointed to see that Prophet Lehi was not out front on his black horse, leading this gathering party. With the soldier despatching every one of his assassins that the Prophet sent back east to stop him culling the stragglers and feed-gatherers and convert hunters of the Fair-skinned Nephrite tribe, it had become too dangerous for their leader to range too far from Zion. The soldier had cut, shot, or smashed down some thirty-three Nephrites to date; another thirty he'd found dead, killed by other hands, including their leader's; over forty more he'd found withered to husks from starvation along the trail he'd tracked them on to Utah. He doubted there could be more than forty left in the congregation that had reached the Great Dead Sea.

The man who sat up front in the waggon was not Lehi either, who he had only seen three times and at a distance. The Prophet was taller and more horribly thin than any man he had ever seen. He always wore a black suit, gold watch chain, short preacher's cape, and a hat of good quality wool felt, with a tall crown, curved brim, and matching hat band ribbon around the base of the crown.

Behind the figure driving the carriage through the ravine, the soldier saw a collection of whitish hair and dowdy bonnets. He waited for the preacher to appear, because he had always been near the waggon on previous sightings. Waited, cursing under his breath, until the black carriage with those big narrow wheels was fifty yards away from him and the driver saw him plainly. As the driver pulled-up on the reins of his train, the soldier shot him back into the bucket seat. Caught him up high in the chest and punched him sideways in his seat, where he sat with his papery maw just snatching at the air.

The sound of the carbine bullet echoing through that ravine set off the passengers into a terrible shrieking, accompanied by the throwing of their long arms up and into the early red sunlight.

As he reloaded the carbine, he heard Lehi from further back out of sight, issue an order. And the passengers, three women and one man naked from the waist down, stood up and tottered in the carriage like they were in a rowing boat that was sinking fast. They disembarked over the sides quickly and scuttled away to either side of the ravine.

When he'd reloaded the carbine, beside the shot driver who was still swallowing at the air and holding his throat, all that was left to see of the Nephrites were suggestions of sprightly dark shapes, crawling upwards. There was no clear shot to be had. The trooper swore and holstered the carbine. Then swung up and into his saddle. He drew his sabre and kicked his horse forward, to a canter that she knew preceded a charge.

And down that valley he thundered, his sabre forward, angled down so he could see the flat slotted throat, level with his charge's bit. And he passed that carriage in a slipstream of dust. His sabre flashed but once before returning to position, and the head and forearms of the drive came asunder from his brittle body as the trooper was already passing away from him.

Above him the soldier received the sense that four dark figures had gone scratching like ocean crabs in flight from a sea bird's sharp beak. They were unarmed save for one Mississippi musket he saw the male drag off behind its long legs. But as this was the closest he'd ever come to Lehi, the soldier kept on the charge like it was those Mexican gunners he was riding down at Palo Alto. The Prophet dropped from his thin horse and ran to the right side of the ravine as the cavalry dragoon rode upon him.

The Prophet's black horse reared and shook a terrible yellow mouth from which no spittle would ever froth again. The dragoon aimed his mount right at it. Then cleaved its bone muzzle and skull in two great parts with Old Wrist Breaker as he passed its shuddering angry shape.

The dragoon inclined his charger to chase the scrabbling Prophet into the rocks, but his horse buckled, and then slid sideways, before he even heard the shot from somewhere behind his right ear.

In the rushing cold of the dawn, the crimson world of dust and stone was all a blur about him, and he jumped from his horse before she bumped and skidded across the valley floor.

He rolled and came to his feet with his sabre up high like the French Hussar taught them back east. He hobbled back to his horse who was shot bad through the neck by two balls from one barrel. Took from the saddle his carbine and ran to the closest side of the ravine opposite from where he'd been shot at.

He went up the ravine twenty feet, and no more in case the shooter had reloaded and could sight him in the open. The soldier dropped down behind a big red boulder that showed him the way in and out of the valley from each side. Three Nephrites were somewhere up above him. Another two, one of them Lehi, were on the other side. "Son of a bitch," he said.

"That you Trooper Ephraim Lisle?" It was Lehi calling out from where he hid like some black spider in the rocks.

"You know it." The trooper peered across the ravine to see if the Prophet had poked up his white face.

"Little Mercy Lisle I keep close, Ephraim. I think you know that. Real close out here on those cold, cold nights. Your uncle may have made her a woman, but I been ploughin' her like a dry field, soldier. You hear me?"

The soldier gritted his teeth and two of them broke their tips clean off at the back of his mouth.

"But I'm a generous man, Ephraim. I might be willin' to let you stud little Mercy yourself. Now, how about that, soldier blue?"

"You tryin' to get a move out of me, preacher. Well it's nearly workin'," the soldier said to himself, and had to bite down so hard on his sleeve and fill his mouth with wool to stifle his sobs of such rage that all he could see was hot red blood pumping through his eyes. And it was all he could do to keep himself nailed to the earth and not to rise up with his pistol and sword and run at the Nephrites across the wash.

"God in heaven," he prayed. "Lord who has walked beside me through the valley of the shadow of death, I ask you now, just one more favour. That you keep me strong and breathin' long enough to send these devils back to the mouth of the hell they come crawlin' right out of... After that my lord, I am happy to come home and take good care of my sister like I never did that last time."

And on the last word of his prayer he saw the long shadow of the first Nephrite come crawlin' through the dawn for him. Like the long shanks of a scarecrow put up in a Missouri corn field, and about as well put together as some bird-frighter too, it was coming down the wall of the ravine. Head first, body after. Hopping and jerking quick, like a bat he'd once seen moving across some dirt.

The soldier used the instincts only a man used to being put under plenty of gun fire can call upon, and he stayed put. Never twitched a muscle even when the raggedy thing's shadow covered him up completely. They rarely made a sound; the Nephrites when stalking. Lest a man saw them comin', or got some sign from a shadow, it was all over for that man, and he had no choice but to convert right there and then as their dirty teeth baptised his flesh. But the soldier had learned from the Indian scouts in the army, as he had learned from the Indians who made those drawings in that cave on the Hill Cumoreh; had learned how to follow signs in the dirt and to move without leaving any himself; learned too how to be still and to wait as all the killers on the plains and in the desert wait. Before he struck.

He saw it as he turned and lengthened the arm holding Old Wristbreaker; saw it readying to leap like a starving man upon the carcase of a horse in a famine. And before the black eyes in the paper-dry face had a chance to blink, and adjust to the sudden whirl of dust and sunlight on steel before it, the Nephrite was looking up at the indigo sky. And three feet away from the workings of its jaw in the dirt, and the attempts to twist that terrible head on a scrawny neck severed, lay its long body, so thin and hard among the loose folds of clothes it no longer filled so well.

The soldier looked up the wall of the ravine and saw two more, hanging like black shadows upon the red rocks. They paused, then reached down their yellowy faces, snake-like, with threadbare heads pushed forward like geese with no feathers, as if to sniff at the sudden commotion they had witnessed below and not yet fully understood.

Their hesitation gave the soldier time to raise his pistol and shoot the closest one clean off the rock. It came out of the air shrieking, but thumped so hard against a boulder next to him he heard its back break like a tomato cane. He saw that it had once been a woman. The ball from his pistol had shot most of its black bonnet away, and half of the skull along with it. The washed-out grey eyes rolled up. A small sigh like a hiss escaping from a kitten, came out of the pale, lipless muzzle. It never moved again.

Up on one knee, carbine butt packed into a familiar embrace of his shoulder, just like a cavalry trooper down off his horse and ready to fire in battle, he sighted the other one. It turned and skittered like a long rat, back up the red rock wall. Strands of white hair had come loose from the bun on the back of its head, and streamed down the dusty cloth of its dress. He'd seen this one before, a long time ago, eating a snake in a valley in Wyoming. Maybe she'd been the wife of a miller back home, but he couldn't be certain.

It was hard work crawling upward on that sandy rock this second time and the Nephrite struggled. It made a pitiful keening sound in its throat, like a goat, because it must have known the tables had been turned on its sneaking approach down that dawn-lightened rock. The trooper shot out its back in a great puff of dust.

It hung on for a few seconds before dropping straight down, close to the face of the cliff, before hitting a promontory and bouncing away, over his head, and further down toward the valley floor.

Their was a terrible strangled cry of rage and anguish from across the ravine, and he heard the pounding of thin hard feet over the rocks and through the dust. One other voice cried out: Lehi's. "Brother be still!" the Prophet commanded, but the last of his congregation still standing was so driven by fury and grief, there was no delaying its desire for an immediate retribution.

Calmly, the soldier reloaded the carbine; working quietly with steady hands. Then peeked over the ridge of his position and saw the female Nephrite he'd just shot from the cliff face crawling slowly back toward either the black carriage or the other side of the ravine where Lehi had been taunting him. One of its stick arms was twisted backwards and flopped across the ruin of its exposed spine. The legs were useless. Even if it made it back to the Prophet, Lehi would not let it live. He'd often found the bodies of those Lehi had saved him the trouble of despatching; whatever the insult caused to bring about apostasy the soldier could but guess, but mad Lehi often killed his own by bludgeoning their skulls with something blunt; almost certainly his boot heel.

The soldier guessed the husband of the broken-backed female was the thing now racing across to him. He smiled when he saw that it carried the musket the Nephrites had in the waggon. The soldier remembered the sudden sideways fall of his horse, shot out from under him, and he stopped smiling.

Leaning up on to his toes, one blue knee pressed into the rock, he sighted the carbine at the hopping fright that came at him through the ravine. Its long arms were thrown into the air and it carried the musket like a club. The sleeves of its black jacket and the hair shirt beneath it, appeared too short for the length of its thin pale forearms. Its trousers were long gone, as was its underwear. A pelvis papered with mottled skin topped two shanks thin as oars, that strode its clawed yellowish feet through the dust toward him.

At fifteen feet the soldier shot off the bereaved husband's face, along with the top of its head, leaving just the jaw hanging down beneath the backward spray of black juice, pinkish drops and dusty skull bone that pattered amongst the dry rocks like an unexpected rain.

As he reloaded the pistol and carbine without once looking at his hands, the soldier peered over his cover and watched the other side of the ravine. He holstered the pistol, sheathed the sword and leapt over the rock; he followed the scratching the female Nephrite had made in the dust as it crawled away, only to then see its husband blasted off its hoary feet.

The trooper stamped on the back of the wounded female's head to stop its mutterings, and felt the skull give way like a cabbage underfoot in a farmer's field. Then cut the head free with two sawing swipes of Old Wrist Breaker, before mounting the greyish ruin of the head upon the point of the sabre and holding it aloft.

"Lehi! See what comes to the Fair-skinned Nephrites. Nary one of your flock will see another night. By the Lord and all that is righteous, you will be smote down. And you will see your flock cut like wheat afore you go. I promise you that, you son of a whore's cunt!"

There was no answer from across the ravine. No movement, save a trickle of pebbles and sand from somewhere up high. The Prophet had been making his retreat while the trooper despatched the last two of his congregation, who had unwittingly gathered here that morning for a cleansing by steel and iron ball. Lehi would be gone now, the soldier guessed, retreating on foot to his ramshackle Kingdom of God.

The two mares that pulled the black carriage were nothing more than bone heads covered in dusty hide, rotten manes and ribs sticking through skin so thin and cluttered with moving blow flies it looked and smelled like they'd been dead for months. Their eyes were milky sightless orbs, hanging with bunches of white ticks. Their smell was of graves freshly interned in the eternal black fields of Hades. Their distended bellies were peppered with tooth marks, from where the faithful had bled them down to these sorry, tired husks.

He cut through each long neck with one stroke of Old Wristbreaker and they fell swift, with a clatter of old bones within their bridles. The black carriage would roll no more across God's earth.

There was little inside the bed of the waggon. Some metatarsels; three bibles that had been chewed down to the bindings by old dirty teeth; a child's bonnet, stamped into the dust; and two long thigh bones from either a man or a steer, he couldn't be sure, but they had been whittled by a fastidious gnawing to thin flutes of scratched bone, bleached white.

The dragoon looked at the sky: indigo turned to blue cut with pink striations. In the west a great yolk of hot sun seemed to be peeking beneath the horizon like a fire at the hem of a tent's skirt. The Nephrites would be inside when the sun burnt this desert white. He'd rather fight them in the open. But it would now be a race on foot between him and the Prophet to the promised land.

He went back to his horse, where she lay, so quiet and solemn in the dust. She licked his hands and looked up at him with more love than he'd received from any living thing, save his sister, in this sorry unfeeling life he oft' wished he'd never been born into.

He kissed her warm forehead, and trickled water into her open mouth. Then shot her still with the pistol.

Wiping at his eyes, the soldier slung the saddle bags over his shoulders. The bottles of kerosene bumped together, inside their oilcloth wrappings. The rest of his ammunition was inside the bags too. He took two canteens and tied them to his belt; threw his dragoon's cape over the saddlebags. And started walking toward Zion.

They had kept slaves, captured along the trail through three states. Had used them to erect the hopeless wooden buildings of the Prophet Lehi's Zion on the shores of the Great Dead Sea. Once their labours were complete, the Nephrites had eaten them alive where they sat exhausted in their chains. Amongst the dozen sets of dirty bone, the soldier moved a few greyish heads with the toe of one boot. The slaves were not the chosen and had never been converted. He moved out of the black barn and onto main street.

Beside the barn where they'd been keeping the black carriage and the three hell mares, they had another three wooden shacks barely upright and facing the shimmering white sand that stretched to the ravines he'd passed through that morning. To the end of the row of wooden buildings were a dozen tents, their dirty grey canvass sides billowing from the wind that came off the long salt water behind.

The settlement appeared empty. Desolate. Damned.

The soldier had made good time out here; was sure he'd beaten that long-legged Prophet back too. Nephrites tired easy; were always hungry; their salvation as the chosen seemed to amount to nothing more than scratching in the dust to gobble down any living thing that had blood inside of it. He'd once found one buried from the waist inside a skinned bear carcass, feeding hard.

He guessed the population of Zion were all resting inside the broken down buildings and loose tents, until their Prophet returned with something warm and squealing in the back of that black carriage.

The soldier smiled. Laid down his bags outside the building beside the barn. "I will be avenged sevenfold. Yes sir." He sprinkled the kerosene oil around the wooden foundations of the building, and peppered the liquid with gun powder. Nary heard a sound from within. Not even a whisper. He'd burned three Nephrite infestations out of farms they'd occupied in Wyoming the exact same way. Nephrites did not like fire; must have reminded them of home, he often mused.

He lit a cigarette and dropped the match into the oil, which lit off in a trail of blackish smoke, the flames invisible in the sunlight. The timber they'd used for the buildings was so worm-eaten and dry, and mostly cobbled together from waggon beds, it took to fire quick and with a furious relish.

Outside the front entrance that was covered with a dirty muslin sheet, the soldier laid down his carbine and drew Old Wrist Breaker. And waited.

But not for long. Deep inside, back someways in the darkness they had all been laying inside, he heard the rustlings of their thin limbs. Then a bumping of bony feet, and a chattering from dry teeth sounded out, getting nearer to the entrance as they came through the house of rotten wood, not yet warmed by the bright sunlight, but roused by the thick smoke.

They came out into the light of dawn, blinking and coughing and whimpering; three raggedy females. The one in the round dress—once a tan check, but now filthy and hard with black blood down the front—came out first, its whited-out eyes blinking within the tatty bonnet. It paused momentarily to fight another behind it; a thing wearing a stained night gown, trying to push around the wide skirts of the other female. They snarled at each other and there was a brief raking of long yellowy nails against leathery faces, until they became aware of the dragoon close by.

With two swift downward strokes, as if striking from the saddle at fleeing artillery men, he caved in their skulls like he was breaking crockery pots with a hammer. The third one he skewered back against a wall, where it kicked out with its long sharp feet and whipped that wispy skull back and forth and showed him its black tongue before he shot it full in the face with his pistol from two feet out.

At the next building, he worked faster with the kerosene on account of the gun shot. Smashed three bottles in the first room, by throwing them against the far wall. Upstairs, on the next level, and just after he lit the place up, he saw a parched face grin down from a window without glass. Looked like the townsfolk were stirring. But the lower floor of the building went off blazing with them all still inside it and nervous about coming out to face him; and he prayed to God that if his sister were inside, she would be taken by the smoke so he would not have to see her in the morning's white light.

Through the dance and beat of the flames inside the building, he eventually saw insubstantial outlines of partially-haired heads bobbing in the smoke, before they rushed at the front door. Two females came out coughing and he slew them swift because their heads were practically bowed for the task before him. Another, without a hair on its patchwork skull, came through on all fours in petty coats and a filthy shawl, and he took from its narrow shoulders its foul head.

Two children, not yet twelve he reckoned when they were bit, tottered out blind from the heat and heavy black smoke they'd woken into. He took each down from behind with quick cross body cuts, then stepped away to the carbine. He glanced back at the great white desert that shimmered into the far hills, and then adjusted his gaze when he thought he saw the lope of a thin black figure coming hither. But once he'd shielded his eyes and squinted hard again, he saw nothing out there but the flat hard salt that could hide not so much as a coyote upon it.

From the third building, a nervous evacuation was in progress, and he scanned the starved upright devils for weapons. A gangly male in braces and a top hat held what looked like a flintlock the French had left behind from when they fought the English. Using the carbine, the soldier shot three parts of its head away; in the smoke-blinded confusion another ragged figure trod on its hat with a clawed foot.

Taking advantage of the two neighbouring fires, the thick black smoke that dropped on to the tented area, and the litter of wasted head-smashed bodies about the ground, the soldier calmly reloaded without looking at his hands, both pistol and carbine. And came up from kneeling, firing steady at those that took it upon themselves to race at him upon a sighting of their nemesis. Two crones that were dust as much as bone came apart like sticks and straw in their bonnets and pinafores. And then Old Wrist Breaker cut down the two teenage girls that tried to scatter before him like hens.

He lit up the third building from inside, keeping his sabre ready and up high. It was dark in there and under his feet, the chewed bones and hollowish skulls of the unfortunates that had been fed upon, crunched and rolled away as he stamped into the Godforsaken dark and dust.

He came out coughing and looked to the tents.

A weary line of dark silhouettes, he counted no more than five, tottered in the bright sun. Two of them wept, which made the other three females take up a wailing like they knew the time of the Great Awakening was all but done. One of them struck its naked head with long thin hands and pulled from its skull the last wisps of colourless hair.

At his back the three temples of Zion, a new Jerusalem to the congregation of Lehi's Fair-skinned Nephrites, burnt red and black and high into the deep blue sky. The soldier walked toward the tents and reloaded as he went. There was little fight left in those that remained and though they snarled like guard dogs they seemed reluctant to move far from whatever was behind them under canvass.

One finally came out to him, low on all fours, its long bone legs kicking up the dust behind it, and he shot most of its neck and cheek away on the right side. It set up a howling that only ceased when he crunched a boot heel down upon its forehead. Of the remaining four, he shot down one, right where it stood, hollerin' at him; hitting it full in the bark-crinkled face from ten yards. The other three scattered away into the tents.

The soldier turned about, Old Wrist Breaker out before him. Something with little cold feet had run up the back of his neck and given him the widdershins he knew he could trust.

Something low to the soil, wearing a tall-crowned hat, had scampered behind the barn like a stray dog.

Prophet Lehi must have circled his own Zion and come in due west across the desert; a slower and more indirect route, but one better at evading the eyes of the dragoon. The soldier knelt down and reloaded the carbine, the pistol. Holstered the pistol, stood up and trotted to the barn in search of a Prophet.

"Lehi! You cocksucker —"

But from out of smoke and fire in the building beside the barn came a sharp orange crack of light and something like a fist punched the trooper right from his feet. He felt three ribs snap like wheel spokes, lost all his air from his lungs, and knew he was hit. Hit wet through his side. And when he tried to drag in a breath, the pain was so bad it would not even let him scream.

He scrabbled about in the dust to get himself at the carbine he had thrown away as he fell.

From behind the burning buildings, the Prophet let out a cry of triumph and fury, and called his decimated congregation to perform a service long overdue. "And he will atone, my brothers, my sisters. And he will atone with his blood that we shall let on this holy shore!"

Up popped a trio of dreadful raggedy heads from among the tents. They weaved from side to side as they tried to sight him with their dim milky eyes, and then dropped and scurried to where the soldier lay blind and sick white through with pain.

He snapped his head up twice, when the black swoops came into his burning eyes and tried to put him down and to sleep. He checked the sopping hand that clutched his right side. The bullet had ripped away the skin and muscle below his nipple and smashed some bones. He prayed the ball had not fragmented down and into his belly because he could feel a hundred little brands burning inside a stomach he might never eat with again.

The Nephrites came at him quickly, seeing he was down and winged bad. They could also scent his hot blood in the dust and all over his white skin, which made them prance and skip and yowl like hungry cats, and cry stark like starving black crows, as they skittered and hopped madly at him from out of the tents.

To his other side he heard the preacher's boots in the dirt.

He clenched his teeth and drew his pistol, looked back at the blaze beside the barn, but Lehi was using the smoke as cover while reloading. The trooper turned and shot out the face of something on all fours that was the first to the feast. The other two broke around him, and shrieked at the sound of his gun.

He got up to his knees and then his feet. Unsheathed Old Wrist Breaker with his left hand. The ground swooped and swooned around him.

Something landed on his back and bit deep through his hat, and he felt his scalp come up and off his bones in a whole mess of dirty chewing teeth. He threw the Nephrite over his shoulders and stamped on its neck to hold it still in the dirt. The second one leaped up at him, long fingers going for his eyes, but he ran Old Wrist Breaker through its grubby bodice and held it away from his body, watched it writhe like a serpent. Put it down and stamped it still and off his sabre with one quick boot, like he was trampling dry kindling flat.

Lehi showed himself then. All teeth under a black hat and one long arm out front with a long pistol waving in his white hand. An old cavalry pistol and not accurate; likely to blow a man's hand off as hit a target at no more than twenty yards. The Prophet had been lucky with that first shot from out by the barn. He aimed to make certain with the second and came in close to do it.

"Looks like I need to start up a new congregation here, Ephraim." A few wisps of hair moved gently as Lehi came up closer on him. One knee that was mostly bone was put through the preacher's trouser leg.

The soldier tottered, sweat soaked and bleeding out. He held his sabre up, but doubted he had the strength to use it again, or even the strength to curse himself for getting so far but failing to behead this false prophet, this corrupt messiah, before his last breath.

Deep down beneath the burning pain and flooding away of his life, the soldier still found an ember of hatred so hot for this devil, that he managed to spit at it.

The devil grinned from under the brim of its black hat. Its voice was soft, and gentle and almost feminine. "Soldier. I might jus' start a new followin' with you. You'd make a fine fightin' apostle. Whaddya say, trooper? I bit your sister good on our weddin' night, in your uncle's bed. She tasted sweet. Bet her brother done taste like milk and honey. She bore me two, soldier. And your nephews lie out yonder, waitin' for the sweet red milk o' life."

The soldier shook his head; his eyes blurred by tears, his heart burnt to a husk by the still-more, never-stopping horrors that confronted his weary eyes and scorched his ears.

The Prophet aimed the long heavy barrel of the pistol between the dragoon's eyes. "Or maybe I should jus' cut you down here and swallow you like the fish and loaves our saviour put out for the five thousand. Yes, I do believe I may rightly —"

And the Prophet was jerked off his feet. Twisted in the air. Hit the sand with a great dusty thump. Then the soldier heard the musket break the desert air further out.

Down in the sand, the Prophet wrenched himself about in the sand, like a man having a fit; his gun arm was twisted out and away from his body.

His eyes mostly closed, the soldier turned about, his sword dragging through the dirt. And saw the small old prospector with the filthy beard coming across the white sand slowly, his musket longer even than he was.

The soldier turned back to the Prophet Lehi; who had turned round and got to its thin knees. Was trying to take the pistol from its right hand with the left. The musket ball had hit its chest and smote through the back of its jacket and cape, which smoked whitish around a dry hole.

Using both hands; holding the weight of the sword with his left and guiding with his right, the soldier raised Old Wrist Breaker, but it made him cry out and then drop the sabre's point. The pain in his side was too great for vengeance to have its way and he cried out in his despair, and his wretchedness, and for the blood that fell from him and for the sister that was took from him. He bent double and held himself up on his feet with the sword as a crutch. Then rose with the last of himself and let that sword fall hard into the Prophet's scrawny neck.

It knocked Lehi flat down in the dirt, but did not severe his head.

The old man came up to him. "Easy. Easy. Easy," he said. Then looked at the preacher and spat a long stream of tobacco and saliva across the back of that white skull. Trod a foot in a dirty moccasin on to the Prophet's gun hand. "Shee-it. I'll be. Man ain't alive nor dead. How can that be? Sweet Jesus."

"My pistol. Load it," the soldier said.

"Yessir." The old prospector took the pistol and loaded it with powder and ball and handed it to the dragoon.

"Lehi. My sister. Where is she?"

The Prophet spat and gasped, his mouth wet with black blood. And his face twisted and every tendon stretched inside that long neck and sharp jaw and the jabbering that came out of that mouth and into the air in the thin high voice of a child, were words that no old prospector and soldier would ever make sense of. So the soldier terminated the interview. He was close to fainting and needed to know before he left the world, that the Prophet was truly dead. So he put the dragoon pistol against the back of that pale cold skull and shot it all apart like a pumpkin off a fencepost.

"Them tents yonder, old man," the soldier said.

The old man got his self under the dragoon's left arm and walked him across to the tents. And there the old man then dragged the sagging dragoon from one yellowy interior of flapping canvas to another.

"What God hath wrought this, soldier? What God?" the old man asked him in the final tent. But by then, the soldier who had fallen into him; had already closed his tired eyes and left the foul tent and the foul world, and gone far from what lay grey and dry and mewling in the filthy bedding in the dirt beneath their feet. The dragoon had gone to another place to look for his sister who he never did find among the Fair-skinned Nephrites on the shore of the Great Dead Sea. The dragoon's last words were: "You know what to do. Use my sabre."

The old man took the young soldier outside the stench of death, soon to be heated by the white desert sun, and laid him at peace upon the dust; closed his eyes, said three lines from the prayer he could remember. Or was it a hymn? He didn't know, but he did what he could for the man. Then sawed the dragoon's head clean off with his own sword, which was so heavy and long he marvelled at the arm that had wielded it like a switch about the godless.

The prospector walked back to the twelve tents, and went in to finish the cavalry man's dreadful work.

In the last tent, as he carved off the tiny shrivelled heads of what was already dead or mostly dead, at what had rustled from out of the dead wombs of Nephrite mothers, the sabre's keen edge scraped at stone. Again and again, as if these birthing tents had been laid upon a stone floor in all of this sand.

Curious, he kicked aside the tatty bundles of headless young, and then scraped his foot through the dust. What lay beneath the sand in the

WHAT GOD HATH WROUGHT?

tent was smooth, undulating, like a water-smoothed boulder in a clear mountain stream.

Accustomed to digging in the dust for wonders to behold, the old man dropped the sword and wrapped some foul swaddling raiment about his left moccasin and began to sweep his leg back and forth across the hard rock.

After a few minutes, he uncovered a great eye, curved like an almond, and shielded by a heavy lid.

One hour later, he had swept the desert sand and grit away from what was an entire face.

By the end of the day, the Nephrite remains of young and old were all burnt to ash within the burning buildings of Zion, on the shore of the Great Dead Sea, and their tents were all cut down from the ground and dragged away from the campsite and left like a pile of dirty rags; also soon to be ignited, for the prospector felt that was what the solider would have wanted. And as the sun set across the glittering ocean of lifeless water, and the buildings were nothing more than blackened smoking bones upon its damned shore, the old man stared down at what he had uncovered beneath seven of the tents; at what had been hidden under the weightless husks of dead babes in the plague hospital, and under the sand.

He looked at the six colossal basalt heads, each measuring eight to nine feet in height and weighing, he reckoned, about forty tons. Stared searching into their great open eyes that, in turn, watched the sky darken and fill with bright stars. And when he eventually walked away, carrying his musket and the dragoon's pistol, carbine and sabre, not wanting to linger at these ruins in the darkness, he wondered if they were the faces of Gods. The Gods that had wrought all of this.

Adam Nevill was born in Birmingham in 1969 and grew up in England and New Zealand. He is the author of three novels of supernatural horror: *Banquet for the Damned*, *Apartment 16*, and *The Ritual*. His next two horror novels will be published in 2012 and 2013. He lives in London and can be contacted through www.adamlgnevill.com

"Many men who experienced a seventies childhood were interested in the wild west in the same way they were interested in WW2; films set in these periods were on television every weekend when I was a boy (can't believe I'm old enough to now write that) and often

Gutshot

involved a great deal of action and gunfire to which we were drawn like the male of the species. And I was no exception to the allure of the wild west; as well as owning boxes of toy figures, a Timpo frontier train set, a set of (alas) replica weapons, I was given encyclopaedias and books on the American west that I still own. My lingering interest in this period of American history might account for why I also consider *Deadwood* to be the finest television series I have ever seen.

"What barely merits a mention, though, in the popularised culture and history of the West, are the origins of God's Chosen People, the Mormons (never saw Mormon figures in the Airfix catalogue). But Jon Krakauer's *Under The Banner of Heaven* changed my perception of the American west of the 1800s. Despite all I'd read, I knew almost nothing of The Second Great Awakening of the 1840s, or its most celebrated prophet, Joseph Smith; and this was a tumultuous period of American history with a flavour of the apocalyptic Anabaptist sects of the old world of Europe.

Formed by a con man, Joseph Smith, a dabbler in the occult, mysticism and necromancy (which led to the Angel Moroni imparting the legendary gold tablets to him to establish the faith), the Mormons have grown into America's biggest cult, with a fundamentalist doctrine that exceeds, or at least matches, the excesses of any other millenarian organisation. Back in the 1800s it was defined by exodus, persecution, and apocalyptic prophesy equal to the Old Testament, from which it takes its inspiration. It even came close to all-out war with the American government, whose army it could nearly match, in The Utah War of the 1850s. Its entire history has been festooned with violence, embezzlement, deception, polygamy, fraud, child abuse, spin-off sects, insane beliefs even Islam would struggle to match, persecution, and a general craziness in the heart of America. At their current rate of expansion, by the last decade of this century it's estimated the Mormons will number 300 million. It may yet prove to be the country's biggest inner threat and an ominously major influence in its political future.

So instead of the Seventh Cavalry, the outlaw, or the North American Indian tribes, I wanted to explore a facet of the American west that resembled an amalgam of the European middle ages, the biblical middle east and the American Gothic. Breaking away from the martyr Joseph Smith and the deified Brigham Young, I created my own Mormon sect, The Fair-skinned Nephrites, and suggest that anything but the Christian God provided a hand in their creation. Stylistically, I also wanted to use an idiom to suggest the period, which is always a risk for a writer in the way regional or historical dialect falls upon the modern reader's ear, but who can read *Blood Meridian* by Cormac McCarthy (perhaps the greatest western prose writer) and not fall under the spell of his language?

THOSE WHO REMEMBER
Joel Lane

Night had fallen when I reached Oldbury. The best time for coming home: when the new developments fade into the background and the past becomes real again. Over the years I'd seen expressways carve up the landscape and titanic, jerry-built tower blocks loom above the familiar terraces. The town was boxed in by industrial estates built on the sites of old factories. Instead of real things like steel and brick, the new businesses manufactured 'office space' and 'electronics'. Only the night could make me feel at home. The night and seeing Dean again.

He took some finding this time. The windows of his old house were boarded up, and two short planks had been nailed across the front door: one at the top, one at the bottom. If they'd been nailed together, I could believe it was still his home. It was hard to imagine him leaving the area, but maybe he was dead or in prison.

I walked around the streets for hours. Everything had changed except the people. The teenagers had designer tops and mobile phones now, but they fought in car parks and fucked in alleys just as they had when I was a teenager. Local industry was dying then; it was dead now. Opposite a new multi-storey car park, I saw the old cinema where Dean and I had gone to see *Butch Cassidy and the Sundance Kid* when we were twelve. The doorway and windows were bricked up.

The next morning, I checked the phone book. Dean was living in one of the tower blocks north of the town centre. Where the council stuck people who had, or were, problems. It saved the social services a lot of petrol. I could see the towers from my hostel room: three grey rectangles cut out of the white sky. Gulls flying around them like flakes of ash, probably drawn by the heaps of rubbish on the slope.

I walked through the town, past the drive-in McDonald's that was now its chief landmark. A narrow estate, with tiny cube-shaped flats in rows three or four deep, seemed to be in process of demolition: half of the cubes were broken up, their blank interiors exposed to the weak morning light. It had been much the same three years earlier. I try to come back every now and then, without letting Dean know my plans. I prefer to surprise him. At least the wasteground with the remains of a derelict house, where he and his mates Wayne and Richard had beaten me senseless in 1979, was still here. I walked through it, glancing around for the teeth I'd lost. One day they'd turn up.

Climbing the bare hill to the three towers, I passed a few children who were stoning an old van. They'd taken out most of the windscreen. I waited at the entrance to the second tower until a young woman dressed in black came out; I slipped in past her. It seemed colder inside the building than outside; the stone steps reeked of piss and cleaning fluids. Dean's flat was on the ninth floor. While climbing, I rehearsed what I was going to make him do.

After ten minutes of ringing, the door finally opened. He was looking rough, less than half awake. The kind of piecemeal shave that's worse than none at all. Shadows like old bruises round his eyes, which were flecked with blood. "What are you after?" he said. "I don't feel too good. Come back later."

"Not a chance." I took his shaky hand off the door and pushed it further open, then walked in. The smell of despair washed over me: three parts sweat, two parts stale food and booze, one part something like burnt plastic. The curtains were shut. I raised a hand. "Miss Havisham, I have returned—to let in the light!"

Dean laughed. "Gary, have you seen the view?" He probably had a point. I shifted a few dusty magazines to make space on the couch, then sat down. "It's been a long time," he said. "Why have you come back? I don't need you."

"Yeah, you're doing just fine on your own." I looked around his living-room. Boxes and suitcases were stacked against the far wall, under a stain like a deformed spider. "Have you just moved in, or are you leaving?"

It took him a while to get the point. "Been here a couple of years," he said. "Lost my job, tried to sell the house but it needed too much work. Council found me this flat. It'll do while I get myself sorted out."

"Sure." The burnt plastic smell was troubling me. "Have you had a short circuit or something? Cable burning out?"

Again, he had to think for a bit. "I was cooking up some breakfast."

"Excellent. Haven't had a bacon butty in ages."

"Oh, I've put it all away now. In case . . ." His eyes closed.

I stood up wearily and walked over to him, looked closely at his face. His eyes opened again; he looked away. "Dean, there were three things you could never keep. A promise, a bank account and a secret. What is it this time?"

"Nothing." He put a hand to his mouth, then staggered. "Fuck."

"I'd rather have a coffee to start with."

Dean gave me a look of utter contempt, then staggered through a side door. I could hear him throwing up in the toilet. The magazines on the couch were his usual blend of soft porn, war and the paranormal. He came back after a minute, looking sweaty. "Need to go out for a while," he said.

"Sit down first. I want to talk to you." He shrugged and balanced his lean arse on a plastic chair. "Have you done any work since you moved here?"

"Building . . . sometimes. More demo than building. It's all casual now, you take what you can get." I remembered he'd started a one-man repair firm in his twenties. Hadn't lasted long. He'd kept a horse tethered to his gate.

"What about Richard and Wayne? Do you still work for them?"

I saw a flicker of recognition in his eyes. Maybe he was starting to remember. "I never worked for them," he said. "Just the odd bit of business. You know?" I nodded. "Look, I need to go out now. Got a job interview."

He was wearing a torn grey fabric top, stained jeans and trainers without laces. They might have had a certain urchin appeal if he'd been sixteen instead of forty-one. But he'd always been sixteen to me, so it didn't matter. An employer might feel differently.

I reached out, gripped his hand. It felt cold and thin. I pulled his sleeve back to the elbow and saw the tracks. He didn't try to stop me. He was drifting off again. "Dean, I'm going to help you," I said. "And that means you're not going anywhere for a while. Tough love. We'll get through this together. And afterwards, I need you to help me."

Dean leaned forward and held onto the wall. A thin stream of drool ran from the corner of his mouth. Then, suddenly, he ran for the door. I stopped him. "Fuck off, fuck off, fuck off," he kept repeating. I held him until he curled up on the floor, his hands over his head, and went to sleep.

The next three days were hard work. I took Dean's keys and kept the flat locked. He wasn't that likely to jump out the window from the ninth floor. A search of his bedroom revealed a battered set of works, a couple of syringes and a plastic bag with few meagre traces of powder. I destroyed all of it. While he was asleep I slipped out to buy bread, milk and bleach, then cleaned the flat as best I could. While he was awake I listened to his rantings, his promises and threats, his explanations and frantic pleas. I cleaned him when he shat and threw up over himself. I wiped the sickly, malodorous sweat from his face and body. And yes, I gave him a couple of handjobs when he became aroused. I have to take some gratification where I can find it. Though I got rather more pleasure from throwing his mobile phone out the window, not even hearing it strike the gravel far below.

After three days, I decided he'd got through the 'cold turkey' and was ready for the next stage. Of course, he'd only keep off the smack with ongoing support to help him fight the craving. But to be honest, that wasn't my concern. He was always in trouble: the last time it had been diazepam, and a couple of times before that he'd been drinking himself blind. I always did what I could to clean him up, put him back on the path. But he'd never had much sense. Like some historian said, those who forget the past are condemned to repeat it.

And those who remember do it anyway.

When I gave Dean back his keys, he was a different man. His clothes were washed and he'd had a healthy breakfast. His flat was still a dump, but it was a cleaner dump that smelt only of pine-scented bleach. He smiled at me, and I could almost have kissed him. "Now I need you to do something for me," I said. He waited. "First we're going out for a decent coffee. Then I want you to find Wayne and Richard. And help me kill them."

○ ○ ○

Dean made the call from an infected phone box on the estate of broken cubes. Said he was clean but had debts to pay. He wasn't kidding. Richard said Wayne was away cutting some overgrown grass. He'd be back tomorrow. They could meet in the usual place. That was the derelict house, Dean explained to me; or rather what was left of it. I was touched to realise I wasn't the only person trapped in the past. The death of religion has left us all to create our own rituals.

We walked out past the Homebase to the new junction, a twisted structure gleaming with light. The gateway to the future. Cars streamed above us as I explained to Dean what he was going to do. "It's not just what they did to me," I said. "You'll never have a decent life while they're around. They know far too much about you. That's why you can't leave this shithole. It has to end. Ten seconds and we'll both be free. Then I'll leave you alone."

He stared at me in a confused way. The years of alcohol and drugs had taken their toll. And he'd hardly been the brightest light on the tree to begin with. "There's no other way," I said, and handed him the knife. He touched his finger to the blade, licked the blood off his fingertip. Then he turned the knife over and over in his hands, gazing at it. I think he knew where it had come from, but I moved us on before he could think too much.

"I need money for a new mobile," he said as we walked back through the town. I had no idea what they cost, but took fifty quid from my old wallet and handed it to him. We passed a branch of Dixon's, but he didn't stop. He was trembling. For a moment I could see him as a teenager, walking up that mountainside in North Wales.

As we neared the estate, I asked him: "What about that mobile?"

"I need a date first," he said without looking at me. "Now I'm off drugs, I've got the urge back. There's a girl on the fourteenth floor of my block. She'll do everything for fifty. Tomorrow could go wrong, Gary. I deserve it."

"You always were the romantic type." I briefly considered just pushing his face through a window. But that wouldn't be enough. "I'll leave you to it, Romeo. Be outside your block tomorrow morning at twelve. Or fucking else."

The town streets were jammed with traffic, workers on their lunch break, pensioners hunting for cheap food. The air was getting warmer, but I was too cold inside to derive much comfort from that. I bought a four-pack of Diamond White, took it back to my hostel room and drank off all the bottles without a break. Thinking about the derelict house: four shattered walls, a few heaps of timber, flakes of plaster, exposed wires. Then I thought of some tents on a hillside in Wales, stars glittering in the open sky like flaws in ice. Finally I drew the curtains, lay down and pretended to sleep. That was the only way I could make myself think of nothing.

"I'm not doing it." He was wearing a battered leather jacket, but still shivering. The sky behind the three tower blocks was the grey of dead skin. He cupped his thin hands and blew into them, shaking his head.
"Are you back on the fucking horse?"
"No, I told you, a date. She fucking loved it."
"Spare me," I said. "The most romantic thing a girl's ever said to you is 'Is it in yet?'"
Dean gazed down the hill at the shattered boxes where people had lived. Where they maybe still did. "They're my mates," he said. "What do you know about friendship?"
"I know a gayboy when I see one."
"Why, you look in the mirror? I like women."
"Gail didn't love it, did she?"
He looked at me then, confusion and panic in his face. "What are you talking about?"
"I'm talking about the one chance you've got to show you're a man. A human being of any kind. Those two don't deserve to walk the streets, and you know it. Or are you just going to spend the rest of your useless life in that derelict house, the two of them taking turns to come in your mouth?" He started walking down the hill towards the estate. "Don't need a fucking syringe, do I? You never give up jabbing the needle in."
At the edge of the wasteground, he stopped again. "Can't see them. They're going to jump on us."
"You wish." I was losing patience. "I'm with you, remember. It's two against two. I know you prefer three against one. But we've got the advantage. Let's get this over with, for fuck's sake." I shoved him forward. "Loser. Coward. Fairy. Don't you know what the knife is for? You used to."
He walked on fast over the wet, uneven ground. The remains of the derelict house were on the far side: a blackened structure only four or

five feet high, with part of an empty window-frame in one broken wall. The doorway had long since collapsed, and you had to climb over the crumbling bricks to get through. There was no longer any roof. Two figures were waiting on either side of the few mouldering stairs. They'd put on some weight.

"Who's this fucker?" I wasn't sure if it was Wayne or Richard speaking.

"I think you know," Dean said quietly. "He's been here before."

"You're fucking kidding," the other one said. Dean whipped the knife out of his coat pocket, gave a wordless cry, and charged at him. Richard, I think it was, kicked him hard in the stomach. Wayne grabbed his right arm and snapped the wrist with a single carefully-aimed karate chop. The knife dropped soundlessly onto the rotting stairs. Dean fell to his knees and vomited. I stood outside the ruin, watching through the empty window-frame.

The two men worked him over for a couple of minutes, doing no serious damage, but inflicting as much pain as they could. They left him lying on his back, twitching and drooling blood. As an afterthought, Wayne pissed over him. Then they walked out without glancing in my direction. They walked away fast, as if they had other business to attend to.

It took Dean an hour to regain consciousness. Bruising had closed his left eye, and blood had crusted over his mouth. He looked like a poorly made-up circus clown. He lifted his right arm and moaned with pain. Then he saw me standing inside the half-wall, watching him. All his memories were coming back. "What's wrong?" I asked. "Don't you like it that way?"

His damaged mouth tried to say something, but I couldn't tell what. "Why don't you finish it?" I said. "I'll let you off the fuck this time. They beat you up too much. Just use the knife." I picked it up and wiped the flecks of plaster from the handle, then put it in his left hand. Dean struggled to his knees. I slipped off my jacket, turned my back to him and put my hands on the window-frame.

The knife went in between my ribs, just to the right of the spine. It was more a carving than a stabbing action. My back arched in the ecstasy of release. I saw my last breath like a scar on the petrol-tinged air. The knife struck me again, but the tissues of my body were already corroding and flaking apart, the bones melting like ice in spring. By the time he let go of the knife and began his long, painful walk to the town, there was nothing left of me.

○ ○ ○

Dean was the only one of the three who went on the camping trip to Wales where we climbed a mountain and put up cheap tents in a sloping field. I shared a tent with a boy called Alan. In the night some of the boys visited the girls' tents. I just lay there, pretending to sleep.

Long after midnight, someone crept in through the tent-flap. It wasn't Alan, who'd gone out an hour before: it was Dean. He told me Gail, the red-haired girl, had refused him. "I'm not good enough for her. So I thought, I know who I'm good enough for."

He fucked me slowly, without spit or tenderness. Afterwards he lay there as if stunned. I asked: "Aren't you going to finish me off?"

He laughed as if I'd made a joke, then grabbed my arm. "Come with me." We got dressed and left the tent. I'd never seen night outside the city before, couldn't believe how bright the stars were. Dean led me to a footpath that curved away from the field into a wooded area that reached up the mountainside. It was midsummer, but I felt cold. His sperm was trickling into my underpants. I no longer wanted any reciprocal contact. But I kept walking until the footpath led us out of the trees to a ridge overlooking a steep rock face and a tree-lined valley. "Stop here," he said.

I turned to face him. He was breathing heavily, and wouldn't meet my eyes. "You want me to finish you off?" I didn't answer. "Turn round."

A terrible chill spread from between my shoulder-blades through my whole body. The knife stayed in my back as I fell towards the dark trees. I was still alive when I hit the ground, and for hours afterwards. But nobody found me. Nobody ever found me, or the knife.

That's another reunion done with. I'll be back next year, or the year after, or a couple of years after that. I like to surprise him. But the scene is decaying. Maybe next time they'll kill him. Or else he'll kill himself, with drugs or booze if not with violence. Nothing lasts forever, and there's no eternal. Everything falls apart in the end.

Joel Lane lives in Birmingham. His work in the supernatural horror genre includes three collections of short stories, *The Earth Wire*, *The Lost District* and *The Terrible Changes*, as well as a novella, *The Witnesses are Gone*, and a chapbook, *Black Country*. He has also written two mainstream novels, *From Blue to Black* and *The Blue Mask*; three collections of poetry, *The Edge of the Screen*, *Trouble in the Heartland* and *The Autumn Myth*; and a booklet of crime stories, *Do Not Pass Go*.

"*Those Who Remember* attempts to set a Western in the West Midlands (of England). It stems from two bad memories: visiting a friend in Oldbury in the 1990s and a weekend camping in Wales in the 1970s. Both experiences seemed on the edge of becoming much worse than they were. The story is also an indirect tribute to the Black Country crime writer Wayne Dean-Richards."

Thanks to the editors: Stephen Jones, Ellen Datlow, Peter Crowther, Karl Edward Wagner. Thanks to the writers: Ray Bradbury, M John Harrison, Christopher Priest, Ramsey Campbell, Cormac McCarthy, Stephen King. Thanks to the people who helped during the compilation of this book: Pete and Nicky, Pat Cadigan, Bob Booth. As ever, thanks and love to Rhonda, Ethan, Ripley and Zac.

A Note on *Gutshot's* Cover Artist

Caniglia's art has been featured in the *Washington Post*, CNN, Spectrum Fantastic Art Annuals and on many magazines, books and CD covers. He has worked with such authors as Stephen King, Ray Bradbury, Peter Straub, Douglas Clegg and F. Paul Wilson. Caniglia was nominated in 2003 and 2004 for the International Horror Guild Award for best artist in dark fantasy and horror. In 2004 Caniglia won the International Horror Guild Award for best artist. In 2005 he received his first World Fantasy nomination. He continues to illustrate, paint, and work on design concepts for movie companies and various publishers.

Many of his surreal paintings from the last ten years can be found in the book *As Dead as Leaves—the Art of Caniglia* from Shocklines Press. He currently teaches at Creighton University and The Kent Bellow Center for Visual Arts. Visit Cangilia's website for more information: www.caniglia-art.com

Conrad Williams

Conrad Williams is the author of seven novels, including *The Unblemished* (winner of the International Horror Guild Award), and *One* (winner of the British Fantasy Award). He has also written four novellas including *The Scalding Rooms*, which beat his own *Rain* to the British Fantasy Award in 2008. He has around 100 short stories to his name, some of which are collected in *Use Once then Destroy* and, forthcoming from PS Publishing, *Open Heart Surgery*. As Nuala Deuel, he ghost-wrote *Princess Spider: True Confessions of a Dominatrix*, which was translated into German and Italian. He lives in Manchester with his wife, three sons and a big Maine Coon. His latest novel is *Loss of Separation*. Find out more at www.conradwilliams.net

Guts